# Shadows and Relics

L.L. Gray

Heroic Rose Publishing

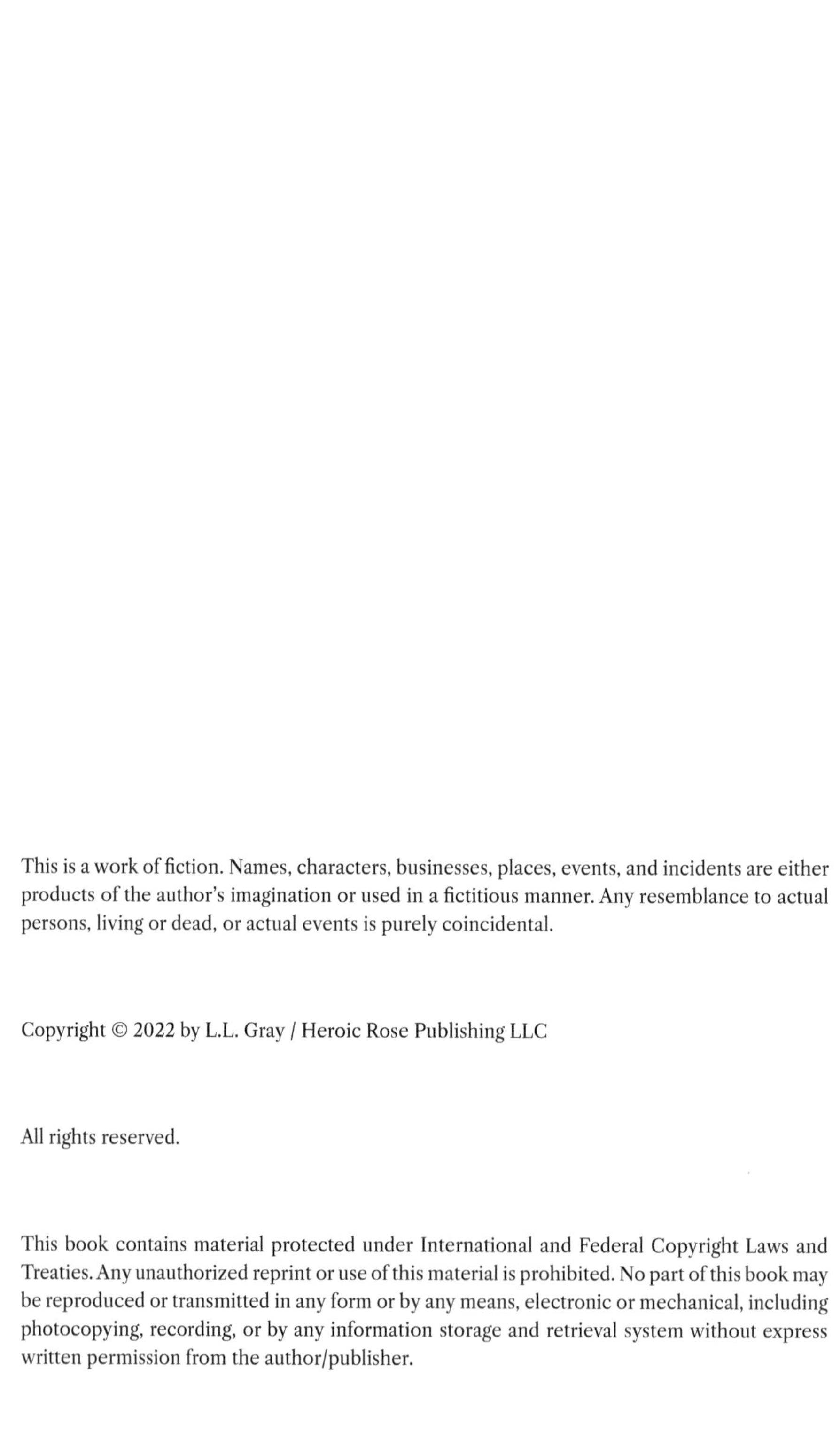

This is a work of fiction. Names, characters, businesses, places, events, and incidents are either products of the author's imagination or used in a fictitious manner. Any resemblance to actual persons, living or dead, or actual events is purely coincidental.

Copyright © 2022 by L.L. Gray / Heroic Rose Publishing LLC

# Contents

# Your FREE book is waiting

**A killer pair of shoes, a party of a lifetime, and a demon. What could possibly go wrong?**

Cameron Blaze owes a demon a favor and what better way to pay off a debt than to have a girl's night out? The plan was simple. Find a killer pair of heels, go to a great bar, and party into the early hours of the morning. Cameron thinks that she has everything planned. The shoes on are, the drinks are poured, and the party is in full swing. She just forgot to account for one small thing. Magic going haywire.

Suddenly, gods are out of control, myths are throwing punches, and Cameron is running for her life. Will she be able to stop the magical mayhem in time or has the clock run out for Cameron and her friends?

Sign up here to get your free book!

https://www.subscribepage.com/llgray

# Chapter 1

I crouched on the cold tile floor, nearly eye to eye with my nemesis. The vicious creature scraped a wickedly taloned foot against the tile with a disconcerting screech. The sound flayed the sensitive membranes of my inner ear and I winced. The creature cocked its head blinking one solid black eye at me. Its head bobbed, weaving through the air like a prize fighter waiting for a fight to begin. My fingers splayed at my sides. Slowly, deliberately, the beast scraped his talons against the tile again sending another screech echoing across the battlefield to assault my eardrums.

Shouts and cheers erupted behind me, but I ignored the spectators. This was between me and the beast. I considered my options as I examined my opponent. I knew from experience that he was fast. The deep gauges on the back of my hand bore testimony to the sharpness of his talons and beak. I grimaced and wiped the blood onto my black jeans.

Hadn't I heard somewhere that these monsters were closely related to dinosaurs? Specifically, the tyrant king of the dinosaurs, the T. Rex? Judging him solely by his fierceness, I could believe it. I shook my head and refocused on the beast in front of me. Purple and green iridescent highlights shimmered over its feathered body and a droplet of my blood hung off its needle-sharp beak. It shook its head, flinging the droplet up into the air and scraped at the floor again with a screech of talons.

A hoot of laughter sounded from behind me. "Get it, girl!" shouted a raspy male voice.

"Don't cock it up!" A woman's voice this time, followed by a peel of laughter.

I grimaced, eyeing the rooster across from me. He was wilier than I'd originally given him credit for. Faster too.  I could probably wear him down, given enough time and maneuvering. However, with the jeering audience at my back, I didn't want to lose any more of my ragged dignity. Whatever I was going to do, I needed to do it fast because my legs were starting to cramp.

I flexed my fingers and called on my magic, pulling the shadows from around the room to pool in the palm of my hand. I felt them tickle at my bare skin like cobwebs. Pulling more shadows to me, I felt the magic coat my arm like an ephemeral sleeve. I imagined what I needed in my mind and my magic eagerly jumped to obey, molding the shadows to my whim. The rooster bobbed his head, scuttling backwards as my form seemed to shift and morph. I bared my teeth at him.

*Let's dance, mother clucker.*

Before the rooster could get out of range, I leapt forward, waving my arms wildly. Except I didn't have just two arms. From the rooster's point of view, it looked like I had six. I made myself as big as I could, waving my shadow arms menacingly at him as I corralled him against a wall. The rooster's beady eyes lit on the nearest arm. He darted forward, intent on tearing into my flesh once more. Except there was nothing there.

The rooster stumbled through the shadowy illusion, expecting to meet resistance where there was only thin air. I cackled and trapped his plump body against the wall with my leg. With my real hands, I carefully pinned his iridescent black wings to his sides and hefted the creature aloft. The rooster wriggled and tried to attack once more, but I was careful to keep that beak facing out and as far away from me as possible.

Cheers erupted behind me as I hoisted my trophy into the air. Smiling and nodding for the small crowd's benefit, I carefully passed the feathered menace back to his owner. I studied the pale red-haired woman discretely from under my lashes as I passed the rooster over. Her vibrant purple top was cut low enough to show an ample amount of pale bosom and a sheer green shawl hung lazily from her elbows, accentuating her inherent fluid grace. She was utterly feminine, innately sensual, and dangerous as hell.

She was also my mark. The whole reason I was here tonight. I swallowed hard, trying to work moisture into my dry mouth.

"Oh, thank you! I don't know what got into him! He's usually so well behaved, aren't you?" The pale woman lifted the rooster aloft and cooed at him in a baby voice, "Yes, you are! You are the best-behaved cock in the whole wide world, aren't you Cluck Norris?"

I choked back a laugh, hiding it behind my fist. The woman's intense green eyes snapped up to me and she arched an imperious eyebrow. I cleared my throat. "Interesting name, that's all."

The woman tucked the rooster under an arm and stroked its feathers gently. "Yes, well, it's fitting, don't you think? I mean, he's the only bird I know who could roundhouse kick the sun clear into tomorrow without so much as a cocka-fucking-doo." She tickled the rooster's back and he preened under her affectionate attention. I hid another smile as she turned back to me. "But speaking of names, I don't believe I caught yours."

I cleared my throat again. "Cameron. Cameron Blaze," I murmured, keeping my voice low to hide my mirth as I solemnly nodded a greeting at her.

"Maman Brigitte," she returned, dipping her head slightly. "And thank you for the help," she added, petting Cluck Norris affectionately.

I schooled my face into a polite smile and nodded in return. "A pleasure."

I hadn't needed the introduction. Maman Brigitte was a legend in New Orleans. Supposedly, she was loosely associated with Saint Brigid of Ireland, hence her distinctive looks. However, Maman Brigitte was no saint. She was a loa, an intermediary between humans and the divine. She wasn't a demon, but definitely not an angel either. With her husband, Baron Samedi, Maman Brigitte acted as a guide for the deceased, guiding them to the other side. She was kind of like the Greek Ferryman, Charon, but way more attractive. She also had the reputation of being rowdy, religious, rude, foul mouthed, and the life of the party. Which was why I was here.

Well, more precisely, the small bottle of dark rum infused with hot peppers that never ran dry that was tucked in her small purse was why I was here. Apparently, someone was willing to pay top dollar to retrieve a small taste of the divine drink. That's where I came in. Cameron Blaze. Supernatural jack-of-all trades. Procurer of the impossible. Lifetime miscreant. And now, rooster wrangler for the immortals of New Orleans.

*Impossible, my ass. Tom Cruise has nothing on me.*

With the escapee back in custody, everyone resumed their places around the poker table tucked into the surprisingly spacious backroom of a bar. As far as I'd been able to discover, Maman Brigitte was a regular at the weekly underground game. It had taken me two weeks to uncover the location of the poker game and another ten days of heavy drinking in the dwarven-owned bar to wrangle a spot at the table. Now, three hours in and a rooster-gauged hand later, all of my hard work was about to pay dividends. Or go sailing off down the river. It all depended on how the cards fell.

I drummed my fingers against the worn green felt tabletop as the snap and riffle of cards filled the space between the murmurs of small talk around the table. The dealer shuffled the deck with expert flair, but I couldn't spare the focus to appreciate his skill. Not with so much of my time and work on the line.

The dealer flicked his wrist and sent cards spiraling around the table. My eyes followed the spinning cards as my stomach churned. The dealer continued to fling cards to each player with dexterous ease. My fingers increased the tempo on the tabletop. The warty brown imp next to me shot a look of such withering scorn from his brilliant scarlet eyes that I froze momentarily before consciously laying my hand flat on the table.

The two tipsy witches on my right had their heads together and were giggling loudly as they clinked glasses of white wine together. The silent vampire next to them leaned back in his chair. He tipped it onto its back two legs and rocked gently as he waited for the final cards to be dealt. He hadn't engaged in any genial banter this evening. I doubted he would start now. The pale red-haired woman across from me rounded out our party at the illicit poker table. She delicately sipped on a tumbler of dark rum and petted the rooster in her lap as she watched the witches with bored interest.

The dealer slapped the deck on the table and said, "Blinds in, please." His tone was professionally detached. He eyed the players attentively as he adjusted the cuffs on his immaculate white shirt.

The imp tossed in the small blind and Maman Brigitte casually flung the big blind into the pot. The rooster squawked at the sudden movement. I eyed the creature distrustfully, fingering the tacky blood forming scabs on the back of my hand. The vamp and witches all threw chips into the center of the table, indicating a desire to play. Before I knew it, the bet traveled around the table to me. Mentally elbowing myself, I tucked a thumbnail under my cards and peeked at my hand. A pair of red eights. Not a horrible hand, but not great either. Luck hadn't been turning my way tonight. Unfortunately, this was the best hand I'd seen in more than an hour. I glanced at my dwindling supply of chips and schooled my face into stoic blankness.

"All in," I said coolly, shoving my pile of chips towards the dealer.

A rumble of disgruntled curses rolled from everyone around the table. Except Maman Brigitte. She raised her tumbler in my direction. "Ignore them. You carpe that frickin' diem if you want to, love," she purred.

"Really?" whined the blonde witch on my right.

Green eyes glittered dangerously at the tipsy witch. "Really *what*, Kimberly?"

"The *swearing*, Brigitte. Can't we get through one evening without you ruining it with your language?" The witch, Kimberly, let out a dramatic sigh.

"Personally, I don't find swearing offensive," Brigitte said, taking a sip from her tumbler. She extended the index finger of the hand holding the glass, cutting Kimberly off as the witch opened her mouth. "However, I do find backstabbing, lying, cheating, and fucking people over offensive, but not swearing. Never swearing. Besides, nothing inspires the words 'fuck off' like someone asking me to watch my language." Amusement flickered in the depths of Brigitte's eyes as she regarded the witch over another long sip of rum.

Kimberly clawed for her glass of wine, clutching it tightly as color rose up her neck and blossomed in dark splotches across her cheeks.

The imp ran a hand through his sparse wiry hair and cleared his throat, interrupting the unfolding drama. "I fold," he said loudly, tossing his cards to the dealer. With a smirk bordering on wicked, he added, "I need a damned drink."

Kimberly's face darkened from dusky rose to puce. The imp blew her a kiss as she started to sputter incoherently. He pushed back from the table wandered off to the dark wooden bar snuggled into a corner on the far side of the room. The dwarf who owned the place leapt to attention, bobbing his long beard as the imp ordered a drink.

The vampire shoved his cards at the dealer as well, folding out of turn and joined the imp at the bar without a word. Brigitte eyed me carefully as she thoughtfully rolled a chip across the knuckles of one hand. A small smile curved her lips. "I really shouldn't, but c'est la vie," she said, waving a hand at her massive pile of chips. "What the hell? I'll call."

Kimberly's face darkened even more. "Don't you care what people think of you? A *lady* doesn't speak like that!" the waspish woman snapped.

Brigitte met her eyes coolly. "Giving a fuck doesn't really go with my outfit," the redhead said, spreading her arms and showing off an impressive amount of décolletage.

Kimberly's friend leaned over and whispered urgently in the blonde witch's ear. Unsurprisingly, both witches folded in short order. Kimberly drained her wineglass and muttered something about needing a refill.

"Aww," Brigitte intoned. I'd never actually heard sarcasm drip off a single syllable so eloquently before. "Are you sure you don't want to play?"

"No," Kimberly said shortly, moving towards the bar in search of alcohol and space.

"You know, 'fuck that shit' is a perfectly acceptable replacement for the word 'no'," Brigitte called cheerfully after her.

I snorted out a surprised laugh. Kimberly's back straightened from starch to ramrod. Her friend grabbed her elbow before the prudish witch could respond and steered her straight towards the wine.

"And then there were two," Brigitte said softly, focusing her intent green gaze on me. "Dealer, if you please?" She waved a hand at the table.

"Of course. Would you like to show your hands?" the dealer asked diffidently.

"Oh, let's keep the mystery alive a little while longer," I demurred.

Brigitte chortled. "I knew I liked you," she said raising her glass my way as the dealer flipped over three cards face up.

The eight of clubs, three of spades, and five of hearts. The little tense knot inside my chest eased slightly. Unless she got extremely lucky, it was unlikely she'd beat my three of a kind with that kind of flop.

"Shall we make this even more interesting?" I asked, striving to keep my voice level.

"Bets are closed," the dealer said, keeping his voice professionally level, but I noticed he paused before flipping over the next card.

"A side bet then," I offered. "If you are interested that is. If not..." I let my voice trail off with a slight shrug.

Brigitte smiled widely. "You do not disappoint, Cameron Blaze. Tell me what you're thinking."

I reached into my leather jacket and extracted the keys to my Honda Rebel. I'd bought the motorcycle secondhand for a song. After some long hours and a lot of elbow grease, she was a sexy piece of machinery. I jingled the keys at Brigitte. "Let's Casino Royale this shit. Are you game?"

Her eyes lit up at the challenge. "I don't have a motorcycle..." she started to say as she shook her head.

"Well, then, this can be the first of your collection," I interrupted her, tossing my keys into the center of the table. My gut gave a little jerk. I'd worked hard for that bike. "Trust me, once you go bike, you never go back."

She snorted a laugh. "Fine. You've got a hefty pair of balls on you. What'd you want?" She sipped on her drink as I pretended to study the table in front of her. My eyes lit on the small bottle of dark rum in her purse.

"What about that?" I asked, pretending the idea had just occurred to me. I jerked my chin at the bottle.

Brigitte's eyes widened in surprise. "This? You're willing to trade your motorcycle for some rum? Who do you think you are? Jack Sparrow?"

"That's Captain Jack Sparrow to you."

The loa threw her head back in surprise as delighted laughter filled the room. "A great big pair indeed! Hopefully it's enough to see you through. You've got yourself a bet." She yanked the bottle out of her purse and shoved it toward the center of the table.

I nodded and returned her smile, but my palms started to sweat. I surreptitiously wiped them on my pants as the dealer placed a card face down and then flipped another card face up. The two of hearts. My heart started doing a tap dance of joy. The dealer didn't hold us in suspense. He quickly burned another card face down and turned up the final card. The two of spades.

I let out a small hiss of relief as I snapped my own cards face up, showing my full house. Given the cards on the table, the only thing that could beat me was if Brigitte had pocket two's, giving her four of a kind. Highly unlikely, but with the way my luck was going, I wouldn't have been surprised. I held my breath as Maman Brigitte considered me briefly before flicking her cards across the table towards the dealer to land face down among the pile of chips.

She'd folded. I won.

I wanted to do a victory dance, but I kept a tight rein on my emotions. Brigitte nodded at me. "And with that, I need a drink," she said, raising her tumbler and draining it. The rooster wriggled in her lap at the movement. The dwarven proprietor leapt to his stubby feet, literally jumping at the chance to serve Maman Brigitte now that I was tucking her personal stash carefully into my jacket pocket along with my keys. In his haste to serve, the dwarf appeared suddenly at Brigitte's elbow. Surprised by the unexpected movement, the rooster freaked out. Loudly. The bird squawked and flapped his wings wildly. The startled dwarf stumbled away from the ferocious bird and straight into the table, sending chips and cards flying. A chorus of displeased shouts rang out as chips scattered across the floor. Maman Brigitte kept a firm hold on the rooster as the dwarf and the dealer hit their knees simultaneously, shouting apologies over the noise of angry patrons.

I ignored them, frozen to my seat. When the dwarf jostled the table, Brigitte's folded hand tipped to expose the loa's cards. A pair of twos stared up at me. My astonished gaze flew up to meet the loa's. She tipped the empty tumbler at me and winked as the dealer swept up the cards, oblivious to the exchange.

*What the hell? She'd let me win?*

As pressing as those questions were, there was a more important one that jammed its way through the turmoil in my head.

*Why?*

# Chapter 2

I extracted myself from the poker game as quickly as possible. Luckily for me, no one wanted to continue the game after the dwarf's faux pas. I glanced at my phone and groaned. I barely had enough time to race across town to get to my next job. Two jobs in one night was unfortunate timing, but it couldn't be helped.

I hurried out of the secluded backroom and into a lively bar full of drunken tourists. I kept a hand firmly over my jacket pocket to protect the small bottle of rum as I shoved my way through the crowd. A live band belted out a pop cover from the small stage and the crowd shouted along with a very loose relationship to the actual pitch of the tune. The room stank of sweat, booze, and broken dreams, but the crowd looked happy enough. Or drunk enough. It was hard to tell.

I pushed out the front doors onto Bourbon Street and the humidity hit me like suspiciously moist towel to the face. It was late October, but Mother Nature's cruel practical joke on curly-haired people never really disappeared from New Orleans. I huffed out a sigh and broke into a brisk jog. I kept my eyes on the ground, dodging questionable puddles. Dodging mysterious liquid on the pavements of Bourbon Street was as natural to any local in New Orleans as the jazz that spilled out of the brightly lit bars. There was a reason you should never wear sandals on Bourbon Street. I focused my attention on the ground in front of me, keeping a wary eye out for the cheap beaded necklaces that usually littered the street. The last thing I needed was to step on one of those and smash the small bottle in my pocket in an untimely fall.

I heaved a sigh of relief as I finally turned right off the suspiciously sticky party road on to Conti Street. I increased my pace as the crowd thinned. I turned left onto Dauphine and hurried to the parking lot where I'd left my bike. By the time I'd tucked the bottle of rum inside the small, lockable space under my seat and jammed my helmet on my head, a light sheen of sweat had coated my skin. Not all of it was due to the hot humid evening. I was cutting it close if I had a prayer of making it to my next job on time.

I tore down the congested roads as quickly as my Rebel allowed, which bordered on the edge of sanity for most people. An unexpected traffic jam on Decatur slowed me down, but I wove through the cars with the ease of long experience. After all, I'd been navigating these streets ever since I'd moved from the small, secluded home I'd shared with my mother into the city of New Orleans five years ago at the tender age of nineteen. When she'd died. I swallowed hard, shoving the unbidden memories aside. I needed to concentrate.

A couple of less than legal maneuvers and one lucky light later, I popped out of the snarl of traffic onto Magazine Street. I revved the engine and sped down the road until I reached the corner of Notre Dame. A familiar dark SUV was parked outside an unassuming gated entrance to what looked like an alley smashed between two buildings in the middle of the block.

I cursed softly under my breath as my motorcycle rumbled to a stop behind the SUV with unnecessarily dark windows. I jerked my helmet off and ran a hand through my long hair, trying to tame it into something a little less like a bird's nest. I hurried toward the SUV. The driver's side window whirred down to reveal a huge man crammed behind the steering wheel. He looked uncomfortable in a stiff black suit and a plastic wire curling from his ear into his collar. He glared at me as I jogged up.

"You're late," he growled.

"Five minutes. Don't get your panties in a twist, Hank," I said to the half-ogre as I shoved my helmet at him.

"Late is late," he grumbled, taking my helmet, and tossing it casually on the empty passenger seat.

"Lucky for me, bodyguarding isn't an hourly rate," I said, expertly flipping my long hair into a quick, if somewhat disheveled up-do that might pass for a rumpled sexy look. If the light was dim.

"It is when I do it," Hank muttered.

"And that's reason fifty-three why you should come over to the dark side," I said, shooting him a saucy wink.

"Never," Hank replied, shaking his massive head. "I like the benefits. I mean, we even get dental." He bared his teeth at me to prove his point. Teeth that looked like he ate gravel for breakfast and boulders for dinner. No wonder he liked the benefits.

The backdoor popped open, and another big guard held the door wide. A beautiful, lithe High Fae woman slid from the back seat, all grace and sex appeal. She flipped a strand of long blonde hair over her shoulder as she regarded me, carefully scanning me from head to toe. I knew what she saw. An average, if athletically built, brunette with caramel skin and gold eyes. I'd opted for skin-tight black jeans, a black lace corset top, and my trusty leather jacket. I'd picked my outfit specifically to get past the bouncer and then blend into obscurity within the darkened nightclub.

The woman, on the other hand, had dressed to stand out. She was tall and willowy, with curves in all the right places. With her height and figure, any high-fashion runway in the world would've welcomed her with open arms. A scrap of pink fabric that might have generously been called a dress drew attention to all her assets. Killer silver gladiator sandals elongated her slender legs and completed her stunning look.

"Really, Cameron? Combat boots?" The Fae woman raised a perfect eyebrow at my footwear.

"All the better to protect you with, Letitia," I said, not bothering to hide the snark in my tone.

Letitia sniffed. "That's *Lady* Letitia to you. Well, I suppose that we can go now that you are finally here." She turned to Hank, lifting her other haughty eyebrow to meet its twin.

"Yeah. Cameron will have your back inside, but we'll be right out here if you need us," he said, keeping his voice cool and professional.

"I'm aware. This is not our first outing, after all," she said with an eloquent roll of her eyes. She turned without another word and sauntered across the road. A bouncer appeared out of the shadows and swung the gate wide for her before she'd even taken three steps. I widened my eyes at Hank at the prissy fae's behavior. He shook his head slightly and jerked his chin after Lady Letitia, indicating I'd better catch up or get left behind. I grimaced but turned and jogged after her.

"You don't have to treat him like that, you know. Hank's just doing his job," I muttered as I caught up to her in the middle of the road.

Letitia sighed. "Yes, I know, but sometimes it is just so *stifling*. I spend all day being the perfect niece for my uncle at the Embassy. After all, it wouldn't do to have a scandal descend upon the New Orleans Ambassador from Fae." Her tone implied she was reciting an often-heard refrain.

I snorted, "You? Perfect? I mean, no offense or anything, but I can't imagine you playing that role. I mean, look at you." I waved a hand at her party-girl attire.

"Yes, well, looks can be deceiving, can't they?" A serious look flitted across her face. Shaking her head, Letitia grabbed my arm and smiled brightly at the bouncer as she dragged me into the nightclub. "But enough about that. This is my night and I'm going to have fun if it kills me."

I rolled my eyes but allowed her to drag me into the packed nightclub.

As soon as we entered the dim club, Letitia waved a hand at someone across the bar and shimmied her way to the dance floor. Knowing the routine, I scouted out a place at the bar near the entryway that was marginally quieter than the cacophony that passed for a good time on the dance floor. I waved a familiar bartender over and shouted my regular order to him over the pounding bass. He nodded and returned a moment later with a club soda and a slice of lime. I slid some money across to him as I settled in for a long night of watching Lady Letitia dance the night away while the throbbing electronic music eroded my hearing.

# Chapter 3

Three club sodas later, I slipped off to a nearby bathroom to relieve myself. I sighed in pleasure as the heavy door muffled the pulsing thrum from the dance floor. I might be twenty-four, but this definitely wasn't my scene. Don't get me wrong, I liked a good party. I just preferred one where I wouldn't suffer permanent hearing damage. Call me old-fashioned.

When I pushed back out into the bar, I gazed at a sea of blackness. A throbbing bass line pulsed through the air like furious thunder, vibrating me to the core. I peered into the dark as fingers of indigo lights glowed, faintly pushing back the blackness. Suddenly, neon lights from the DJ stand strobed into the inky darkness. I'd grown accustomed to the dim lighting and I wasn't ready for the ocular assault.

Never having developed much in the way of ladylike behavior, my natural reaction was to swear. Rubbing at my eyes, I shouted curses that were immediately lost amid the deafening music. I tried to paw away after images of the strobing lights that flashed against the inside of my eyelids. I stumbled, crashing into something hard. Strong arms wrapped around my waist and pulled me tight against a hard-muscled male torso.

Instinctively, I reached for my shadows as I struggled for equilibrium. I shook my head sharply, reminding myself that I couldn't do that here. Using magic in front of Norms was the first cardinal sin for any Supernatural in New Orleans. Instead, I relied on my speed, strength, and training. I turned to face my attacker. I flattened my palms against his chest and pushed hard to gain some space. He let go immediately, throwing his hands wide. Unexpectedly free, I dropped into a crouch to lower my center of gravity, cocking back my fist for a swift uppercut. Then I looked up.

The man in front of me should never be punched in the face. To break a nose like that would be a crime against beauty. His straight, almost noble, nose sat in perfect symmetry between gray eyes that were currently laughing down at me. His cheekbones should have been gracing magazine covers instead of dingy nightclubs.

I tipped my head to the side, considering him cautiously before starting a brawl in the nightclub. Although, in my defense, he *had* grabbed me without permission, so I wouldn't take a nasal reprimand off the table. Yet. This man's future reconstructive surgery bill depended on what came out of that mouth, currently curved into a roguish grin over brilliant white teeth that flashed in the strobing lights from the dance floor.

*Down, girl.*

He held his hands out in front of him. "Whoa! *You* crashed into *me*. I was just doing the gentlemanly thing and helping you not fall on your ass."

Yep. That decided it. I wanted to punch him in the nose. I glared up at him, not dropping my fist. "A gentleman wouldn't have mentioned my ass," I growled as menacingly as possible over the swelling music.

His eyes twinkled. "A lady wouldn't have jumped into my arms ass first." His grin widened. "You can hardly fault me for noticing a lady's *ass*ets," he said, unnecessarily stressing the first syllable of the word. The gorgeous man leaned to the side, trying to sneak a glimpse of my backside. Which was likely on display, thanks to the squat I still maintained.

I rolled my eyes and pushed back to a standing position. This guy was obviously focused on flirting rather than fighting. I cocked a hip and folded my arms. "Really? Bad word play is the best you've got?" I asked, allowing the disdain to drip off my words.

He threw his head back and laughed. I couldn't help but notice how the muscles in his shoulders and pecs responded to the sudden movement under his tight T-shirt.

"Well, you haven't given me much time to come up with clever word play between jumping into my arms and trying to cold-cock me. All in about three-point-one-four seconds."

"No excuse for bad behavior," I returned swiftly.

"Oh? And what *would* be an excuse for bad behavior?" His eyes gleamed wickedly. He took the time to scan me from head to toe. The slow smile that curved his lips told me he enjoyed what he saw. When his eyes finally met mine, laughter danced in the warm gray depths.

I rolled my eyes but couldn't help but smiling back. Something about the handsome man whispered to me of genuine mirth. When you go to as many bars as I've frequented for my various jobs, you get a sixth sense for a stranger's smarmy flattering mumbo jumbo. I got none of that from the man smiling down at me. This guy was all sincere charm, or I missed my guess.

"What brings you here? This doesn't really look like your scene," he said and then held up his hands in self-defense. "Not that I'm complaining, mind you."

"What, prying into a girl's secrets already?" I said with a wink that I hoped came across as flirty.

He jammed his hands in his pockets and shrugged. "It wasn't my intention. Based on the other women here, the dress code seems less leather and more skin," he said, jerking his head towards the dance floor.

I spun, spreading my arms to put my carefully-constructed noncha-lant-chic ensemble on full display.

*Oh, this? I just threw this on...in three hours, with several YouTube tutorials, and whispered promises of fulfilling sexual fantasies to un-named gods if the thing would just. Freaking. Go. On.*

When I faced him again, I slapped on an overtly innocent expression. "I have no idea what you mean. You're telling me that this place isn't a black leather and biker boots kind of bar?"

He snorted. "I'm pretty sure that you're the only one here in that ensemble and I'm one hundred percent confident that you're the only one who could pull it off."

I chuckled, "Lucky me, then." I craned my neck, searching for a free bartender at the nearby bar.

The man noticed the direction of my gaze. "At least let me buy the prettiest girl here a drink," he said, smiling charmingly down at me and offering me his arm like a proper Southern gentleman.

I debated brushing him off as I glanced out on the dance floor. Letitia shimmied to the beat with a bunch of girls I didn't recognize. She looked like she was enjoying her night. There was no reason I couldn't do the same. Smiling, I placed my hand in the crook of his arm and allowed the stranger to lead me to the bar. He patted my hand and held onto it as he steered us through the crowd, keeping me close to his side as we slid up to the tall wooden bar. He threw an arm around me casually as he waved down a bartender. I bit my lip. Talk about muscle definition! I could almost hear his biceps shouting at me about reps and increased weight routines from where our arms briefly touched before he shifted away. I looked at him through my lashes, entirely aware of the effect my unusually brilliant golden eyes had upon men.

"What is your pleasure this evening, milady?" he asked with a courteous little bow. A smile crinkled the corners of his eyes as his warm gaze suddenly turned up the temperature in the bar.

"Club soda, please," I managed past the flutter that sprang to life in my stomach. I needed to give my knees a stern talking to, because they were not doing their job, the traitorous bastards.

The hunk of a mystery man raised an eyebrow but ordered the drinks. The bartender ducked away in search of the libations as the stranger turned back to me. "Tell me again, what brings you to a place like this? I can't believe that this is your regular Friday night, Miss...?" he eyed my well-worn black leather jacket again as he left the sentence hanging.

"Cameron. And how do you know what my scene is?" I answered primly, turning to stare out at the crowd on the dance floor. I had to admit that my jacket was out of place in this club, where most women were showing as much leg or cleavage as possible; sometimes both.

He held up his hands to protest his innocence. "Just making an observation, that's all. A beautiful woman doesn't usually come to a nightclub to stand by herself on the edge of the dance floor and drink soda water. At least not in my limited experience of the mystery that is the fairer sex."

"I'm working," I said. I turned my back to the bar and put my elbows on the top, surveying the crowd. Letitia was still bobbing away to the beat of the throbbing bass. It would be a miracle if she didn't have a wardrobe malfunction soon in that skimpy excuse for a dress. The way some men were eyeing her up, I could tell that they were hoping for just such a happenstance.

I stood up straight, eyes focused on the blonde bouncing away on the dance floor. "I'm working," I repeated as a sluice of cold awareness awoke something in my subconscious. I scanned the crowd again, this time with an intense professional detachment. One by one, I clocked three men moving in concert towards Letitia. I'd been on too many jobs to assume they just wanted a dance. No, I knew better in my bones. They were hunting her.

The handsome man grabbed my arm as I shoved away from the bar. I shook him off roughly. "I'm *working*," I said shortly.

He held his hands up in surrender. "Another time?" he called out as I pushed my way onto the dance floor.

"Find me later!" I shouted over the pulsing bass, waving a hand over my shoulder. I put an extra wiggle in my hips so that my assets were giving him an eyeful as I walked away. Balance. Life is about balance. I could add in a little flirtatious fun to compensate for working on the weekend.

My gaze locked on the blonde bouncing to the beat in that gravity-defying dress and all thoughts of frivolity fled. I scanned the room and located the three guys I had noticed earlier. If I got her away from them unscathed, I would have to ask Letitia for her secret to keep her secrets, well, secret. Victoria had nothing on her.

Pointy elbows and accidentally smashing toes in my heavy combat boots got me through the crowd fast, but not as fast as I would've liked. Cold sweat dripped down my spine as I stretched onto my tiptoes, hoping for a glimpse of one of the men. I needed to get to Letitia before they did. I craned my neck, peering around the gyrating bodies and saw a tall wiry guy with dark kinky hair reach my hot pink target.

*Damn it.*

The wiry guy jammed along to the pounding bass, towering over Letitia as he approached her from behind. I watched helplessly as he wrapped his hands around her tiny waist; lean muscles danced along his exposed forearms as he smiled down at her. I hissed in anger, shoving through the crowd with more urgency to get to her. Letitia smiled up at the newcomer, happy to have a dance partner. The wiry guy started grinding on her, pushing her towards the DJ stand and the back of the club.

I gritted my teeth. I hadn't been monitoring her alcohol intake this evening, so I didn't know if she was drunk or stupid or both because she went right along with him with a grin and a sexy little wriggle of her hips.

My blood boiled. I hated unfair fights. A big guy with backup against one slim woman was my definition of unfair. Unless, perhaps, the woman was me.

I glanced around, searching for the wiry guy's two friends even as I kept forcing my way through the densely packed dance floor. I saw them, closing in on their friend and Letitia. Instinctively, I pulled on the dark shadows at the corners of the room, blurring out my form like water dripped on a charcoal sketch. It worked. Both men continued scanning the crowd, watching for any signs of pursuit or angst from the party people getting their late-night groove on, but their eyes slid right over me. The men hustling Letitia out of the club couldn't pick me out of the press of bodies, but I had an easy enough time keeping tabs on my charge, thanks to that little pink dress.

It was unusually hot in New Orleans for late October, but I was genuinely concerned about her catching pneumonia dressed like that. And being kidnapped. The latter was probably a more urgent issue.

The crowd of sweaty, wriggling bodies jiving to the beat got denser the closer I got to the DJ. I lost sight of my quarry in the mass of dancers. Just as I pushed past the corner of the DJ stand, a steely hand grabbed my upper arm. I quickly scanned the room again as I dropped my shadows.

*Shit. Shit. And triple shit.*

Only two guys with my blonde target. Which meant that number three was likely my unwelcome suitor. He should have known better. No one likes a grabber.

As I spun towards the guy holding my arm, I feinted an open-handed slap towards his face with my free hand. Guys always assume that girls will go for the dramatic face slap. Not me. I'm one of those women who actually knows how to fight, not pose dramatically after cracking some man across a cheek.

The guy holding me in place was already moving to block my feint, so he didn't see my foot, encased in my favorite combat boots, lash out towards his knee. I love high heels for what they can do for my ass, but no shoe can quite match the damage of a combat boot, especially when it connects with an unsuspecting knee.

He fell, and I twisted out of his grasp to put him in an armlock. Now, I had the advantages of height and gravity. I raised a fist, but hesitated. The face looking up at me caught me by surprise. My assailant was in the awkward phase between boy and man. His dark features had hints of unrealized strength and good looks, but damn. He still looked like a teenager. How did he even get into the club?

Not my problem. My problem was in a pink mini dress being hurried out of my field of vision by two large, likely violent, men who were going to wonder where their buddy was really soon.

Mentally shrugging, I jabbed a fist into the young guy's face. I had zero qualms about breaking *his* nose. I threw another quick jab to his throat, making sure that trying to breathe was going to be his top priority for the next few minutes.

The DJ moved his headset to the side and raised his eyebrows in surprise as the guy thumped down next to his kit. I lifted my thumb to my mouth, miming taking a drink, and then shrugged with a wry grin. The DJ gave me a thumbs up and turned away before he saw the blood gushing down the goon's face.

*Gotta love New Orleans*! I chuckled darkly as I dove through the crowd, hunting the hunters.

# Chapter 4

I pushed through the heavy metal door at the back of the club and the hot, humid night air wrapped around me like a warm embrace after the artificially arctic air conditioning inside. A second later, the fetid smell of rotting garbage in the club alley mixed with a muggy New Orleans autumn night.

*Why can't nightclubs ever open onto a nice thoroughfare or a park?* I thought, trying not to breathe through my nose.

The two men wheeled round as the heavy metal club door banged against a crumbling brick wall. I let the dim light from the single overhead bulb above the door illuminate me as I stepped into the dank alleyway. I knew what they saw. A slim but attractive brunette with tanned, almost caramel skin, honey highlights in her wavy dark hair and shockingly golden eyes.

I also knew how they perceived the potential threat. To put it mildly, I didn't intimidate most men at first glance. Or women. Or large-ish rodents, for that matter.

I tried to compensate for my stature with threatening fashion choices. I was wearing a black leather jacket, black leather leggings that looked painted on, my black lace corset top, and my trusty combat boots. Black, of course. When I was working, I liked to keep it simple and, above all, easy to move in. Just in case I found myself in a fight in a stinking club alley, for example.

"Let her go," I purred softly.

The big bald guy with a couple of visible scars peeking out from under a tight T-shirt let out a rumbling chuckle. He looked like he had more muscles than brains, but I wasn't about to assume the worst without a proper introduction.

The tall wiry guy with kinky hair kept a firm hold on the blonde's arm. I made a bet with myself that the New Orleans humidity was not kind to his haircare routine. He looked content to hold on to the girl and let his bigger buddy take care of the angry little woman.

The meathead faced me with a growl. "Get outta here."

"No," I said calmly, letting the word hang in the fetid air between us.

He waited for me to continue. When I didn't, he grunted in surprise.

There are some people who use words as weapons. Don't get me wrong, I've used them a time or two myself. At tea parties. But in my line of work, I've found that a quiet woman just unsettles people, especially men. Especially the big ones.

I use it to my advantage from time to time. If you can call being quiet while facing a man who is a foot taller than you and nearly two hundred pounds heavier an advantage.

Meathead growled again. His brain must have shorted out at my monosyllabic answer. Then he rushed me. My brain stutter-stepped for a moment. It seemed like he was going to grab me, or maybe just throw me around a bit. He wasn't trying to take me out or even hurt me.

Unfortunately for him, I didn't harbor those same sentiments. I wanted him out of my way. Now. To do that, I was going to hurt him. Quickly and violently.

As he ran at me, I slid to the side, pulling on up my magic and using the shadows to distort my form as I dodged. The trick worked. Momentum suddenly wasn't on the big guy's side as I was there one moment and gone the next. He struck headfirst into the door frame behind me. He shook his head dazedly and turned just in time to see the heavy metal battering ram of a door shatter his nose. I slammed the door into his head twice more.

Glancing down, I noted he would not be enjoying consciousness any time soon. I pushed him out of the doorway with my boot. He rolled into a pile of pungent, oozing garbage overflowing from the dented and rusting metal trash cans. One down, one to go.

I turned toward the lanky guy with kinky hair as I gently shut the club door behind me.

Tonight, my score card read: two guys down, two broken noses. I turned my attention towards the third guy and suddenly craved a clean hat trick to round off my evening.

The wiry guy shoved Letitia into a wall as I turned my focus on them. She stumbled over her high heels with all the grace of a newborn baby giraffe on ice. I heard a crack as her head struck the brick wall and winced. I cringed again as she crumpled, unconscious, into a puddle of what I hoped was water. But we were facing off in a nasty alley at the back of a club. Experience told me that the liquid soaking into her pink mini dress was a lot more disgusting.

The wiry guy crouched and shuffled slowly forward, avoiding the scattered debris dotting the alley. *Damn it. Why did the smart one always come last?*

He shuffled towards me; hands raised in a grappling stance. I have no idea why. With his reach, he could have easily put his palm against my forehead, locked his elbow and reduced me to uselessly flailing my arms as in every cartoon sibling fight ever. I mentally shrugged. No use waiting forever.

I grabbed a metal trash can lid from the pile of dented canisters to my right and hurled it at him like a discus. He batted it aside with his left arm but was too slow to deflect my fist as it connected with his temple. The strength of the punch combined with my speed spun him to the side. The speed and strength of my attack surprised him. He hadn't expected either. That was likely because I was faster and stronger than any normal human should be. Why, you ask? Well, because I am not strictly a normal human.

As the wiry goon was stumbling to his left, I kept the momentum from my first punch going and spun around to land a second punch to his kidneys. He then ran into my third and favorite fist. The pavement.

He lay on the pavement moaning. I stepped back, watching carefully until he tried to push to his feet. Then I kicked him in the stomach.

Twice. Honorable? Not a chance. I can do honor. In a gym with rules. In a dingy club alleyway, I check my honor at the door.

Wiry surprised me and knocked my non-kicking leg out from under me as I was readying a third kick. See? You always have to watch out for the smart ones. Being on the ground with a larger opponent lunging to his feet over you is never a great option when you are a petite woman. I rolled back on my shoulders and flipped to my feet with a groan. I was going to have to get my jacket professionally cleaned again after this. Annoying.

Wiry took a big swing at me, but I ducked under his arm and served him a couple of quick jabs to his lean gut. He instinctively grabbed to protect his already bruised and battered middle. I took the opening with an uppercut to his nose. A fountain of blood cascaded down his face. Yes! A hat trick for me!

He reached up to staunch the blood coursing from his broken nose. I grabbed his shoulders to brace myself and rammed my knee between his legs. I needed him incapacitated, not coming after me on some revenge quest for a damaged dong.

Wiry was on the ground, moaning and grabbing his face with one hand and his nuts with the other. I twisted to check over my shoulder and grinned. Meathead was still unconscious. In a pile of rotting club refuse. I doubted he would be happy when he woke up.

I crouched next to the wiry guy rolling around on the pavement. "You want to tell me what that was all about?" I asked. "Why did you grab the girl?"

"Fwuck ewu," he groaned, spraying blood through the fingers clutching his face.

"No," I chuckled darkly, "fuck you." I punched him in the side of the head, sending him into the comforting darkness of unconscious.

# Chapter 5

I looked down at my hands and sighed inwardly. Dark sticky blood from three different guys' broken noses covered them. I know that accent colors are important and all, but I'm not sure any fashionistas would approve of my current dripping crimson statement. This is why black is my favorite color: It doesn't show the blood. I wiped off what I could on my top, trying not to get any more blood on my leather jacket. My dry cleaner kept telling me that blood is not a leather treatment, but I'm still not convinced.

I shuddered as I took another look at Wiry. He looked hairier than when I opened the alleyway door. A *lot* hairier. Either he had the worst case of body hair I had ever seen, or that was fur peeking out of the neckline of his shirt. I peered closer at his hand holding his junk. It looked more paw-like than hand-like.

*Shit.*

It was a good thing I had followed the first rule of fighting that any girl learns: Take the other guy out fast and hard. Otherwise, the werewolf on the ground in front of me might have finished his shift.

I cursed inwardly. *Werewolves? In New Orleans?* There was no Pack here. These werewolves must be rogues. I quickly rifled through their pockets. Damn it. No IDs. They must be smarter than they looked at first glance. I pulled out my cell phone and snapped a picture of both unconscious guys for later inspection.

I didn't have time to mess around and I needed to get my target to safety. Keeping a careful eye on my surroundings in case there were more wolves around, I went over to Letitia and did a quick visual evaluation. She didn't seem grievously injured.

I crouched just outside of the questionable puddle and dug a small envelope out of my jacket. Ripping it open, I waved it under her nose. She woke up, coughing and spluttering, pushing away my smelling salts.

"Come on," I grunted, pushing to my feet. "We need to get out of here."

Letitia looked up at me groggily and then at the unconscious wolves, caught mid-shift. She noted the partial paw with a slight widening of her blue eyes before imperiously reaching out an arm for me to help her up.

I shook my head, crossing my arms over my damp top. "Nuh-uh, princess. I'm pretty sure that ain't water you're sitting in. I'm already looking down the barrel at a steep dry-cleaning bill. No need to add whatever that is." I waved a hand vaguely at the puddle surrounding her.

She looked down, wrinkling her nose at the foul-smelling liquid. Carefully, touching as little as possible, she slid smoothly to her feet. She ran careful hands over her dress and hair, checking for injuries. Her bedazzled pink fingertips emphasized the silkiness of her gorgeous blonde hair falling over smooth, perfectly tanned shoulders to tickle the top of her ample cleavage, and the shape of her beautifully curved figure that was lovingly embraced by her hot pink mini dress. Her teeny dress rode up ever so slightly to further elongate already long, tanned legs. My gaze skimmed down the long expanse of leg to dainty feet tied into killer silver gladiator sandals. I took a shaky breath. I was getting hot and bothered just watching her examine herself.

I decided now was a good time to strategically scan the darkened alleyway for additional threats. Because I am a professional.

Apparently satisfied by her lack of injuries, the blonde bombshell took a dainty step out of the puddle of questionable origin. She grimaced at the dirt staining her dress and splattered over her body. She waved a perfectly manicured hand and her form started to shimmer. Recognizing the Fae glamour magic, I looked away before my night vision was completely ruined. Just in time too because a brilliant flash flared around Letitia a moment later.

"Hey! Princess Lightning Bug! Keep the fireworks down! Someone might see us!" I grouched, keeping my eyes averted until the light dimmed.

She sighed, "For the last time, Ms. Blaze, it is *Lady*, not Princess. Lady. Lady Letitia of the High Fae Spring Court. But you are right about one thing, it would have been a tragedy if someone had seen me looking so disheveled. Appearing as anything less than perfect is unacceptable."

"Could've fooled me, the way you've been carrying on all night," I muttered, rubbing the last of the magical shimmer from my eyes.

*Damn Letitia's vanity and her attention-grabbing glamour magic.*

When I focused on my blonde companion again, she no longer looked like someone had knocked her unconscious in a puddle of unmentionables.  She looked, well, *hot*. My pulse pounded again, and I forced myself to look away.

She caught me and gave a naughty little grin. "Careful, Ms. Blaze, or I might promote you from bodyguard to something more." A wicked gleam danced in her eyes as she took her time scanning my figure even more closely than the guy in the bar who had been admiring my...assets.

"You're not paying me for my services," I mumbled towards the wall, still dazzled by her overt use of magic in the dark alleyway in the middle of New Orleans.

"And I never would. That's my uncle's job," she quipped, the corner of her mouth curling up. "Come," she commanded, extending her arm. "I am no longer in a festive mood. Take me home."

"Never in a million years," I muttered too softly for even her delicately pointed Fae ears to hear. Her head whipped towards me. *Whoops.* Not soft enough, apparently. "Right away, milady. Your wish is my command," I amended.

I added a slight bow and what I hoped was a courtly wave towards the mouth of the alley to suit her Hoity-Toity-ness. The darkened street at the end of the alley beckoned us. I needed to get Letitia out of here before the werewolves woke up. Or anything else attacked us.

# Chapter 6

I gave the unconscious werewolves a cursory examination once more. Their fur had receded and there wasn't a paw in sight. Good. At least I didn't have to worry about a drunk frat boy stumbling onto irrefutable proof of the existence of the supernatural world when he slipped out to have a whizz in the alley. Satisfied that I'd covered my tracks as much as time allowed, I hurried Letitia away. I hoped Hank was still waiting for us. Waiting and werewolf-free.

I stuck out an arm to keep Lady Letitia behind me as I peered around the corner of the alleyway onto Camp Street. The narrow road was deserted except for a few parked cars and one lone man poking through a restaurant's dumpsters in another nearby alley.

I let out a shallow breath in relief, having imagined the worst. Namely, an entire pack of wolves waiting on the other side of the road.

Letitia craned her neck to peer over my shoulder, "Why'd you stop?" she murmured, her honeyed breath and intoxicating perfume sweeping over me, distracting me from my surveillance. "It reeks," she added with what I imagined was an annoyingly cute wrinkle to her nose.

I scanned the dark street again, making sure I hadn't missed anyone lurking in the shadows cloaking the sidewalk. Only a few of the street-lights were working, so there were plenty of places to hide. The shadows were so deep that you could walk right up to one before you could tell if there was someone lurking, just waiting to pounce. I was loath to walk into an ambush but needed to move us out of the werewolf-infested alley. Fast.

"Just checking for more assailants, your Highness," I whispered, as satisfied as possible with my surveillance.

"Ladyship," she corrected absentmindedly, following my gaze and trying to pierce the gloom with her heightened supernatural senses.

When it came to seeing in the dark, there were few that could best me. Normals had no chance, but I had yet to meet a Supernatural that could see better than I could. I didn't advertise this fact. In fact, I obscured knowledge of my powers from the supernatural population of New Orleans whenever I could. But on a night like tonight, I freely utilized my bonus of being able to see in the dark regardless of potential exposure.

Reassured that there was no one else on the street except the homeless man, I pulled slightly on the shadows surrounding us. I felt the shadows brush my fingertips like soft velvet. I wrapped them around us as tightly as I could before grabbing Letitia's elbow to keep her close. We hurried down the road and took a quick right onto Girod Street. A hiss of relief escaped me as I saw the familiar black SUV parked on the corner. I pounded on the back door on the passenger side with my fist. It immediately popped open and the same burly man in a black suit with a curling plastic earpiece peered out at us.

"Lady Letitia wishes to return home," I informed him with as much arrogance as I could manage. He nodded and scooted over to make room for her.

Hank rolled down the passenger-side window and passed me my bike helmet as Letitia settled herself in the SUV. "Run into any problems?" he asked.

"You know me, Hank; nothing that I couldn't handle," I shot back with a cocky smile.

Hank grunted. "That means you did. Boss won't be happy." He clicked open the glove box and passed me a small pack of wet wipes.

"Tell him to come and have a chat with me," I said, accepting the wipes and using them to clean the residual blood from my hands.

He shook his head. "You know that will never happen, Cam. He likes you. Or rather, he likes your work. That's why he keeps using you for these special occasion gigs. But he is never, *ever* going to meet with you."

I shrugged. "His loss, your gain, Hank," I said, with a waggle of my eyebrows and a smirk.

Hank winked at me, smiling past a nose that had obviously been broken more than once in the past. "Follow us home?" he asked.

"Anytime, sugar," I drawled in my best, saccharine-sweet Southern affectation.

I jogged back to where I'd parked my motorcycle. I crammed my helmet on my head as I swung a leg over my Rebel. It was significantly easier to navigate the narrow roads and snarl of one-way traffic on my bike than the massive SUV in front of me I sighed, settling into the slower pace as I followed Hank to the Fae Embassy.

As we wove through the darkened streets of New Orleans, I kept a wary eye on the road behind us in case we were being followed. I let my subconscious paranoia take control of surveillance as I turned the situation over in my mind.

Letitia's uncle was the Fae Ambassador to New Orleans. He hired me for this routine bodyguard gig. He often used me to be the muscle where burly muscle would be out of place. I blended into club scenes to watch over his party-loving niece much better than the half-ogre Hank with his professional wrestler physique, stiff black suit, and curling plastic earpiece. Lady Letitia, like her uncle, was a lesser noble member of the High Fae. Except for the extraordinary beauty and pointed ears, High Fae could pass for human more easily than most Supes.

Letitia took advantage of this and liked to mix it up with the Norms, despite her uncle's misgivings. She said that hanging out with mortals helped her to remember to live life to the fullest or some such tripe. I didn't really care. She was a party girl who loved to dance. The money was good, and it had always been an easy gig. Until tonight.

I kept up my surveillance as I trailed the SUV to a swankier part of town. A grand old mansion, complete with white columns and climbing ivy, housed the Fae Embassy. It was far away from the loud, drunken tourist scene in the French Quarter that most people associated with New Orleans. This part of town oozed Southern sophistication and charm. Seriously, a movie crew could have walked into any house on the block and filmed a period drama piece with no need for set dressing.

Our small caravan pulled up to the gates surrounding the mansion. I dropped a foot to the pavement, letting the Rebel rumble as I watched the heavy gates swing open. I still hadn't figured out how they made the gates look like the famous New Orleans wrought iron. They couldn't actually be iron because all Fae creatures seemed to have a destructive allergy to metal, in varying degrees ranging from developing painful blisters on contact to death from prolonged exposure. This was especially true for the High Fae. No, that's not right. High Fae despised the metal. *Loathed* it, in fact. I had heard rumors that iron could do anything from making them sick for days, to killing one on contact. Touch the wrong utensil with a high iron count? *Poof!* You're dead.

I had my reservations about believing the rumors. They sounded ridiculously exaggerated to me. I mean, how could High Fae function in the modern world if they were deathly allergic to the slightest hint of iron? There were alloys of the stuff everywhere, not to mention all the wrought iron decorations scattered throughout New Orleans. It all seemed a bit extreme to me.

Come to think of it, that summed up the High Fae nicely, in my experience. In everything they did, they were an extreme bunch. My experiences with other fae creatures like fairies, brownies, pixies, elves, or goblins were usually much more predictable. Hell, even Hank was a cool dude and he was half-ogre!

I watched until Hank tapped the brakes on the SUV twice to let me know they were in for the night and my services were no longer needed. Letitia's uncle would pass along my payment for the evening through the guy who always arranged my jobs, Logan. We already had a meeting on the books for tomorrow to settle up tonight's fee. I sighed and pushed off the pavement, tired from the long night. I turned my bike back towards the heart of New Orleans, already fantasizing about my soft, warm bed.

Twenty minutes later, I was still wound up, despite the comforting cruise through the empty streets of the Big Easy. I hated to admit it, but I was too jazzed to head back to my apartment. I usually just rode out any residual adrenaline after a job by cruising with my Rebel, enjoying the New Orleans scenery. But the appearance of werewolves at my gig tonight threw a wrench into my plans for a calm cup of tea and a book.

*What the hell were werewolves doing in New Orleans?*

We weren't a werewolf kind of place Vampires, sure, given the history and location of the city. I hadn't run into a crazy number of vamps in my seven years here, but I knew a couple. Vamps and wolves got along about as well as oil and water. Cats and dogs. Knowledge and Jon Snow. You get the idea.

New Orleans was a tried-and-true vampire hot-spot Which meant that it didn't have a Pack. Sure, there was a Pack up in St Louis. A huge one, in fact. There may have been a couple of small ones scattered between here and there. Who knew? But a Pack in New Orleans? Not a chance. I would have heard.

That meant the three guys from the nightclub were rogues just passing through my fair city, or they were staking a claim trying to take over territory in New Orleans. Either way, by interfering in their plans to grab Letitia tonight, I had painted a giant neon target on my back. And werewolves didn't need a flashing sign to track someone down. I sighed, slowing for a red light. This was going to complicate things for me. I did not like complications.

Neither did my job-broker, Logan. He was wound a little tight. To be fair, that was an understatement. Logan made a Swiss watch look like a chocolate bar at the beach. In the middle of summer. He liked things to go precisely according to plan. I was confident that he had not planned on werewolves interfering in tonight's gig.

Despite the unfortunate timing of doubling up tonight, jobs were currently few and far between. I couldn't afford to piss off Logan and miss out on a future paycheck. Sure, I wasn't destitute, but neither was I swimming in money. I needed the work, which meant I needed these wolves to disappear. I groaned, rolling my shoulders under my leather jacket to relieve the tension creeping up my back.

I needed to talk this out. I needed a drink. Perhaps not in that order. I smiled, knowing where to go. Making a right turn, I set a course for my best friend, her bar, and a stiff drink to calm down before bed. Nothing bad ever happens from just one drink, right?

# Chapter 7

I pulled the Rebel around back at Sloane's place. Sloane O'Shea owned and operated the Forge, a local watering hole for Supes. It was a bar with character, which was saying something for New Orleans. It was close enough to the French Quarter to do a brisk business, but far enough away that tourists rarely stumbled through her doors. Especially at this hour. The tourists who came down to New Orleans to get smashed wouldn't waste their time on the walk to the Forge, and those who came for the local New Orleans flavor went to bed hours ago.

Sloane was a stunning leprechaun, an excellent bartender, a Star Trek fanatic, and my best friend. Perhaps not in that order. When I'd moved to New Orleans, I'd made some bad choices and worse acquaintances. Thankfully, I'd also met Sloane in those early days. She'd helped me navigate the complexities of being a Supe living in a city full of Norms. She'd lived in New Orleans long enough to offer invaluable advice about not drawing the wrong kinds of attention.

Sloane owned a refurbished old blacksmith shop and turned it into a bar that she christened the Forge. Creative with names, Sloane is not. Her drinks, on the other hand? That's a completely different story. What the girl can do with some liquor and a shaker was magic, I swear. But she also used her contacts to put me in touch with my job-broker, Logan.

I parked my bike next to the two spaces reserved for employees and grabbed my helmet. Shaking the ride from my legs, I walked around to the front rather than slipping in the back of the Forge. Sloane has a policy about unannounced people coming in the back of her bar. Namely: shoot first, ask questions later. It is a policy that I helped co-author and fully supported. One thing I liked about Sloane was that she was a woman of her word. Consistent. Steady. In a situation like this, I wasn't about to test her. She'd shoot me and then laugh and call me a "bloody eejit" as I lay bleeding on her floor.

I cracked open the front door. A smile immediately curved my lips as the sound of jazz drifted through the dimly lit bar from one of the interior rooms. Sloane had done little to adjust the bones of the building. She had kept the low ceilings and irregular walls and tucked tables into the resulting nooks and alcoves. It gave the place a cozy, secretive ambiance. Like those drinking here weren't just drinking, they were holding clandestine meetings so scandalous that they needed to huddle over tiny tables and blend into the smoke-stained walls of the old smithy so as not to be overheard.

I dragged the fingers of my left hand across the wood worn smooth by time. I had never been able to pry out of her if the walls and ceiling were actually smoke-stained or if it was just a dramatic effect that her interior decorator had concocted. Hell, she kept the old anvil as the centerpiece in the middle of the largest room. I wouldn't put it past her to amp up the character of her bar by engaging in some exaggerated decorating. However, I've learned over time that Sloane runs her bar how Sloane runs her bar and if you are smart, you don't question her aesthetic choices. At least, not where she can hear you.

These days, the anvil in the middle of the main room served as a table for her guests to get hammered instead of hammering iron. It also served as a massive deterrent to the High Fae community of New Orleans. They couldn't stand being in the same room as that much iron for long, let alone leaning up against a massive anvil made of the stuff while sipping Sloane's creative cocktails. The Forge was not somewhere Lady Letitia would have spent the night shimmying away in her little pink dress.

Sloane preferred it that way. Like I said, she's a leprechaun. The High Fae had hunted her people even more than the humans had hunted them. The way Sloane tells it, they hunted, tortured, and brutally murdered leprechauns whenever they got the chance. Whether for sport, for luck, or for the rumored gold at the end of the rainbow, it was unclear. Although it was centuries ago, the stories Sloane told me made my blood run cold.

Sloane hated the High Fae and did not want them anywhere near her bar. Hence, the big-ass anvil in the middle of the bar. I wove my way through the dim rooms, rubbing the polished tip of the anvil for luck as I passed.

Even though it was late, the Forge was still lively. I guessed that was because of Billy. From the piano I heard tickling in the background, he was the musician on staff tonight. He probably pulled in more cash at his other gigs around town, but he always played piano a couple of nights a week here.

Billy drew in just as many people as Sloane's concoctions and the atmospheric setting. I swear, the man was a genius with the ivories. The way his fingers danced over the keys was bewitching. I could sit and watch him play for hours. Pure magic, and not the supernatural kind.

I finally reached the bar at the back of the Forge. Billy's piano was tucked up in the corner opposite the bar and surrounded by a moderately sized crowd. The piano man gave me a small jerk of his chin and a wink before turning his attention back to his adoring fans. I raised a hand in return, my nerves settling. The familiarity of the music worked on my anxiety like a warm bath, soothing away my unease so I could think straight.

I waved over the short, stocky man behind the bar. "Hey, Rudolph," I extended my hand across the bar. "How are you doing tonight?"

Rudolph took my hand and performed a courtly little bow over it. "Fair to middling, Miss Blaze."

I rolled my eyes at the wood elf. Wood elves were just one variant of elves you could find hiding in plain sight. However, they were some of the finest brewers of beer I had ever had the pleasure of meeting. Sloane scored a coup when she snagged Rudolph as a bartender and in-house brewer for the Forge. He brewed my favorite beer and kept a stash behind the bar for me.

"How many times do I have to ask you to call me Cam, Rudolph?"

His eyes twinkled. "At least once more, as always, Miss Blaze."

I snorted. "Same old, same old, Rudolph. Is she in?"

He jerked a thumb towards the tiny back room, snuggled into a nook behind the bar. "She's finishing up some paperwork. She's been at it a while and could likely use a break. Shall I let her know you are here?"

"Please. That would be great, Rudolph. In the meantime, could I have a beer?"

He nodded and retrieved my favorite. From the lack of a label, I knew he had brewed it himself. He popped off the top of the chunky brown bottle and slid it over.

I saluted him with the bottle. "You're the best. Let Sloane know I'm waiting?" I asked. He nodded again before heading down to take care of the other thirsty patrons.

I made my way towards a secluded table that I had dubbed *mine*. I wouldn't go so far as to call it *my precious*, but give me a few drinks more and it might happen. The table was in a quiet little corner near the back of the Forge. It was far enough away from the bar that I could enjoy some privacy but still close enough to the piano to keep my toes a-tapping. I turned the corner, already taking a long pull from the bottle. I froze, cold beer trickling down my throat. Someone was sitting at my table. Given the events of the evening, I was paranoid enough to assume that it wasn't a coincidence.

# Chapter 8

A sultry redhead was sitting, no, *lounging*, at my table. I doubted that this woman did anything so mundane as to *sit*. Her pale skin seemed to reflect the dim light from the flickering fake candles. Wavering light sent shadows dancing around the room, highlighting the depths of her dark eyes. She raised a delicate glass containing a dark red liquid to her lips and sipped, and the bewitching shadows emphasized the curves of her face, her neck, and her cleavage.

For a split second, I thought Maman Brigitte had somehow tracked me down, but then, on closer inspection, realized this woman was a stranger. The redhead lowered her glass, catching me staring. The intensity of her deep eyes was startling. For a moment, I thought they were completely black. She blinked and smiled pearly white teeth at me. Nope, her eyes were definitely a chocolatey brown. It must have been a trick of the light. Or the start of an adrenaline crash messing with my usually sharp eyes. On the plus side, I hadn't upset a local deity to the point that she felt the need to track me down.

The woman carefully set down her glass and licked a droplet of blood-red wine from her lower lip with a delectable pink tongue, never breaking eye contact with me. I lowered my beer bottle, watching her cautiously. You never knew who or what you would encounter at the Forge. There were a fair number of powerful beings running around New Orleans, Maman Brigitte just being the most recent one I'd encountered. Regardless of power levels, Sloane got pissy when I broke things in her place. The last time it had happened, she'd banned me for a month. Rudolph's beer was too good to abstain for a month by choice, so I needed to proceed carefully. For the sake of the beer.

The redhead gestured invitingly at the seat across from her with long, elegant fingers tipped with blood-red nails. I glanced behind me to make sure it was me she was inviting to join her. Me, in my blood-spattered jeans and smelling like the wrong end of an alleyway. This beautiful—no, *intoxicating*—stranger wanted me to have a drink with her. I glanced surreptitiously around but couldn't see any other open tables. Finally, I shrugged and slouched into the seat she had indicated, knocking my knees intentionally against the table hard enough to make it wobble as I placed my helmet on the floor and sat down.

She grabbed her wine glass as it almost toppled over, moving so quickly that not a single drop of wine spilled. She smoothly raised the glass in a toast, ignoring my faux pas. "To new friends," she murmured huskily.

I grinned toothily, tapping my sturdy beer bottle gently against her elegant wine glass. "Or to new enemies."

She shrugged a smooth, pale shoulder and tossed her long, luscious red hair to the other side of her head. "Two sides of the same coin, wouldn't you say?" she said, taking a sip of her wine. Her smirk revealed teeth that were perhaps a little too sharp.

I made a show of patting down my pockets. "Damn. I don't really carry coins anymore. It's all plastic these days. Care to flip one of your own?"

Her smirk bloomed into a crafty smile as she correctly identified my not-so-subtle ploy to gather information about her. "Perhaps another time." She took a long drink from her glass, almost draining it. Interesting. She was nervous. That, combined with the speed with which she grabbed the wine glass, made me guess she was from my side of the fence. A Supe. An uncomfortable one, for some reason. Which meant this was likely not a chance meeting.

I decided to play along with my new drinking companion to see what information she was willing to reveal. "What are you drinking? Perhaps I can get you another?" I offered courteously.

I knew Sloane kept a supply of bloodwine on ice in case vampires wanted a drink out of a glass rather than a much warmer vessel in one of the back alleys of New Orleans. The tourists thought that we just poured stiff drinks down here. Little did they know that seven times out of ten, they had been a midnight snack for one of the local vamps. From what I'd been told, hangovers from stiff drinks compounded by vampire-induced blood loss were the *worst*.

Her smile widened, deducing what I was attempting. "Oh, I *like* you. This is going to be fun," she purred.

I shrugged, lifting my bottle to my lips for another sip.

She tapped a long, manicured finger on the table, waiting for me to speak. I examined my beer bottle like it was the most important thing in the world, just to see what she would do. People get uncomfortable with silence, even Supes. They like to break it, to fill it with something, *anything*, but the dreaded quiet. The more comfortable you are with silence, the more you learn with very little effort. Me? I'm lazy as hell. I sat there, enjoying Rudolph's beer, and waited.

The redhead sitting across from me arched an eyebrow; her furrowed brow cracking her elegant façade. I smiled and nursed my bottle, sensing victory.

The redhead sighed, tracing a finger around the edge of her almost empty wine glass. "I heard you were competent. I didn't know you were infuriating."

I smirked and indulged in another malty sip from the bottle in my hand. Damn, Rudolph brewed a fine beer.

She rolled her dark brown eyes expressively, allowing them to make her point. "Well, since you aren't much on conversation, I suppose introductions are in order." She extended her dainty manicured hand across the table. "I am Meridiana. And I drink." She pronounced her name like 'Mary-Diana'. I'd heard of Mary-Lou, Mary-Anne, and a host of other hyphenated names. This was the South, after all. But I'd never heard of a Mary-Diana.

I grunted in acknowledgment of her limited introduction, my mind flashing to my favorite dwarf from an epic fantasy series. He had said something similar once. I took her hand cautiously and gave it a brief shake.

"Cameron Blaze," I returned and then added quickly, "And what are you precisely?"

She raised a delicately shaped eyebrow. "Straight to it then?" she smiled, revealing those perfectly straight, pearly white teeth. On closer inspection, they were too sharp to be entirely normal. Her scarlet lips closed, obscuring my view. Her dark eyes flicked up to my right shoulder. I took a quick look behind me to see what had captured her attention. Nothing was there.

When I looked back, she was tapping her finger against the corner of her mouth. "Now, if I answer that, the next logical question would be 'What are *you*?', my dear Ms. Blaze. Since you don't really know the answer to that, this hardly seems like a fair exchange of information, does it? Daddy issues, am I right?"

Shock at her words rocked me to my core. "What do you know about my dad?"

Meridiana shook her head. "Not much." I let out a little sigh and wasn't sure if it was one of frustration or relief. She held up a slender finger. "But I do know your mom."

I froze, my heart clenching painfully in my chest. *Mom*. I sucked in a breath and let it out slowly. "Knew," I corrected softly. "She died five years ago." Memories threatened to overwhelm me. I forcefully shoved them back into the little boxes in my mind, focusing on the stranger across from me. The unexpected swell of emotion caused my response to come out harsher than I'd intended. "You really expect me to believe that you knew my mom and, what? Just popped out of nowhere to give me condolences, did you? You're five years too late, lady."

"She said you'd be suspicious. Fine. Your mom, Sophia Blaze, was a powerful mage. Bold, beautiful, and brilliant. She was on her way to achieve great things but threw it all away to move to a small nowhere place in backwoods Louisiana."

"Abita Springs," I murmured. An image of my childhood home flashed in my mind, and I smiled fondly. Mom had done her best to raise me on her own. We'd been comfortable, but there was nothing ostentatious or flashy about my childhood. Just Mom and me and lots of love.

Meridiana continued, ignoring my interruption, "She raised you on her own in that little backwoods town until she died."

"Pneumonia."

"Well, it didn't help things, no."

I shook my head, rousing myself from the trip down memory lane. Suspicion flared. "What kind of game are you playing, showing up here and claiming you know me? That you know my mom? Everything you've told me so far you could've googled about ten minutes."

The redhead drummed her fingers on the tabletop, long nails clicking a staccato rhythm. "She said you'd be skeptical, but she didn't mention pig-headed." Meridiana *tsked* under her breath and then leaned forward, speaking softly. "Fine, we'll do it your way. Your mother was a mage, but you aren't. When you hit puberty, you developed an affinity for shadow magic, which you got from your dad. When she realized she was out of her depth, your mother invited contacts from her past to come and help you develop the skills you'd need to survive. Contacts including a certain Coraniaid dwarf named Dougal. Does that ring a bell?"

One eyebrow crept toward my hairline in surprise. My mom refused to take me to one of the magic academies for training when my powers manifested, opting to invite tutors she knew and trusted to live with us for anything from a few weeks to a few months. Dougal, the Coraniaid dwarf who'd stayed the longest of all the tutors, had been my weapons master. Coraniaid dwarves have insanely sharp hearing and are immune to blades, which made him an ideal teacher for a clumsy teenager equipped with knives. I studied with him daily. He was the toughest trainer I've ever had. Other than Mom, that is.

I folded my arms across my chest to hide the trembling in my hands. I took refuge in stubborn denial. "So? Again, with enough digging, you could've uncovered that on your own."

Meridiana reached under the table and withdrew a heavy, worn cream colored envelope from the bag tucked next to her chair. She placed it on the table with a small *thunk*. "Your mom didn't die of pneumonia. Like I said, it didn't help matters, but that's not what killed her."

"What are you talking about?" I asked, my mouth turning dry.

"When she saw how your powers were developing, she knew she had to do something. She created and powered a high-level spell, but it required more power than she anticipated, draining her reserves to deathly levels. That spell left her susceptible. When she got sick, she couldn't shake it off and eventually succumbed to the illness, much to the sorrow of everyone who knew her."

My vision blurred as unshed tears pooled. "Why? Why would she do that?"

Meridiana looked at me, a sad smile turning up the corners of her mouth. "Why, to protect you, Cam. She did all of this to protect you."

Everything went hazy and spots danced in front of my eyes. "I don't believe you," I whispered.

Meridiana caressed the envelope in front of her. "Your mother loved you so much that she gave her life to cast a powerful protection charm over you."

"Why?" I barely got the word out past the sudden lump that appeared in my throat at the thought of my mom giving up her life. All to protect me.

"She knew that there were people out there who would love to get their hands on your father's daughter. On *you*. The charm was the only thing that she could think of to buy you time."

"Time I could've had with her?" I shot back.

Meridiana shrugged a slim shoulder. "Perhaps. But then again, perhaps not. Without the charm, your burgeoning power would've eventually drawn unwanted attention from powerful supernatural creatures. Creatures who would've done anything to get their hands on you for their own ends."

There was a ring of truth in her words, but a little part of me wasn't ready to accept all that this strange woman was selling. If I did, it would mean that I was responsible for my mother's death. "This is all very convenient, you showing up here with this story, claiming to have known my mom. Why should I believe you or any of this? What do you want?"

Meridiana smiled gently. "I just want to pay a debt," she said, sliding the heavy cream envelope across the table to me. "Which I now have. As for whether or not you believe me, you don't have to take my word for it." She nodded at the envelope.

"Cam!" Sloane's voice cut through the conversational buzz of the bar. I turned my head and raised my arm to wave her over. When I turned back, Meridiana's glass was wobbling on the table, but the woman had vanished.

# Chapter 9

Sloane wove through the crowd to get to my secluded table, holding two beer bottles in one hand. She was petite. An inch taller and some might have even generously called her short, a fairly common trait for leprechauns. Sloane's black hair was so dark that it almost looked like it had deep blue highlights running through it. She kept it chopped short in an edgy, fashionable cut. It contrasted beautifully with her luminous dark blue eyes. She could have passed for Black Irish if not for her delicately pointed ears, which she typically hid with clever styling of her ebony locks.

I understood Sloane's desire for privacy. In a world gone mad with posting every detail of life for public consumption on the worldwide web, a little privacy was nice. Sometimes, like in Sloane's case, privacy was essential. If anyone knew there was a leprechaun living in New Orleans, things wouldn't end well for her. People would flock to hunt her down for some illusionary pot of gold.

Sloane had told me once that she felt trapped in the leprechaun communities. 'Claustrophobic' and 'suffocating' were her precise words. According to her, they were traditional, conservative, and slow-paced communities. Everything that Sloane was not. I could appreciate wanting to taste freedom. Freedom inherently had risks attached, but Sloane had long ago decided that the risks were worth the reward. She guarded her freedom as jealously as any dragon would guard its treasure hoard.

Sloane stuck out her hand, and I smiled, returning the grip. A mischievous grin curved her lips and our fingers flew through a complicated series of gestures on instinct. We'd developed our secret handshake not long after I'd moved to New Orleans. I was young, stupid, and hungry to prove myself. Sloane needed a hand dealing with some vandals who were trying to drive her out of town. The short version is that we'd met, joined forces, and bonded during some long, uncomfortable nights staked out on the roof of the Forge as our butts grew numb and our legs cramped.

I can't tell you precisely why, but sometimes, you just meet someone and something inside you picks that person to be *your* person. The person you'll go on adventures with. The person you'll call at three in the morning because you need to talk. Your friend. The person who might as well be family because they know you so well. That was Sloane.

Sloane slipped into Meridiana's recently vacated seat across from me, eyeing the empty wine glass. "Company?" she queried with a raised brow.

I grunted in response.

"Well, I know this isn't a social visit. You never show up at this hour just to see me, which means you either want to celebrate or commiserate." She slid a fresh beer across the table to me. "Drink up while you tell me which one it is."

"You are seriously the best bartender in New Orleans," I said earnestly. I chugged the remainder of the beer in my hand before reaching for the cold bottle.

"You only say that because you get the family discount," Sloane said with a roll of her eyes and a smile.

"That doesn't hurt," I joked. We clinked bottles, sipped, and sighed in appreciation of Rudolph's fine brew. We spent a couple of minutes just enjoying the beer and each other's company while catching up on the insignificant details of life.

Sloane waved a server over and ordered another round. When he delivered the beer, Sloane leaned back in her chair and stretched out her legs. "Okay, I'm ready for whatever you came in here to talk about. Lay it on me."

I told her everything. Taking the bodyguard gig for Lady Letitia as she kicked up her heels. The recalled memory in the club that had disoriented me enough that I had missed the initial signs of trouble. The guy I had knocked out who had partially shifted to wolf. My suspicions that the other two were also wolves. I showed her the photos I had taken of the guys in the alley to see if she recognized them. She didn't.

I wrapped up my tale with my concerns about the wolves coming to New Orleans. I didn't know what their presence here meant, or, more immediately, what it meant for me. After all, I was the one who had kicked this hornets' nest. Or tugged the wolf's tail. Whatever.

Sloane listened attentively. She let me tell things in my own way, without interrupting. I found the retelling helpful. It helped me look at the situation through fresh eyes. I tried to see if I had missed anything important in the adrenaline rush.

Sloane sighed and sat back in her chair. Ever logical, she asked, "Right, so what's the next move?"

I mirrored her posture, leaning back in my own chair. It was a good choice, because the room was starting to spin. "Well, I have a morning meeting set up with Logan to get paid for the Letitia gig. I could ask him about the werewolves then, but I'd prefer to do some digging on my own before involving him. Get just a little more information first, you know?"

Sloane nodded. "Seems about right. He always struck me as a little—I don't know—slimy? Sleazy?"

"Slick," I interjected. "The word you are searching for is *slick.*"

Sloane pointed an index finger at me. "That's the one. He's just a little *too* slick. Best stick to probing as discretely as possible for information on werewolves."

"Hey now!" I protested, "I don't think probing Logan or werewolves ends well for me."

Sloane rolled her eyes at my juvenile joke. "As long as you are *searching* for werewolf info, you should go see Mama and Ben. You never know with them. They have been here—well—forever, it seems, and have a lot of esoteric knowledge. They might know something about new Supes coming into New Orleans."

I banged the heel of my hand against my forehead. "Of course! Why didn't I think of that? I'll go visit them first thing in the morning. I can stop on my way to meet Logan. Three wolves, one stone. That's the saying, right?"

Sloane shook her head slowly. "Remind me why we are friends again?"

"Because you loooove me," I cooed, raising my voice an octave, and reaching across the table to grab her hands.

"What about that?" Sloane asked, nodding at the heavy envelope in front of me.

I spun the unmarked paper around absently. I could feel something more than paper was inside. The envelope spun out of my hands and off the table, hitting the floor with a solid *thunk.*

Sloane chuckled. "You're turning into a lightweight. Do I need to cut you off?" She shot me a wink and her eyes twinkled merrily.

"Killjoy. When are you going to stop the smothering?"

"Looking out for you," Sloane corrected.

"Whatever. When are you going to stop?"

"When you stop needing it. So...never?" She grinned widely at me.

I rolled my eyes and nabbed the envelope off the floor. Sloane had gotten me out of a fair number of scrapes over the years. To be fair, she'd also gotten me into a few, but she always had my back, no matter how bad things got.

"The mysterious wine drinker left you that?" Sloane prompted, interrupting my wandering thoughts. I realized I had forgotten to include Meridiana in my story. I caught her up on the disappearing stranger as quickly as I could.

Sloane stared at the envelope in shock. "Do you really think that could be from your mom? Why the hell haven't you opened it yet?" she demanded.

I shook my head. "I don't know, and I don't know. I guess, maybe because if I don't, there's the possibility that it could be from her. And that makes me happy. Like she actually is sending me a message from beyond the grave, you know? But that can't be. That Meridiana lady *has* to be crazy, or a charlatan, right? And once I open it, the possibility that it is from Mom vanishes. It's like that Schrödinger box thing, but with envelopes and mysterious redheads."

"Well, sitting and staring at it won't change the reality. It's either from your mom or it isn't. Don't you want to know?"

I hated when Sloane was logical. Especially when I was all fuzzy with emotion and beer. I flipped it over and slid a nail under the flap. The adhesive holding it down gave way under the pressure easily. I tipped the envelope and shook out the contents. A small piece of paper and a thin, gold necklace with a carved oblong charm about the size of my thumb tumbled onto the table.

I pushed the necklace to the side for later inspection. The paper looked old and crumpled. I fingered it tentatively, suddenly feeling like my heart was beating loudly enough to rival the drums in a marching band at a Saints' football game. I drew in a deep breath and opened the folded scrap of paper.

"Well?" Sloane asked eagerly.

The words jumbled and blurred as tears flooded my eyes. I couldn't make sense of what was written on the page past the watery haze, but I recognized the handwriting. I looked up at Sloane and said one word.

"Mom."

# Chapter 10

*My darling Cameron,*

*I wish I could've been there to tell you all of this in person, but time is short, my darling. Forgive me. By the time you read this, I will have passed on. The protection spell I wove to mute your powers and give you a chance to grow up demanded all I had and then some. I know you, my darling, and you will try to blame yourself. Don't. It was my decision, born of a mother's love. Given the choice, I would do the same thing again.*

*It is imperative for your safety and survival that you keep your powers secret. Your father was a powerful Supe, and I fear that if it became known that he sired a child, you would never be safe again. If they learn of your existence, the power hungry will do everything they can to harness your power or to kill you for your parentage. I did what I could, but the protection magics I wove around your aura, your powers, will fade over time until they disappear completely. By my closest estimate, I've bought you roughly five years. I just pray that is enough for you to develop the strength you need.*

*Included with this message is a small token from your father; a charm he carved himself. He gave it to me the last time I saw him and told me it was for you. He said it would help you to understand your powers. I've tried everything I can think of and used every spell I knew to uncover its mysteries, but to no avail. Perhaps you will have better luck where I have failed. I've debated keeping this from you, but fear what might happen if you cannot figure out how use your powers to your full potential. I pray I am not making a mistake by sending the charm to you now.*

*I know you, my darling. You are headstrong, intelligent, driven. I know you will want to pursue finding out about your father. Don't. Digging up the past will only bring unwanted attention from dangerous people. Please, my darling, do this for me.*

*I wish there was more time to tell you all that is in my heart, to watch you grow up. You are my precious, beautiful daughter. No matter what happens, that will always be true. I love you, my darling. Now and forever.*

*Mom.*

*P.S. You can trust the woman who delivered this message. She has proven herself to be a true and loyal friend. I trust her with my life and with yours.*

# Chapter 11

I woke up coughing. My throat was raw. Had I been screaming, or had I just dreamed it? I rolled over and grabbed my phone off the nightstand. I squinted at it, trying to make sense of the glowing numbers. They flashed brightly in an order that I barely recognized, which meant it was too early to be awake. Especially after the long night and the drinks. I groaned. There was no way I was getting back to sleep now. Not as everything that had happened the night before came rushing back.

*Mom.*

Sloane, seeing that I was in no fit state to drive had brought me home. I'd read and reread the message my mother had sent me what seemed like a hundred times while we discussed the possibilities of what it all meant. Unfortunately, neither of us had come up with any answers to the cryptic message from beyond the grave. Eventually, Sloane had gone back to close up the Forge for the night. I'd stared at the paper covered in my mother's elegant scrawl until my eyes drooped and my mind was fatigued beyond functioning. Reluctantly, I'd tumbled into bed and slept until dawn just kissed the horizon.

I fingered the carved gold charm I now wore on a chain around my neck, wondering what my father had been thinking when he made it. My father. That was a bizarre, foreign concept to me. He'd always been a shadowy figure in the recesses of my history, but never more than that.

I glanced at the clock again, noting the time. I had a meeting with Logan this morning that I couldn't afford to miss. Another groan emerged as I remembered I wanted to stop by Mama's, too. I would have to get moving if I wanted to do both this morning.

I stumbled my way to the bathroom and turned on the shower as hot as possible. As it was heating up, I stripped out of my clubbing outfit, sighing in relief as I finally peeled off the corset. I really shouldn't have slept in it, but exhaustion made my choices for me when I got home. I've learned not to argue with that particular mistress. She can be a bitch when angry.

Or was that me?

The hot shower was rejuvenating. I lathered up my hair and washed away the residue of the previous night. The glorious sluice of warm water cascaded down and helped to kick start me in the right direction. Towards my tea. Craving my morning hit of caffeine, I stepped out of the shower, dried off quickly and slipped on a worn black silk robe that hit mid-thigh, showing off a long expanse of tanned, bare leg. It was a shame no one was around to see it.

I tossed my dirty clothes in the hamper and smoothed the wrinkles out of my bedspread on my way to the kitchen. I liked to keep things tidy. In a place as small as mine, a little mess got out of hand quickly. Ten steps out of the bedroom and I was within arm's reach of caffeine. I sighed in contentment at the glorious aromatic brew steeping in my favorite mug. Tea in hand, I wandered back into the bedroom. It was going to be a busy morning, and I wanted to be well equipped for every eventuality.

I tugged on some cotton shorts and a bright blouse. Black leather and sexy low-cut tops are perfect for a club, but weren't comfortable during an unseasonably warm New Orleans autumn. Contemplating my shoes, I opted for my favorite combat boots. Much more comfortable than heels and way more ass-kickery stats than sandals.

I tossed my long, wavy hair up into a high ponytail. Looking in the mirror, I settled on a cute, easy vibe today. I swiped on a quick coat of mascara and lip gloss between gulps of tea that was just shy of boiling. Peeking in the mirror again, I declared myself passable, even after the long night.

Dressed, and ready for the day earlier than I expected, I decided to distract myself with a little research on werewolves. I made myself another cup of tea and powered up my laptop.

Norms don't get everything right when it comes to Supernaturals, but they don't get everything wrong, either. Trawling websites of fantasy nerds is a great way to cultivate a rough understanding of Supernaturals. Admittedly, you usually have to fill in a couple of blanks here and there that the Norms missed, but those nerds knew their mythology.

I pulled up one of my favorite fan-fantasy wiki-sites. The author spent a lot of time researching the more obscure supernatural elements and wrote clearly and succinctly. I found the werewolf tab and wrapped my hands around the warm mug of tea as I became engrossed in the lore.

Apparently, werewolves weren't the only werebeasts out there. There were werebirds, werecats, wererodents, and so on. According to the website, they grouped by animal species and even exhibited some of the same traits as their animals. For example, canine weres were more likely to form Packs whereas feline weres were more likely to be solitary.

The author noted that animals which exhibit social behaviors, such as wolves, either function in an organized hierarchy, like a Pack under the leadership of an Alpha, or they run alone as rogues. Rogues differed from the more solitary creatures and flaunted Pack rules and regulations. They made and broke allegiances as it suited them, were less likely to adhere to societal norms, and were more violent and aggressive.

*Gulp.*

That type of structure seemed to be normal for most breeds of Supernaturals, werewolf or not. An organized hierarchy helped curb some more aggressive personalities, whereas a solitary existence usually ended violently. I suddenly hoped that a werewolf Pack *was* moving to town. I didn't like my odds against three rogue werewolves bent on revenge.

But what would happen if a Pack moved to town? If I pissed off a new Pack, where would that place me in the supernatural hierarchy of New Orleans? Sure, I'd been here a while, but I wasn't part of any sort of hierarchy because I operated on the fringes of Supe society. Being an independent allowed me a certain amount of freedom in my operations.

But it also came with more risk because there was no iron fist backing up my velvet glove. I just had my fists. They were serviceable, but against a Pack of werewolves? I was probably punching above my weight class.

I shook my head, interrupting my musings with more werewolf neighbors and my past. I wasn't likely to get any answers about *that* today. Instead, I took a sip of tea and read on.

According to the author of the article, werewolves weren't restricted to shifting during a full moon. They likely found it easier when the moon was full, but lunar events weren't mandatory for a shift. Instead, the author claimed that shifting was more like an urge. Werewolves got itchy, restless, if they didn't let their animal out regularly, usually about once a month.

The article continued, detailing common mythology or stories from around the world about wereanimals and werewolves, in particular. I scrolled through the page, scanning for any other useful information. A wealth of blue links at the bottom of the page glowed at me, promising to connect me to further interesting information about the mythology of werewolves. I bookmarked a few out of curiosity and then shut my computer before I got lost down the digital rabbit hole and found myself doing quizzes on which house I belonged to or what color my spirit animal was at two in the morning.

Draining the last of my tea, I walked back to my bedroom and threw open my closet to select the most important part of my outfit. Polished metal from weapons of every kind glinted at me in the morning sun. I liked to keep my swords wickedly sharp, maintained a vast collection of knives of all shapes and sizes, and had a respectable variety of firearms neatly organized in my closet. Every accessory a girl could possibly want was neatly tucked away in its proper place where nosy neighbors couldn't see it or report me for having an entire armory in my apartment.

Opting for discreet today, I grabbed my karambits. I'd splurged to buy myself an excellent pair. The curved, double-edged knives mimicked a tiger's claws, both in look and damage capability, but the handles were coated in a patented blend of magic infused rubber polymer and ended in a safety ring that I could loop around a finger when fighting. It made it hard to disarm me. I'd paid an extortionate amount to a warlock who spelled durability and sharpness into the weapons. On top of that, they were also easy to carry without being noticed. I strapped the sheaths for the two knives across my lower back and slid the blades home. I tugged my loose blouse over the top to hide the blades. No need to scare the tourists.

Like me, most Supes favored blades over guns. Don't get me wrong, guns had some advantages, but there were also tremendous disadvantages. One of them was the attention that gunshots drew. Also, unless you were a master marksman and could guarantee a head shot with every bullet, there were too many things out there in the supernatural world that could heal too quickly to be kept down by a handgun. Hell, there were some things that even head shots couldn't keep down. Then there was the fact that guns didn't even function in some of the realms connected to Earth. I'd never left this plane, but I knew from Sloane it was possible. I also knew that mixing modern technology and magical worlds resulted in catastrophic results, usually for the wielder of said technology.

Swords had survived the test of time in the supernatural world for a reason. For one, they never run out of ammo. They also don't blow up in your hands when mixed with magic. You couldn't beat a sword when it came to decapitations. Decapitation was still the tried-and-true method to make sure your enemies stayed dead. Except when it came to vampires. You had to burn those suckers to ash.

I contemplated my swords for another moment before shaking my head and closing the closet door. The only way to explain carrying a sword in public was to claim some sort of LARPing game, and that wasn't me. I got tired of playing that role whenever someone confronted me about my swords. Give me my knives any day. They held the same damage consistency as swords in the supernatural world and were much easier to explain in the human world. Excuses for carrying knives were also much more believable than excuses for carrying swords.

*"Oh, this knife, officer? I use it to gut fish at the weekend. My bad! I forgot I had it with me. I'll just run along home and put it back."*

Versus *"Oh, this sword, officer? I was just playing a game with my friends. Why is it razor sharp? Because I believe in verisimilitude."*

Yeah. You tell me which one would keep you out of prison. Or a psych ward.

I grabbed my bag, checked that my taser was tucked safely inside. I stuffed the bottle of rum that I'd thankfully remembered to grab out of my bike before I left the Forge into the bag as well. Logan would be thrilled to have the rum sooner than promised. I shouldered the bag and locked up the apartment, setting and resetting my locks seven times. It was a neurotic habit I'd picked up when I'd moved to New Orleans, but I didn't fight it anymore. If I didn't lock my door seven times when I entered or left the apartment, I felt unsettled and twitchy all day. It was better just to do it, for my peace of mind. I trotted off down the stairs heading off to see Mama and Ben. One way or another, this was going to be an interesting day.

# Chapter 12

New Orleans is a great place. The sights, the smells, the culture, the music, the *food*. I loved this city. I loved walking through the different neighborhoods and waving at the folks on their front porches. The crazy, fun tourists were lively, but the colorful local characters gave New Orleans its life. It was probably a good thing that I didn't mind a walk because I realized when I opened the door of the apartment building and saw my Rebel was missing. I smacked the heel of my hand against my forehead. That's right! I hadn't driven myself home last night. With a sigh, I breathed in the sunshine and set out towards Mama's. I could always swing by the Forge later to grab the bike.

There was always something to discover in New Orleans. A new musician trying out his chops in the Big Easy for the first time. A chef reimagining a popular classic dish. An old timer spinning yarns on a park bench for the youngsters. I took it all in as I strolled down to the road. A brilliant burst of colorful flowers at a local corner store caught my eye. I decided a bouquet would make Mama smile and popped in to grab one for her.

Mama Atli and Ben lived on Treme Street, around the corner from St. Louis Cemetery No. 1. I loved strolling past the city of the dead with its crumbling, above-ground graves that were slowly sinking into the marshy ground. Once, this cemetery straddled the divide between the city limits and the marsh, but as New Orleans expanded, this cemetery became part of the city's heart. There are hints of stories about the larger-than-life personalities entombed within, such as the voodoo queen Marie Laveau, making the veil between the past and the present seem thin.

I eyed the bank of wall vaults where a tour guide in a wide-brimmed hat was leading a pack of sweaty tourists through the tombs decorated with flowers and trinkets. She rolled her eyes at me as one tourist started complaining about the heat. I smiled in return. Some things never changed.

As I spied Mama and Ben's house, I sped up in anticipation. They owned a big, old house painted a cheerful yellow. I started smiling as soon as I saw it. I couldn't help myself. It's the kind of place that radiated its own sunshine. Even though it was almost November, their back gate was open, like they were welcoming in the world. I turned the corner into the courtyard at the back of the house and sighed with happiness at the peaceful beauty.

You could see Mama's influence everywhere. There were comfy wicker chairs with colorful cushions big enough to swallow you in a warm hug. A large round table with too many mismatched chairs to count sat in the grass, surrounded by a variety of potted flowers. Brightly colored scarves danced in the morning breeze, decorating the ancient oak tree that held the place of honor in the center of the courtyard. Its shade welcomed anyone who was lucky enough to visit Mama and Ben on warm Louisiana afternoons. Lights nestled among the gently swaying leaves to provide illumination on the lazy summer evenings.

I'd spent a fair share of evenings here, chatting over a cup of tea with Mama or shooting the breeze with Ben. It was a place of peace and joy. I smiled, just taking it all in as the back door opened.

"Cameron! Good to see you, child. I've just put the coffee on. C'mon in and grab yourself a cup." The woman framed in the doorway shaded her eyes, looking out over the courtyard at me. I hustled over. When Mama offered you a cup of her famous chicory coffee au lait, you'd best hurry; only a fool would turn it down.

Mama Atli, as she introduced herself to everyone, was on the short side, but was far from petite. If she'd have been an inch taller, she'd be round. Even though I'd never be mistaken for tall, I towered over her.

Her wrinkled face creased even more with a giant smile as I approached. Her skin was the same color as her chicory coffee and her eyes were like melted milk chocolate, just as deep and just as sweet. I hurried up the steps. You didn't have to ask me twice when it came to caffeine or Mama's company.

Mama opened her arms wide. "Give us some sugar, child." Mama's hug enveloped me in cozy comfort. I leaned down to give her a quick peck on the cheek as I offered her the bouquet I brought.

"Morning, Mama. How are things?" I asked, straightening.

"Getting by, getting by," she replied, accepting the flowers with a beatific smile. "That was kind of you, child. Thank you for these, they're beautiful. I had an inkling you'd be around today, so I made extra coffee. C'mon in and set yourself down."

Mama grasped my hands warmly and gently pulled me towards her kitchen. The inside of her home was just as bright and welcoming as the courtyard. She got me settled at the big wooden kitchen table before she set her brilliantly colored skirts to swinging as she sashayed around the kitchen. Mama grabbed some oversized mugs for the coffee and a plate of what looked like fresh cinnamon rolls. My grin stretched even wider. She was living her best life, and I was going to enjoy the fringe benefits of her joy of baking.

I looked around at the odd assortment of items piled in every available space in the kitchen. Herbs were hanging in bundles from the window frames. Vegetables and fruits were stacked haphazardly in baskets. There were even four, no make that five, vases full of random flowers and vegetation. I was pretty sure some of the greenery in those vases were weeds. But with cinnamon rolls on the line, who was I to judge?

I knew some items in the kitchen were mundane, used to make things like the chicory coffee or the cinnamon rolls that I planned on devouring shortly. The others? Not so much. If you weren't careful, you could inadvertently do some nasty things to yourself in Mama's kitchen. It was best to keep your hands to yourself and let her take care of you.

Mama Atli served the supernatural community as a healer of sorts. Her tinctures, potions, and poultices helped to mend the body and soul. When she wasn't working with Supes, she entertained the Norms by reading tarot cards, spinning tales about voodoo practices, and making the best lemonade this side of Heaven.

Mama had vast experience with all sorts of supernatural beings. For the rare instance where she couldn't pluck information from her memory, she had an exceptional library that took up almost the entirety of the second floor of the house. It was filled with both mundane and magical tomes. Good luck trying to find anything in there, though. It seemed to be categorized in a way that only made sense to Mama.

The bangles on Mama's wrists tinkled as she set a mug of steaming chicory coffee with milk and the plate of cinnamon rolls in front of me. Mama was never one to scrimp on portion sizes. The rolls were just about the size of my face. My mouth was watering already at the sweet, spiced aroma wafting up from them. She grinned and pushed them closer to me. I took one and bit into the gooey deliciousness. *Ohmygawd*. It was still warm from the oven and smothered in cream cheese icing. My favorite.

Mama sipped her own coffee, enjoying the sight of her baking making someone else so obviously happy. She let me devour the first cinnamon roll and start on the second before broaching conversation, which was kind of her. I had forgotten to grab anything to eat with my lackluster post-shower breakfast of tea at home. Mama's cooking put mine to shame. No, that's not fair. Mama could fry an egg on the street better than I could make, well, anything. We sat in companionable silence for a while as I ate.

"So, what brings you here at this early hour, Cameron?" Mama always used my full given name. She said she liked the sound of it rolling around her mouth.

I licked a rogue droplet of frosting from my fingers, savoring the sticky sweetness that contrasted wonderfully with the bitter tang of the chicory coffee. Knowing how she liked to cut straight to business, I jumped right into it. "I was on a job last night and I think I ran into some werewolves. Have you heard anything about a Pack moving to New Orleans?"

Mama shook her head. "We haven't had a Pack in New Orleans in an age. It's been a mostly vampire-run city with a healthy sprinkling of magic users. However, a particularly strong vampire ran off to St. Louis recently. Perhaps there was a void, and a Pack is moving into the power vacuum?" she mused. She tapped a finger against her lips, thinking out loud.

"Maybe. What if they are rogues?" I asked.

"They could be. Rogues have set up Packs before, but they are also known for their ability to cause a ruckus. Especially when there's no Alpha who keeps them in line," she replied.

"The vampire who left created that big of a vacuum?"

"Who can tell? Vampires and their politics. Not something I want to get involved in. Nor should you," Mama said sternly, waggling a finger at me.

I held up my hands in protest. "I have no intention of getting involved with vampires or politics," I said truthfully.

Mama stared me down for a second longer. She was as close to an actual mother as I had in New Orleans. She was never afraid to give me advice or a piece of her mind if I'd been stupid. "I suppose your werewolves could just be passing through," she shrugged, seeming unconvinced by her own theory.

"You haven't heard anything, then?"

Mama shook her head. "Would you like me to do some asking about, child? If a Pack were moving in, they would need a special dispensation from the Collective. I haven't been paying a great deal of attention to the Collective of late because they've been relatively quiet, which is usually a good thing," she said with a frown.

"For everyone," I added with a shiver.

I didn't want to mess with the Collective. Hell, I didn't even want to draw their attention if I could help it. Most large cities with a substantial supernatural population had some sort of regulatory body of powerful beings to ensure Norms remained ignorant of the Supes living among them and it was best to not draw the ire of such a body. In Louisiana, a group called the Collective ensured the secret of our supernatural society remained undisclosed to Norms. They're a scary bunch, made up of reluctant representatives of all the major supernatural players in area. If you put a toe out of line where the humans could see, you'd best be packing your bags, because the Collective will find you and make you an example. If a Supernatural was flaunting powers where Norms could see, the Collective would swoop in and put them down. Hard. The gorier the example, the less often the Collective had to make their point to the supernatural community.

Luckily, my powers didn't fall neatly into any category the Collective recognized. The major power players in New Orleans mostly ignored me unless they needed to hire me for a job and when that happened, they contacted my job-broker, Logan Wilder. He acted as a middleman for the supernatural set, contracting all sorts of jobs throughout the region by matching up interested parties with independent Supes with the right skills. Between keeping my head down and using Logan to maintain a semblance of anonymity, I'd managed to avoid the Collective entirely.

Speaking of Logan, I looked at the time on my phone. I was meeting him soon and didn't want to be late.

Mama noticed me looking. "Do you need to get on your way, child?"

"Soon," I said. "I have a work meeting at Kenzie's Kafe, but I need to swing by the Forge first."

She nodded, collecting the dishes. "Do you want the rest of your coffee to go, then?"

I grinned. "Yes, please. I can finish it before I meet with Logan for a cup of tea."

She returned my grin. "What number will this one be?"

"Only number three. You know I can't really function before my fifth cup of the day."

She shook her head, turning to grab a to-go cup for me. "Child, you have a problem."

My grin spread. "It's only a problem if you can't find the solution."

"Oh? And have you found the solution?" she asked, arching an eyebrow in that way that only mothers can do.

"Yep. More caffeine. See? No problem."

Mama rolled her eyes, handing me my cup filled with caffeinated joy. I gave her another quick kiss on the cheek. "I want to say hi to Ben before I go. Is he around?"

Mama nodded and pointed to the front of the house. "He's pottering about in the front with Goliath."

"Thanks! And thanks for the coffee and the chat." I walked towards the front of the house, but turned in the doorway, remembering the other thing I meant to ask Mama. "I ran into someone last night and had a drink with her, but she vanished before I could repay the favor. Maybe you know her and could help me find her?"

Mama shrugged, turning towards the sink with her handful of dishes from my impromptu breakfast. "Sure, I know a lot of people in this area. What's her name?"

"Meridiana."

"Hmm, I'll have to check my books. I'll let you know what I find," said Mama, speaking over her shoulder.

"Thanks, Mama, I'd appreciate it. And thank you for the cinnamon rolls. They were delicious!"

"Anytime, child. Tell Ben that his cinnamon rolls are ready or he'll get cross with me," she said as she wrapped me up in a warm hug. I bent to hug her back, feeling like I was on solid ground for the first time since I'd read the note from my mother the night before. I hurried off to find Ben before unanswered questions could intrude on my slice of peace.

# Chapter 13

I walked out the front door to see a tall and lanky elderly man on his knees amidst piles of freshly turned earth. He was muttering absently to himself as he shifted piles of dirt with a little green toy rake, obviously quite distressed.

"I know I put them somewhere. Where are they?" he murmured under his breath.

I reached out to touch him on the shoulder. "What are you looking for, Ben?" I asked.

He leapt up in surprise, but lost his footing on the uneven terrain, toppling over on his backside and staring up at me. "Well, butter my butt and call me a biscuit! Cam! It's you! How're y'all doin' this fine day?"

I laughed, reaching out a hand to help pull him to his feet. He stood up about as gracefully as a baby deer on skates and brushed the dirt from his trousers with one hand while simultaneously smoothing his unruly white hair into a semblance of order. He failed miserably on both counts but looked so adorably cute that I just had to smile.

"Just fine, thanks. How are you, Ben?" I asked.

"Oh, fair enough, fair enough. The sun is shinin', the plants are growin'. Now, if I could just find my glasses, all would be right with the world." He spun around in a circle, patting himself all over in search of the missing bifocals and looking like a gangly puppy chasing his own tail. He almost tripped over the toy rake he had been using just a moment before. I caught his elbow, steadying him before he could crash to the ground in a tangle of lanky limbs.

Looking around, I spotted a small white mouse with beady red eyes dragging a pair of slightly bent gold-framed glasses out of the zone of destruction. I pointed towards the little creature. "I think Goliath has found them for you."

Ben spun around, looking for Goliath. This time his feet got so tangled that he did tip over on to his hands and knees, which brought him nose to nose with the mouse. The furry white creature held up the wire-rims to his master. I imagined the little mouse letting out an exasperated sigh and felt silent laughter bubble in my stomach.

"Oh! Thank you so much, Goliath," Ben said courteously, taking the proffered glasses and wedging them in place on his long, narrow nose. He extended a palm to the little mouse. Goliath clambered aboard and scampered up to his normal place on Ben's left shoulder. He was the same color as Ben's rather wild hair and often blended in. It was unnerving to see those beady, red eyes peer at you from what you assumed was unoccupied hair.

Ben absentmindedly raised his hand to pet the mouse. Ben was a necromancer. Goliath was his familiar. The little mouse was never far away from the old man. I didn't know if it was because Goliath needed to stay close to the necromancer to maintain his reanimation or if it was because he genuinely liked the old fella. Perhaps Goliath was simply the necromancer's version of a peeper keeper. Regardless, they were almost inseparable.

"It's good I ran into you, Cam." He gave me a warm hug, which smudged dirt all over my clean blouse. I sighed and squeezed him back. "I was hopin' that I could ask a favor of you?"

"For you, Ben, anything." I stepped back and grinned up at him. I really loved the lanky klutz.

Ben put his hands on his hips, looking up at the sky. "Well," he drew out the word to be almost three syllables long, "this is gonna sound as crazy as a soup sandwich. Hold on to your panties."

I just smiled, waiting to see what classified as crazy to the slightly befuddled necromancer. Perhaps he had misplaced his hoe or something.

Ben leaned down towards me. He whispered, "The ghosts. They're disappearing."

It took all the self-control I had not to laugh in his endearing, overly concerned face. I took a sip of Mama's coffee to give myself a moment. "Umm, isn't that kind of in their job description, Ben?" I asked kindly.

He shook his head sharply. "No, not disappearin' like 'Poof! I'm invisible!' That happens on the regular. One perk of being a ghost, but not the only one, mind you?"

I couldn't help myself. "Being a ghost has perks?" I asked.

Ben waved a hand dismissively. "Oh sure, loads of them. But that's not the point. Ghosts are disappearin'. Gone. No one can find them. Not in this realm or any of the others. Even *I* can't sense them with my powers. The other ghosts can't find their friends anywhere and I do mean, *anywhere.* They're just...gone."

I shrugged, not understanding. "Maybe they're just haunting another cemetery?"

He shook his head. "No. If that's the case, one of the other spirits would've seen them and told me. Trust me, there are *a lot* of rovin' spirits in New Orleans. Someone would've seen something. I would've heard."

The old guy was genuinely upset, bless his heart. I needed to do what I could to ease his mind. "Well, could they have, I don't know, passed over? Gone to their eternal rest? Ceased being a shade? I don't know what the appropriate terminology is for a ghost who has moved on."

"Passed over is fine," Ben said absently, waving a hand. "But I don't think that any of them have. I've checked with my contacts on the other side, and no one has seen them."

"Do you talk with these contacts regularly?"

He blinked at me through his spectacles. Given the conversation, maybe they were specter-cals. Heh.

"Of course! I had tea with Fred yesterday. Or was it the day before? I mean, Fred didn't have tea. That'd be ridiculous, wouldn't it?" he asked, tipping his head to the side, and looking like a bespectacled owl.

I smothered a chuckle behind my cup. "The ghosts, Ben?" I prompted the old necromancer.

"Right. We started noticin' some absences last month. You know. Ghosts missin' the local tours." He started pacing, dragging his hands through his wild hair. Goliath hung on to his collar to keep from being dislodged.

I interrupted again, "Those things are actually haunted? I would've guessed that the local ghosts would have been more, I don't know, local?"

Ben held a hand flat out and swayed it back and forth in a *kinda-sorta* gesture. "Haunted might be a bit of an exaggeration. Consider the tours more like ghost fan clubs. The spirits like to hear humans tell stories about them. It's an ego boost, you know."

"Sure. Of course. Naturally," I said, taking another sip of coffee. *Ghosts maintained egos after death?* This conversation was blowing my mind.

"Well, things've been escalatin'. There are maybe twenty, twenty-five ghosts missin' now. It's hard to be sure. They can be kinda hard to keep track of sometimes."

"Of course," I nodded. I was doing my best to sound knowledgeable, but dealing with ghosts was completely over my head. Ben seemed to buy my act and continued.

"I wouldn't bother you, Cam, if this wasn't important. But we can't find them. It's like someone's taken them. They are just...gone. They aren't here and they definitely aren't *there*," he motioned with one finger, like it was hopping over a fence. I assumed he meant 'the other side,' whatever that was.

I took a deep breath. "Okay. Let me get this straight. There are ghosts missing. Roughly twenty of them. You, a necromancer, can't find them, but you think I can? Where would I even start looking? What would someone even do with kidnapped ghosts? It's not like you can hold them for ransom. I mean, what would the kidnappers say? 'Give me all your money or I will kill your already dead ancestor'. That doesn't inspire a great deal of fear, does it?" I ran a hand through my hair, shaking my head. "Look, I want to help, Ben. Really, I do. But I feel like I'm missing some pieces to the puzzle."

Mama cleared her throat from behind me. She walked on past to Ben, giving him a mug of steaming coffee. "If that many ghosts are going missing, someone is harvesting them. Based on the time of year, I would guess that whoever is doing this is aiming for some sort of dark ritual. Probably timed to coincide with Halloween."

I did some quick math in my head. "That's next week!" I blurted out, interrupting her.

Mama nodded grimly and continued, "Best-case scenario? Whoever is taking them will use their energy to fuel a relatively minor ritual." She waved a hand, sending her bangles jangling again. "A crossover spell to the other side, a short-term power enhancement, a lesser spirit summoning, that type of thing. Ghosts aren't powerful energy conduits for ritualistic magic because there's not enough life force left in them."

I sucked in a breath. Spirits weren't something I wanted to mess around with, lesser or not. "That's the best-case scenario. What's the worst case?"

Mama took Ben's hand, clasping it tightly. She looked me square in the eyes. "The worst-case scenario? This person uses an animal or kidnaps a person or, gods forbid, *people*, and uses a sacrifice to power the spell."

I bit my lip, trying to put the pieces together. "And that would be bad not only because of the kidnapping, but also because, if this kidnapper sacrifices someone, there is more life-energy to power a more powerful spell?"

Mama nodded seriously. "You asked for worst case. Kidnapping and sacrifice seem a bit farfetched, but unfortunately, it has happened before. Not all Supes are peaceful folks." She gestured around the yard, sending her bangles jangling discordantly.

"Gods forbid that this person, whoever they are, capture and sacrifice a Supe," Ben interjected.

"Why would it matter if they sacrificed a Norm versus a Supe?" I asked, shaken by the dark turn this had taken. I hadn't expected such a disturbing conversation on this brilliant autumn morning.

"Because Supes are inherently more powerful. Using a Norm to power a ritual would be like pouring gas into a car. A Supe powering that same spell would be the equivalent of using nitrous," Mama stated calmly.

Wait. Did I just hear confirmation that Mama watched *The Fast and the Furious?* I shook my head. *Focus, Cam!*

I didn't want to ask, but I had to know. "You said *sacrifices*. Plural. What kind of spell would require the energy of twenty-ish ghosts and human sacrifices?" I asked.

Mama's gaze bore into mine. "Think of the very worst situation you can imagine."

My brain gleefully opened a box of nightmares and I raced through horrible imaginings. Things that I had only heard whispers of around a campfire that gave me the heebie-jeebies. Summonings. Opening portals to forbidden realms to allow creatures of myth and legend free rein in the human world. Absolute power upgrades that corrupted absolutely.

And those outcomes were only if someone completed the spell correctly. When a spell powered by this much potential dark magic went wrong, well, it was almost better when they went right. At least you knew what the repercussions were then. When they went wrong, I didn't even want to think about it. My eyes finally latched back onto Mama Atli.

She nodded grimly. "Whatever you just thought of, multiply it by seven and you are getting an idea of how bad the situation is."

Ben spoke up. "A threat like this isn't just about the ghosts of New Orleans. If there's some sorta ritualistic-crazed kidnapper bent on human sacrifice on the loose, no one's safe."

"If Ben is right, this is a potentially cataclysmic event that threatens the entirety of New Orleans," Mama said.

"Umm, why?"

Ben cleared his throat, "Again, talkin' about worst case scenarios here. If someone wants to go so far as kidnappin' and killin', you can bet your last dollar that they ain't about to be workin' a spell that makes daisies pop out all over town, if you get my drift."

Mama nodded. "Precisely. In this hypothetical worst case, the spell goes right and something horrendous is unleashed or summoned. If the spell goes wrong, the accumulated power has to go somewhere. It usually disperses in some sort of explosion or something of that nature. The magnitude and type of destruction would be inherently linked to the type of spell, of course."

"So, let me get this right. There's a ticking magical time-bomb in the form of a crazed sorcerer somewhere in the city?" My mouth went dry. This city had been through so much already. Magical disasters were the last thing New Orleans needed.

"Well, that's only worst case scenario, remember," Ben said.

"What happens if its best case again?" I asked

"Then the trick-or-treaters will have nothing to worry about on Halloween night apart from cavities and New Orleans loses a few ghosts." Mama met my eyes; I could tell that she believed the old necromancer.

I left Mama and Ben standing in the front of their yard, surrounded by the calming backdrop of a leisurely day. Despite the gorgeous day and the vibrant setting, goosebumps were pebbling my bare arms. I was scared by what I had just heard. Werewolves yesterday, ghosts today. My week was not going how I had planned.

However, that did not take away from the urgency of my next meeting of the day. Logan. My job broker and holder of the purse strings. I chugged my chicory coffee as I walked, not even registering the delicious flavor. I hoped that the minor act of normality would help snap me back into reality so I could deal with Logan. And then deal with the werewolves. And then the ghosts.

Damn it. Maybe I should have stayed in bed today.

# Chapter 14

I let out a shallow sigh of relief as I rounded the corner and saw the welcoming blue door of Kenzie's Kafe. It was a hippie-turned-vegan type of place. It served everything in ceramic dishes with wooden cutlery. Local artists' paintings covered the walls. Most of it was pretty good, too. There were at least five different milks that weren't milk at all. I still didn't know how you could milk a nut; I left that one to wiser minds to ponder. There were vegetarian, vegan, gluten-free, sugar-free, and egg-free options for just about everything on the menu. From the dishes I'd tried, nothing was taste-free, which was probably a sound business model for a café.

In short, it was *the* pretentious, environmentally conscious, over-priced place to see, be seen in, and get your morning caffeine fix in. And the Fae freaking loved it. The reason was obvious; there was no iron to be found in this place. At all. I'm pretty sure they even skimped on the spinach offerings for that very reason.

I waved at the curvy blonde behind the coffee bar as I entered. Kenzie was one of the High Fae who had a permit to live and work full time in New Orleans. Most of the Fae creatures who passed through were tourists, just like the human visitors. They came to town for a good time and then returned to their regularly scheduled lives, which was better for everyone. Creatures from Fae could be wild if they were not used to hiding in plain sight among Norms.

Letitia's uncle, Aldrich Kingsley, ran the Fae Embassy in New Orleans for the region. It was a glorified passport control for those using New Orleans as their transportation hub to pass in and out of Fae. Kenzie and other agents scattered throughout the city kept tabs on the tourists from Fae to ensure that nothing got too out of hand while during a visit. I wouldn't be surprised if the agents from Fae who lived in New Orleans full time were also highly skilled and could handle themselves in a scrap. I didn't really want to find out. Currently, I just wanted a cup of tea, to find Logan, and get paid.

I scanned the small ground-floor seating area. Kenzie squeezed small tables around glass counters displaying a variety of treats to tickle any craving. Almost every seat was taken, but I couldn't see Logan. I moseyed up to the bar and wiggled my fingers in greeting at Kenzie.

She smiled widely at me and bustled over. She was pretty, with a smile for miles and dimples big enough to go fishing in. Her blonde hair was pin straight and never looked out of place, no matter how busy the café was.

"Morning! What can I do you for, Cam?" Kenzie asked, leaning her forearms on the top of the bar, which emphasized her cleavage in her already low-cut top.

"Morning, Kenzie. Have you seen Logan come in yet?" I asked.

"Nope," she replied. "Not yet. Expecting him?"

"Yeah, morning meeting. I'm thinking we'll take it upstairs to the balcony. You look busy this morning," I said, glancing around at the nearly full café.

She grinned, "We've got a new pastry chef in from Fae. A half-pixie, half-brownie. His beignets are out of this world. You've gotta try 'em before they disappear."

I was already salivating even though I had polished off two of Mama's huge cinnamon rolls. Must be that supernatural metabolism. Or I am a sugar fiend.

"Sounds delicious. I've always heard that brownies are outstanding bakers, but haven't had the chance to sample their work. Will you send two of those beignets upstairs? With two black teas please?" After all, a meeting without food might as well be an email.

Kenzie nodded, "Sure. I'll grab those for you right away. I'll even put some macadamia nut milk on the side if you're feeling brave." Kenzie laughed as I eyed her suspiciously. As much as people swore by the nut milk of their choice, I didn't trust it. "Shall I let Logan know where you are when he gets here?"

"Please. Oh, and Logan will pick up the check."

She gave me a thumbs up and went to prepare my order. I made my way upstairs and selected a table in the shade on the balcony. The heat hadn't kicked in fully yet, but the shade was nice, anyway. What I really liked was the idea of having my back to a wall and an unencumbered view of the street. A little paranoid part of me was on the lookout for werewolves although I doubted they'd been able to track me this far. However, I'd been wrong before. Regardless, I had a magnificent spot for people-watching while waiting for my broker to appear.

Logan Wilder was a professional middle-man and my job-broker. He arranged for things to happen. You needed something smuggled? Logan would find you the crate and the driver. You needed a loan? Logan knew where they kept the gold. You needed to find a particularly elusive person of interest? Logan knew all the hidey-holes. He had more contacts than there were drunks in New Orleans during Marci Gras. Everyone knew Logan and Logan knew everyone, or at least, that's the way it seemed. On top of that, Logan ran a slick operation. If he took a contract, he'd source one of his freelancers, like me, to complete the job. Guaranteed.

I loved working with Logan because he tolerated bullshit about as well as a Southern debutante. He made sure the job was always done, the client always paid, and my name was never mentioned. Logan was the primary reason I'd been able to avoid the notice of the Collective for so long. No one powerful gives a shit about you if they don't know you exist. Discretion came with a hefty price tag in the form of paying a percentage of every job to Logan. The arrangement cut deeply into my profits, but the price was worth it. However, with jobs so few and far between lately, that meant that I needed to contract another job or choose between rent and food this month.

Two minutes later, a man came upstairs carrying a briefcase and balancing a tray with the beignets, tea, and a small pot of milk. He was average in just about every way. Good-looking, but not good-looking enough to warrant a second glance. Fit, but not ripped. Non-description brown hair cut in a fashionable, but not fashion-forward manner. I could say the same about his clothing choices. It was like he had designed his entire appearance to fit in well enough to be completely ignored.

I had a running bet with myself that he was some sort of magic user, but I had never discovered what kind of Supe he was or how strong his powers were. Other than a past mysterious enough to rival my own, the only thing abnormal about him were his incredibly sharp green eyes. They burned with intelligence. I could imagine him playing entire games of chess in his mind before his opponent had even made a move. And winning. Every. Single. Time.

Logan set down the tray and took a seat across from me. "I hope you don't mind me ordering for you," I said by way of greeting.

"Good morning, Cameron. It was a pleasant surprise and surprisingly courteous, so thank you very much for thinking of me. I'll admit, I'm looking forward to sampling the new pastry chef's creations. I've heard good things," he said as he carefully set the full tray on the tiny table.

"C'mon Logan, call me Cam."

A slight frown formed between his eyebrows. "No, thank you. I like Cameron. It suits you."

I shook my head and reached for my tea. Kenzie made it strong and typically added mixed spices to her house blend, based on the season. Today, it smelled like cloves and cardamom. I inhaled deeply and took a sip. It wasn't bad. I gave the small jug of milk the side-eye and pushed it towards Logan with the tip of a finger.

"Thank you," he murmured, pouring a generous splash into his tea. Of course he would. The traitor to all things dairy.

I pulled the bottle of rum out of my bag and passed it over to him. "Delivery ahead of schedule," I said.

Logan opened the top and inhaled deeply. He coughed slightly at the potent combination of strong rum and hot peppers, but nodded in appreciation. "You always do good work, Cameron. The buyer will be grateful for the early delivery."

"Grateful enough for a bonus?" I asked hopefully.

Logan's brows furrowed slightly. "I don't work on bonuses. A job is a job. End of story." His tone was frosty.

I sighed, "Can't blame me for trying."

He ignored me, reaching for his briefcase instead. "Here are your payments for the High Fae body-guarding job as well as the liquor acquisition, minus my cut of course," he said, extracting two envelopes and sliding them across the table to me. I wasn't surprised he was uber-prepared. It was *Logan*, after all.

I thumbed through the bills inside each quickly. I ran some quick calculations in my head. There was enough to pay some interest on some of my outstanding debts, settle up my late rent, or eat. Good Lord, I hated those kinds of choices. I took out a couple of the bills and tucked them in my pocket before sliding the wad of cash back to Logan.

"For rent and the interest on the debt of that warlock enhancing my blades. Any extra can go against the principle I still owe," I ground out.

"I shall see that it gets to the proper people," he said, sliding the money back into the case and closing the locks with a snap. He picked up his tea and stood.

"Logan," I protested, "Sit. Stay a while."

He looked down his decidedly average nose at me. "I'm not a dog, and this isn't a social visit. Good day, Cameron."

I sighed. "I need to talk to you."

He glanced at his watch. An actual watch, not one of those smart does-everything-short-of-making-you-breakfast wrist devices that also tells the time. He settled back into his chair.

"I have ten minutes," he said, his words clipped and precise.

I nodded, knowing that he wasn't joking. It wasn't worth the time to push his buttons. If Logan said he had ten minutes, he had ten minutes. He was out the door at ten minutes, plus one second. Regardless of where I was in conversation.

"Okay. Thanks. I appreciate it." A little courtesy never hurt with him. "Something happened last night. Some guys targeted the High Fae girl. There was a confrontation."

His eyes hardened. He did not like complications. "What kind of confrontation?" he asked, his voice dropping a few degrees.

"Don't worry," I said hurriedly. "I handled it and I protected the primary at all times." A little white lie. Letitia had suffered no permanent damage, after all.

Logan leaned back in his chair. "Thank you for your honesty."

I tried not to wince.

He continued, "Why are you telling me this? As long as you completed the job per the contract, I have no need or desire to hear details."

I nodded. Another of his quirky policies that he strictly adhered to. "Then I won't bore you. The only real pertinent thing you need to know is that I'm pretty sure these guys were werewolves."

His eyes widened slightly. For Logan, that was the equivalent of a long, creative, expletive-filled sentence.

I pulled out my phone. "What do you know about werewolves in New Orleans?"

Logan looked at the pictures I was showing him of the two guys with broken noses, unconscious in the club alleyway. "Your handiwork?" he queried. I shrugged, letting a small grin do the talking for me. I was never one to pass on collecting bad-assery points.

He sighed. "Why are you asking me?" He leaned back in his chair, eyeing me speculatively over his cup of tea.

I leaned back in my chair as well, interlacing my fingers across my stomach. "You're the only person I know who has regular contact with members of the Collective. If I'm remembering the rules right, any new Supernatural groups who want to settle in New Orleans need the Collective's permission. If they gave permission for werewolves to move to town, you'd know it about ten seconds later," I said. Flattery worked wonders with Logan.

He nodded along silently with my assessment, but didn't volunteer any additional information.

I leaned forward. "Logan, I pissed these guys off last night. Not only did I stop them from kidnapping Lady Letitia, but I also beat them up. So, I need to know. Do they play by Pack rules or are we going to have ourselves a rogue-y rumble one of these days? Are they going to be my new neighbors and we have to play nice? Or are they passing through and can come after me without fear of repercussions? Hell, is the Collective using them to get rid of me? Or vice versa?"

He exhaled noisily through his nose. He understood what I was saying. If I upset the werewolves enough to come after me and I wasn't ready for an attack, things could get ugly, fast. If the Collective were scheming to get rid of me, I needed to run. Now. To get as far from New Orleans as possible.

Logan took a sip of his macadamia-milk-flavored tea and frowned at it. He set it down carefully. "I don't know much, but what I know points towards the Collective giving special permission for a small werewolf Pack to settle in New Orleans for a trial basis of three months. Upon completion of those three months, they'll either be instructed to leave, forcibly removed, or invited to join our community. As far as I know, they did not bring your name up as part of the deal." Logan kept a neutral mask in place the entire time he spoke. Damn, he was good.

I groaned. "In other words, I need to make nice with the widdle cutesy-wootsy doggies," I said, adopting the vocal timbre of adoring doggie mommies everywhere.

He nodded. "It would be prudent. Especially for the next three months. I might also suggest not calling them little or cute or dogs. Werewolves don't strike me as jovial creatures who'd enjoy your infantile talk about their noble and honorable species."

I grimaced. He had a point. If the Collective had invited a Pack to New Orleans, I'd best smooth any fur I'd inadvertently ruffled. If they had been invited, that must mean having a Pack in the area would likely bring some major perks for the Collective. Why else would the Collective be willing to upset the power balance in the region? I wasn't sure how I measured up in a contest of value against a Pack of werewolves to the Collective. An unknown, potentially dangerous Supernatural or a group of highly skilled shifters? I know which one I'd pick to keep if I were the Collective in the hypothetical situation.

Logan moved to gather his things again. "If that is all, Ms. Blaze, I really must be on my way."

I reached out a hand to stop him. I hated that I needed to ask, but there weren't any other good options available to me.

"Look, Logan. I need a job. With better pay. The jobs you are throwing me, minus your cut, are barely covering my expenses. I need something more or I'll have to do something drastic. Like become a line chef." What I didn't say was that having a little extra money in my pocket also wouldn't hurt if things went poorly with the werewolves. I was partial to the advice: Always plan for the worst and you'll never be disappointed. It had never done me wrong.

Logan shuddered. He had good reason. He had tasted my cooking. Just once. Apparently, it had been enough to leave an impression. He opened his briefcase and shuffled through some papers, muttering to himself. After passing on a few jobs that were obviously not suitable for my skill set, he looked up.

"How do you feel about a trip to Florida?" he asked.

I shrugged noncommittally. I honestly didn't know much about the place.

He looked back at his papers. "How are you with animals?"

"What kind?" I asked, curiously. "We both know wolves are not high on my buddy-list at the moment." However, I could do a pet-sitting gig. I could keep the little menace alive. Probably.

"Crocodiles," Logan replied absently, scanning the page with the job details.

I nearly choked on the tea I was drinking. "Umm, pet-sitting croco-diles?" No. That sounded ridiculous. "Hunting them?" That sounded at least possible for my skill set.

"Locating, trapping, and smuggling them. Internationally. It would be of great assistance if you could also aid in breeding," he said, serious eyes flicking up to me.

I blinked in surprise. "Breeding. You want to know if I can breed crocodiles."

"Precisely."

I stared at him. He must be joking.

Logan stared back at me and blinked. Once.

*Okay. So not joking.*

"Hard pass, Logan. For future reference, I'll likely pass on anything involving crocodiles," I said, working hard to keep my voice level.

His mouth quirked in a quick, annoyed twitch. "You said you wanted something that pays well, Cameron. The pay for this job is excellent."

"So is the chance of mutilation! Why crocodiles? Who wants crocodiles shipped internationally? Scratch that. How do you breed a crocodile? Wait. Do *you* know how to breed a crocodile? Good Lord, Logan, how did you learn how to breed a crocodile?"

He blinked.

I leaned forward conspiratorially. "Are you trying to breed a super race of crocodile fighters? Kind of like TMNT, but with crocodiles?"

Logan blinked again. "I didn't follow most of that, so I'll just assume you are passing on this opportunity?"

I nodded firmly, but my mind was already drifting towards mutant crocodiles. Would they walk on two legs and engage in martial arts like the turtles of fame? What artists could you name a crocodile after? Turtles are cute. Any artist, dead or alive, would be thrilled to have a turtle named after them. But a crocodile? Maybe they could be named after...

Logan went back to shuffling through papers, oblivious to my musings.

"It looks like the only thing that fits your parameters is another acquisition request. The details are sparse, but I'm confident that there are no crocodiles involved. The pay is..." his eyebrows lifted. Both of them. For anyone else, that was a long whistle followed by a lot of cursing.

He cleared his throat. "The pay is generous," he finished.

Wow. That said a lot. I know he'd given me all the details he was at liberty to share prior to accepting the job. I took a quick mental tally of my resources. Pulling down a quick payday would buy me some breathing space. And food. Always a plus.

"What's the time frame?" I asked. I couldn't very well spend months traipsing after a random knick-knack some rich so-and-so wanted, waiting on a payday that might not come.

Logan checked his stack of papers. "It looks like three days."

"Local?" I didn't mind travel, but preferred jobs close to home if I could manage it.

"Yes," he confirmed.

"Sounds perfect!" I grinned at the potential of a big payday. "Sign me up."

Logan pulled out yet another envelope. This one was thin and tightly sealed. He handed it over to me, giving me the pertinent details in professional tone, "All the details they gave me are here. The person making the request is expecting a phone call by noon from my agent. I've been informed that they will arrange a meeting, and will share all pertinent details then," he instructed. I nodded and tried not to snatch the envelope from him.

Logan paused and cleared his throat. "I'd usually give this to one of my more experienced agents, but you've proven yourself time and time again. However, this client isn't one you want to upset."

That made me pause. Logan never gave me warnings. He just gave me work. He carefully matched jobs and agents based on skill set. Whatever the acquisition was or whoever it was for had shaken him. For Logan, to be nervous? Well, that meant I should probably be shaking all the way down to my cute little combat boots.

# Chapter 15

As predicted, Logan left precisely within his ten-minute window. Either the acquisition job or the werewolf situation must have thrown him because he seemed nervous when he left. Nervous enough that he forgot to eat his beignet. His lack of appreciation for the pillowy pastry would have caused me to gripe most days. Today, however, his loss was my gain. I moaned slightly in pleasure as I sank my teeth into confectionery heaven.

I opened the envelope Logan had left as I munched on the bonus beignet. All that was inside was a single sheet of paper with a printed phone number. It was local, but I couldn't deduce anything more than that. I glanced at my phone, realizing that I had some time to spare before the noon deadline. I decided to spend the next few minutes people-watching and enjoying my tea before calling the mysterious phone number.

New Orleans draws an interesting crowd of people. The locals come from many colorful and flamboyant backgrounds. They are the lifeblood of the city, what keeps it pumping all night, every night. I love to watch them go about their daily routines, living it up and enjoying their time in the Big Easy. They're what makes this city a special, crazy, amazing place to be. Sure, the architecture is monumental, and the drinks are, well, intoxicating. But you can find both those things in other places all over the world. The people, though? That was a different story.

I sat up straight. A man had just turned off the street and entered the café below while I was soaking in the beauty of a perfect Southern morning. Something about him jogged my memory. I thought hard. He didn't match up with Meathead or Wiry from the alley the night before. Was he the third guy? The one I had put down in the bar? I dredged my memory, but all I recovered was an impression of a dark-haired youth. The guy downstairs didn't look young, but I had been more focused on rescuing Letitia than remembering a face.

With my spidey-senses on high alert, I dashed inside and crept to the edge of the stairs. I peered over the railing, trying to sneak a peek at the guy below. *Damn it.* I could only see the back of his head. If it had been one of the guys from the club, his broken nose would have given him away. Wouldn't it? Did werewolves heal supernaturally quickly? I hadn't asked Mama about that, but there were better than even odds they did. Most Supes I knew had better speed, strength, and healing than the Norms.

I decided it was better to avoid the front room and the mystery guy just in case he was a caffeine-addicted werewolf. I hurried down the stairs and out the back door. I turned the corner, jogged another block, and turned again. Then I waited on a city bench to see if anyone was following me. Nothing. My nerves must be reacting to this morning's caffeine intake.

I pulled out my phone, checking the time. It was five minutes to noon. Might as well set up the job while I watched my back trail. I yanked out the phone number Logan had given me, dialed, and waited.

Three rings later, a female voice answered, "Yes? To whom am I speaking?" Refined. Indeterminate accent. Not Southern though. Interesting.

"I'm calling on behalf of Logan Wilder. I was told there was something that you needed help acquiring?" I tried to match her detached tone.

There was a slight pause. The voice simply said, "Connecting." Nondescript hold music jangled over the line as she clicked off.

The four caffeinated beverages that I'd consumed this morning were catching up with me, making me jittery. I stood and paced down the sidewalk, needing to move as I listened to the tinny music.

A male voice with the same smoothly refined accent interrupted the repetitive jangling that passed for music. "To whom am I speaking?" he asked in a business-like manner.

"I'm Logan Wilder's agent. He informed me you needed assistance in acquiring an item?" I repeated my introduction.

"Yes, indeed, I'm aware of the arrangement I made with Mr. Wilder. But to whom am I speaking?" He sounded mildly annoyed at having to repeat himself.

"Cameron Blaze." I rolled my eyes at the haughty potential employer, secretly glad that he couldn't see me.

There was a pause on the line. "Cameron Blaze," he mused. I could almost hear him tapping a finger on his chin. "Now, why does that sound familiar? Oh. I know. You were the extra bodyguard hired to protect my niece last night."

I groaned inwardly. Aldrich Kingsley? My potential big payday job was for *Aldrich Kingsley*? Besides being Lady Letitia's uncle, Aldrich Kingsley was High Fae nobility. I couldn't remember which court he belonged to. Was he of the Spring Court like Letitia? Did all Fae family members belong to the same court? I was certain it wasn't Winter. I doubted a member of the Winter Court would have opted for an ambassadorial posting in this hot and humid region.

Regardless of which Court he belonged to, he was noble, ergo powerful. He was also the Fae Ambassador to New Orleans and, if rumors could be believed, a member of the Collective. I couldn't see how I'd be of any help to someone like him. To be honest, I wasn't sure I wanted to get mixed up in things at his level. He outclassed me in every way. I'd have to be very careful on this job. Very, very careful.

"Wonderful!" he exclaimed enthusiastically.

*Wow. Not the reaction I'd expected after the kerfuffle last night.*

"My niece and head of security both speak highly of you. It's reassuring to know that Mr. Wilder has referred such a capable agent for this matter," he continued, unaware of my surprised reaction.

"Yes, sir." Now that I knew who was doing the hiring, I wasn't above pulling out my best manners and dusting them off. "How can I help you today?" I asked politely.

"This isn't a matter I'm comfortable discussing over the phone. Are you available for a meeting today? Would two hours give you enough time to arrange your schedule and rendezvous at my estate? I can send Hank or one of the other security team to collect you if you need assistance in finding it," he offered courteously.

"No, I know where to find you. No need to send anyone. And yes, two hours is just fine," I assured him.

"Brilliant. I look forward to meeting you soon, Ms. Blaze," he said, sounding pleased.

He hung up, and I stared at my phone in mild disbelief. I never thought that Aldrich Kingsley would talk to me directly. He usually worked through intermediaries whenever he needed my services. To be honest, it surprised me that he even knew my name. This day just kept getting weirder and weirder.

And that's when a freight train of muscle knocked me into a brick wall.

# Chapter 16

I'd been so distracted by my conversation with Aldrich Kingsley that I hadn't been paying attention to my surroundings. Rookie mistake. The back of my head cracked painfully into the crumbling bricks. Stars danced in front of my eyes. I blinked rapidly, trying to focus. Before I could regain my equilibrium, large hands pulled me roughly around the corner of the nearly deserted street into an empty alley. Well, almost empty. I slapped away the guy's hands and spun away, taking a few steps deeper into the dead end. Which put me face to face with Wiry, the werewolf from last night.

I dropped my hands to my sides, trying to keep an already dangerous situation from escalating. Wiry stood in front of me with the young guy, Grabby Goon, off to his right. Presumably the one who had propelled me into the wall was Meathead. I snuck a look over my shoulder. Sure enough. I was standing in the middle of a werewolf triangle and they all looked wound tighter than a piano wire.

The icing on the cake in this shitty situation was that werewolves were apparently quick healers. The noses I had broken the night before were straight and the black eyes were fading on all three of the guys surrounding me. I took a gamble that their feelings were not mending nearly as fast.

This was bad. This was very bad.

"Morning, fellas. Looks like you had a rough night. Didn't sleep well?" I said with faux sympathy.

Low growls rippled through the alley.

"Looks like you still have bags under your eyes. Have you tried herbal tea in the evening? I hear it works wonders for relaxation."

Meathead took a step closer and let out a snarl. The sound vibrated in my ribcage, ending in some nervous fluttering in my stomach. I had to remind myself: *You are not prey.* Yeah, right. I'm pretty sure that is exactly how they saw me.

Wiry narrowed his eyes. "Where is it?" he asked softly.

"Where is what?" I said, confused. I decided to needle them a bit to see if I could shake out some additional information. "Or did you mean *were* is it? Like the werewolf is IT? Are we playing tag, and you guys didn't tell me? Is that what last night was? Just a friendly, little game?"

Stunned silence met my ridiculous diatribe.

I shot Wiry a brilliant smile and a wink. "I *love* tag!" I nearly sang at them.

The growls that met my words practically rattled the bricks right out of the walls. Wiry gestured towards his buddies to calm down.

He turned back to me, keeping his voice low. "You're working with the High Fae. They have something that is...important to us. We want it back. Now. Where is it?" He looked like he was fighting hard to stay calm.

Whoa. Not a promising sign. I decided to stop poking the wolf. "Look, man. I don't work *with* the Fae. They hired me for a protection gig. A one-off. I don't know what you're talking about or what you're looking for." I kept my latest phone call with the Fae Ambassador out of the conversation. After all, I hadn't officially accepted the job yet.

Wiry stalked forward a couple of paces. "Tell me why you were on the phone with Aldrich Kingsley. From what I hear, he's not one to talk to underlings."

Whoops. There went that bit of privacy.

"Wow. *Nosy* much?" I winked as I thumbed my nose at them.

Wiry took another menacing step forward.

I folded my arms over my chest, refusing to give into intimidation tactics. "Two problems. One: I don't kiss and tell. Part of my policy."

"Pretty fancy for a freelance Supe to have a privacy policy, isn't it?" he asked. Did Wiry's mouth quirk into a smile for a second?

"Something like that," I said softly, letting menace creep into my voice.

"What's the second thing?" Wiry tipped his head to the side, unintentionally imitating the pose of a curious canine. I had to push down the chuckle that suddenly burbled to life in my stomach.

I looked him straight in the eye, not afraid of playing domination games with a wolf. "I am no one's underling," I spoke firmly, refusing to break eye contact.

He snorted out a chuckle at what he perceived as bravado. Wiry took another few steps closer, looking like he was going to continue our repartee. He inhaled to speak, and that's when things went to hell. Literally.

Abruptly, he snorted, grabbing at his nose as if something truly offensive had assaulted his olfactory senses. "Why do you smell like demon?" Wiry demanded, trying to paw the scent from his nostrils. I could have sworn I saw the fur starting to sprout from the backs of his hands as he tried to bat away the offensive smell.

"What the hell?" I shouted as the werewolves tackled me to the ground.

They shoved my face into the cement and the burn of a friction rub tore open my cheek. Like I said, these guys were big. Much bigger than I was. They were also hyped up on wolf-juice. I was only hyped up on strongly brewed tea. Sure, I had my own set of talents and skills, but that just barely put me on a par with werewolf strength. I had to train my ass off to hold my own. Surprised and pinned to the ground by three strong, angry Supes? I didn't have a chance.

They flipped me over, wrenching my left shoulder. Despite my struggles, Meathead soon had my arms pinned over my head, and Grabby was sitting on my legs. The knives strapped to the small of my back wouldn't do me any good in this situation. I tried to inch my hands close to my bag. I had both lethal and non-lethal options in there. If I could just reach them. Although, trying to move was like fighting against bands of iron. These guys were *solid*.

"Exactly my point. What the hell?" Wiry panted. Sweat beaded along his forehead, dripping down his long nose. I didn't think it was from the autumn heat. He looked like he was trying to hold back a flood with will alone and that tenuous dam was cracking. From what I heard, when werewolves lost control, bad things happened.

"What's going on with you and demons and Aldrich Kingsley? And where's the relic?" He was shouting by the time he reached the end, spittle flying in my face.

I turned my face to the left to dodge some of the spray. Which was when a series of brilliant flashes accompanied by the clicking sound of a camera app erupted at the mouth of the alley.

The wolves must have been as surprised as I was because their holds loosened. Even though I wanted to rub the spots blurring my vision, I blindly used the momentary reprieve to my advantage. Heaving up with all the strength I could muster, I threw my hips up and wriggled like a fish out of water. The sudden movement tossed Grabby back on his rear. I quickly hinged my lower section up, catching Meathead's neck between my legs like a pair of scissors and twisted to the side, forcing him off my arms. I scrambled to my feet, clawing at my bag. I had my hands on my taser when an unfamiliar voice interjected.

"Morning, boys. Ma'am," a man's voice drawled.

This time *I* growled. I *hated* being called 'ma'am'.

I finally blinked away enough of the spots dancing in my vision to focus on the man standing in the alley's mouth. He held up his phone like it was a freaking sword. His tight black T-shirt emphasized the defined muscles of his chest and arms as he raised his technological rapier. He looked familiar, but I couldn't quite place him.

This guy must have a death wish to walk into what the three wolves would consider their territory. I took a couple of steps backwards, trying to keep my three attackers in sight. All three wolves took menacing steps towards their newest chew toy. The stranger's gray eyes flashed dangerously.

"Nuh, uh, uh. I wouldn't do that if I were you," he said as he waggled the phone at them like a teacher scolding naughty students.

They stopped as if someone had jerked a leash. I'm not sure if it was from curiosity or from shock at the confrontation.

The newest member of our little drama continued. "You see, boys, I have a series of photos that show you in a less than respectable position with this young lady. What would the public have to say about it if I were to, say, send these to the local news outlets? Especially of the ones where you look like you are in dire need of a trip to the barber?"

The insinuation froze the werewolves in place. All four of us stared at the stranger, waiting to see what he said next. If he had been a Supe, surely he would have attacked or used his powers or *something*. Right? So why wasn't he? Unless he wasn't a Supe. Which meant that he was stupid. And a Norm. Great. Looked like I was going to have to save my savior before the werewolves picked a bone with him.

The gray-eyed man struck a musing pose, a finger laid alongside his cheek. He wiggled the phone meaningfully. He lowered his hand and voice to issue a more dire threat. "What would your Alpha say if he saw? One press of a button and those photos go viral. Your choice, boys."

Well, that answered that question. No Supe I knew chose technology over a weapon when confronting angry werewolves. He had to be a Norm. What was his game?

I kept my hand in my bag, close to my taser. I felt more confident with my weapons within reach and a couple of steps away from my attackers, but I didn't want to pull anything out yet.

The gray-eyed phone warrior held up his weapon of choice. "I respect your skills enough to press 'send' if you take one more step. You may get me," he added with a shrug, "but your Alpha will want a word with you if he sees these. He won't like the heat it will bring down. Hell, maybe your Alpha's boss will want a word or two as well."

"You're bluffing," Meathead rasped. Wow. He was afraid of his boss. Or his boss's boss. Or the Collective. All viable contenders for a tightening of the sphincter in my estimation.

Steely gray eyes swung towards Meathead. "Try me," he said simply. There was no give in the man. I had no doubt he would follow through on his threat.

Apparently, the wolves reached the same conclusion. Meathead looked nervous and Grabby went slightly green around the gills. The three wolves shot nervous glances at each other. Whoever held their reins must not be one to mess around.

The phone suddenly bobbed up and down as the guy shrugged. The wolves watched it in horror, like they had just discovered a bomb with mere seconds left on the timer.

"Or you guys leave now, and I don't need to send these pictures anywhere," the gray-eyed man offered.

Meathead tried to rally, "Let's just smash the phone. Problem solved."

The handsome man with the phone sighed. "It's already uploaded to the cloud, you cognitively challenged cretin."

"Huh?" grunted Meathead.

"Dumbass," I offered helpfully from behind the wolf. "He just called you a dumbass."

The Norm's gaze flicked to me. Was that amusement I saw in his piercing gray eyes?

He swiftly refocused on the three wolves in front of him. "If you smash the phone, it won't destroy the photos, but I will take it personally. I'll upload these photos in retribution for not treating a lady with respect," he said, gesturing my way.

I gave him a small nod of acknowledgment. A flicker of a smile tugged at the corner of his mouth.

"What I do next will be recompense for the inconvenience of having to get a new phone. And trust me, I'll enjoy every second I spend destroying your lives," he murmured menacingly.

I swear, that man's eyes dropped the temperature in the alley by about ten degrees.

Wiry tried to save face. He turned to me. "We'll be in touch," he muttered.

"Why wait?" I shot back, aggressively stubborn, and not willing to settle for them jumping me again. "Let's finish this, man to man. Woman to dog. Mano e paw-o. Whatever."

A low growl resonated ominously off the alley walls. This one was distinctly human. Wiry took another glance towards the man holding the phone.

"Another time," he muttered as all three wolves backed slowly out of the alley, careful never to turn their backs to either of us.

# Chapter 17

The gray-eyed Norm stepped back and to the side, allowing the werewolves plenty of room to pass. I noticed the Norm didn't turn his back to anyone either; me included. Cautious. I liked it.

The wolves ducked around the corner and vanished. We continued to stare at the empty street, waiting for a surprise attack. When nothing happened, the man turned his gaze to focus on me. He tucked his phone carefully into his pocket.

"Are you okay?" he asked, keeping his distance, his empty hands at his sides.

I nodded, watching him for any sudden movements. Even though he'd just saved me, I was wary.

"Okay," he drew the word out. "It's just that you have your hand in your purse still. The way you grabbed for it as soon as you could makes me think there is something in there that could, I don't know, put holes in my body or something. I prefer my body un-hole-y."

I chuckled. I couldn't help myself. He had a body that practically begged to have unholy things done to it.

He grinned slightly himself, catching the meaning behind my chuckle. "So? What do you say? Am I safe?" He held up his hands to show his lack of threat.

I released my hold on my weapons. "Safe? Good Lord, you just knowingly faced down three werewolves. You're anything but safe," I snorted in disbelief.

He waved his hand dismissively. "Those puppies haven't even found their milk teeth. They backed down from a flash from a camera," he said easily.

"Oh, so you're a flasher now?" I quirked my eyebrows suggestively.

"Only in the right company." His smile was downright devilish this time as he met my eyes squarely.

I may be dense sometimes when it came to men, but I was at least ninety percent sure he was flirting. I brushed some of the alley grime from my clothes. His eyes followed the movements of my hands, appreciating my curves. Well then. Make that ninety-five percent.

"Thanks for the help. It was handy that you were in the right place at the right time." I tried to keep my tone light and breezy.

"No problem." He brushed it away easily, like he had done something as mundane as holding a door instead of facing down freaking were-wolves.

"Well, I should probably be on my way then. I have to get home and clean up before a, uh, work thing." I stumbled through the sentence. Why was I so awkward? Was it because I was used to doing the saving instead of having to be saved? Or was it that this insanely good-looking man seemed interested in me? No, I wasn't that shallow. Was I?

"Sure, let me give you a ride. My car's just around the corner," he offered.

My spidey-sense suddenly flared to life again. Why? This guy seemed perfectly normal and he'd just saved my ass. What about him was making the hairs on the back of my arms stand on end? I mean, I supposed it was convenient. The "rescue" could have been an orchestrated plan to gain my trust and get me alone with this stranger. This beautiful, beautiful stranger.

"No. Thanks, though. I live close by. It's an easy walk." I said, trying to slide out of the alleyway into the relative safety of a lightly populated sunlit street.

He courteously stepped to the side. "Sounds good. I could use a walk," he said easily.

He fell into step beside me on the sidewalk. Not close enough to invade my bubble, but matching my pace. He stuck his hands in the pockets of his jeans, looking for all the world like he was just enjoying a morning stroll. Huh. Was my spidey-sense doing me wrong?

We walked in silence for a few paces. I took a gamble. "So, how long have you been following me?" I watched him carefully out of the corner of my eye for a reaction.

He shrugged easily, not seeming upset or surprised by my question. "Thought I saw you leaving Kenzie's Kafe. I wasn't sure and didn't want to be creepy, so I thought I would scout it out to see if it really was you."

I rolled my eyes. "Yeah, stalking a girl is one hundred percent not creepy. Well done, dude."

He grinned, not rising to the bait. "Is it still stalking if you issued an invitation first?"

I stopped in the middle of sidewalk, hands on my hips. "I did no such thing!"

He walked forward another pace or two before looking over his shoulder. "I don't know. I'd interpret 'find me later' as an invitation. Cameron." He continued forward and put an extra waggle in his hips as he walked. His ass looked mighty fine in those jeans. My memory jogged. Ass. *Ass*ets.

"Wait! You're the guy from the club?" I was simultaneously relieved and on edge. At least my spider-sense hadn't let me down, but his awfully convenient story didn't convince me. Not yet, anyway.

He stopped and turned, "I mean, you can call me that if you like. 'Magnus' is easier, but your choice." His gray eyes twinkled merrily down at me.

I folded my arms over my chest. "And you expect me to believe that you just *happened* to be in my regular coffee shop this morning at *precisely* the right time to catch a glimpse of me? Then you followed me for blocks just to see if I was really a girl you bumped into for a moment at a nightclub. Is it your habit to stalk people you've just met?"

He grinned again. Wow, he didn't ruffle easily. "I admit, when you put it like that, it sounds pretty convenient. But it's also the truth. When I'm new in town, I like to try out the local places. I get enough of chain stores when I travel, so I like to indulge in the local ambiance when I can. So, to answer your question, yes, it was lucky happenstance." His grin took on a roguish quality. "And I freely admit to stalking people, but I usually do it like everyone else does."

I raised an eyebrow.

"Via social media," he clarified. "However, you didn't leave me with a lot of information, so I trusted fate. When I thought I saw you turning the corner, I took a chance. I'm glad I did." His easy-breezy attitude blew away. "It looked like things were moving from a frying pan to a fire situation for you back there."

I looked back over my shoulder at the alley. He was right. If he hadn't been following me, that little tussle with the wolves could have ended badly for me. I tried to suppress a shiver. I didn't like feeling weak and ineffective. Like a victim. Hard pass.

I turned back to face him. "Well, Magnus No-Last-Name, all things considered, you may walk me *close* to home. But when I say the walk is over, you go," I said sternly, trying to channel my inner schoolmarm.

"Deal," he said instantly, lips curving into a grin. "And my last name is Donovan."

I wasn't going to turn away an attractive guy who might be genuinely nice; the light stalking aside. After all, he'd faced down three werewolves for me. That moved him far along in my vetting process. However, even with all that, there was no way that I was showing a stranger where I lived after the events of the last twenty-four hours. I was pretty. Not pretty stupid.

I caught back up to him and we started off in the general direction of my apartment. I'd have liked to stretch out the walk a bit to gather as much information about him as possible, but I did have that meeting with Aldrich Kingsley. There was no way I was showing up looking as scruffy as I did right now. A change of clothes and a shower were in my immediate future. Even with a slightly pressing time frame, I wasn't above enjoying the mid-morning sunshine and a stroll with a beautiful stranger. I mean, through a beautiful section of town.

Magnus snuck a glance at me. "I'd ask you any number of questions right now, you know, just out of polite conversation," he said suggestively.

"Really. Like what?" I asked drily.

He faced forward again, a smile hiding at the corner of his delicious-looking lips. "You seem like a fascinating woman. At the very least, you keep fascinating company between the High Fae and the werewolves."

I gave a noncommittal grunt of acknowledgment, but my nerves stretched tighter. *How did he know Letitia was High Fae? Did he see her ears? How does he know about the Fae anyway? The same way he knew about the werewolves?*

The corner of his mouth twitched upward again and he spoke before I could voice the questions racing through my mind. "But I wouldn't want to be accused of stalking, so I'm in a difficult position. What's a guy to do?"

I smiled tightly. He was charming, I'd give him that. Not in the fairytale-prince kind of way, but more in the good-guy-next-door-who-also-happens-to-be-ridiculously-hot kind of way.

"I'm never one to leave a man in distress," I quipped, "but it's not a very long walk."

Magnus shrugged easily, "That's cool." He just left that there, allowing me the freedom to offer as much or as little as I chose.

I weighed my options. "How about we play a game? I'll ask a question and then you ask. We swap until we run out of time." I gave myself an out with the last part. I could call time whenever I wanted to because he didn't know where exactly I lived. We continued walking, and I steered us right at the corner.

"Deal." Magnus stuck out a hand.

I laughed. "Deal," I echoed, shaking his hand briefly.

Was my heart thumping a little louder? Wow, he must be getting to me.

I pounced on the opportunity. "I'll take the first question then. What are you?"

He shrugged easily. "Just your run-of-the-mill, all-American, good guy next door."

I snorted in disbelief. The guy who lived next door to me was in his fifties, balding, and had a beer belly. I was also fairly confident he was Dutch.

"But you know about werewolves." I was careful to phrase it as a statement and not a question. I wasn't about to give him any freebies in our small game. "You didn't seem bothered by that at all. Most normal guys I know would've run screaming if they found out that the things that go bump in the night are real. Werewolves in particular."

"You must know many normal guys," Magnus stated drily.

I rolled my eyes, noting that he'd avoided phrasing it as a question. Well played, sir. For now.

"My turn. What do you do, Cameron?" he asked, continuing to stroll along. The man gave every appearance of enjoying the beautiful autumn morning. Was it that simple? Was he just a guy who was taking a stroll with a girl on a lovely day? Did people still do that?

I decided to play my cards close to my chest under the guise of being coy. "Oh, lots of things, here and there, for lots of different people. I'm a jack-of-all-trades," I waved my air vaguely through the air, keeping my tone light.

He nodded, taking the information on board without trying to pump me for more details.

It was my turn again. "How do you know about werewolves?"

Magnus sighed as if in preamble to a long story. "I'm in IT. Not the phone call support 'Please check if your computer is plugged in, sir' kind of IT. I work with a company that focuses on cybersecurity. Which gives me the ability and the access to all the spooky corners of the dark web. There are plenty of people who wonder about the existence of supernatural beings. Some even fantasize about it or write stories about mythological creatures inhabiting the real world. If only they knew."

I smiled, acknowledging the point.

He continued, "However, if you look hard enough, you can find evidence of the existence of Supernaturals hidden in the binary code. Also, I used to live in Chicago. You don't even need to go trolling around the dark corners of the internet. Some wizard up there advertises through the Yellow Pages, of all things. That is, if you can even find a phone book nowadays."

I let out a small chuckle. The Supes I knew wouldn't be so obvious for fear of bringing down the wrath of the Collective. Then again, I didn't know any wizards. From what I'd heard, they were a crazy bunch. Just take that Temple guy up in St. Louis. His shenanigans would get him in hot water down here if he ever traveled this way.

Magnus' voice grew a little more serious. "I've seen enough to convince me that humans have either evolved, mutated, or, more likely, we simply co-exist with other species. Regardless, I don't believe that regular humans are the dominant beings on this planet anymore. Even though most would like to keep pretending that's the case. However, direct proof of the existence of many mythological creatures is difficult to uncover for a Norm." He gave me a quick glance with a small smile, "Except for werewolves and now, a jack-of-all-trades."

I shot him a glimmer of a smile in return, trying to mask my feelings. Magnus seemed like a genuinely good guy even if he was a Normal. I couldn't really hold that against him, especially since he was aware of the supernatural side of the world. But something wasn't sitting right with me yet.

"Were you following me today?" I asked, searching for a reason for my paranoia to be flaring up.

He chuckled and re-focused on the street ahead of us. "I'll give you that one for free, even though it's my turn. Truly, only from the coffee shop. Like I said, it was just luck that I ran into you. I wasn't even sure it *was* you. Thought I'd take my chances though. I had nothing to lose but a few minutes of time." His eyes crinkled up with mirth as he faced me squarely. "And what I gained through the adrenaline boost today could make me swear off caffeine for a week, so win-win, I guess."

I grabbed his arm in mock horror. "No! Don't do that! Never do that! It's not worth it! Caffeine is possibly more important than air!"

I hammed it up for dramatic effect to make him laugh. He had a boisterous, booming laugh. It made me want to laugh along with him. I liked it when he threw his head back, chuckles rolling out from deep in his chest. Which also sent his muscles quivering under his tight tee.

There were no wimpy muscles of the desk-bound computer nerd there. Suddenly, I found myself wondering what exactly that muscled body looked like underneath his clothes.

*Whoa, easy girl. Slow down for a second.*

If I wasn't careful, I would be in danger of catching feelings for this guy. He chortled as we resumed walking, taking the next left. When he had regained his composure, he continued the game.

"What happened in the club?" Curiosity laced his voice.

I stutter-stepped. "What do you mean, exactly?"

He lifted an eyebrow at the question.

I raised my hands in self-defense at answering a question with a question. "I could give you some bullshit answer about drinking and dancing."

He nodded, "Yes, you could. I didn't phrase it well."

"Yeah, that one's on you." I nudged him with an elbow. "I'm giving you a pass on this one though, since you just gave me a freebie. Would you like to rephrase?"

"I think I would, thank you. Prior to you crashing into me..." I elbowed him harder this time.

"Ow! Prior to you crashing into me just like that," he said, rubbing his ribcage where my elbow caught him, "what happened in the club? It looked like you zoned out and were moving around a bit. Not jerking like a seizure or anything, just...I don't know, *responding* to something no one else could see. Then you dumped your drink down your front. Not that you'll find me complaining in the least." His eyes took on a wicked gleam, and shamelessly scanned me from head to toe. He made sure I knew he appreciated what he saw.

Rather than giving in to my budding flirtraction or the desire to dodge the question, I honored the bargain I'd made. "To be honest? I'm not entirely sure what happened in the club."

Magnus tipped his head and squinted at me. I held up my hands in protest. "That's the honest answer! Besides, we're getting near the end of the line." I let the corner of my mouth twist into a smirk to break whatever tension might have been lingering. "For you."

He sighed dramatically and pulled out his phone. "Let me arrange a ride since you're ditching me in the middle of the street." He started tapping away on the screen.

My hand flew to my chest in a mocking imitation of sophisticated Southern debutantes. "Why I never! I, sir, am a *lady*." I laid the Southern drawl on thick. "Good Lord, I would never leave a helpless man in the middle of the road all by himself. He might get hurt! Or run into something awful like a werewolf! How'd a single man ever be expected to take care of himself? Heavens, man, I'm not a monster!"

He chuckled and tucked the phone away. "You should go into acting."

"Why? You think I'm good?"

"No, you suck," he said drily.

I swung a mock punch his way, which he dodged easily.

"But it's cute." He grinned down at me.

I might be dense, but I wasn't blind. He was absolutely flirting and enjoying every second.

He crossed his well-muscled arms over his broad chest. "I have a couple of minutes before my lift gets here. One more question each?"

"Sure. My turn," I agreed easily.

I took a gamble and decided to see how much he knew about the supernatural community of New Orleans. Maybe I'd get lucky, and he'd give me some new insights. "Tell me everything you know about Aldrich Kingsley?"

He stuck his lower lip out in thought, nodding slightly to himself. "Okay, I didn't see that coming. Fair's fair, I guess. Aldrich Kingsley. Hmm." He paused, gathering his thoughts. I waited, trying not to let my impatience show.

"Fair warning. Most of this is guesswork backed up by tidbits I've uncovered in trawling the web," he qualified.

"Noted. Give me what you've got. Guesswork and all," I said.

His eyes rolled up to the left, trying to recall what he had read. "He's a Fae. My best guess is that he's a noble in either the Summer or the Spring Courts. I wouldn't have guessed Winter, but that's purely because of the Louisiana heat. He's also likely high up enough in whichever Court to have some significant influence in Fae. Again, just a guess since he seems to oversee the Fae happenings in this town."

I bobbed my head in agreement. That aligned with what I knew or could surmise.

Magnus continued, "Extrapolating from that, he can't be royalty or hold an insanely powerful role in the Court because he isn't required to stay in Fae full time. Although I haven't done a deep dive into him, I'd also venture that most of his dealings are on the up and up. A man in his position would have to present a respectable front to both the mortal and the Fae worlds to maintain a prestigious post in this realm. However, it wouldn't surprise me if he had some more nefarious side hustles. Although I've no outright proof to that extent."

I nodded along thoughtfully, digesting his information. Most of it matched up with what I either knew or guessed myself. Magnus was surprisingly well-informed for a Norm.

"I suppose I could do you a favor and look into him. If you wanted me to," Magnus suggested easily.

I contemplated his offer. It would be beneficial to have as much information as possible about Aldrich Kingsley. I liked to be well-informed before accepting a job. Usually, I knew a little about the players, especially if they were supernatural or affluent members of the New Orleans community. If I didn't know them, I might go ask Sloane. Possibly Mama Atli, given the situation. However, Logan usually provided more information on jobs and outcomes when doling out assignments. The information on this job had been sparse. It would be prudent to gather as many details as I could, even if it was just educated guesswork.

"Okay. If you do it discreetly. You've already called enough trouble down on yourself by tangling with the wolves. You don't need any more trouble by attracting unwanted attention from the Fae." The earnestness in my voice surprised me. I really was concerned about him. I must be going soft or something to be worried about a stranger. Albeit a very handsome one.

"Discretion is the name of the game." His smile flickered again. "I'm happy to do you a favor, but there is a price."

I instantly grew wary. "Which is?"

"Lunch. Have lunch with me tomorrow?"

Lunch with an attractive man? My mama didn't raise no fools. With a smile, I agreed. Just as we were finalizing our lunch plans and exchanging numbers, a shiny black Tesla pulled up to the curb.

"That's my ride. I'll see you tomorrow." Magnus waved as he slid into the backseat of the car. It silently pulled away from the curb and into traffic.

A tingly feeling built in my stomach that felt deceptively like butterflies. I had a good feeling about Magnus. After our conversation, something in my gut told me he was a good guy. After a life of doing what I do, I trusted in my gut instincts the way I trusted Louisiana to be humid and full of mosquitoes. Neither one had let me down yet. And right now, my gut was on Magnus' side.

And not just because he offered to buy me lunch.

# Chapter 18

I made sure that the Tesla was out of sight before turning and retracing my steps. We'd passed my apartment a block and a half ago, but I'd wanted to make sure that Magnus was being truthful. He hadn't blinked twice when we passed my place, nor had he given any indication that he knew where I lived. I was probably being unnecessarily paranoid, but I'd rather that than face down in an alleyway. For the second time today. I'll admit, it hadn't been my finest moment.

I flicked open my phone to see that I didn't have much time to get cleaned up before my meeting with Kingsley. A message from Sloane pinged on my home screen. I opened my door and went through my security protocols, re-locking my locks the requisite seven times before reading her message.

*I found something. Call me ASAP.* Brief and to the point. Just like Sloane.

I dialed her number as I stripped off my shirt and shorts, tossing them towards the hamper.

Sloane answered right away, "Cam, are you okay?"

"Yeah. Why?" Had she heard about the werewolf attack already?

"Are you sure?" Sloane sounded flustered, worried even. Very much not like Sloane.

"Yes, I'm sure. What's going on, Sloane?" I asked.

She took a deep breath. "You know that lady you asked me to look into? The one with the tequila? Mary-Diana or whatever?"

"Yes, Sloane. I remember the favor I asked you to do for me last night." I rolled my eyes as I hopped into my favorite skinny black jeans. I loved the butter-soft fabric and the flexibility of movement that the jeans allowed me, but good Lord, they're a pain to get into.

She sounded flustered. "Cam, she disappeared."

I grabbed a clean top from my closet and tried to keep any trace of condescension out of my tone. "Yes, Sloane. I remember. I was there."

"No, Cam. I mean, she *disappeared* disappeared. At first, I thought she was just cloaking herself." Sloane sounded agitated.

"Like an invisibility cloak type of thing?"

"Exactly. That's what I thought too. When I went over the security footage visually, she was just gone. One frame, she's sitting across from you, sexy as sin. The next, she's gone. I assumed it had to be magic of some sort. A spell or artifact or something. When she vanished from visual, I switched over to my other set-up."

Sloane did a brisk business with supernatural customers. Beings that didn't always behave in ways traditional security measures could track. Therefore, she had installed creative, hidden security features in her bar. Some of them were purely observational, whereas others were defensive wards to protect innocent onlookers. Sloane had even upgraded her security recently to include some aggressive offensive spells to counteract any overly belligerent behavior. I grimaced, rolling a shoulder. I'd been on the receiving end of one of those offensive spells in an incident that'd resulted in a dislocated shoulder and a month-long ban from the Forge. I'd mourned every day, distraught to have missed out on all of Rudolph's beer for an entire month.

Sloane's voice snapped me back to the present. "When I switched over, I tried everything in my security arsenal. Infrared. Heat sensors. Wards. Runic resonators. Hell, I even tried running the feed through a high-tech sound filter to catch some sort of sign that she was walking out of the room."

I'd been touching up my make-up while I listened. I was going for coldly professional, a vibe that required more make-up than my morning look. At her words, I stopped messing with my face. This was big.

"Cam, there was *nothing*. When I say that she disappeared, I mean she *disappeared*. One minute she was in my bar, drinking with you, and the next moment, she was gone. She wasn't invisible or hiding. She was just...gone." Sloane sounded frightened. That scared me worse than the information of Meridiana's disappearance.

I let out the breath I'd been holding. This was much worse than I'd imagined, but I needed to hear my suspicions confirmed.

"Tell it to me straight, Sloane," I said softly.

"Cam, she wasn't using magic. I've never *heard* of someone being able to just vanish like that. As far as I know, it's not even possible." Sloane's voice wavered slightly.

"What does that *mean*, Sloane?" I insisted. I needed to hear her say it.

My best friend let out a shaky breath. "It means, whatever she is, she is massively high-powered. More powerful than anyone I've ever encountered. And for some reason, she is *very* interested in you."

# Chapter 19

I flew through the rest of my preparations on autopilot, trying to process what Sloane had shared. Who was this Meridiana lady? What strange powers did she have? Most importantly, what did she want with me? She hadn't seemed threatening at the Forge. In fact, she seemed pleasant. A good drinking buddy, at the very least. She had given no indication of wanting to hurt me or mine. However, I've hung out with enough Supes to know that being able to do high-powered spells no one else is capable of was its own kind of threat.

Perhaps now wasn't the best time to be taking an unknown job. Especially when the client was a High Fae. They're tricky as a rule. Come to think of it, the werewolves had said that the Fae were looking for the same thing they were. I wrinkled my nose, trying to recall what the wolves had called it. I snapped my fingers. Right, a relic. They'd said the Fae were after the same relic they wanted.

It was possible that the acquisition job Kingsley was hiring for was something else altogether. Perhaps he just wanted the best sandwich in Louisiana. I doubted it, but there was always a chance. I was willing to bet one of Rudolph's excellent beers that the Fae Ambassador was after the same relic that the wolves wanted. It might be hard for some people to believe in coincidences. When it came to Supes, it was even harder to believe in anything else.

I grabbed a few things that might come in handy and shoved them in a bag, thinking hard. I could back out of my meeting with Kingsley. Not taking the acquisition job would remove the conflict between me and the wolves if my hypothesis was correct.

I took a quick look around my apartment. My place wasn't much, but it was mine. I reminded myself that my last paycheck covered the rent, but not much else. If I wanted to continue to live and, you know, eat, I was going to have to find work somewhere. Fast. Otherwise, I'd have to go back to Logan and take that crocodile job.

I sighed. Heavily.

Some shady deal involving werewolves and the Fae or crocodile smuggling. Shitty choices all around. Taking the meeting with Kingsley would at least give me some more information. There was always the chance that what he wanted had nothing to do with the wolves. My gut told me it was a slim chance. My gut also told me I liked food.

I sighed again. When faced with a field of shit and nowhere else to go, it's best to pull on your boots and get to walking. I shrugged into my leather jacket, slung my bag over a shoulder, and reset my security as I hurried out the door.

I dialed the number for a cheap car service I'd used in the past to take me to the Forge to pick up my bike. I pondered the situation on the ride over.

What was this relic that the wolves wanted? If the Fae were after it as well, it must do some really hinky stuff. Perhaps it was better if it was left wherever it was. Hidden from the Supes who wanted it.

No, I knew better than that. Powerful magical items never seemed to stay hidden. If they weren't placed somewhere for safekeeping and guarded, they fell into the wrong hands at precisely the wrong time, likely twisting some important, world-saving moment into a world-shattering disaster.

I paid the driver and ducked inside to grab my helmet. Unfortunately, Sloane wasn't in, but one of the bartenders recognized me and grabbed my helmet from her office. I slapped it on my head as I jogged out the door to collect the Rebel.

My thoughts turned back to the mysterious redhead as I sped towards the Fae Embassy. How did she figure into this? She had obviously known who I was, but the timing of her appearing out of nowhere was awfully coincidental. What did she want with me? Was she really just doing a favor for my mom five years after her death? Or was it even me she was interested in? Was she after the same relic that the werewolves wanted? I suddenly grew cold, and it wasn't from the autumn wind whipping through my hair as I roared through the streets of New Orleans.

A lost relic, presumably powerful, and a woman with mysterious magic were in town at the same time. Sloane was convinced that this Meridiana was capable of spells well above what Sloane had ever *seen*. Hell, she'd done something that Sloane hadn't even thought *possible*. Add in the wolves and the missing relic. Yeah, right. I didn't think for a second that all these things just *happened* to crop up at the same time. If you believed that, I have some swampland in Florida to sell you.

I revved the Rebel's engine and zoomed around a corner. I didn't have to do this, I reminded myself. I could just take a step back and let someone else deal with all the supernatural, spooky, crazy shit. Spooky. Why did that sound familiar?

Oh! If I hadn't been driving, I would have face-palmed myself. I had completely forgotten about my promise to Ben to investigate the disappearing ghost thing. If he and Mama were right, they could be the battery for some really messed-up magic. I wondered if all of this was linked somehow. I felt like I was on the edge of a whirlpool just waiting to get sucked in. And I'd forgotten to pack my floaties.

I sucked in a deep breath as I pulled to a stop and examined the gorgeous, white-columned mansion. It was a now or never kind of moment. One of those roads diverging in the woods, as Robert Frost would say. I looked down the literal road in front of me. I could hop on my Rebel and ride straight back home. I could figure out the money thing. Probably.

If not, there was always the open road. I could try my hand in a new place, see what I could do there. However, the few roots I had were in New Orleans. My family was here. My family of choice, at least. Sloane, Mama, and Ben, to name a few. They held a large part of my heart here and I couldn't just abandon them.

I also had a feeling, deep in my bones, that if I wanted to shed any light on my shadowy past, that the answers were here. Somewhere in New Orleans. I just had to shake them loose.

My gaze swung back to the mansion in front of me. If I chose this path, it'd be more exciting. Which is just another word for dangerous. Or fun. I grinned. Sounded like my kind of party. Besides, it might provide me some answers. There were too many unanswered questions in my life right now. For better or worse, I was curious. Cautious, but curious. I kicked the stand on the Rebel down and put my feet on the path I had decided on. It led right up to Kingsley's front door.

# Chapter 20

The floral knocker on the front door sent a resonant boom echoing through the old house. A stuffy-looking butler in a full morning suit opened the door a moment later. He took in my windswept hair and bug-smeared helmet with a disdainful sniff. Turning on a heel, the uptight butler ushered me through a lavish foyer decorated with expensive-looking statues and framed art. They must've been switching some pieces because there were a few framed works stacked carefully to the side of the room, waiting for removal.

The butler silently led me to a sitting room near the back of the house. He waved me inside and shut the double doors behind me, leaving me waiting for Ambassador Kingsley.

The room was decorated in a functional, decidedly masculine manner that elegantly suggested good taste and wealth. The dark, heavy wood furnishings and plush red leather chairs nestled in a deeply luxurious carpet looked more expensive than everything I owned combined. Heavy bookshelves lined two of the walls from the floor to the high ceiling and proudly displayed sophisticated-looking tomes. The only picture in the room was an old-fashioned oil painting hanging directly across from the door. A beautiful young blonde High Fae girl with striking green eyes smiled out at me. A man, presumably her father based on his matching eyes, stood behind her, gazing down adoringly at the lovely girl.

An unexpected spear of regret ripped straight through my heart. I wondered if my own father had ever looked at me like that. I couldn't remember him. He'd vanished from my life before I'd been born, and my mother never spoke of him. I fingered the charm pensively as my thoughts drifted to my shadowy past.

A man cleared his throat behind me, startling me from delving any further into the pool of self-pity within my soul. I turned, trying to mask my emotions. The well-dressed man with a silver-tipped cane in one hand stood framed in the doorway like he was posing for the cover of a gentleman's style magazine. His impeccably tailored three-piece suit emphasized the elegant lines of his slim frame. He styled his silver-blond hair longer than fashionable to hide the telltale pointed tips of the High Fae's ears. The longer style suited him, highlighting his strong, noble features. His green eyes bore straight through me. He easily could have passed for human, but even though I couldn't see his pointed ears, I knew that this was the Fae Ambassador, Aldrich Kingsley.

I tried not to fidget or straighten my helmet hair. Despite what commercials would have you think, salon-perfect hair didn't just fall out of biker helmets.

"Ms. Blaze, I presume." His voice was softly accented with breeding and money.

"Yep. That's me." My own voice rang out a little too loudly in the lavish space.

He gestured elegantly to one of the opulent red leather chairs. "Please, do make yourself comfortable," he invited.

I plopped down in the nearest chair. The leather squelched at the unexpected assault. Kingsley glided to the other, cane tapping quietly on the hardwood floor. He loosened the button on his jacket and sat elegantly, leaning the cane against the side of his chair.

His calculating, cold eyes appraised me, measuring my worth in that single gaze. I squirmed. Somehow, I knew I didn't measure up.

I wriggled in the chair, causing it to squeak again. "Umm, is that your daughter? She's pretty," I said, tripping over my tongue.

Why was I so uncomfortable? I was more at home beating the hell out of the werewolves in a club alley than I was in the luxury of the

Fae Embassy. That said something about me that was not particularly flattering.

His perfectly formed lips twisted into a sad smile under his slightly hooked nose. "Yes, that's my Blythe." His intense gaze focused on the painting, drinking in the sight of the beautiful child. An air of melancholy seemed to settle over him like a shroud.

"Blythe is a pretty name. Is she here with you at the Embassy or does she live in Fae?" I asked curiously.

He shook himself slightly, bringing himself back to the conversation. "I believe you're here at the request of Mr. Wilder. About the acquisition I require?"

Interesting. He dodged an innocuous question about his child. Parents usually loved to talk about their little angels. Why didn't he?

I decided to see what kind of information he was willing to volunteer. "Yes, but I need the specifics of the job before I accept."

"I'll provide you with the details I'm comfortable sharing. In return, I'll need your immediate commitment or refusal. I don't have the luxury of time in this manner." Kingsley leaned back in his chair, steepling his fingers and waiting for my agreement.

It wasn't ideal, but the more information I could gather, the better. I nodded my acceptance of his terms.

Kingsley rested his steepled fingers against his chin, pondering his words carefully. "Before I begin, I must pry into your bona fides. Mr. Wilder was cagey about providing your personal details. He flat out refused to divulge your, shall we say, gifts?"

This was the reason I worked with Logan, despite his outrageous cut. He commanded respect among the New Orleans Supes, and his discretion kept my powers and name secret.

"I can hold my own. With Norms and Supes alike." I purposely kept my answer vague.

A faint line of irritation appeared between the Ambassador's brows, marring his otherwise alabaster face. "I'm afraid I'll require more details."

I sighed and spread my arms. "You're welcome to scan me with whatever sort of sensors you like," I said, knowing my response would annoy him. He wanted a defined answer. About me and about my powers. To be fair, I'd love to have the same answers. It looked like we'd both be frustrated for the time being.

The line between his brows grew deeper as his eyes flicked up and down my body, focusing on a spot over my right shoulder. "Interesting," he mused, "you're potentially powerful, but are hiding your powers behind a powerful spell. One is forced to wonder why?"

I let him stew in my silence. Mostly because I wasn't about to explain complicated family history to him. Although, this *was* the first time I'd allowed someone with magic to scan my powers. It was a rare trait, even among Supes. Most Supes would've used a portable charm purchased from the local coven to get a power reading, but those charms were rare and expensive. It was much easier to just do it yourself if you could.

He mused under his breath. "Your magic, while muted, unlike anything I've ever seen. Fascinating. It's too bad that the ward is obscuring a closer inspection."

"Umm, thanks. I think."

He refocused his attention on me. "Ms. Blaze, I would very much like to continue this conversation at another point in time. There seems to be more to you than meets the eye."

I shrugged, allowing my silence to settle over the room.

Sensing that I would not volunteer any more personal information, Ambassador Kingsley sighed dramatically. He dropped his elegant hands to his lap, leaning forward earnestly. "I'm interested in locating an ancient High Fae relic. It's powerful and cannot fall into the wrong hands. It must be under my protection by midnight on All Hallows' Eve. If you can retrieve it and bring it to me, I will pay you twenty thousand dollars. In cash."

I mirrored his body language, subconsciously telling him I was on his team. I took a beat before responding. He wanted this item fast. Two and a half days was a short time frame to find something and return it. However, the pay was excellent. Choices, choices.

"I'd like to ask some questions prior to agreeing to the job," I said after a brief pause.

He dipped his head, allowing me the freedom to continue.

"How powerful is this relic?" I asked.

"Powerful," he said simply.

Inwardly, I rolled my eyes, but kept my face an impassive mask. "What does it do?"

Kingsley smiled and leaned back in his chair, steepling his fingers again.

I almost let out an exasperated sigh, but restrained myself. "Okay. So that's information I only get upon agreeing," I mused aloud.

He nodded almost imperceptibly.

I tried my luck and hit him with a series of rapid-fire questions. "Well, what does it look like? How do you expect me to find it? Do you know who has it? Why can't you go after it yourself? What's with the three, no sorry, two-and-a-half-day deadline?"

Silence.

This time, I did sigh in frustration. "I take it I will only receive that information after committing to retrieve your relic as well?"

He nodded again.

I sat back and ran my hands through my tousled hair. This was a tough decision. I didn't like all the secrets, but I needed the money, and I was curious. Damn curious. Which was worse for me, all things considered.

Kingsley leaned forward. "Time's up, Ms. Blaze. What's your decision?"

# Chapter 21

As the saying goes, curiosity killed the cat. Which might very well be me. After my recent run-ins with the werewolves, I doubt they'd classify me as a dog person. If I took the job, I might even get some answers regarding the wolves' presence in my town. At the worst, I would get paid. Very well. But I had a gut feeling that something was off. As much as I wanted the money, at the end of everything, I needed to walk away from this situation intact.

I started to push to my feet. "As fun as this has been, Kingsley, I'm going to have to pass," I said, having to work to keep regret out of my tone. It was an enormous payday. One I could really use.

"Wait!" Was that desperation I heard in the High Fae Ambassador's voice? Aldrich's fevered green eyes were intense, bordering on un-balanced. "I know how these things go. Discretion is big business in our world, but anonymity comes with a hefty price tag. Logan and his practices are well-known to the Collective, but we tolerate his presence in our city because he always delivers exceptional work. However, what would it feel like to be out from under his thumb? To choose jobs because you *want* them instead of *need* them? To take a vacation once in a while or treat yourself to the finer things in life? How does that sound?"

"Expensive," I said drily.

"I'll pay you double. Forty thousand dollars for two days work."

My breath caught in my chest and my knees gave out. I hit the chair with a smack, barely registering it. Kingsley threw out the offer like it was pennies, but that kind of money would be life changing for me. I looked up at him, stunned. There was no way I was passing on this job and he knew it.

"Let's make a deal," I whispered hoarsely. "A *sworn* deal." High Fae cannot break a sworn oath, although if you leave them a loophole, the slippery bastards will figure out a way to slither through it, no matter how small.

The Fae Ambassador closed the distance between us, cane tapping on the floor. He grasped my forearm, pulling me to my feet. Staring deeply into my eyes, Aldrich Kingsley swore an irrefutable oath, "I swear on my power, on my name, on the life of my daughter, that I'll pay you forty thousand dollars upon receiving the relic I've described. However, if you're late or cannot recover it for me, you will never work for me again, in any capacity. I will not abide incompetence."

I bristled under his tone, but when I met his burning eyes, I held back my biting retort. He wasn't on the brink of madness. He'd already fully embraced it. He'd just lifted the veil long enough to show me the truth. I shuddered, already knowing I had made my decision. I was going to dance with this devil and pray to anyone who would listen that I didn't get burned.

"I agree to find, retrieve, and bring the relic that you've described to you within your given time frame. I agree to fulfill these terms in return for *fifty* thousand dollars. Half now and half to be paid immediately upon delivery of the relic." It was always good to set clear parameters when dealing with the High Fae. They could be tricky and would find even the smallest of loopholes if given the chance.

Kingsley's thin lips curved into a predatory smile. He hadn't missed the increase in the fee. I matched his smile with a cutting one of my own. I knew when I had someone by the short and curlies. He wanted this relic as badly as I wanted the promised payday. And he needed it fast. Which meant that he was desperate. I wasn't above some friendly extortion in a situation like this. Whatever this relic was, I now wanted to find it as badly as he did. Scratch that. I wanted to find it more.

Kingsley met my eyes. "You'll be paid in full when I have the relic. Fifty thousand in cash."

I didn't like it, but had a feeling that this was the best I could hope for. "Fine. Agreed."

"Agreed," he intoned solemnly, giving my arm a jerky shake.

A thump radiated out from my chest and resonated through my entire body. Like someone had just amped up a subwoofer to the max and played a test bass guitar chord in a stadium and I was standing next to it.

Wow. Now *that* was power.

Kingsley had obviously experienced something similar, but didn't look nearly as shaken as I was. Perhaps this was a normal occurrence for the High Fae. Perhaps phantom guitars always signaled a deal being struck. I didn't know. I'd never made a deal with a High Fae directly. Sure, I'd worked for them. Repeatedly, in the case of Lady Letitia. But we'd always arranged the deals through intermediaries.

Attempting to cover my surprise, I leaned forward in my seat. "Now that we're in this together, lay it on me. I'm on a deadline."

A serious, regretful look swept over the Ambassador's face. He stood and strode towards the windows, gathering his thoughts. The rhythmic tap of his cane marked his journey from the plush carpet, across the hardwood to the window.

"A long time ago, my people, shall we say, misplaced a relic and we've been trying to recover it ever since. It's a powerful item that needs to be returned to its rightful owners as soon as possible," he said, turning to face me. His eyes shone with fevered intensity.

"Right. Got that. Why the deadline?" I said, trying to remember what information I needed under his unnerving scrutiny.

Kingsley stared out the window at the beautifully manicured garden basking in the sultry Southern fall afternoon. "All Hallows' Eve is coming. I must have the relic before it passes. For protection."

Was it my imagination, or had he paused over that last part?

"Okay," I drew out the word, bringing his attention back to me. "But why?"

"For my own reasons. There are matters, High Fae matters, which I'm not at liberty to discuss. Suffice it to say that your deadline is set." He gestured towards the door, "If you have no further questions…"

Deliberately, I leaned back in my chair, steepling my fingers in a posture reminiscent of his own.

He smiled, reading the gesture for what it was. "My dear Ms. Blaze, I'm beginning to enjoy your company. You bear a stubborn streak to rival my own, but do we really have the time for trivial games?" The smile did not reach his eyes.

"We can discuss my stubbornness at another time. You've just hired me to do a job. Give me the information I need so that I can get your relic for you." I left out the 'so you can pay me,' bit, but it sat at the forefront of my mind.

Refusing to rise to my antagonistic behavior, Kingsley leaned on his cane, considering me. "Let's see if I can answer all your questions. The relic I require is a pink crystal. It's about the length of your forearm and contains an ever-shifting light inside, easily identifying it from mundane quartz or the like. The relic acts as a reservoir. A powerful one that enhances the wielder by storing power. I have a tracker that will help you find it. Unfortunately, it is the only one I have, so don't lose it."

He reached into his pocket and gently tossed me a small silver orb. I easily plucked it from the air. He continued as I examined the engraved silver ball. "That tracker latches onto the power signature from the relic. They have assured me it will glow and vibrate when you are within one hundred meters of the relic. The vibrations and light will intensify as you close in on the relic's hiding spot."

I interrupted, "How far is a hundred meters? Speak American, man!"

He sighed. "Such an inefficient system of measurement," he muttered. Kingsley ran his hand through his long, silver-blond hair, which fell perfectly back into place. Naturally. "Fine. The tracker will notify you when you are roughly a football field away. Do you understand that unit of measurement?"

I nodded in satisfaction. Both at riling him up and the distance clarification. I really wasn't great with the metric system.

"I'll never understand the stubborn desire to find value in a measurement system that is ancient, impractical…" he said huffily under his breath.

"Kind of like valuing an ancient and impractical relic?" I interrupted rudely, still trying to poke at him to see if he revealed something out of sheer frustration. "After all, you'd have to be fairly powerful for a relic like that to make any sort of difference. From what I've known of magic, you'd have to spend weeks or months drip-feeding power into it for a one-time use spell. Even then, the power would be directly proportional to the source and the time of accumulation."

Cold green eyes snapped to me. I could tell I had surprised him. He must've initially placed me in the capable-but-dumb category. Whoops. I wasn't there now.

"Something like that, Ms. Blaze." He purposefully turned his back on me, looking out the window again. I allowed him a moment to gather his thoughts, inspecting the tracker. It was about the size of a golf ball. Tiny runes were carved all over the silver surface. No iron here, that's for sure.

"Any further questions?" His voice rang with the chilly finality of someone ending an interview.

"Sure," I drawled. "Why can't you go after it yourself if you have this fancy tracker?" I waggled the silver ball at him for emphasis.

The Ambassador started pacing, his cane tapping rhythmically against the floor. "We've tried. Either the relic is warded specifically against Fae, or we aren't looking in the right places. Either way, that's where you come in. I am grasping at straws. Stretching for any semblance of hope. Namely, that you'll get lucky where I have not."

"Fair enough." I pocketed the tracking orb. "Do you know who has it? Or can you suggest a place to start looking?"

His intense gaze locked onto me once more, and I had to work to suppress a shiver. "I'm unsure if anyone is currently in possession of the relic. Someone may have it. Or it may be lost." He shrugged elegantly. "Either way, you can assume that there'll be other people looking for it. Although it is Fae made, any Supe can use it. We know it hasn't left New

Orleans. Other than that," he shrugged again, "your guess is as good as mine."

"If anyone can use it, how discreet do I need to be in my retrieval process?"

"Don't proclaim it from the rooftops, but if you need assistance, I value speed over secrecy in this matter."

Standing and stretching my back slightly, I said, "Right. I'd better get to work then."

"Good luck, Ms. Blaze. Do not fail me." I couldn't tell if he was making a heartfelt plea or a veiled threat.

I nodded and, with nothing more to say, turned to leave the study. Ambassador Kingsley stood staring out the window, anxiously fiddling with the silver knob on top of his cane as I walked out of his study. As soon as I shut the door behind me, I let out a silent sigh, leaning my head back against a door. The High Fae I'd met were intense as a rule, but this Kingsley guy took the cake.

Muttering from inside the room surprised me. Confident that I'd left the Ambassador alone in there, I pressed an ear against the door, curious as to what was going on. My sharp hearing could discern his precise accent through the heavy wooden door easily. It sounded like he was praying.

"Oh, Carina, we're one step closer. I swear to you on my life I'll make this right. Our daughter will not suffer anymore. All I need is to get my hands on the Shard and everything will be as it was..."

A throat cleared behind me, and I slowly turned from my eavesdropping to see the butler standing at the entrance to the hallway, glaring at me. I think he wanted to cross his arms to add to the weaponized disapproval wafting off him, but his rigid training wouldn't allow it. I pushed away from my lean against the door with a sigh and followed him as he led me back the way we had come. As we walked, I tried to pry more information from the Fae man. After all, Kingsley hadn't sworn me to secrecy.

"So, the Ambassador wants this relic pretty badly. Any idea why?" I asked, forcing innocence into my voice as I pretended to study the paintings that adorned the walls.

The butler's face did not twitch in the slightest. "I really can't comment, Miss."

"Can't or won't? Two different things, Jeeves," I said, keeping a careful watch for any tells.

"I really can't comment, Miss," he repeated in precisely the same tone of voice as we entered the foyer.

*Damn it.*

The unflappable butler moved to collect my helmet, intent on ushering me out of the Embassy as quickly as possible. He walked past the stack of paintings leaning against the wall.

I did a double-take, recognizing the top one. It was a copy of the painting that I had seen in the sitting room. The artist had centered the lovely Fae child in the portrait, with Kingsley gazing down at her adoringly. However, in this version of the painting, there was a gorgeous Fae lady who was staring with equal adoration at the beautiful child. Interesting. Who was she? Aldrich's wife? The child's mother? More importantly, why had the lady been removed from the painting in the sitting room?

# Chapter 22

With nothing better to do and no brilliant ideas striking, I trusted to luck. I shoved my helmet on my head, threw a leg over my Rebel and patted my jacket pocket to make sure the tracker was still there. Reconsidering, I moved it from the outer pocket to an inner pocket with a zip. Not only would this keep the little tracker safe, but I could also discern any vibrations it made over those made by the Rebel.

I started the engine and began to weave through the streets of New Orleans, hoping Lady Luck would take pity on me. I really should have known better. Based on the events of the past few days, she was a bitch who had a personal vendetta against me.

Nine long hours, two greasy burgers, and one pit stop at a dodgy gas station later, I admitted defeat. I'd driven all over New Orleans proper and the surrounding area, trying to get the damn tracker to vibrate. My mind was so tired that it was hard to focus. I scoured the map in my mind, trying to guess where the relic might be hidden. When I ran out of ideas, I pulled off to the side of the road and used my phone to plot a careful track through some of the more rural areas, hoping to get a hit. Nothing. Nada. Zilch.

My Rebel rumbled dejectedly up my street. When I got off, my legs were still sending phantom vibrations up to my brain. Not in the good way either. I pulled myself up the stairs, absent-mindedly going through my security protocols and heading for the comfort of the kitchen. Where could the relic be hidden? I eyed the kettle, but wanted something harder than tea. I reached above my mugs and pulled down a bottle of tequila from the top shelf. I poured myself a shot and knocked it back. Then I made myself a cup of tea and slid into the shower while it was brewing to wash off the road grime. I went through the cleansing ritual on autopilot, my thoughts churning.

Kingsley had said that the relic was still in the New Orleans area. I'd covered a huge portion of that today on my road trip. My little Rebel had stood the test well. My ass, on the other hand was still buzzing as I plopped down on the couch with my cup of tea and laptop. I opened a browser page to a map of the city. Sipping my tea, I contemplated my next move.

I had roughly fifty hours left to find the relic and bring it to the Kingsley. I rolled the silver tracking orb in my fingers, considering my options. The problem was there was just too much land that was too far away from public access points. Private property, gated communities, business parks—hell, even things like golf courses required some sort of special access. I was confident that, despite my charming personality, I wouldn't be able to sweet talk my way into each of those properties to check them out for a missing magical artifact.

*Please, sir, take pity on a poor girl. All I want to do is take my little ball on a walk through your facility to see if it vibrates. If it does, I'll kindly remove the item of immense power that is probably worth a lot of money on the supernatural black market. Don't mind me. I'll be out of your hair in two shakes!*

Yeah, that would work about as well as a frog frying flapjacks; a whole lot of flailing about to only land face first in a frying pan.

Those gated properties were just the start of my problems. There were miles of swampland and bayou surrounding New Orleans that a road couldn't reach, even with something as durable as my Rebel. To get to those places, I would require either specialized vehicles or specialized boots. Probably both. Either way, time wasn't on my side to clear every patch of swamp in New Orleans with one tiny tracker.

I rolled the orb across my knuckles, trying to brain my way to a solution. No. Think. The word was think. Good Lord, I was tired. Maybe *thinking* hard enough would produce more results than my haphazard trek across New Orleans. Was there a way to replicate the tracker? More trackers meant more area covered in the same time. I examined the ball. The rune work on the sides of the orb looked intensely detailed. It wasn't my field of expertise, but I could imagine that carving those tiny markings into metal with such precision took a long time. I shuddered. I had once seen what happened when runes were drawn in haste. An extra swirl cost a man his leg. And that was *drawing*. Carving into metal would be infinitely harder.

If multiple trackers weren't an option, I wondered if there was a way to increase the range on this one. One hundred yards wasn't terribly far, given the area I had to cover in the time left on Kingsley's deadline. I considered taking the tracker to Mama Atli tomorrow. She might know a way of helping me increase the radius. I should also call Sloane. She'd been in New Orleans a while and might have contacts who could help. I wasn't holding my breath, though.

I stared at the screen of my laptop, zooming in and out of the map until the images blurred. I looked at the time and cursed softly under my breath. It was coming up to midnight. Two days left on my deadline. With a sigh, I decided I wasn't accomplishing anything productive by staring at my screen. I drained the cold dregs of my tea and shut down the laptop.

I poured myself into bed. Best to get some sleep while I could. I'd approach the problem fresh in the morning. Just before I drifted off, I remembered to set the alarm on my phone. Six o'clock in the morning wasn't a time of day I usually saw. However, I couldn't afford to waste time. Not with this deadline. I planned to get enough sleep to be functional. I needed to be awake bright and early, ready to go relic hunting. Lara Croft had nothing on me.

# Chapter 23

Sunlight splashing golden radiance across my bedspread woke me up. I was disoriented, clawing my way to consciousness from the comforting oblivion of sleep and the cozy cocoon I'd made of my blankets. Stretching with an audible groan, I rolled over, grabbing at my phone. I sat up straight in bed. What the hell? Ten o'clock?!? How had I slept through my alarm?

I scrubbed at my face, trying to wake myself up. I needed to be on my A-game today, so I padded to the kitchen to make myself a cup of tea strong enough to stand a spoon up in. The bottle of tequila that I had left beside the kettle tempted me. No. Better not. I needed a clear head this morning. I pushed it to the side and switched on the electric kettle.

Flicking through my messages while I waited for the water to heat, my body jerked upright. I had forgotten all about my lunch date with Magnus today. I should cancel, but I really didn't want to. Could I justify spending an hour or two on frivolous fun when I was on a tight deadline with an almost impossible location task? I typed out a message, postponing lunch plans with Magnus. My finger hovered above the 'send' key just as a message from Sloane popped up.

My best friend seemed insistent on meeting with me as soon as I read her message. She also emphasized the need to meet in person. Interesting. Whatever she needed to share must be a doozy. I shot her a quick text suggesting that we meet at Mama's in thirty minutes. Her affirmative response dinged up less than a minute later as I was adding milk to my tea.

Based on the past few days, I had a feeling that werewolves were going to be dogging my steps. I vowed to prepare better this time, which meant that I needed something functional for the day that could also hide my weapons. I settled on a cute, lightweight pullover that hung off one shoulder, showing off the strappy sports bra I wore underneath. It was baggy enough to hide my karambits in their sheaths at the small of my back. Black leggings and my trusty combat boots completed my look. On reconsideration, I tucked an extra knife in a custom sheath on one of my boots. It felt like a three-knife kind of day.

I fingered the necklace with the carved charm on it. I hadn't taken it off yet. It simultaneously felt like a tangible connection to my mother and an infuriating enigma. I ran over the letter in my mind again, wondering if I should be heeding my mom's advice and just lying low. But she'd said that she didn't know when the charm would dissipate. Also, I had to make a living somehow. I traced the carvings on the charm absently, my thoughts drifting to my dad. I wondered what he would make of me. Would he be proud of the woman I'd become?

I mentally shook myself. What he thought didn't matter. He'd abandoned us. Why should I care about what he thought? Still, I didn't take the necklace off, opting to tuck it under my shirt as I headed to the bathroom.

I threw on enough make-up to ensure I didn't look like I had just rolled out of bed five minutes ago and tossed my hair into a simple but secure updo, complete with small, sharply pointed hairpins to hold it in place. There had to be some benefits of being a girl. We had ladies' nights and extra-weapon-hiding-places going for our gender.

My bag hung on the kitchen chair, still packed with my taser from the day before. I grabbed it, flew through my security protocols, and raced down the stairs. I had just enough time to make it to Mama's. If I jogged.

The New Orleans morning embraced me. It really is a beautiful town. However, I didn't have time to appreciate my surroundings as I rushed to Mama's house. By the time I knocked on her back door, I had a faint sheen of sweat at my hairline. I tried to wipe it away without mussing my hair as Ben opened the door for me.

"Cam!" The warm greeting from the cheery necromancer made me smile despite the adrenaline coursing through my veins. "How y'all doing? C'mon in here. Mama's got the kettle on and some blueberry scones in the oven."

A smile split my face. The smell of the baking scones welcomed me into the house as warmly as Ben had. Well, nearly.

Ben led me through to the cheerful kitchen, where Mama was bustling around. The sequins sewn into her brilliant skirts caught the sunlight pouring through the windows. They sent multicolored specks of light dancing around the room whenever she moved. She looked busy, but paused so I could give her a quick hug and a kiss on the cheek.

Ben plonked a full mug of one of Mama's homemade tea blends in front of me. I took a deep breath of the ginger chai. It smelled like cozy nights and popping fires. In two shakes, Mama had steaming blueberry scones on the table and was drizzling icing over the top. I swear, that woman never met a calorie she didn't love.

Sloane's voice rang out from the back of the house. "Morning! Any-body in?"

"In the kitchen! Just follow your nose!" Ben shouted over his shoulder as he brought another pair of tea mugs to the table.

Sloane appeared at the kitchen door and sniffed appreciatively. "Are those blueberry scones? They smell amazing!" Mama smiled at the compliment as Sloane wrapped her arms around the older woman and kissed her wrinkled cheek.

Ben whisked her into a kitchen chair, muttering, "Quit all that non-sense. Mama done been hangin' those scones over my head for the last hour or so waitin' for you girls to show up. I'm so hungry I could eat the north end of a south-bound goat right about now." He turned away to grab her a mug of tea.

Sloane and I shared a smile at his familiar griping. The little lep-rechaun came over and gave me a warm hug. I wrapped my arms around her and a piece of my heart clicked in place. This place and these people felt like home.

Mama finally settled into her chair. "Well, don't stand on ceremony, girls. I know y'all are hungry. Get to it." She waved her arm at the scones, sending her bracelets tinkling. We grinned, not needing any more encouragement, and each took a scone. Ben took three.

We passed a couple of minutes catching up. Sloane's business was doing well, and she was looking to expand to include a beer garden soon. Speaking of gardens, Ben had eventually finished tending his garden out front and swore it would attract all the butterflies in New Orleans when the flowers bloomed again in the spring. Mama just smiled, content to have a kitchen full of family.

Ben tried sneaking a fourth scone while we were talking, but Mama had slapped his hand away. "Well, Mama, I have to say, if you put those scones on top of my head, my tongue would damn well beat my brains out trying to get to 'em."

Sloane leaned over and stage whispered, "Does that means he liked them?"

"Liked them?!" Ben roared. "Why girlie, are you disparaging Mama's fine baking? Did you even taste those scones? They're sent straight from Heaven, they are! And I should know!" The elderly necromancer jabbed a thumb at his chest.

Sloane held her hands up in surrender, giggling at his antics.

I couldn't help but grin myself. Even though I was twitchy to find the relic and claim the information Kingsley had promised, I enjoyed the familial banter. It was moments like this that I knew what love was. When I was surrounded by people who had adopted me as family when I had no one and nothing. They were the ones who made the sun shine a little brighter each day. I was humble and grateful to have them in my life.

Mama turned away from the silliness at the table to face me squarely. "Alright, child. Let's get down to business, shall we? I can see that you have pressing matters weighing on you." Just like that, the clouds on the horizon darkened the sunshine of the moment.

# Chapter 24

I caught all three of them up on what had happened since I'd seen them last. The run-ins with the werewolves, Meridiana, Magnus' intervention, Kingsley and his mystery relic, and my fruitless search with the magical Fae tracker. All three listened carefully, not wanting to miss an important part of the story. I finally wrapped up my tale by pulling out the silver orb and passing it around the table for inspection.

Ben took the tracker from Sloane and poked at it with one callused finger. I watched him investigate the Fae tracker as I spoke. "The way I see it is that I either need to get the tracker to lengthen its radius of detection or figure out a way to get it to the secluded areas of New Orleans."

Sloane choked on her tea. "Wait, you are telling me you need a longer ROD to get to secluded areas so that your little toy can vibrate?"

I glared at her. "Yes, Sloane, I need to expand the radius of detection to get to some difficult to reach areas. Of New Orleans."

Sloane laughed out loud, and Ben chortled along with her. Even Mama cracked a smile. I scowled at them all.

Mama held out a hand for the tracking orb, and Ben passed it over. She scrutinized it while Ben and Sloane got themselves under control. When she finally looked up, her wrinkled brow furrowed even more deeply than usual.

"Child, Fae magic isn't my forte. Looking at the runes, this is a complex and delicate spell. I'm not comfortable attempting to copy or alter it." Mama handed the orb back to me and I slipped it into my bag, making sure that the zipper was firmly closed. Sloane and Ben grimly nodded their agreement.

I tried not to let the disappointment show on my face. "I thought as much, but it was worth a try."

"Can you reach out to Kingsley and ask him for another?" Sloane interjected. "Or another hundred?"

I lifted a shoulder. "He said it was the only one."

Ben raised his hand. I had to suppress a chuckle so as not to hurt the old guy's feelings. "Yes, Ben?"

"I hate to rain on your parade, but what if this is just a pretty silver ball?" He gestured towards my bag where I'd secured the tracking orb. "Stick with me here. What if he wants you busier than a cat coverin' up crap on a marble floor?"

Mama laid a hand on Ben's arm. "To what end? What does he gain from sending Cameron all over town on a fool's errand?"

"I dunno," grumbled Ben, slouching in his chair and folding his arms. "Just tryin' to see all the angles here."

I smiled and patted his shoulder affectionately. "I appreciate that, Ben. That's why I wanted to talk to all of you. To get your thoughts and formulate a plan. But I am inclined to agree with Mama. I don't see how Kingsley sending me all over New Orleans looking for something that doesn't exist is beneficial to him. Besides, you didn't see him. He wants this relic. *Bad.*"

Ben snapped his fingers, sitting upright again. "Wait. You said that he described this crystal relic thing as a storage device, right? It stores energy. Kind of like a battery?"

I nodded, not sure at what he was trying to say.

His voice dropped. "Cameron. There are ghosts missing all over town. They can be used to power any number of spells if someone had, oh say, a magical battery to harness their energy."

A chill passed over the table.

Sloane voiced the question looming large, "Who has the relic right now?"

My voice infused extra chilling frost into an already tense room. "And what are they planning to do with it?"

The four of us stared at each other. This shit storm had just gone from bad to epically messed up.

*Damn it.*

Mama reached across the table for my hands. I extended them to her, searching for some comfort. "Cameron, you won't like what I say, but I would beg you to hear me out."

I nodded. Mama's advice was usually sound.

"Cameron," she cleared her throat, obviously uncomfortable. "You need to leave."

I raised my eyes to hers, confused. Was she kicking me out?

"You need to get out of New Orleans as soon as possible."

I recoiled at her words, jerking my hands away.

"Just for a few days," she said placatingly. "Get on your bike and go see something new. It's a big country. Drive. Explore. Come back after All Hallows' Eve has passed."

Her words shocked me. I came here looking for help, for guidance to help me find the relic. To help me uncover the truth about my past. Not to be told to run away. I glanced over at Sloane and then Ben. Both were nodding in agreement.

"Cam, it's for the best," Sloane said. "Let things calm down here. Besides, if Kingsley can find out something about your past, that means that we can too. We just have to keep trying."

Blood rushed to my face, and I struggled to keep a lid on my emotions. The throbbing of my pulse in my temples made it hard to concentrate.

Mama chimed in, "If you leave, then we can bring the relic and the disappearing ghosts to the attention of the Collective. Your standing with them is tenuous at best. It wouldn't be good for you if they found out you were involved with something this dangerous."

"I'm trying to help *fix* it," I protested, anger and frustration getting the better of me.

Ben touched my arm. "I know you are, sugar. But they won't see it that way. If the Collective gets involved, they won't care who's on what side. All they'll care about is wiping the slate clean. If nobody's messing with relics and ghosts, the Norms can't find out about anything. That keeps us all safe." His voice dropped, "They won't hesitate to kill you, and everyone involved, to keep the supernatural world a secret."

I rose from the table abruptly. "I came here for advice, for help. And you're telling me to run away? How does that help anyone? The ghosts? Me? New Orleans?"

Sloane murmured softly, trying to diffuse the tension. "It helps keep you alive, Cam. You can't fight to free the ghosts if you are one. All the money in the world won't matter if you're dead."

Her cool logic doused the flare of my anger. I took a breath, trying to see things from their point of view. They saw danger at every turn with no good way out. I got it. If the situation was reversed, I might also advise them to get out of town. But I knew, deep in my soul, that I had to do this. I was like a hooked fish, slowly being reeled in. I couldn't leave. I could dance on the line all I wanted, but I still had a hook in my mouth, and someone was pulling on that line.

I raised my eyes to them, taking in their concerned faces.

"I'm not running," I stated simply.

Mama took my statement in stride. Ben looked deflated. He'd obviously been hoping that I'd run from the danger. When I saw Sloane's face, my resolve nearly crumbled. She looked scared. This leprechaun, my best friend, the woman who supported me with unwavering devotion and had seen terrible things in her constant struggle for freedom, looked terrified.

I sat down at the table again and reached out to take Sloane's hand on one side and Ben's on the other. Mama completed our little circle. "Let's hope for the best," I said. Then, smiling grimly, I added, "But plan for the worst."

I had a feeling that the latter was what I was going to be facing soon enough.

# Chapter 25

I left Mama's bright and cozy kitchen unsettled and disturbed. The plans we had hashed out over the kitchen table were rough and sparse. We were all going to pursue our different contacts to track down information about either the ghosts or the relic. Anything we found would be texted to a group chat.

I was surprised that Mama and Ben even knew what a group chat was, but Mama had suggested it. She'd also set it up. Never underestimate your elders. They've been through more shit than you can imagine and made it out the other side to survive on liquor harsh enough to cause liver damage and complain about arthritis.

We'd also set up a fail-safe system to ping each other's locations via the GPS on our phones. Ben had suggested checking in every hour. That seemed excessive, so we agreed upon every six hours. Failure to send in an all clear would result in a check-up. Not the friendly kind with a doctor in a big red clown nose with a lollipop. More like the kind where you shot first and asked questions later.

I pulled my phone out as I walked down the street away from Mama's, glancing through my messages. I realized I hadn't ever sent that message to Magnus, but I really needed to reschedule. It wasn't fair to drag him into this mess. Especially because he was a Norm. Hopefully, he wouldn't see it as canceling so much as postponing. Just until after Halloween and this whole werewolf-ghost-relic malarkey was resolved.

Just as I was pulling up his number to text my apologies, a horn sounded behind me. I whirled. I was wound tight, tense after the dark conversation at Mama's kitchen table. A Jeep Wrangler rolled up to the curb and Magnus hopped out. After the pick-up in the Tesla earlier, I was surprised at the vehicle choice.

"Hey!" he greeted me, a warm smile flashing across his handsome features. He leaned on the open driver's door, smiling over the roof at me. "I know I'm early, but I thought I would save you the walk when I saw you. Ready for lunch? I have a table booked at Galatoire's."

My stomach rumbled, and my mouth watered. Galatoire's had a reputation for making some of the best food in New Orleans. I hadn't had much in the last twenty-four hours that could be described as nutritious. Mama's food was always delicious, but you could only go so far on pure sugar, and I wasn't sure I would classify the greasy burgers from the night before as food. Surely, I could pause for some excellent eye candy and shrimp cooked to perfection, right?

Magnus misinterpreted the distress on my face. "Oh, is the restaurant not good? I read the reviews and thought they were excellent."

I waved his concerns away. "No, they're awesome. Some of the best food in New Orleans. Something just came up and I'm distracted."

He shrugged easily. "That's okay. How about we grab a coffee or something? We could walk while you tell me about whatever is distracting you? We can always grab lunch another time." His smile was bright after being lost in my own dark thoughts.

Wow. On a shitty day like this, Magnus turned up like a freaking rainbow to brighten my mood. I took a surreptitious look around, waiting suspiciously for the other shoe to drop. When nothing happened, I nodded slowly, accepting his offer.

Magnus pulled the Jeep into an open spot on the side of the road. He beeped the lock with the fob in his hand as he jogged around the car to join me. We started walking down the street and I steered us towards the Louis Armstrong Park.

"Alright," he said. "Lay it on me. What's got you so distracted that a fabulous lunch with me couldn't tempt you?" He spread his arms wide, showing off his excellent physique.

Oh, it tempted me alright. I just wasn't about to tell *him* that.

I sketched out the important details for him. He already knew about the supernatural world and at least some of the creepy-crawlies inhabiting it. I even included the advice that Mama, Sloane, and Ben had given me to leave town for the next few days. During my narration, we walked through the iconic white arch at the front of the park. I led Magnus towards one of my favorite statue installations, a wrought iron jazz band marching along the path. We sat on the stone ledge under the upraised iron trombone, taking in the pleasant scene of children playing as I shared dark and scary matters.

He shook his head when I paused. "Respectfully, I have to disagree with your friends. I've always found that facing my problems is the best way to resolve them. It's hard to confront anything when you're running away."

I had to agree with him.

"Can I see this tracker?" Magnus held out his hand.

I considered for a moment. After what I had told him, he was still willing to try to help. He was a brave guy. Or stupid. Or both. There was definitely room for both in this equation.

I dug around and handed it to him. He turned it over in his hands, examining the runes and muttering to himself. We got a couple of odd looks from passersby, but Magnus didn't notice. He was too engrossed in examining the orb.

"This is a beautiful piece of work. You say that it'll notify you when it's roughly within a hundred yards of this mysterious relic?" Magnus asked, glancing up.

I nodded in response to his question. "Give or take. I asked Mama Atli if there was a way that she could up its detection radius somehow, but she said it was dangerous to mess with the magic."

Magnus bobbed his head, refocusing on the tracker in his hands. "I'm not surprised. I'm not great with identifying runes. Magic isn't my thing, but if it's anything like coding, you wouldn't want to mess with something this complex because you'd probably blow something up."

"Yeah, that's about what Mama thought too." I looked at him sharply, remembering he was into technology. "Is there, I don't know, some sort of computer mumbo-jumbo you could do to amp up the power on this thing?"

He slowly shook his head. "As far as I know, magic and tech don't exactly go hand in hand. Although now that you mention it, experimenting with combinations of magic and technology might be interesting. It'd have to be relic-based, though, nothing innate..."

I could almost hear the gears turning in his head. "Umm, Magnus?" I queried as the silence stretched.

His intelligent eyes snapped up to me and he shook his head. "Sorry. I got excited by the possibilities for a moment. Something to explore later. But the answer to your question is still no. I don't think I could increase the power of the tracking spell to reach a broader area."

My shoulders slumped in defeat. It looked like I was facing a long couple of days on my bike, hoping that my luck would bring me through. That was a shitty tactic, but what else did I have?

Magnus interrupted my pity party. "However, I may have a way to help broaden your search without increasing the range of the detection spell."

My eyes widened as hope surged through my chest. "How would you do that?" I blurted out in surprise.

"Have you considered drones?"

# Chapter 26

Magnus' eyes lit up in excitement as he explained his plan. I was just glad he used small words so I could follow the gist of it. I wasn't a Luddite with technology, but I wasn't anywhere near his advanced level either.

"Based on the size and weight of the tracker, I could likely attach it to one of the company drones without difficulty. Our drones are more heavy-duty, more durable than your average commercial drone. If I can get the tracker hooked up to a drone, we could fly it into some of those more restricted areas to get a look around." He was talking fast, obviously excited.

"Okay," I drew out the word, considering his idea. "But the tracker vibrates and glows when it is near the relic. If it's on a drone flying around New Orleans, how could we see it?"

"You could hook up a transmitting camera to the drone with the camera facing the tracker." He continued, almost to himself, "We would have to remain within signal range of the drone to monitor the tracker, and to change batteries when necessary. But, yes, I think it's possible." He nodded firmly.

I was getting excited by the prospect of a solid plan. "What sort of time frame are we looking at here? You said that the drone was company equipment. Is it stored close by? Would you be able to get the tracker and the camera mounted easily enough? I'm on a deadline."

He grimaced. "That's the snag. The company houses its equipment out of town. I could probably get the tech, get the drone rigged, test out the compatibility and range of the equipment, and get back here by tomorrow morning. I know that is cutting it close. Especially with a lot of territory to cover."

I took a deep breath. This was the best solution I had heard so far, but it meant cutting a short time frame even shorter. "Well, sounds like it's the best idea we've got. While you are off doing your techy thing, what should I do? Want me to come with you?"

Magnus smiled down at me. "I'm not sure a long car ride under these conditions would be an ideal second date."

My heart gave a little flutter. It had been a long time since I'd been on a date. Let alone a second one.

Magnus continued, oblivious to my tangential thoughts, "No, I think it's better that you stay in town. See if you can cover some more ground with the tracker. If you get a buzz from it, great! Call me and I'll come right back."

"Okay. And if I don't?" I asked. I was next to useless if the best I could do was driving around New Orleans hoping to get close enough to the relic to trigger the tracker.

"Work on a map," Magnus suggested. "Start by crossing out where you've already searched and come up empty. Then rate the remaining areas by ease of storage for a magical relic and likelihood it is being kept there. That should make our search more efficient when I get back with the tricked-out drone. We'll do a quick flyover of the places you mark in order and clear each one by one. If we don't find it, we move on to the next spot until we do."

"Right." I still had my concerns despite his logical-sounding plan. "That might be okay for the public spaces such as the bayou or coastline. What about private areas? The ones with the 'No Photography or Trespassing' signs or the 'Have Guns, Will Shoot' ones? To be honest, the latter is more likely down here."

His mouth twisted into a wry smile. "Most places will give you a warning if your drone goes into private airspace. Even if it flies into a private area and we get shut down, we should be able to collect it from security."

"But what if they won't give the drone back? Or they shoot it down?" I really wanted his help. His plan seemed like a decent one and it was something I couldn't manage on my own in this time frame. However, that didn't mean I wanted him to get in trouble at work for damaging company property on my behalf.

He shrugged. "It'll be easy to show them the feed from the camera to prove we weren't trying to spy or anything. Most places that are concerned about a drone flyover are trying to protect company secrets. In my experience, those types of places would prefer to use a gun for protection over anything else. Bullets are cheaper and more reliable than any non-kinetic options I am aware of. Regardless, you're right, I'd better bring a couple of back-ups along, just in case." He was nodding to himself. He looked like he was making mental notes as he talked.

"It sounds like it could work," I mused. Actually, it sounded brilliant. It impressed me that he developed the idea on the fly. "The only catch I can see is that your boss might get pissed if you wreck expensive company property. Especially if their drones are better quality than commercial ones. Drones are already pricey, aren't they?" Completely out of my price range, I was guessing, but I wasn't going to let on to that fact.

"That should be easy. Let me ask him." Magnus tipped his head up contemplatively and then looked down at me with a grin. "Boss says it's fine. In fact, he told me to make sure I leverage my help into a second date with you."

The shock at his admission clearly registered on my face. "I didn't know that you owned the company," I managed. To be fair, I didn't know much about Magnus. The more I learned about this man, the more impressed I became.

He gazed out at the children running around the park chasing a ball. He smiled faintly as their joyful giggles reached us. "My origin story isn't much to talk about. I got into computers at a young age and excelled. I moved from writing code for others to writing for myself. Eventually, I built a small security company. We create and maintain security systems for just about anyone and anything."

"Saving the world, one desktop at a time?" I quipped.

"Exactly. I'm just your average knight in shining microchips," he said. "Speaking of, this knight had better go find his loyal steed and set off to get those drones ready."

I walked him to his Jeep and waved goodbye. Part of me felt bad for using our date to commandeer him into helping me find this relic. A very small part of me. He had volunteered, after all, so not really my fault. Right? I may have been rationalizing.

I could at least take him out for dinner for all the trouble he was going through on my behalf. I'd have to think of something big to repay him if his drone idea paid off. Wicked thoughts danced through my head as I imagined all the ways to say 'thank you' to the handsome Magnus. Shaking my head to clear it, I set off to narrow down the search area.

I took Magnus' advice and pulled up a map of New Orleans on my phone. One look was enough to convince me that whilst scissors might beat paper, paper beat phones in this case. I gathered up my things and headed to the nearest shop that might stock paper maps of the region.

I finally found what I was looking for three shops later. A series of paper maps of New Orleans that zoomed into street view close enough to provide tourists with a good view of the buildings and shops in the city center. I added a ruler and a highlighter to my basket. Grabbing my purchases, I headed back to my apartment to start plotting my next move.

# Chapter 27

Close to an hour and two highlighters later, I groaned, looking at the sheer amount of space I had still to search for this damned relic. Sure, I'd narrowed it down considerably on my nine-hour trek of a bike ride through town and the surrounding areas. I'd even tried to measure the distances carefully to make sure I was presenting Magnus with as much information as possible when he returned with the drones.

With a sigh, I pushed myself back from the table. I needed a quick break before trying to rank the possible hiding spots for Magnus. I poured myself a shot of tequila and knocked it back. Why live in New Orleans if you can't enjoy the Bukowski drinking lifestyle? All day, all night, baby.

I let my head fall back, muttering to myself, "I would love some damned help on this damned relic hunt."

"Someone ask for some damned help?" a cheery voice piped up from behind me. "That's my specialty."

I spun around, grabbing for a kitchen knife. I quickly took the two steps needed to close the distance to the kitchen table before I recognized who was sitting there.

Meridiana. Red-haired, sexy as hell, and sitting in my apartment like she owned the place. She watched me carefully with her deep, rich chocolate eyes. She kept her hands in the open and didn't make any sudden movements as she waited calmly for me to regain my composure.

"What the *hell?*" I shouted, throwing the knife back to the kitchen counter behind me with a clatter. My chest was heaving, and adrenaline was pumping through my veins at the shock of finding her sitting at my kitchen table. Despite my security precautions. Damn it! That shouldn't have been possible!

"How'd you get in here? You scared the ever-loving life out of me!" I had to work to keep from shouting at her again.

Meridiana winked at me. "Oh, I very much doubt that. *That* would require a fair bit more than a mere scare if I don't miss my guess. I'm here because you invited me, my dear. Admittedly, it is a loose interpretation of an invitation, but nonetheless, I come when I'm called." She winked at me again, lasciviously licking her lips. "Sometimes twice."

I took a deep breath, trying to calm my racing heart. "I'm going to have to choose my words more carefully in the future."

Meridiana pointed a scarlet-tipped finger at me. "Now, that is the most sensible thing I've heard you say. Words have power. Especially your words."

I plopped into the chair across from her. "Right, I'll make you a deal..."

She hissed at me. Literally hissed. Like an angry cat. "No! No deals!" Her hand sliced through the air in front of her.

"Okay." I raised my hands in a placating gesture. "No deals. How about you tell me how you got in here? I'll get you a drink, regardless. No obligations, no deals."

Meridiana relaxed, regaining her composure. "A drink would be nice. Some of that swill you call tequila." She eyed the bottle on the counter dubiously. "I don't suppose you have anything a little more top shelf, do you?" she asked hopefully.

I shook my head, but retrieved an adequate, mid-range bottle from the cupboard where I had been stashing it for a rainy day. I poured two generous glasses and slid one over to her. We raised our glasses to each other. I sipped my drink. She pounded hers.

"Want to tell me what's going on?" I asked, trying to stay calm.

Meridiana raised a slim shoulder in an elegant little shrug. "You called; I came. I thought you might encounter some, shall we say, new experiences since we last met. So, I kept an ear out, so to speak, in case you got in over your head and needed help. Or a distraction." She waggled her eyebrows suggestively and winked.

"Look, as much as I like the people who come to New Orleans and I'm usually in for the all-day-all-night parties, I don't have time right now. I'm on a job. Perhaps you could come back in, say, a couple days? My schedule is wide open then. Happy to have vague conversations, a girls' night out, whatever you want. Then. For now, get the hell out." I gestured to the door that she obviously hadn't used to enter my apartment.

Meridiana clapped her hands in excitement, doing a little sexy bounce in her seat. "I'd *love* a girls' night out!"

"Great. In two days. Get. Out."

Instead of leaving, she took in the markings on the maps strewn across the kitchen table. "You're looking for something?" she asked.

"Bingo," I said, pointing my index finger at her then flicked it to the door. "Out."

She ignored the command. "Tell me." Her voice raised ever so slightly at the end, almost making it a question.

I considered. Kingsley hadn't sworn me to secrecy, and I had already discussed finding the relic with my closest confidants. And Magnus. Why not add the disappearing lady to the mix?

Never one to miss an opportunity, I said, "First, how'd you get into my apartment?"

"Magic," she said, wiggling her fingers in my direction with a small smirk.

That told me a big fat nothing. Not in the supernatural community, at least. I tried again. "Tell me what you are."

She tapped her fingers on the tabletop in an agitated rhythm. "I can't."

"Why not?"

"I can't say," she said, frustration simmering in her voice, her posture tense and erect.

Interesting. Something was preventing her from sharing the information with me. Some sort of binding promise? An oath or geas, perhaps?

"Okay, can you signal me instead of answering? Nods and shakes work fine for me." I was happy to play a little twenty questions if it got me some answers.

She rolled her eyes in exasperation. "It wouldn't be much of an agreement if it was that easily circumvented."

I shrugged. "I'm willing to waste a little time if you are." Could I wrangle this to my advantage somehow?

She inhaled deeply and let out a resigned sigh. "Do your best," she said, waving a hand.

"Do you know who my father is?" I was going for broke. Might as well start big.

"Yes," she said, staring significantly into my eyes, like she was attempting telepathic communication.

You could have hit me with a pillow and knocked me clean into next week, I was so surprised. I hadn't expected the direct response.

"Who is he?" I followed up quickly.

Nothing.

"Do you know what kind of Supe he was? What kind I am?" I pressed.

She narrowed her eyes and did a little lateral wiggle in her chair that I took for a 'yes and no' answer.

"Okay, so partially? Or at least, you have a theory?" I said, testing her reaction. Her eyes resumed their normal appearance. I guessed that meant yes.

"Why are you here?" I asked.

Meridiana let out a relieved sigh. I must have hit on a question she wanted me to ask. "I'm here to help you. Much like I did in the bar. However, I can only guide you. You must uncover certain truths in your own time. To do otherwise would be...detrimental. To both of us."

I narrowed my own eyes, considering. "Let's try out this scenario. Hypothetically, of course. Let's say that you want to help me. Someone doesn't want you going all gung-ho and swears you to secrecy."

Meridiana nodded encouragingly and then flicked her eyes around the room. Strange. She looked on edge, like someone was watching. I tried to navigate my way through this seemingly dangerous discussion while walking a conversational tightrope. With my hands tied behind my back. In the dark. And there was a bomb on a pressure plate somewhere underneath me.

I continued hesitantly, "But, whoever this is, they don't want you spelling things out for me, so they're watching you. Closely."

She nodded again, gesturing with one hand for me to continue.

"If you go against this mystery person-slash-being-slash-thing's wishes, you or I, or both of us, will end up hurt or dead." I tried out the theory. Yeah, that felt right.

I tried to simplify the situation in my head. "So, someone has sent you in here with a proverbial suicide vest and a transmitting earpiece. You can help me but are being monitored while you do it. One wrong word and boom!" I made an explosion gesture with both hands.

Meridiana allowed a small smile to curve her lips. "A crude analogy, but apt. Hypothetically."

# Chapter 28

My mind was reeling. This was the closest I'd gotten to answers about my past in years. The answers were right there, sitting across the table from me. Locked inside that sexy little redhead's, well, head. And I couldn't get them out. Yet. I was a stubborn asshole, though. I wouldn't let a little thing like mutually assured destruction get in my way.

"So, what *can* you tell me? Without, you know..." I made the explosion gesture again and accompanied it with sound effects this time.

Meridiana leaned forward intently. "You should take careful note of anything abnormal occurring in your life right now. Now that the charm warding your powers is unraveling, you may be able to access more of your magic soon." Her eyes sparkled with intensity. "Have you experienced anything like that?"

"Maybe?" My thoughts flashed back over the past few days, trying to remember if my magic had felt any different. Nothing sprang to mind, but I also hadn't been actively monitoring my powers either.

She nodded in satisfaction, leaning back. "As your magic trickles back to you, I suggest you note anything that seems strange, extraordinary, or bizarre. Perhaps you can put the puzzle together as you gather more of the pieces."

I snorted, "Lady, my whole life is strange. Especially now. Werewolves are chasing me, I'm working for the High Fae, trying to find an impossible to find..."

Meridiana cut me off. "*What?* Why on Earth would you work for those," her cute little nose wrinkled in disgust, "*things?*"

"The High Fae? My client promised me a buttload of money for helping him find something." I waved a hand at my cramped apartment. "I'm not exactly swimming in cash. Unless you want throw a little green my way, this girl's gotta work," I said. Her eyes narrowed. What was her deal? Had a High Fae stood her up for a date sometime or something?

"Tell me everything. Be specific. Words matter," she reminded me, urgency lacing her voice.

I wracked my brain for as many details as I could remember from my encounter with Ambassador Kingsley. I felt no compulsion to obfuscate as I tried to remember the precise language of the agreement I reached with Kingsley. He'd told me that speed trumped secrecy after all, and perhaps Meridiana could give me a clue that would help find this relic.

"Aldrich Kingsley, the Ambassador from Fae, wants me to locate a lost relic and bring it to him before midnight on Halloween. In return, he promised me enough money to make working for a member of the Collective well worth the risk. Besides, it's not like I'm getting any help on untangling my mysterious past other than a cryptic note from my mom."

I left off what I really wanted to say. *Things you know and could tell me.*

Meridiana was clever. She read between the unsaid and shot me an apologetic look.

Shrugging, I checked my phone. "Which means I have just about two days to find this thing."

Meridiana leaned back, looking relieved. "As far as deals go, that could have been much, *much* worse for you. At least there's some wiggle room there."

I raised an eyebrow.

She continued, "I would suggest that you be very careful in making any sort of deals in the future. Until you establish a firmer grasp on your powers and the inherent benefits and limitations of your unique gifts."

"For all of those reasons that you know, but *cannot* say?" I couldn't quite keep the bitterness out of my voice.

"Precisely." At least she looked as infuriated as I felt. That assuaged my ego. Slightly.

"Is there anything that you *can* tell me?" I asked, gritting my teeth to keep from growling at her.

She cocked her head to the side, appearing to consider what she could safely say. "It sounds like this Kingsley person is looking for a Shadow Shard."

At my questioning look, she elaborated. "Shadow Shards are rare, but not one-of-a-kind magical artifacts. They harness energy, usually collected over time. Sometimes from multiple people, sometimes from one person."

My confusion must have been evident because she rolled her eyes up towards the ceiling, searching for an apt comparison. "Think of a Shadow Shard like a blood bank. People donate blood to be stored and used at a later point in time. Sometimes, multiple people donate to the same blood bank. However, a person can also save his or her own blood for emergency purposes."

"So, Kingsley is blood-doping? I mean, magic-doping?" I interjected, "Saving up his own magic over time to increase his power for a future spell?"

Meridiana waggled a flat hand back and forth. "Perhaps. There are other ways to harvest power for a Shard. None of them are pleasant. Most are deadly. All of them require a great deal of power. How much power does this Fae have?" She cocked her head to the side inquisitively.

I shrugged, "I'm not sure. I don't have a way to gauge his power."

"Shame." Meridiana murmured, rubbing her forehead with one perfectly manicured hand.

I tested out a theory. "Wait. Is there a way that ghosts could power the Shard? There are rumors that some have gone missing in the area."

Meridiana clapped her hands, a glow of respect lighting her eyes. "Actually, that would be an ingenious way to power a Shard. Few people would notice missing ghosts, whereas a missing Supe or Norm would raise an almost immediate search party."

"Okay, let's assume, hypothetically, that Kingsley is the local ghost-napper intent on using the Shard to power some dark ritual. My necromancer friend says that a ritual like that could have catastrophic consequences for the entirety of New Orleans. Unleashing monsters or something equally dire."

Meridiana nodded solemnly. "It would be prudent to stop such a hypothetical occurrence as quickly as possible."

"And how would you advise me to go about doing that?" I asked.

"This could've been so much easier if you'd just waited a few days. You would've had more knowledge, more access to your powers. I might have even been able to share more openly instead of this ridiculous cloak and dagger dance." She almost shouted the last part, directing her venom out my living room window. I wondered who our mysterious eavesdropper was.

I rolled my eyes. Loudly. "Look, not that this hasn't been vague, tantalizing, frustrating and all, but I have shit to do and a deadline to meet. Is there any, I don't know, *helpful* advice you can offer before I leave?"

Meridiana leaned forward. Her body language emphasized the importance of her next words. "Pay attention to everything, *anything*, that might be your magic coming back in full. And for all that's unholy, don't go making any more deals."

I formed both my hands into finger guns and pointed them at her, "Dea..." I started, with a smug smirk.

She disappeared. Literally vanished before my eyes. One blink, there. Next blink, gone.

"Well, that's one overly dramatic way to make an exit," I muttered, leaning back and finally downing my glass of tequila.

With nothing better to do, I returned to work on the map. I finished marking it up for Magnus as I replayed my confusing conversation with Meridiana in my mind. Unfortunately, I didn't shake loose any new information upon review, so I focused on the map, contemplating options. I had a good ten hours to narrow down the search zone. There was always the possibility that I got lucky and found the damn relic before Magnus ever got back. I wasn't holding my breath on that one though.

With nothing much better to do, I packed a bag and sent a text to the group chat to let the team know what I was doing. I was halfway out the door when a thought struck me. I rushed back to my computer and pulled up a search engine. A few minutes later, I was grinning broadly. I had found a map of the no-fly zones for drones in New Orleans. I took a quick photo of the map on the screen for reference, set my security, and left to try my luck at relic hunting.

Six hours later, I had nothing but road-grime and a sore ass to show for my labors. I'd cleared most of the no-fly zones for drones, though. The ones near the airport were easy. Mostly shipping warehouses with easy road access. The area near the naval air station was harder to clear. I got as close as I could, but eventually had to settle for the fact that if someone was hiding a supernatural, super-charged relic on or near a US naval station, they were either brilliant or suicidal. Possibly both.

I parked up at the Forge. Sloane met me in the small lot behind the bar, her blue eyes taking in my dirty, tired visage in a single, concerned glance.

"How'd things go?" Sloane asked, offering her hand. I smiled despite my fatigue and gripped her hand, fingers flying through the familiar motions of our secret handshake. The mundane action wove its own kind of magic around my heart, buoying me despite the frustration of not finding the relic.

I shook my head. "No luck, unfortunately. This seems like a needle in a haystack situation. And I don't know what to do. There is just too much area to cover."

"Let me help," Sloane said, holding out her hand for my keys.

My eyes widened. "You hate driving the Rebel."

"I know, but it's more practical than driving the car I don't own for this type of thing. And you need the help."

"Don't you have a business to run?" I asked.

Sloane waved her outstretched hand back at the Forge. "I trust Rudolph. He'll be fine. Besides, you need me. I'd drop anything, anytime, when you need me."

A warm feeling swelled up inside me and it was hard to speak past the lump forming in my throat. "Thanks, Sloane."

"C'mon, you're my girl. Stop trying to do everything on your own." Sloane closed the distance between us and wrapped her arms around me. I hugged her back, leaning my cheek against her silky dark hair and drawing strength from her.

I handed over the keys to my bike, the newly annotated map, and the tracker, explaining how everything worked. Sloane reacquainted herself with the Rebel. When I was confident she wouldn't crash, I threw a leg over the bike behind her. We cruised through the streets slowly, giving Sloane a chance to regain her confidence on the motorcycle as she drove me home.

I waved as she roared away from my apartment before dragging myself upstairs. My everything was exhausted. I carefully went through my security procedures. I didn't have the energy for any more surprises this evening. After a quick shower, I shot a text to the group, checking in before I hit the sack. Then I closed my eyes, waiting for sleep to drag me under. It didn't take long.

# Chapter 29

An incessant buzzing invaded my dream, waking me. My phone was dancing right off my nightstand. I grabbed at it before it could fall, flicking the 'accept' icon to answer Sloane's call.

"I've been knocking for ages," she complained. "Come grab your stuff."

I rolled out of bed with a groan and pulled a pair of shorts on under my sleeping tee. Mostly presentable and somewhat functional, I unlocked my door.

Sloane tossed the tracker my way as she slouched into the apartment. I relocked the door behind her as she set my helmet and keys on the coffee table. Sloane didn't comment when she heard the locks click over and over. She was familiar with my habits.

"Any luck?" I asked, already knowing the answer. If she had found it, she would have told me straight away. Call me a masochist, but I had to confirm the bad news.

"No, sorry. But I've narrowed the search area at least."

Sloane pulled the map out of her bag and handed it to me before she plodded towards my tiny kitchen, heading straight for my kettle and the tea stash. I opened the map. It was starting to look like a toddler had stolen it, found some markers, and went to town. At least the colored sections were growing. That meant we were making progress, even if it was slow.

Sloane spoke over the noise of rummaging for mugs. "Whoever hid this thing did a good job. Needle in a haystack doesn't even begin to describe it. At least a haystack is contained in one place. The bayou, on the other hand..." She left the sentence hanging, but I felt the futility of the situation all too well.

"I know, I know," I muttered.

Her nose wrinkled as she sniffed the air. "What's that smell?"

"What smell?" I asked distractedly. I was still poring over the map she had given me. She had covered a lot of territory last night. I was impressed.

"I don't know. It smells like burned paper or something. Have you been lighting candles?" Sloane brought two mugs of tea over to the table. Black and strong for me. A sleepy-time tea for her.

"Not lately." I shrugged, still focused on the map in front of me. "This is great work, Sloane! you really narrowed down the search area."

She shrugged with a smirk. "I do what I do."

We spent the next few minutes discussing the likelihood of various locations. Sloane agreed with me that the relic was unlikely to be hidden near the US naval base. There were too many people who were well trained and on high alert. If a Supe wanted to hide something, maintain anonymity, and have easy access to it when needed, we agreed they would choose a more secluded location, so we focused on the wilder areas surrounding New Orleans.

There were a few wildlife parks and refuges in the area. We debated the pros and cons of hiding the relic in one of the parks, but ultimately agreed that the chance of accidental discovery was high. An area of open, unprotected marshy bayou was a more logical hiding place. The slow-moving water would act as a natural barrier to drunken tourists. The bugs and gators would keep most of the locals away as well.

"Seems like we've got a plan," I said, rubbing my hands together.

Sloane drained the rest of her tea. "Yeah, except there are literally hundreds of miles of bayou. And you have one tracker."

"Killjoy."

"Realist," she returned. She let out a yawn that cracked her jaw as she stretched her arms over her head. "I'm beat. Can I crash here?"

"Sure."

Sloane stayed over often enough that I kept a toothbrush and a set of clothes for her. She headed for my bedroom as my phone buzzed. I glanced at the text. Magnus. He was back and wanted to know where to meet.

"Looks like my tech support is back," I said towards her departing back as I sent Magnus my address. "I'll go see what we can uncover while you catch a nap. Don't forget to message Mama and Ben."

Sloane raised an arm in acknowledgment and disappeared into the dark recesses of the bedroom.

"Don't forget to lock up when you leave!" I shouted after her. I think I heard a grunt of agreement and then the water in my shower switched on.

I decided that today was a good day to get my full kit out and hurried into my bedroom to get dressed before Sloane crashed. I pulled out my specially designed leather pants and tugged them on. Although I wasn't a fan of the way the leather stuck to me in the Louisiana heat, the leather provided protection that jeans couldn't match. These pants had extra armored panels, enchanted by a war mage for strength and durability, over the major arteries in my legs. I debated the benefits of my lightweight flak jacket, but decided wearing it all day in a car wouldn't be comfortable. Opting for my favorite on-the-job aesthetic, I pulled on a black tank, my leather jacket, and combat boots. That should be good enough protection for driving around with a drone all day, even if things went sideways. Paranoia, my old friend, convinced me to throw the body armor into a bag for the day. Just in case.

With defense taken care of, it was time to outfit myself for offense. I drew the curtains before flinging open my closet doors. My weapons stash glinted at me in the dim light from the bedside lamp. I weighed my options and settled on throwing knives. Easy to conceal, easy to carry, easy to replace. I concealed as many knives as I thought prudent on my body, including my karambits at the small of my back. Deciding that there was no such thing as too much when it came to safety procedures, I tucked a couple of small throwing knives into their hidden sheaths in the top of my boots. Upon further consideration, I slid a couple of handguns and extra ammo into the bag to keep my body armor company. No sense in scaring the tourists by carrying openly. Or Magnus.

I took careful stock of my weapons and decided I was as prepared as possible for the day. Just as I was finishing up, my phone buzzed again. I glanced at it. Magnus was here and waiting.

"Bye, Sloane!" I called.

"Be careful out there!" she shouted from the shower.

I smiled, grabbed my bag, and headed out the door. I relocked the doors seven times so that Sloane could sleep in peace. As tired as she looked, I doubted anything short of a jazz band in the kitchen would wake her. I clattered downstairs, armed to the teeth and ready to find this relic.

# Chapter 30

By the time I reached the front door of the building, Magnus had opened the passenger door on the Jeep. He was holding a to-go cup that he extended to me with a flourish, like it was a bouquet of flowers. I took it with a grateful smile and slid into the Wrangler. He closed the door behind me and jogged around to his side of the car.

I pulled the map and the tracker out of my bag as he slid behind the wheel. Handing them over, I said, "You are the boss today. I am out of my depth with this level of technology."

He grinned. Damn, he had a nice smile. Paired with the rugged stubble darkening his cheeks and his gray eyes twinkling at me, well, let's just say the heat I was feeling was not just from the morning sun. Nor was it located solely on my head and shoulders.

"No worries. Do you have an idea of where we should look first?" He turned the engine over as he spoke. He sniffed deeply. "Do you smell something burning?"

"No," I said, a little too quickly.

"Hmm. Well, as long as it's not the engine," Magnus replied, sniffing audibly again before cracking a window.

I took a surreptitious whiff of my shirt as I leaned over to point at the map and caught a hint of charred wood with underlying tones of sour eggs. Eww. Had I forgotten to wash my gear from my last job? Well, there wasn't much I could do about it now.

I pointed out all the annotations to the map Sloane and I had made. "Well, I know where *not* to look."

Magnus let out a low, appreciative whistle as he examined it. "You've been busy," he commented.

"To give credit where it's due, Sloane picked up where I left off last night. I think we've cleared most of the populated areas. I hope you brought some bug spray today because we're heading in towards the bayou. And that means bugs. Lots of bugs." I grimaced. I liked New Orleans, but I could do without the insects.

Magnus grinned and reached into the back of the Jeep, pulling out a bag. Inside was everything a girl could want on a trek through the swampland of Louisiana: Flashlights, sunscreen, bug-spray, snacks, and more.

Magnus jerked a thumb towards the back. "I grabbed you some galoshes as well. I didn't know your size, so I had to guess. Hope they fit."

"I'm sure they will be fine," I murmured, touched that he was so well prepared. Most girls would love a guy to show up on their doorstep with flowers. Give me a guy who brings drones and galoshes any day.

Magnus flicked on his turn signal and pulled out into the slow morning traffic. "Right, where are we heading?" he asked briskly.

I glanced back at the map. "I thought we'd start with the closest locations and work our way out from there in one direction. Hopefully, we get lucky. If not, we come back to center and start again."

"Sounds like a plan. Which direction first?" Magnus asked as he turned towards the highway.

"Let's go southwest towards the national parks around Lake Salvador. I hope that whoever had hidden this made it at least somewhat accessible. If not, we are looking at a lot of browsing through the bayou, I'm afraid," I said.

Magnus nodded and programmed our course into the GPS on the dash. I inhaled deeply from the cup in my hands. Hot Earl Grey tea, which meant tons of caffeine. Perfect.

We passed the time on the drive on getting-to-know-you small talk. He kept me laughing at the pranks he and his siblings pulled on each other in their small town in the middle of Ohio. Things involving cows, dogshit, random wildlife left in secret places in their family home. You get the idea.

A pang of loneliness stabbed through my heart at his stories, but I did my best to hide it from Magnus. Before my mom had died, it had been just the two of us against the world. When she had passed, a gaping hole had been torn in my heart. It had never really healed. I just got better at masking the pain.

I kept those thoughts locked inside, choosing to share the mundane things about my life instead. Girls' nights with Sloane. Devouring Mama's baking. Laughing at Ben's endearing colloquialisms, of which I usually only understood about half.

Magnus chuckled. "It sounds like you have a pretty amazing family as well."

"I really do," I said, choosing to focus on my New Orleans family. The gentle, persistent mourning of my mother's death would never fully vanish and recent events had just stirred up painful memories. I carefully closed the lid on my grief, tucking it away in a corner of my mind for a later time.

I'm not going to lie, other than the conversation with Magnus, the first few hours of searching were boring as hell. Sure, I learned a lot about drones. I even tried flying it once or twice. However, when I saw how much faster Magnus was at manipulating the controls and keeping the drone on a level trajectory, I happily let him be in charge. Which means I had a lot of time to sit. At least Magnus was pretty to look at. I mean, the bayou. The *bayou* was pretty. But I wasn't the least bit upset when Magnus suggested stopping for lunch.

We agreed burgers would be a good idea and stopped at the first diner we saw. Magnus locked the Jeep, but I grabbed the tracker from its harness on the drone and the map so that we could game plan over lunch.

We placed our orders of burgers, fries, and milkshakes with the waitress as soon as we hit the vinyl upholstery of the booth. Magnus stretched his arms, working the kinks out of his back from the drive.

"It's nice to be with someone who doesn't just eat rabbit food," he said as the waitress departed.

"You don't make friends with salad," I sang at him, quoting a line from one of my favorite shows.

He grinned back at me, "Burgers for the win!"

Our food arrived quickly, for which we were both thankful. After devouring the massive burger and slurping down the milkshake, I pulled out the map again and groaned. Even with all the territory we had examined this morning, there was a lot of space left to cover. Part of me began to give in to the gnawing doubts that had made base camp in my amygdala and were starting what looked to be a successful campaign throughout my cerebral cortex and beyond.

Magnus must have been experiencing similar doubts because he muttered, "That's a lot of ground."

I groaned again and dropped my head into my hands. "I don't think this is going to work. Unless we get lucky, and the dumb schmuck buried the relic one hundred and one yards outside of this diner or something."

Magnus slurped up the last of his milkshake thoughtfully. "I've got an idea, but I'm not sure you'll like it," he said.

"Try me," I said, not raising my head from my hands.

He sounded like he was talking through a problem and getting more excited as he worked out the kinks. "Well, it's kind of frowned upon, but I could operate the drone from the Jeep while you drove. We'd go down one side of the highway here." His finger traced the LA-1 down to Grand Isle, jutting out into the Gulf of Mexico. "When we get to the, what is that at the end? The Grand Isle National Park? Then we'd turn around, and I'd run the drone along the other side of the highway."

I raised my head, peering at him through my fingers. "Will that work?"

He waggled a hand back and forth. "I've seen it done, but never tried it myself. It should be okay if the Jeep doesn't go much faster than the drone. If you stay about forty miles per hour, we should be just fine."

I tried to ignore the spark of hope that leapt to life inside me. This was a long shot, but at least it would speed up our search of the area. "Okay," I said, shaking my head. "I'm game if you are. Let's go."

# Chapter 31

Magnus' idea of flying the drone a hundred yards off the highway over the bayou from a moving Jeep worked surprisingly well. I drove the Jeep while he manned the drone. I'll admit, his skills impressed me. He controlled the drone and kept half an eye on the camera feed transmitting to the laptop in his lap as we cruised along.

"Anything yet?" I asked for about the fifteenth time.

"Not yet," he said, unperturbed by the repetitive nature of our conversation over the last thirty minutes. "How about on your end?"

"Nope," I said dejectedly, glancing in the rearview mirror. Cars had been passing us regularly. I liked to give them as much room as I could by squeezing the Jeep onto the narrow shoulder of the two-lane road.

"Wait!" Something drew my attention behind us. "There's an SUV back there. It's just hanging out behind us. Most cars have passed us in short order. This guy? Just moseying along."

"Could he just be enjoying the scenery? A family out for an afternoon pleasure cruise?" Magnus asked, not looking up from the laptop.

My eyes flicked back to the rearview mirror, checking out the dark SUV behind us. "Maybe? I don't know. I don't like it."

"Well, keep an eye out and let me know if anything changes. We can deal with a look-y-loo if need be." Magnus kept his attention on the monitor in front of him, searching for any hint of vibrations from the little tracker. Nothing.

My nerves continued to ratchet up with every mile. The SUV was still behind us. I was already making plans to pull off and stage an ambush when the SUV following us turned off at the Grand Isle Beach. I sighed in relief, releasing some tension from my shoulders. It must have just been a family out on a day trip.

Magnus glanced up at me. "We only have about five more miles until we run out of road," he said, waving the map.

I cracked my neck, keeping my focus on the road. "Well, let's drive until we get to the end. Then we can take a quick stretch before starting back."

Magnus murmured his agreement, returning his attention to the camera feed on the laptop.

It turned out that the end of the road was in the middle of the Grand Isle National Park. We followed the ever-narrowing pavement until the road spit us out into an empty parking lot surrounded by sand dunes covered in long grass, blowing in the sea breeze. I could taste the salt on the air and saw a smudge of water peeking out above the green of the beach grass. Two buildings framed the entrance to a weathered boardwalk that stretched towards the Gulf, ensuring any visitors didn't trample the delicate flora on their way to the beach.

Magnus jumped out of the car and neatly landed the drone on the pavement as I pulled to a stop.

"Might as well use the stop to change out the batteries so we can make a longer return trip without interruptions," Magnus said, already pulling equipment from the back of the Jeep.

"Sure. Need a hand?" I offered.

He snorted. "No offense, Cam, but your 'help' would probably put us further behind schedule and cost me valuable hardware."

He was right. I was happy enough to leave the tech to the master. "I'll have a quick walk and stretch my legs while you get things sorted," I said, strolling towards the dunes rolling into the Gulf of Mexico.

Magnus waved at me distractedly, already engrossed in checking the drone for any damage and getting it ready for its return flight.

I tucked the keys of the Jeep into a pocket and slung my bag across my body. A sign told me that there was a fishing pier ahead. It also warned me to keep to the boardwalk to avoid disturbing the plants and animals of the dunes that surrounded the walkway. I strolled along the boardwalk, enjoying the salty sea scent on the back of my tongue as the wind washed in from the Gulf, tangling my long hair behind me.

Magnus called out to me as he jogged up, drone in hand. "I've got everything set. Ready for the drive back?"

I waved at him as he came up. "Yeah, just give me a minute or two more. I've never been one for sitting for long periods of time. If I enjoyed that, I would've taken a desk job with a regular paycheck rather than doing what I do."

Magus set the drone on the boardwalk carefully. He leaned his forearms on the railing, which emphasized his sexy ass and well-muscled legs. I mirrored his posture so as not to be caught staring. Together, we looked out at the beach dunes covered in vibrant vegetation as waves crashed in the distance. It was peaceful and quiet, leaving me alone with my thoughts. Which drifted towards the handsome man next to me. Magnus was incredibly helpful, but also damned distracting.

He broke the silence. "You hear all sorts of crazy things about New Orleans. Mardi Gras. Insane all-day-and-all-night parties. Voodoo. Ghosts. Alligators." He snuck a glance at me. "Gorgeous women."

I let a smile flicker over my lips as the only response to his words. Good to know I wasn't the only one who was distracted.

"But they never tell you about this side of New Orleans," he continued.

"The sand?" I quipped.

"The natural beauty," he responded seriously. He pushed himself upright from his sexy lean and gestured towards the wide expanse of dunes, rolling gently down to the waves lapping up from the Gulf.

I followed the trajectory of his gesture, taking in the vista. "Definitely different from Bourbon Street on a Friday night," I murmured.

Magnus gently brushed against my shoulders as he placed his arms on either side of me. Although he didn't lean against me, I could sense the heat radiating off him. I turned to look at him. His mouth was mere inches from mine. I licked my lips reflexively, wondering what he tasted like. I had felt the hard planes of his body the night we met, but now I wanted to run my hands over them. With intention. Taking my time. His eyes dilated as he looked down at me.

His voice was raspy when he spoke. "Like I said; natural beauty."

He lowered his head an inch or two. And stopped. He was letting me make the ultimate move. If I wanted to. It had been a long time since I had allowed a man this close to me without landing at least one punch. I took a shaky breath, enjoying the spicy scent of him as the salty sea wind swirled around me. I raised up on my tiptoes to close the scant distance between us, my hand drifting to tangle in the short hair at the back of his neck. Which is when the tracker started buzzing like a kicked hornets' nest.

# Chapter 32

I jumped in surprise, looking around wildly until I found the source of the noise.

Magnus sighed and rolled his shoulders, muttering something that sounded suspiciously like, "Of all the times..."

I agreed, silently screaming at the interruption. The tingles of our almost-kiss were blowing away in the salty ocean air as my eyes locked on the tracker.

"This is it!" I cried. "The relic must be somewhere close!"

The radius Kingsley had estimated was still a lot of distance to cover, but hope flared to life in my gut, nonetheless. There was still plenty of time to find the relic and make the exchange with Kingsley. I'd have to buy dinner for Magnus in thanks for his help. And who knew? Maybe dinner would lead to...

No. Focus. Find the relic first. The dinner. And afterwards...

Magnus had already moved over to the drone and was releasing the tracker from its nest of wires and gizmos. He held it up triumphantly, the silver orb catching the afternoon sunshine with a sparkle.

"Let's go find some treasure!" he crowed. He leapt over the railing, soft sand cushioning his landing. He turned to reach up towards me. I passed him the drone and jumped down myself.

"I sure hope this thing lights up or something when we get close," I said. "It's an enormous sandbox to sift through if it doesn't."

He passed the tracker over to me. "Well, only one way to find out." We shared a grin and struck off on our treasure hunt.

Luckily, Kingsley had been correct in his description of the tracker's signals. About ten yards into walking through the sand and trying not to trample too much of the delicate flora, the tracker stopped its buzzing altogether.

I shook it, just to be sure. "Looks like we are playing a game of hot-and-cold until we find this thing," I said to Magnus as I showed him the tracker lying still and silent in my hand.

"At least we've got that," Magnus said as we reversed our direction, angling to the side to explore a different area of the grass-covered dunes.

Soft sand covered in salt-encrusted grass does not make for graceful walking, but we slogged through it while keeping a careful eye on the tracker. It started off by vibrating so softly that I wouldn't have noticed it if I didn't have it clasped tightly in my fist. The vibrating grew more intense as we fought our way further along the shrub-covered dunes. I was glad that the parking lot had been empty. There were no rangers to tell us to get back on the path or families to shoot disapproving looks our way.

As the vibrations seemed to shift in intensity, I adjusted our course. After about ten minutes of fighting our way through the sand and the prickly, knee-high grasses, the runes on the side of the ball glowed. We struggled on for another two or three minutes, watching the runes grow brighter. When they dimmed again ever so slightly, Magnus and I turned to each other. We had found it. It had to be here.

Except there was nothing. No crystals, boxes, or bags. Not even something that could have passed for one of those fake rocks where people hide house keys. I swiped the brush aside, looking for anything hidden under the prickly branches or hugging the sandy ground. Nothing.

I looked up at Magnus. "Looks like we are digging," I said with a small shrug.

"I've got some shovels in the Jeep. I'll go grab them and dump this thing," he said, raising the drone. "Be back in a sec!" He set off towards the car as quickly as the sand would allow.

I looked around. As beautiful as this scenery was, there was no sense in waiting for him to return with shovels. If the relic was in a shallow grave, I could likely have it out before he returned. I shrugged and hit my knees, pushing sand out of the way with my hands.

Luckily, it didn't take long to uncover the edge of a dark wooden box. I pawed furiously at the sand. My fingers found the edges of the box and burrowed down alongside, releasing it from its sandy hiding place. It was about the length of my forearm. I traced the intricate carvings on the top that were embedded with sand. They were similar to those on the tracker. Fae design. This had to be it. With the carved oblong box sitting in my lap, I took a quick look around. I couldn't see Magnus yet, so I decided to peek inside.

The box, although intricately carved, had no lock or hinges. The person who had hidden it must have trusted to the remote location to protect the relic. With no metal on the box, it would've been very difficult to find without the tracker. The wood was warped, showing water damage from being exposed to the elements—unsurprising given its hiding place. The lid stuck fast. I reached behind my back and pulled a karambit out of its sheath. I wedged the blade in the crack between the box and the lid to pry it open.

I strained to wiggle the lid off. Finally, with a grunt and a hollow *pop*, the lid slid free. I was relieved to see that the water hadn't damaged the inside of the box. Nestled on a bed of blue velvet was a piece of pink quartz. It was about eight inches long. Instead of being round, each side was squared off, forming a flat irregular hexagon at the base. The other end was shaped into a pyramid with a wicked-looking pointed tip. I held it up to the sunlight, admiring it. The crystal was just slightly kissed by a rosy pink color. When I held it up to the sun, it almost seemed like there were lights inside the crystal, dancing down its length.

I shifted my weight in the sand and the wooden box tumbled off my lap with a clatter. That was strange. It had looked empty. Curiously, I set the crystal aside and lifted the box for a closer look. Nothing. Gently, I shook it. A rattle sounded underneath the velvet lining. Carefully, I pried the velvet away from the box. The warm autumn and the damp ocean air must have weakened the glue holding it in place. The velvet tore away easily. Something silver glinted at the bottom of the box.

I fished it out for a closer look. It was a silver ring with a single, irregular stone set in the middle. The stone was the same color as the crystal and about the size of my thumbnail. Spirals of silver held the oblong fragment of crystal in place on a delicate ring. I tried it on, but the tiny ring wouldn't even fit on my little finger. Kingsley hadn't mentioned anything about finding a ring with the relic, so maybe this was a bonus I'd keep. Speaking of the Ambassador, I suddenly wanted to hand the crystal over and claim the reward he had promised me as fast as possible.

I was practically salivating as I wrapped the crystal relic in the ripped blue velvet and slid it into my satchel. The ring went into an inner pocket with the tracker for safe keeping. If Kingsley didn't ask about it, then I contemplated keeping it as a bonus. I fit the lid gently back on the wooden box and tucked it under my arm as I fought my way through the shifting sands towards the Jeep.

# Chapter 33

The hike back to the boardwalk was faster than the stumbling pace we had taken to the relic's hiding place. I reached up to slide the box and my satchel through the gap at the bottom of the boardwalk. I hoisted myself up and scrambled over the railing. Reclaiming the box and bag, I jogged down the wooden boardwalk towards the parking lot as quickly as I could with the awkward load. I hoped to catch Magnus on his return trip with the shovels.

As I approached the two buildings that marked the end of the boardwalk, I slowed. There was now a black SUV parked in the lot near the only exit. Was this the same SUV that had been following us? My gut said yes. I scanned, looking for Magnus. Shit. I couldn't see him in or around the Jeep.

This was bad. This was very bad.

Thinking quickly, I fell to my stomach and carefully lowered my satchel with the relic nestled inside over the edge of the boardwalk. I gently swung it underneath the wooden pathway, letting it land with a soft plop on the sand. Grabbing the empty box inscribed with Fae designs, I tossed it next to my bag. It landed in the soft sand with a thump. The impromptu hiding place would have to do. If my gut was wrong, I could easily reclaim the recently uncovered treasure.

I pushed to my feet and tiptoed along the boardwalk to the two buildings standing sentinel at the entrance of the wooden walkway. I chose the one casting the deepest shadow, pressing my back firmly against the weathered frame and pulled at the shadows. They sprang to life under my magical pull with such force that I would've stumbled backward if I hadn't been firmly braced.

*Whoa. That was new.*

Usually, calling up my magic felt like pulling open a heavy door. The shadows always responded, but it took effort to make the magic work. This time, however, it felt like someone had pushed open the proverbial door at the same time I tried to pull it. Shadow magic doused my form as easily as water did when I cannonballed into a pool.

Depending on the ambient light, my shadow cloaked form could appear like anything from a deeper section of darkness in low light to a hazy, smudged blur in full daylight. The latter wasn't particularly effective as I just looked like a giant blob of charcoal that a toddler scribbled on a piece of paper and then spilled water over.

Curious to see if the ease with which the magic responded changed the result of my shadow cloak, I held a hand up in front of my face for inspection. Nothing. Huh. In the shadow cast by a building in the afternoon, I expected to see a blurred outline of my hand. Carefully, I extended my arm, crossing the boundary of the shade into full daylight. A shimmer appeared around my arm. I could see a basic outline if I squinted, but it wavered like it as a heat mirage in the desert. There was definitely an arm there, but I had to search for it. I yanked it back into the shade and the heat waver disappeared. As did my arm.

*Magic is so cool! This must be because of the charm disintegrating. I wonder what else I'll be able to do.*

Voices interrupted my musings. I shrank back against the rough wood and pulled my shadows tighter around me as I peeked around the corner of the building, careful to stay fully in the shade.

Magnus was walking across the parking lot towards the boardwalk, surrounded by two men and a teenager. My blood boiled. The werewolves had captured Magnus. I considered and discarded a handful of ways of attacking and freeing Magnus. My hands already gripped the sheathed karambits at my back as they clattered up the wooden steps. No matter how I looked at it, it was three on one. Well, three on one, plus a Norm. But I didn't know how adept Magnus was at hand-to-hand combat or more appropriately, hand-to-fang. He could be more of a liability than an asset.

I was weighing the pros and cons of a surprise attack when they drew level with me, pausing between the buildings. A breeze gusted up, blowing the faintest scent of salt and dog my way. Magnus turned to face his captors, speaking calmly.

"She's right up there and off to the left. If she hasn't uncovered the relic yet, she'll be off to the west in the dunes. We need to make sure she doesn't slip through our fingers this time."

My mind whirled. Magnus was working *with* the wolves?

Magus turned to the wiry guy. "Will, you circle around to the south." The wiry guy, Will, nodded as Magnus pointed at the burly, bald guy. "Julius, you take the north. I'll head straight across and we'll catch her in a pincher movement."

The teenager spoke up. "What about me?" He stood, looking caught between cocky and wanting to prove himself.

"Andrei, we need you to use your speed to patrol the edge of the dunes in case she decides to cut across country. We can't have her getting to the parking lot and escaping. Especially now that she found the relic."

The teenager frowned. "I'm not an idiot. I know when you're trying to get rid of me."

"Protect you, kid," the muscular titan masquerading as a man said, leaning down to ruffle the teen's curly hair.

"Hey!" The teenager juked to the side, batting the bigger man's hand away as he protected his untamed mop. "I'm nearly eighteen! Stop calling me a kid!" Andrei protested.

Magnus shook his head. "We know she can handle herself and, like it or not, your dad would be pissed if you got hurt again. So, you watch our flank. End of story."

"Fine," the teen grumped.

Will interjected, "Don't forget what the Alpha said. Absolutely no shifting. We're on shaky ground with this local Collective. He doesn't want to do anything to upset them. Having someone report a werewolf sighting won't help to ease the diplomatic tensions."

The big guy, Julius, mock saluted. "Got it. Anything else or can we go hunting? By the way you're carrying on, it sounds like you're worried we won't get the job done."

Magnus snorted. "Well, she didn't break *my* nose," he observed wryly.

Good natured banter drifted on the ocean breeze as the werewolves moved off. I let out the breath I'd been holding silently. Magnus had betrayed me. I should've known better than to trust a stranger who'd appeared out of nowhere, but he'd said he was a Norm, hadn't he? I cast my mind back over our conversations. Well, if he hadn't explicitly said it, he'd definitely allowed me to believe it. I wondered briefly if he was also a wolf or just working with them. Regardless, it didn't matter now. All that mattered was retrieving the relic and getting the hell out of here before they circled back.

I waited until the men disappeared around a curve in the boardwalk, all my senses vibrating on high alert. When I was sure they were out of sight, I shuffled along the building until I could peek around the opposite corner. I searched the dunes for movement from the teenager, but couldn't see anything. Perfect.

Keeping my shadows pulled tight around me, I jogged back to where I'd stashed the relic and vaulted over the railing. I wiggled under the walkway and snagged my bag. I considered grabbing the box as well, but decided against it. Instead, I spent a few seconds stomping and scuffing around in the sand before hoisting myself back up onto the boardwalk. I glanced down. To anyone walking by, it was obvious that someone had jumped down here. Tracks led under the walk and grasses were trampled flat. Hopefully, the wolves would spend precious seconds looking around the area and even more time confused by the empty box. Any time I could buy now was invaluable. Speaking of, I dropped my shadows, directly all of my attention towards speed. I sprinted for the Jeep, already pulling the keys out of my pocket.

The engine roared to life and I stomped on the accelerator, spinning the wheel and squealing towards the exit. Sudden inspiration struck as I passed the empty SUV. I put both feet on the brake and screeched to a halt, throwing the Jeep into park and leaving it idling as I flung myself towards the SUV. My karambit blade glinted in the sun for a split second before I drove it viciously into the rear tire of the wolves' SUV. I hurried to the front and gauged another ragged tear in the front tire. The SUV listed slowly to the pavement on a dejected hiss of escaping air. For good measure, I rounded the vehicle and slashed the two remaining tires. The wolves weren't going anywhere soon in the SUV.

Satisfied that I'd done as much as I could to slow them down, I spun back to the Jeep. The sudden movement saved me from face planting into the metal frame of the SUV as something slammed into my back.

I stumbled forward, fighting for balance and hit my knee on the bumper of the SUV. Hard.

"Ouch!" I hissed, spinning on my good leg and blindly slashing out with my blade at my unseen opponent.

"Damn it!" The voice cracked at the end. I instantly realized who must have jumped me. It was the teenage werewolf, Andrei.

"Watch your language!" I snapped instinctively.

"Yeah, like I've never heard the word 'damn' before," he retorted, fingering a fresh tear in his shirt.

"Well, you shouldn't be saying it, kid." I felt the lame dripping off my words as soon as they left my tongue.

The teen snorted. "You may be old, but I'm not a kid."

"Hey! I'm not *that* much older than you."

The kid cocked his head to the side. "What, ten years? Fifteen maybe?" He shrugged like it didn't matter.

I glared at him. "Look, *kid*, I'm gonna get in that Jeep and drive out of here. If you know what's good for you, you're not gonna try and stop me."

The teen, Andrei, crossed his arms over his torn shirt. "No can do. I've got my orders, straight from the Alpha."

"Kid, you don't wanna do this," I said, inching backwards, flicking the karambit on its retention ring in an effort to dissuade any stupidity. I really didn't want to fight him, but if he pushed the issue, I was afraid I'd have to hurt him to make my escape.

"Yes. Yes, I do," he growled. With that obvious declaration of intent, the teen wolf leapt at me.

My left hand already flashed to the small of my back for my other knife before he started to moved. I leaned down low into a side crouch as he sprang at me. The kid seemed intent on using his speed and surprise attack to his advantage. However, he forgot to consider gravity and, let me tell you, gravity *works*. I popped back up just as his arm shot past me. I caught his arm, spinning him to use his momentum against him. In less than a second, I wrangled him into a lock. My right knife curved with barely contained violence to kiss his jugular while the left blade tickled his sternum.

I really didn't want to kill the kid, purely for the complications that his death would bring into my life, but I needed him out of the way. He struggled with all the lean desperation of someone with something to prove.

"Stop it! I grunted from behind him, trying to not to let him go or slice him to ribbons.

He grabbed my wrist. With his teeth. I yowled in pain and rapped him hard on the side of the head with the hilt of my knife. He let go, but so did I. I examined the bloody wound briefly.

"I can't believe you bit me!" I shouted.

"Wolf."

Oh, the snark on this kid! I felt the resolve to not harm a teenager draining away by the second. He launched himself at me again. I flicked the karambit back and drove my fist into his oncoming shoulder, retention ring first. The blow dug deep into the meat just below the joint and his arm flopped to his side like a dead fish. I blocked his wild, retaliatory punch, driving my fist into his stomach. The boy staggered back, clutching at his dead arm and wheezing for air.

"Kid, you tried. No one can fault you for bravery, but you've got a hell of a long way to go before you can hope to match me. Call it a day," I said, watching carefully for any ill-conceived stupidity. I wasn't disappointed.

The teenager drove at me like he was trying to sack the quarterback and he thought my knife was a football. I dodged the mad charge easily. I knew he was just going to keep attacking until he slipped past my guard or until the other wolves came back from their fruitless search for me.

Almost regretfully, I dropped my blade as he flew past me and dragged it across the back of his leg, neatly hamstringing the kid.

He screamed, collapsing to the pavement. I crouched near him, but well out of arm's reach as he writhed, trying to grab at his leg with his dead arm. "Look, kid, I'm sorry I hurt you, but I gave you plenty of warnings. In this world if you pick a fight, you'd better be sure that you can win it." I cocked my head to the side, considering him carefully. "If the rumors about werewolves are true, you should heal up just fine. I wouldn't try to shift though. Who knows what that would do to your leg."

"The relic!" he spat out, pain giving his voice a fraught edge.

"Really? That's what you're worried about right now?

"Give me the damned relic!"

I rolled my eyes. "I made a deal for the relic, but not with you," I said, pushing out of my crouch. I dusted off my knees and tucking my karambits back into their special sheaths at my lower back.

His eyes tracked me wildly, his breath coming in short, sharp pants. "You don't know what you are doing! You need to keep the relic out of the hands of the Fae. Give it to us, don't give it to us. Whatever. Just don't give it to *them*." He said the last word like it left a vile taste in his mouth.

I stared down at him impassively, pasting on the resting bitch face all women develop in their lives. "Look. I don't really care who gets this relic. But when I make a deal, I honor the deal. Above all else. I've been patient with you so far. Enough is enough. Don't try me again."

A shout sounded behind me and I glanced over my shoulder to see three figures sprinting towards us.

I looked back at the kid. "Keep pressure on it. Your friends will be here soon."

With the words still hanging in the salty, humid air between us, I spun and sprinted towards the Jeep. Throwing the car into gear as soon as I slid into the driver's seat, I slammed my foot down and fishtailed out of the parking lot with a squeal of tires. All I left behind was the smell of scorched rubber as I tore out of there like I was being chased by the devil himself.

# Chapter 34

I scrutinized the road behind me as I sped up the LA-1 back towards New Orleans. I knew I hadn't injured the kid too badly. At least, not enough to cause long-term damage. He was a Supe after all. He'd heal up just fine given enough time and enough protein. It was a miracle that the rest of the wolves hadn't shifted in the middle of the parking lot once they saw the injured kid and me fleeing the scene. I didn't know what kind of repercussions I'd face, but I knew better than to think this was over.

What I was worried about at the moment was the wolves getting on the road and catching me before I got to New Orleans. There was only one way off Grand Isle and this strip of Louisiana road was narrow. If they sideswiped me, I'd tumble into the bayou. There was a reason all those cop-chase shows stuck to paved roads instead of murky, alligator-infested, shallow rivers coated in slippery silt.

After thirty minutes and a severe crick in my neck later, I settled more comfortably into my seat, fairly confident that I'd gotten away. At least, for now. I kept an eye on my six using the rearview mirror as I sped along the relatively empty road.

I kept my foot firmly on the gas, but dug my phone out of my bag. Slowly, I punched out a couple of quick texts as I drove through the bayou. The first one went to the group chat, letting everyone know I'd found the relic and was on my way back. Then I tapped out a message to Kingsley requesting a meeting. It surprised me when a message popped up almost immediately arranging a meeting in two hours at the Fae Embassy. I glanced at the clock on the dash It would cut it close, but with the way I was driving, I should be back in time.

My phone buzzed and I glanced at it. A message from Sloane popped up. Rather than continue texting and driving, I thumbed the icon to call her. She answered on the first ring.

"Cam! Are you ok?"

"More or less. I got the relic."

"Ok, that's the more. Why the less?"

I slowed to take a curve before flooring the gas again on the straight-away. "I found out Magnus was working with the werewolf Pack. He set me up."

"Shit," Sloane cursed softly.

"Yeah. I barely got away."

"Where are you now?" she asked.

"On the way back to New Orleans. I slashed their tires so I doubt they'll be able to catch me."

"Good. Glad to hear it. Did you get away clean?"

"Not exactly. But that doesn't matter. This isn't over yet. I have a meeting with Kingsley to hand over the relic. I won't rest easy until I get it into his hands and get paid."

"What can I do to help?" Sloane asked immediately.

"Have you got any werewolf repellant?" I joked, my eyes flicking up to the rearview mirror. Nothing moved on the road behind me.

"I think I can put something together," she said thoughtfully.

"Wait, what?"

"Knives coated in silver. Guns with silver bullets. Body armor. That type of thing." I heard scratching like she was making a list.

"Yeah, that'd be great. I mean, I'd take anything right now with a Pack of werewolves on my heels."

"I'll put a kit together. I should probably get some healing potions and bandages from Mama just in case."

I nodded even though she couldn't see me. "That'd be great, thanks Sloane. Once I hit town, it's going to be a race to see who can get to the Fae Embassy first."

"I thought you said they were stuck behind you," Sloane said.

"They are. But they have phones."

"Right. I'll pull together what I can and leave it for you in my office at the Forge. They might not expect you to go there. Hopefully I can get the gear and get to Mama's before you hit New Orleans. If I don't make it, grab the kit and get that relic to the Fae Embassy. Then the werewolves can chase Kingsley instead of you."

"Sounds like a plan. See you soon."

Satisfied, I settled back in my seat. Despite my casual demeanor, I kept a careful eye on the road behind us. I didn't see the wolves' SUV the entire way back, but I knew they were back there somewhere. The knowledge that I was being chased like prey kept my foot firmly planted on the accelerator all the way back to New Orleans.

I made excellent time, but I was glad for the drive. It allowed me to gather my thoughts and flesh out the plan that was forming in my head. By the time I'd hit the city limits and slowed to a speed that wouldn't get me pulled over, I felt almost confident that my plan would work.

I turned the Jeep into the parking lot outside the Forge. My Rebel glinted in the sunlight like a beacon of hope. I smiled as I parked the Jeep. Shouldering my bag with its precious cargo, I headed towards the back entrance. Rudolph pushed open the door for me.

"Sloane said to keep an eye out for you. I'm to tell you that your gear is in her office and not to wait for her," the wood elf said.

"Fantastic." I tossed him the keys to the Jeep.

"What am I supposed to do with this?" he asked skeptically.

"Don't care. Take it for a joyride. Burn it. Drive it into the bayou. Doesn't matter to me. I never want to see the thing again."

"Who spit in your beer?" Rudolph asked, raising an eyebrow at my tone.

"Werewolves," I replied shortly.

"Ah. I see." His face paled slightly. He clenched the keys and considered the Jeep thoughtfully.

I patted him on the shoulder as I passed. "Have fun!" I said cheerfully before slipping inside the shadowy back hallway of the bar. My eyes adjusted swiftly to the interior gloom after the late afternoon autumnal brilliance. I made my way to the office where Sloane had left me some goodies. Mostly sharp and pointy goodies, I hoped.

As soon as I opened the door, my eyes bugged out of my head. The arsenal covering Sloane's desk put my closet to shame. I closed the door to the office firmly behind me before pulling off my tank. Carefully but quickly, I strapped on the lightweight body armor panels from my bag, doing up the various buckles and ties securely. I selected as many silver-coated knives as I thought prudent for the situation. Then I added a few more. I even slipped a gun loaded with a special magical silver alloy coating and extra ammo of the same into my bag. Feeling much better prepared for what was to come, I slipped my tank top and my leather jacket back on. I grabbed my keys and helmet from Sloane's desk, where she had left them for me. I silently slid out the back door and started up my Rebel.

Things were going to get messy. Soon. I could feel it in my gut.

# Chapter 35

I slowed the Rebel as I turned the corner, not liking what I saw. Two black SUVs were parked on either end of the road leading up to the gated Fae Embassy. They were far enough away to be out of Fae jurisdiction, but could easily monitor guests arriving. They'd also positioned the SUVs for the optimal control of any entry or exit to the Embassy. This was one of those rare instances where my knives were practically useless. I had a gun in my bag but didn't want to pull it out. I couldn't afford to start a firefight that would bring both the mundane police and the Collective down on my head.

*Damn it.*

I slowed the Rebel and put a foot to the pavement. I wasn't sure who was in the cars. Frankly, I didn't care. The relic was burning a hole in my satchel. I just wanted to bring it to Kingsley, trade it for the promised rewards, and call it a day. But it looked like things weren't going to my plan.

*Typical.*

The backdoor opened on one of the SUVs. A distinguished-looking gentleman in an impeccably tailored navy suit emerged. He moved to stand in the middle of the street, blocking my way to Kingsley and my payday.

I flipped up the visor on my helmet in irritation. "Hey! I'm drivin' here!" I shouted over the roar of my engine in my best New Yorker impression.

"I'd like to speak with you, Ms. Blaze. Before you have your meeting with Mr. Kingsley." He slowly moved closer, hands held open and away from his sides. He gripped a slim folder of papers in one hand. Assuming that he wouldn't paper-cut me to death, I switched off the engine, but stayed on the Rebel. Better safe than polite.

"You have five minutes. Start with your name." The growl of my voice seemed to reverberate in the sudden silence of the tree-lined street.

The man in the navy suit continued to move forward slowly and steadily. I could see the silver streaking his elegantly cut black hair and beard. He could have been a hard-lived forty. Or well into his second century. It was hard to tell with Supes.

Ice-blue eyes shone with wily intelligence under craggy eyebrows. He looked like a man who didn't suffer fools. More like he ripped their throats out and then dabbed away any excess blood with a silk handkerchief.

"My name is Damon Lykaios. I believe that you have had some, shall we say, *encounters* with some of my men." He extended a card held carefully between two fingers as he drew closer. It was thick, creamy stock and embossed with the head of a wolf. The only thing printed on the card was a local phone number.

My mind whirled. This handsome, sophisticated man must be the Alpha of the werewolves who had been hounding me.

"You should really keep a tighter leash on your pets. If they run wild, they might get hurt. Hit by a car. Or my knives." I batted my lashes at him, putting as much false sincerity into my words as possible.

He grimaced. "So I've been told. Believe me, their...leashes," he paused over the word in obvious distaste, "have been suitably short-ened."

I folded my arms over my chest. "What do you want, Mr. Damon Lykaios? Your guys have come at me three times now. Left with their tails between their legs three times as well, if anyone is keeping count." I kept half an eye on him and half an eye on the SUVs. I doubted my three little buddies were back yet, but wolves ran in Packs. The Alpha undoubtedly had more goons to back him up, stashed away in those slick vehicles. I didn't like my odds if this situation took a turn for the worse.

"Cameron. May I call you Cameron?" His voice was like a velvet glove over brass knuckles, and I was just waiting for the punch to land.

"Call me whatever you want," I said brusquely. "Three minutes."

"Cameron, they have deceived you. Mr. Kingsley is using you to gain control of an extremely dangerous magical item. It's something he couldn't obtain himself for fear of reprisals from powers higher than all of us. From the scent my wolves picked up on the box you left on Grand Isle, I must assume that you found this artifact."

I winced. I thought I'd been smart to leave the box as a distraction, but it'd turned out to be a careless mistake. One I should've anticipated.

*Sloppy, sloppy, sloppy.*

I raised a shoulder nonchalantly, keeping my voice cool. "They hired me to do a job. That's all. Besides, why do you care?"

"My Pack were selected as the guardians for this relic," Damon said, his voice laced with urgency as he took a step closer.

"You're doing a bang-up job." I tried not to twitch as I allowed an apex predator to come within striking distance. It required all my self-control to not move as he closed the distance between us.

Damon shook his head fiercely, lips tightening. "Someone stole it from the Pack and we tracked it here, but the trail went cold. When we informed the Collective of the matter, it must have alerted Kingsley to the relic's presence. He sits on the Collective, you know."

"Fine. Whatever. Why include me?" I asked, not seeing the connection.

Damon spoke bluntly. "You're disposable, an independent. Not connected to the Fae. If *you* were to retrieve this dangerous relic, well then, Kingsley couldn't be held responsible for your actions, could he? And if you were to be fatally injured in some freak accident and the dangerous relic disappeared to the mists of time again? Well, that couldn't possibly be Aldrich Kingsley's fault now, could it? After all, coincidence is not a crime." He raised one eyebrow to emphasize the point.

He painted a vivid scene; I'd give him that. However, I wasn't convinced. "Why are you telling me this now, after all the...encounters with your guys?"

Damon cleared his throat uneasily. If he had been anyone else, I was laying dollars to doughnuts that I would have seen some squirming. "I tasked them with arranging a meeting. A private meeting. I didn't want to be seen to be publicly consorting with a Fae hireling. Apparently, their diplomatic skills are severely lacking. I'll remedy that immediately."

I could've pointed out that a phone call would have done the same thing as sending werewolves to track me down. Because of the wolves fumbling Damon's message, we were meeting publicly now. Very publicly. What had changed his mind?

"You could always send them to obedience school," I suggested, flicking out a hand to examine my nails as if I was getting bored with this conversation even as I subtly prodded for more information.

A frown line furrowed its way down between his eyebrows. "They have something like that to look forward to soon. I was unaware of their coercion techniques until this afternoon. I'd sent them after you today to pass along some information that I thought you would find valuable." He waved his folder in my general direction.

I let my feigned nonchalance slough away. "Yeah, right. I'm supposed to believe that they were merely delivering messages when they tricked me, stalked me, and then attacked me?"

Real anger bubbled inside me, close to the surface and threatening to boil over into the street. I'll admit, I wasn't taking it well that Magnus had so easily duped me. Or that I let him. All because I started to catch feelings for the handsome jerk.

Damon shrugged. "They saw an opportunity and took it. Their mistake was underestimating you. I doubt they'll make such a blunder again."

*That* was their mistake? Being too slow to incapacitate me? Well, at least I knew where the Alpha stood on the matter. Top priority: retrieve the relic. I doubted my safety even made it on to his list.

"That instills so much confidence of your peaceful intentions," I spat out sarcastically.

Damon waved an arm, encompassing the public street and the Fae guards watching us warily. "That is why I picked this location for our tête-à-tête. If I make a move against you here, it will be the match that ignites the powder keg of smoldering hostility between my wolves and the High Fae pulling your strings."

"That doesn't help me in the slightest. I'm still caught in the blast radius," I pointed out ruthlessly. "Assuming I believe you, what's the point of all this?" I mirrored his gesture, sweeping an arm at the Fae and werewolves alike.

"From what I have been able to discover about you, Cameron, you are an honorable person. You have a moral compass." His lips twitched in the hint of a smile. "Even if it is slightly skewed from time to time. Your current employer doesn't operate with the same ethical standards. But you don't have to take my word for it. As they say, a picture is worth a thousand words."

I took the thin folder he offered me and flipped through the pictures. Damon captioned them all with brief headings detailing the time and location of the photos. My blood ran cold as I continued to rifle through the photos, a crushing weight settling on my chest as I reached the end of the file.

Each picture showed Aldrich Kingsley standing alone in the middle of a ritualistic ceremony in different graveyards, holding a small, glowing object. These pictures were the brass knuckles I had feared from Damon Lykaios and I had just taken a proverbial roundhouse to the jaw.

"You're implying that Kingsley is harvesting ghosts. How do I know these are real and not some digital enhancement?" My voice was hoarse.

"My wolves are creatures of the night and excellent trackers. There are very few beings that can hide from us when we put our noses to the task." His mouth twisted into a wry grin. "Although my wolves would much prefer to fight with tooth and claw, they can fight with other tools when necessary. Including cameras. Besides, it would be counterproductive to upset a major power-player in the area and a member of the Collective when we are attempting to relocate here permanently. Trust me, the photo is real."

I closed the folder and returned it to him. "Why not just give these to me? Hell, why not advertise to the entire supernatural community?"

Damon bared his teeth at me in what could be loosely described as a smile. "We may be a Pack, Cameron, but what about werewolves makes you think we play well with others? What about Supes makes you think they would accept the word of a new group of Supes against that of a highly respected member of the community?"

*What indeed?*

He leaned forward, speaking urgently. "What are you going to do now?"

That was a loaded question. I turned the key on my Rebel, revving the engine.

"I'm going to keep my meeting with Aldrich Kingsley," I said grimly, lips set in a thin line.

# Chapter 36

The butler ushered me through the pristine entryway to the Embassy. Someone had cleared away the piles of artwork since my last visit. The butler deposited me in the same opulent sitting room where I had met Kingsley previously. As I waited for the Fae Ambassador, I turned over the events of the past few days in my mind, adding in the information that Damon had presented me. What the Alpha had shown me in that series of photos aligned too perfectly with the other details from various sources that I had uncovered to be anything but the truth.

Kingsley cleared his throat from behind me. "Ms. Blaze, I assume you have my relic?"

I whirled, startled out of my suspicious musings. Was it my imagination, or was there an air of hopeful desperation about him?

"I assume you have my money?" I countered.

He reached into an inner pocket of his suit jacket as he walked deeper into the room. He placed a thick envelope on the end table next to the luxurious red leather armchairs.

"Everything you require is there," he said, then glided backwards, allowing me unencumbered access to the envelope.

I took a couple of quick steps forward and snatched it. Keeping a careful eye on Kingsley, I flipped it over. The envelope was sealed with an ornate red wax seal. I tried to break the wax seal with my thumbs. It refused to budge. I blinked and used more force. Nothing. I looked up in confusion at Kingsley.

"It's enchanted," he explained. "You have a reputation of being a bit of a wild card, Ms. Blaze. I took precautions against any untoward actions on your part. The seal will not open until dawn on All Saints' Day."

I tamped down on my disappointment as I examined the envelope with its tantalizing promise of fiscal freedom carefully. Finally, I shrugged, trying for nonchalance as I tucked it inside my bag. Surely, waiting one more day for my money wouldn't kill me.

My eyes flicked back to Kingsley. I gave him a curt nod.

His smile was almost predatory. "My relic?" he asked.

I secured the envelope in my satchel and pulled out the crystal relic. Kingsley's eyes glimmered hungrily. I carefully set it on the table, flat on one facet so it wouldn't roll off. I took a few steps back to show him the same courtesy he had shown me.

Kingsley's long-fingered hands flashed out to grab the relic. He examined it eagerly, moving away from me and towards the window. He held the crystal up to the evening sunlight. I took the opportunity to sidle closer towards the door of the sitting room.

"It seems you have succeeded where all others failed. My congratulations, Ms. Blaze. I think this could be the start of a very beneficial relationship." He spoke with his back towards me as he examined the relic triumphantly.

I didn't respond. Kingsley turned back to face me, a triumphant expression suffusing his face. His victorious smile faded when he saw the gun I held pointing directly at his heart.

His eyes flared in surprise. "What is this treachery?" His cultured voice dripped with menace as he clutched the crystal to his chest.

"No treachery. I located the relic and brought it to you, precisely as we agreed. A deal's a deal, after all, and I've fulfilled our agreement to the letter." I tried to mimic Damon's menacing, toothy smile. "Now, we negotiate a new deal."

The Fae Ambassador glared at me. Not that I cared. If what the Alpha werewolf had told me was true, there was no way I was leaving a relic with mystical, magic-amplifying powers in Aldrich Kingsley's control when he already had kidnapped ghosts stashed away and ready to fuel a dangerous ritual. I waved the gun towards the end table between us.

"Put the crystal on the table and back away," I said, keeping my voice low.

He shook his head. "I *need* this. You don't understand." He looked panicked.

I growled at him. "I understand more than you think. The werewolves showed me what you were doing. They took pictures of everything. You're harvesting the ghosts from around town to power up your little ritual. My necromancer friend told me that the ghosts would only provide a relatively minor amount of energy for a spell. I'm guessing that you weren't just going to use the ghosts. No, you were planning on *sacrificing* someone, weren't you? That shit is messed up. Taking someone's mother or father away just so you can have some extra *oomph* in your spell? *Nothing* is worth that price." I was panting with emotion, trying to keep my voice low so as not to alert any other members of the Embassy that their ambassador was being held at gunpoint.

"Just a Norm or two. Why would you care?" Kingsley looked genuinely confused.

"Because they are *people*! No one deserves to be *sacrificed*, no matter what you think you might gain. Besides, what if it all goes wrong? You could unleash a whole lot of who knows what into the middle of New Orleans and I can't let you do that. There are too many people I care about in this town to let you open the gates of Hell and ring the dinner bell."

His mouth twisted in anger. "Moronic, meddlesome wolves! Always sticking their noses in where they don't belong. I suppose you are giving the relic to them?" His cold eyes filled with hatred as they met mine defiantly.

"That doesn't concern you," I spat out. "Within an hour, that relic will be under the powerful protection and safely out of the hands of magic users who want to abuse its power. Like you."

He snarled, curling a lip upward, and took two aggressive strides forward. I raised the gun, aiming it at his head. It was nearly point-blank range. There was no way I could miss this shot. He must have seen the resolve in my eyes, because he stopped instantly.

I almost spat the last words. "Put the relic on the table, Kingsley, and back away."

He glowered at me, but slowly inched closer to the table. Just as he reached out to put the relic on the end table, he fumbled it. We both watched as the crystal spun in horrifying slow motion to crash into the thick carpet. Thankfully, the plush carpet cradled the glowing facets of the relic in rich luxury.

Kingsley let out an audible sigh of relief. I barely contained my own. I didn't know what would happen if a relic that powerful was broken and I didn't want to find out. He scrambled to collect the relic and placed it shakily on the table.

I silently let out the breath I had been holding. "Good. Now back away. I don't want any more accidents."

When he had moved sufficiently far away from the table, I tossed him a set of zip-tie handcuffs. I didn't know what steel handcuffs would do to him, what with him being Fae and all. I didn't know what level of iron could be tolerated in an alloy. Also, I didn't need to add injury to the insult. Kingsley was going to be pissed enough. No need to make it personal.

"Secure your feet," I said, keeping my voice low and my gun steady.

Kingsley sat and bound his ankles with the zip-tie, shooting venomous looks at me. I felt a twitch tickling up the muscle of my leg and tried to relax. Making a mistake now would be deadly.

When he finished, I said, "Great. Now lay on your stomach with your hands behind your back."

He grimaced at me and then at the spotless floor, obviously not pleased about being forced to lie on it. Once he was face down, I moved swiftly. I zip-tied his wrists behind his back, grabbed the pocket square from his coat and gagged him with it. I assumed he would break out of the heavy plastic restraints soon after I left. That was fine. I just needed enough time to get off the Fae Embassy estate. Then the Ambassador couldn't do a thing to me.

Checking his restraints to make sure they were secure, I patted him on the back of the head. "A pleasure doing business with you, Mr. Kingsley."

I grabbed the relic from the table and made sure that I securely stashed it and my gun in my bag as I hurried from the room. As I rushed out the front door, the butler's surprised face poked out into the entryway from an adjoining room.

As I opened the door, I couldn't help myself. I was feeling cocky. I looked over my shoulder at the butler and said, "Thanks, Jeeves! Mr. Kingsley said not to bother him for a while. After our meeting, he seemed a little tied up. Relics." I shrugged and shut the door behind me.

Sometimes, it's the little things.

# Chapter 37

Even though my meeting with Kingsley had been brief, the SUVs full of werewolves were gone. I pulled the Rebel out onto the street and roared away from the Embassy. I drove quickly for a few blocks, making random turns to throw off any Fae pursuit Kingsley might throw after me.

Being extra cautious, I pulled to the side of the road about five minutes later to see if anyone was following me. I scanned the street carefully. No one menacing jumped out of the shadows. Knowing I was out of my depth, I switched off the bike and dialed Sloane's number. She answered on the first ring.

"Did things go as planned?" Sloane asked. I could hear the tension thrumming through her voice.

"Not even close." I said, throwing a leg over the Rebel. I started to pace, finding the movement helped me manage my mounting anxiety.

"Why? What happened?"

I rubbed my free hand across my eyes. "The wolves showed up."

"What?!" Sloane squeaked.

"Yeah. The Alpha showed me some pictures of Kingsley harvesting ghosts in a local cemetery. He claimed that the Ambassador's planning something much worse and the relic is the lynchpin to his plans."

"Are werewolves good at photoshop?"

"I asked myself the same question, but you didn't see the evidence, Sloane. Those photos looked pretty damning." A car whizzed toward me, and I froze, nerves jangling. The man driving the car didn't glance once at me as he kept one eye on the road and strained to hand something to the kid strapped into a car seat in the back of the vehicle. I let out a slow breath.

"Cameron. Tell me you didn't double-cross Kingsley," Sloane said, jerking me back to the conversation.

"Technically, no. I stuck to the letter of our agreement. I brought him the relic in exchange for my fee. I think he expected me to leave the relic with him though."

"*Technically*, you must have a freaking death wish! Don't tell me you gave the relic to the werewolves."

"No. I didn't. Which is why I'm calling. Everyone wants this thing. Badly. I need to figure out what to do with it before someone catches up with me. The way I see it is I can either find somewhere to stash it or find someone more powerful than I am to keep it safe."

"You could just chuck it in the Mississippi. No one will find it in that murk," Sloane grumbled.

"You know that isn't true. Magical artifacts never disappear for good. Who knows? The next person who discovers it might use it for even worse things than Kingsley. No, I can't take that risk."

"Well, you can't keep it either. What about handing it over to the Collective? Isn't this type of thing precisely why they exist?"

I let my head fall back and let out a groan. "Yeah. Except for one teeny, tiny problem. Kingsley is part of the Collective. Giving it to them might amount to giving it back to him."

"What!" Sloane shrieked. I held the phone away from my ear and winced. "What the hell were you thinking, Cam?!"

I cautiously put the phone back to my ear. "I was thinking I was trying to keep him from killing someone. I couldn't live with myself if my actions resulted in someone getting hurt."

"Fine. I can't fault you for good morals, although morality won't keep you safe. What about giving it to Logan? He knows everyone. He'll probably know someone who can keep it from falling into the wrong hands."

"No, he's part of the New Orleans scene. He might be pressured to turn it over to the Collective which would probably result in Kingsley getting his greasy hands on it."

"Who then? Who isn't part of the New Orleans power balance and has enough clout to protect the relic if the Collective or Kingsley presses the issue?"

I groaned as the logical answer to her questions popped to the forefront of my head. "You're not going to like this."

"What are you talking about?" Sloane asked. I heard the dread start to creep into her voice.

"There is a group that might be powerful enough to protect the relic from Kingsley and the Collective. As an added bonus, I'm pretty sure they were the original guardians."

"Who?" Sloane said. "Not..."

"The wolves," I said in chorus with her.

"Cam, you can't! They have it out for you."

"Do you see another option? I can't just keep driving around with this thing. Someone is going to catch up with me eventually. Either the Pack or the Collective or some money-hungry mercenary that Kingsley hires. Besides, despite the opportunities, none of the werewolves have actually done anything to hurt me."

Sloane paused. When she spoke, I heard hard-headed resolution in her voice. "I suppose you're right, on all counts. But you need back up. You aren't going to meet those fleabags without me."

I rubbed the back of my neck, but she made a good point. "Fine. Let me set up the meet with the wolves and then I'll give you a call back right away." I hung up the phone and leaned over my bike to dig Damon's card out. It wasn't optimal, but at least the werewolves and the High Fae would be at each other's throats instead of both coming after me.

I didn't have to wait long. He answered the phone on the second ring.

"Yes?" Damon growled.

"You've convinced me," I said, by way of introduction.

"I see." I could almost hear him nodding in relief on the other end of the phone. "Do you have it?"

My eyes scanned the street, on alert for any pursuers. "Yes. I'm assuming that you would like it back as soon as possible. You know, to save face with the supernatural community. Heaven forbid, word leaks out that the reason you came to town was because you couldn't keep track of one small crystal."

"It was stolen from us! You know that!" His outrage was clear as his volume rose.

I held the phone away from my ear, scrunching up an eye at the roar emitting from my phone. "I know only what you have shared with me. Besides, I don't work for free. I have your relic; if you want I back, you need to pay."

A sigh reverberated through the cell phone in my hand. "How much do you want?"

That took me aback. If he had asked me that a week ago, I would have asked for an extortionate amount of money. Today, I had an enormous pile of cash burning a hole in my bag. So, what was more valuable than money?

"I want three favors," I blurted out. "And honest answers to five questions. And I want you to call off your wolves. Literally. I want a truce between your Pack and me." The answer to what was more valuable than money? Relationships with and knowledge from powerful beings. I learned that from Sloane early on in my dubious career.

Silence met my offer. I could tell that he hadn't been expecting my asking price. Damon cleared his throat. "Three questions, two favors, and a truce," he countered.

"Done. Where should we do this?" I asked.

"Do you know the wharf next to Crescent Park?"

Oh, this was just too perfect. I made sure that my smirk infused my voice. "You mean, next to the Crescent Park dog run? Yes, I know it."

I swear, I could actually hear Damon grinding his teeth over the phone. "Yes. Meet me there in thirty minutes. I will send an exact location to this number. Make sure you bring the relic."

"You got it, Big D." I must have a death wish or something, but I couldn't seem to stop myself. Needling the werewolves in this Pack was just so much godsdamned fun.

I smiled and hung up the call, feeling pretty good about myself. I should've known better. That's when everything went sideways. A strong arm snaked around my chest, pinning my arms to my sides. My phone crashed to the sidewalk as a dark bag was jerked down over my head. I thrashed, kicking out at my unseen attacker. Make that *attackers*. I felt another set of hands grab my ankles, wrapping them in some sort of restraints. A set of plastic zip-ties secured my wrists despite my best efforts to escape. I screamed and twisted helplessly in midair as my kidnappers unceremoniously dumped me into what felt like the trunk of a car. Something landed with a thump next to me and then the trunk slammed shut, shutting out the dim light that barely penetrated the dark bag. A moment later, the car pulled away from the curb. I kicked at the trunk and screamed with all my might as I disappeared into the depths of the underbelly of New Orleans.

# Chapter 38

I tried to use all the survival training I'd learned to wriggle loose and try to escape the trunk, but the zip-ties were too tight for me to break them. It took time, but eventually, I tossed, turned, wriggled, and cursed my way free of the bag over my head. The pinpricks of light seeping through a cracked taillight gave me enough to see by. Except for my bag, which sat near my feet, the trunk was empty. The kidnappers were careful, but not careful enough. They hadn't searched me for weapons in their haste to get me in the trunk. I twisted around until I could dig my fingertips into the top of a boot, inching out the small blade in its hidden sheath. The muscles in my shoulders strained from the awkward position, screaming at me as I worked the blade free. Just as it popped out of its sheath, the car hit a one of the potholes that the New Orleans streets were riddled with and the knife was jarred from my fingertips.

"Shit!" I cursed softly, twisting around to locate the blade again. The car made a wide turn, sending me skidding into the side of the trunk and then pulled to a halt. Realization dawned. That's why they hadn't searched me. My kidnappers must've known that their destination was close. My mind flashed immediately to the Fae. Depending on the speed of travel, their Embassy would've been close enough. Or maybe they were taking me to some black site I'd never return from. Horrible images flashed across my mind's eye as I heard two car doors slam. I needed that knife! I scrabbled over the trunk's carpeting, trying to locate the small blade, but I was too late.

The trunk popped open, sunlight pouring into the dim interior, momentarily blinding me. A familiar male voice spoke up.

"No need for knives, Cam." It took me a moment to recognize the voice as I blinked spots from my vision.

*Magnus.*

I glared up at him. "What the *hell?*" I shouted up at the tall man.

Magnus smiled cheerfully down at me. He leaned into the trunk and I reared up, head butting him in the face. The satisfying crunch of cartilage made the pain worthwhile. Magnus reeled back, out of my line of sight. Another familiar face replaced his. Wiry, or Will as I supposed I should call him, peered down at me cautiously.

"That wasn't very polite," the tall, lean werewolf said, staying out of my limited reach.

"I didn't know that this was a frickin' cotillion. Let me go get my ball gown, gloves, and silver knives. I'll be right with you."

Will chuckled. "Magnus didn't lie. You are a firecracker."

"Magnus did lie. Repeatedly," I spat back.

I heard a sharp snap and a groan of pain from outside my field of vision. Magnus reappeared, blotting blood from his recently reset broken nose. At least my aim hadn't failed me where my good sense had.

"I never actually lied. I just allowed you to believe what you wanted to," he said, rubbing the bridge of his nose gently.

"Amounts to the same thing," I retorted.

Will shrugged. "He was doing his job. You can hardly fault a man for doing his assignment well."

"Oh, I can and I will." I wriggled, trying to find purchase to get my bound arms around my back to where my karambits were still in their sheaths.

"None of that now," Magnus admonished, fishing the small blade from my boot out of the trunk from where it had fallen. I kicked out at him, but he dodged easily. "The Alpha wants a meeting."

"No shit, Sherlock! We just set one up when you snatched me!"

A look of consternation crossed both of their faces. They glanced at each other; trading looks heavy with significance.

"Well, shit," Will cursed softly.

Magnus inhaled a deep breath which caused him to wince in pain. A small part of my pride was restored as he rubbed at his nose again. He slashed through the zip-tie holding my feet with my knife and then reached for my hands. I jerked them away, glaring a different kind of dagger at him. "Look, right now, we both want the same thing. To get you to Damon. Standing here with you tied up in the trunk of the car is going to attract the wrong kind of attention."

Silently, I extended my bound wrists towards him. He sliced through the zip-tie easily. He offered me a hand, which I ignored. I clambered out of the trunk, snatching my bag and shouldering it. Magnus flipped the knife around, extending it to me handle first. I grabbed it without a word and tucked it back into its sheath.

Will cleared his throat. "Great. Now that we're all friends again, it looks like the Alpha's waiting."

I glared at Magnus a moment longer before taking stock of my surroundings. We were in a deserted parking lot outside a generic white warehouse. The type of place that could've house shipping containers, boat repairs, or any number of things. I could smell salt on the air, so I assumed they'd brought me to my meeting at the wharf.

A dented metal door on the side of the warehouse opened, and Damon appeared for a moment, framed by the dark interior of the warehouse. He vanished just as quickly into the gloom. If I hadn't been looking, I would have missed his appearance. Will turned, leading the way into the warehouse. I glanced at Magnus. He sketched a slight bow, waving a hand graciously to allow me to precede him.

"This isn't over between us," I muttered to him.

He grinned. "I never thought it was."

I rolled my eyes and turned my back on him. Cautiously, I walked towards the warehouse full of werewolves. There had to be a joke in there somewhere, but I was too keyed up to find it.

Damon and Will met me just inside the dim building. The taller werewolf locked the door behind us as the Alpha silently led us deeper into the warehouse. Gutsy. I wouldn't have turned my back on an unknown, dangerous Supe. Even with two guys there for back-up. Perhaps Damon was showing me he trusted me. I tightened the strap of my bag and kept a hand close to the knives at my back as I followed him into the shadowy warehouse.

The Alpha rounded a stacked pile of pallets and turned to face me. In a semicircle at his back were about fifteen men and women. Bare bulbs high overhead provided barely enough illumination in the dim aisle between tall stacks of heavy wooden crates. From what I could make out, all of them were ripped. I swear, you could see muscles on their muscles. And they were all staring at me like I had a steak hung around my neck.

*Gulp.*

Staring directly into my eyes, Damon spread his hands to either side, indicating the men and women at his back. "Cameron Blaze, meet the Pack of New Orleans."

My eyebrows shot towards my hairline. I thought they were on probationary status with the Collective. Which either meant that my information was out of date or Damon was making a ballsy claim.

Damon stretched out a hand towards me. "Wolves, this is Cameron Blaze. We have just negotiated a truce, and anyone who breaks it will have to answer to me." A rumble of growls met his words. Shivers danced up my spine.

The Alpha continued without giving me the chance to comment. "I believe you know my beta, Will."

Will stepped around me, joining the rest of the Pack. He nodded in greeting. I returned the gesture.

"And Julius," Damon said. Meathead stepped forward. He smiled cheerfully at me, good humor crinkling the corners of his eyes.

"Nice to meet you, Cameron," Julius said. "I'm going to take advantage of this truce for a little rematch in the gym." He spoke over his shoulder to the rest of the Pack. "I'm telling you; this chick has got some *moves.* I'll bet she can teach your lazy asses a thing or two." He smiled widely at his Pack mates and I noticed good-natured teasing grins met his words. The Pack members looked like they were family rather than joined by convenience. If I didn't miss my guess, Julius was the gregarious, fun-loving life of the party. Julius extended a hand towards me with a guileless grin lighting his scarred, brutish face. I felt the ice in my posture thaw incrementally under his welcoming grin and clasped hands with him.

"I could get behind that. As long as it's for fun and in a gym. No more of this jumping-me-in-back-alleys nonsense."

The big guy threw his head back and roared with laughter. "No way! That didn't work out too well for me the first time around. Besides, the Alpha gave us our marching orders. Officially, we have a truce."

I smiled back at him, "Fair enough. As long as you show me some of your boxing moves. I imagine you hit like a freight train." A round of affirmative noises rang up from the surrounding Pack. I saw a couple of them even cast a glance my way that wasn't entirely hostile. Maybe they were softening towards me. Julius pumped my arm up and down a few times before clapping me on the shoulder and returning to stand beside Will.

"And, as you know, this is Magnus," Damon continued with the introductions.

The ice returned to my spine and I glared at Magnus. He shot me a jaunty little salute. I jerked my chin at him in a gesture that could have been interpreted as "Hello" or "I'll see you out back later."

Damon turned and put an arm around a young man's shoulders. The dark-haired teenager bore a striking resemblance to the Alpha. Cold realization dripped into my consciousness as I put two and two together even as the Alpha spoke. "And this is my son, Andrei," Damon said, pride clear in his voice.

Shit, shit, *shit*.

Truce or not, had I hamstrung the Alpha's son? And then knowingly walked into a building filled with his Pack of werewolves? My life choices were looking in deep need of a re-haul. I hoped I survived long enough to get the chance.

# Chapter 39

The dark-haired young man leaned heavily on his father; his leg not completely healed yet, either. "It is nice to finally, officially meet you," Andrei said, dipping his head towards me, dark curls falling over his brow. A grin split his youthful face. "You're going to have to show me how to fight with those blades. I've never seen anything like that before." He pawed the air in vague mimicry of flicking invisible karambits back and forth before striking an utterly ridiculous pose.

I shook my head, bemused. "As long as you promise not to hold that against me," I gestured towards his injured leg.

Andrei glanced down. "This? Just the price of doing business in our world. I'll heal." The teenager shrugged easily, looking like he didn't' know how to hold a grudge. I snuck a peek at Wiry and Meathead. Sorry. Will and Julius. They were nodding in agreement with the young werewolf's sentiment. I relaxed slightly, glad to know that there were no hard feelings. Business was business, after all. Supes tended to handle their business in slightly more violent manners than their Norm counterparts. I let out a silent sigh of relief, pleasantly surprised at the turn of events. Damon's lips quirked in a smile. Okay, not so silent then.

"It would be my pleasure to show you how to use the karambits, Andrei," I said formally. And then ruined it. "No teeth. I don't want to turn furry once a month. Shaving my legs is enough of a chore, thanks very much."

Andrei's grin split his face this time. "I can handle that. Give me a day or two to heal up. Then you can show me your stuff, Teach." He winked a cornflower blue eye at me.

The cheeky little shit! I wasn't *that* much older than him.

"First lesson, young Padawan. Make sure you can finish what you start," I mock glowered at Andrei.

He gave me a cocky salute, "Whatever you say, Teach."

He grinned at me, and I grinned right back. He was my kind of people.

Damon lightly cuffed his son on the side of his head. "Enough of that. We have business to attend to." Andrei nodded and took a step back into the rest of the Pack. He shot me a look full of mischief, though, once his father couldn't see his face.

*Oh yeah, this kid was okay.*

Damon waved at the Pack, "Spread out and make sure we aren't disturbed. I want a tight perimeter and a wide-roving radius. No shifting." The Alpha nodded at Magnus. "You take point," he ordered.

The Alpha was no fool. He'd most likely sensed the tension between Magnus and me. Sending Magnus out on guard duty meant that emotions were more likely to stay civil. I glared at Magnus as he led the Pack outside. He and I had unfinished business. I didn't like being made to look the fool.

The Pack melted away into the darkness of the warehouse like ghosts. I was certain that nothing supernatural or mundane would disturb our meeting unless Damon willed it. Oddly enough, that reassured me. The only Pack members who stayed besides Damon were Will, Julius, and Andrei. The kid couldn't very well patrol with a dodgy hamstring and the other two were likely high up in Pack hierarchy.

Damon held out a hand, his tone one of command. "Fulfill your agreement, Cameron. Give us back the Shard."

I put a hand on my bag protectively. "I need some answers first. Straightforward answers. The pictures you showed me were convincing evidence, but now I need the back story."

The Alpha rubbed at his face in exasperation. "Is anything ever easy with you, Ms. Blaze?"

I shrugged and rested a hip on a protruding part of the pallet wall behind me. "Rarely. You get used to it." I grinned toothily at him. "Part of my charm."

He cracked his neck, running his hands through his hair distractedly. "It's not a short story."

I settled myself more fully on the pallets and crossed my legs. "The abbreviated version will do for now," I stated firmly.

He sighed and scrubbed at the back of his neck. Will looked tense behind his boss, eyes flicking between us. Julius adjusted the bandages on his hands, refusing to meet my eyes. Andrei just grinned. Apparently, he appreciated a fellow shit-stirrer.

Damon took a deep breath, considering how to condense the information I wanted. "Shadow Shards are a powerful, ancient magic. So ancient that the method for their creation has been lost to the tides of time. There are only a few left, to the best of my knowledge."

I nodded. So far, his information fit with what I had gleaned over the past couple of days.

"Powerful relics are tracked, and the supernatural community often selects certain Supes to protect them. Groups that could not possibly benefit from using the relic's power themselves. Although it isn't a perfect system, it tends to keep the balance of power more or less equally distributed among the various factions of the supernatural world. Like I told you before, my Pack was tasked with protecting this Shadow Shard. A week ago, it was stolen from us. We tracked it to New Orleans and then lost the trail. Until you discovered it." His eyes drifted meaningfully to my bag.

I ignored his obvious hint. "Okay, so that's how the relic got down here. Why were you put in charge of it?"

"Cameron, do you know what the relic does?" Damon asked.

I tried to keep my answer vague, which wasn't hard given the limited information I'd gained in the last few days. "Some kind of supernatural battery, isn't it?"

Damon waggled a hand back and forth. "Yes, it can act either as a power storage unit or as an enhancer. Either way, it only works if you possess magic."

At my confused look, Damon attempted to clarify, "Werewolves and vampires are part of the supernatural world, but most possess no magical abilities. Our abilities are innate. We can't push our speed, strength, or fangs into a Shadow Shard. Which is why we were tasked with guarding it. It cannot benefit werewolves directly."

I nodded slowly in understanding.

Damon continued, "Supes like mages, witches, warlocks, and so on, all possess magic. They can push magic outside of themselves to enact spells, enchantments, and rituals. They can also push their magic into storage devices like the Shard. If they do this slowly, they can build up a sizable power bank over time, with very little impact on their daily magic usage."

This all fit with what Kingsley had shared with me. Moreover, Damon's story convinced me the Shard belonged with the Pack. They could protect this dangerous item far better than I could. Also, I didn't want the heat this thing could pull down on my head. The faster I could hand it over to its rightful guardians, the better. I reached for my bag when Damon's voice interrupted me.

"That's not all, Ms. Blaze. Creating a super-powered magical battery over months is one thing. But Shadow Shards have a bloodier history." The ice in his tone froze my hands in place.

*Of course they did.*

I dropped my hands back in my lap. Damon's face looked grim in the dingy overhead lighting. "Shadow Shards have the potential to literally suck the magic from a magic user. All the magic. It is usually fatal for the victim, but not always. Sometimes, the victim wakes up to find themselves mundane. A Norm. Even though they physically survived, they have suffered another kind of death. From the tales I have heard, these poor souls do not last very long. They succumb to madness or suicide once they realize their powers are gone forever."

I shivered. Those poor bastards. To be stripped of all their powers, to be forced from the only world they had ever known and have to figure out how to survive with knowledge of the supernatural world, but none of the skills that made survival possible? It did not surprise me that some victims of the Shadow Shard ended it all, rather than facing that kind of daily hell.

Damon's voice snapped me out of my thoughts. "That's not the worst part, Cameron. The person who did that, who stripped the magic straight from the soul of a supernatural? That person would have an instantaneously charged relic. One fueled with the entirety of another being's magical potential. The Shadow Shard wouldn't just be a super-charged battery in that case. It would be a magical nuclear bomb. However, unlike a nuclear bomb, the Shadow Shard is endlessly reusable. Assuming the wielder can get his or her hands on more magic users to victimize."

I suddenly wanted this damned thing out of my possession. Now.

I scrabbled inside my bag, finding the oblong crystal. I had no more smart-aleck comments for the Alpha. I just wanted this business concluded.

I hopped down from my perch on the pallets and offered him the relic. He took a couple of steps forward to meet me and laid his hand on the other end of the crystal. I refused to let go. "Three favors, three questions," I stated, reminding him of our deal.

He bared his teeth in a smile. "*Two* favors, three questions, Ms. Blaze, and you've already used two of your questions." I grinned back. I was glad to know that Damon was a straight-shooter who honored both the letter and spirit of a deal.

I nodded in agreement. I let go of my end of the relic and said, "Welcome to New Orleans."

Damon handed the relic to Andrei, who stepped up to take the magical artifact carefully from his father. The Alpha extended his hand to me to shake. "Glad to be part of the neighborhood."

Just as we exchanged grips of welcome and good will, things went from fine to frantic in the blink of an eye.

Andrei took a step forward, holding the crystal his father had given him carefully in both hands. He had forgotten that his hamstring wasn't fully mended yet. His foot landed on a broken piece of a wooden pallet and his injured leg gave out on the teenager, sending him crashing to the floor. The crystal relic tumbled as if in slow motion through the air.

Andrei flailed to catch it, but he only batted impotently at the relic as he fell. One hand knocked the crystal down to the floor in front of him. We all watched in horror as the ancient artifact crashed to the cement floor of the warehouse and rolled to a stop.

The relic hadn't broken. I raised my eyes to see horror melt to relief on the faces of the four werewolves.

A sixth sense drew my eyes back to the crystal. Something had moved out of the corner of my eye. I stared at the relic intently, not realizing that I hadn't released Damon's hand yet. And then the damn thing flickered. Again.

Without consciously realizing it, I pulled Damon towards me, shoving him behind the wall of pallets at my back as my brain raced to catch up with my subconscious.

The relic had *flickered*. Relics didn't flicker. That didn't make any sense. Unless...

Unless it wasn't the actual relic at all, but something glamoured to *look* like the relic.

I gasped in horror as understanding crashed into me. Kingsley, the Fae bastard, had tricked me. He had attached a magical glamour to the fake relic, whatever it was. A damned good glamour, if even I'd missed it. When it had fallen, the glamour must have been dislodged. The spell flickered one last time and the image of the relic vanished. In its place on the warehouse floor was a pipe bomb, roughly the size and shape of the relic. The timer glowing red on the top showed seconds left until detonation.

*The crazy Fae had given me a glamoured pipe bomb?!*

And I had just been driving around with it willy-nilly, all-over New Orleans? In a flash, my mind replayed the events in the Fae Embassy like I was in a movie theatre.

Kingsley turned towards the windows. His body was hiding the relic from my view while I moved towards the study door. He could have easily switched it out for a glamoured item in that time. I cursed myself.

Kingsley had asked me what I was doing with the relic, and, like an idiot, I'd bragged! Like a noob, I'd boasted about my own brilliant plans and unintentionally giving him a rough estimation of time. I almost groaned. Then he had *fumbled* the relic. The ever-graceful Fae had dropped a near-priceless magical relic on the carpet. Why hadn't that registered on my internal paranoia-alarm? That fumble must have been a cover for setting the timer on his little surprise. At least I hadn't told him an exact meeting time. Which meant that I didn't know whether his target was just me or me and my allies, or both. It didn't matter right now. I was going to kill the Fae bastard. If I survived the next few seconds.

With Damon out of the way behind the pallets, he was as safe as I could make him, with mere seconds ticking inexorably down on the bomb. My gold eyes flickered up to meet Will's dark ones. They were full of thanks for saving his Alpha as he pulled Julius to the side, both shifting for more speed and diving for cover behind another stack of pallets. I wasn't sure that either they or Damon were safe, but at least they were further from the nucleus of the blast than I was.

Andrei. *Shit. Damn it all to hell. Andrei!*

My gaze locked on the Alpha's son. There was no way he was getting out of there in time. His hamstring was only partially healed, and he was on all fours, looking at a bomb mere feet away from his face with seconds left on the timer. Even if he wasn't recovering from a movement-impairing injury, I doubt he could have shifted and gotten clear in time.

His cornflower blue eyes locked on mine. He was scared. This over-grown pup was terrified out of his mind. There was nothing he could do to save himself, and he knew it. Resignation settled in, and his eyes glistened with tears. He bent his head as if in farewell.

*No way was I letting this kid die!*

I didn't think. I just acted.

I dove in front of Andrei, pushing him further away from the blast radius as he unleashed his wolf in a desperate attempt at escape. It was futile, and we both knew it. There was no way he was getting out of there in time. I did the only thing I could. I used my body as a shield to protect the kid, landing on top of the bomb and curling around it to contain as much of the blast as I could.

There was a moment of silence. A perfect eternity in a second. I knew that, given the chance, I would make the same decision again. He was a kid with a dad who loved him. He deserved the chance to have a life. A good life.

Who was I? A no one with no family. It seemed like a fair trade. My uncertain life for his, full of potential. I smiled, finding calm in the middle of the storm. I finally had a purpose. For the first time, I *fit* instead of struggling to find my place. I sank into the peaceful sensation.

A concussive *whoomph* rocked me to my core, and then the world flashed white.

# Chapter 40

The white faded from painful intensity to a radiant glow. A lightness buoyed me within the white. I was both there and not there. A place between. My body was no longer subject to the laws of gravity or physics. I looked down at myself, trying to understand. All I saw was shifting shadows where my body should be. I turned my hand back and forth in front of my eyes, sparks twinkling against the smoky darkness surrounding me. Wait. It wasn't all shifting shadows. There, right in front of my feet, was a brilliant flare. I floated down for a closer look.

The flare grew as I approached. It was coming from an oblong metal device. A tube! It was a tube. I poked at the metal tube. It rolled. I reeled back in surprise, unaware that I could do that. I zoomed in closer again. The metal tube had a series of ovals flashing in red on the top. The flare on the opening was now tinged with orange.

A little voice in the back of my mind was screaming. I hadn't paid attention to the voice before. I focused, bringing the female voice to the forefront of my consciousness.

FIRE! RUN! PROTECT!

I looked around, confused. Who was I supposed to protect? There! A face behind me in the smoke. As I focused on him, his features grew more distinct. A terrified young man, barely out of childhood. A protective urge swelled within me. I had to save him. I *needed* to save him. He had so much life, so much potential. I zoomed my body of ever-shifting light towards him. The closer I got, the clearer he became.

He looked so young and so scared. I brushed a lock of curling dark hair from his forehead. *Don't worry, youngling, I will protect you.*

I grabbed his arm and pulled with all my might. His body shifted fractionally, just as the tube had. Then, nothing. No matter how I pushed or pulled, I couldn't get him to budge more than a few inches.

The voice in my head was screaming still. I tried to ignore her, but she was too loud.

NO TIME!

I zoomed back towards the flare, so fast that my body left trails of golden light behind me. I looked down in fascination. The light was no longer white, but red and orange tipped with brilliant yellow.

Flame. Combustion. Fire.

I sighed, stretching my hands out towards the flare of fire. Fire was good. Fire was my birthright. Fire was branded into my bones, my soul. Fire was home.

NOT FOR HIM!

I wished the voice in my mind would stop screaming. She was giving me a headache. I looked back at the boy. Why was he so scared? Fire meant warmth, comfort, life. I looked back at the flare of flame before me, peering through the smoke for a closer look.

The metal tube was rupturing. No, no, no, no. The beautiful boy behind me would be damaged if the tube broke and the fire threw the pieces at him. He would be burned; he would be scarred.

He would die.

He must not die.

YES!

The voice stopped screaming. The cracks in the tube were getting bigger. It shouldn't be going so fast. Not here, not in the light. Panic welled inside me, threatening to overflow and consume my rational mind. What should I do? What should I do? The question played over and over in my mind, blurring into one word.

*WhatshouldIdo?*

PROTECT HIM!

I flew down and pushed at the tube with all my might. It rolled slightly; the flames shifting. Not enough. The cracks grew wider, and pieces broke off. One by one, I flew to each piece and pushed with all my might. I couldn't get any to move away. Not enough.

Inspiration struck and I called up my magic. Shadows flooded joyously into my hands, surging with unrealized potential. I extended my hands, palms first at the tube slowly disintegrating into shrapnel. My magic flowed out of my fingertips, engulfing each piece of flaming metal in a small orb of shadows. I focused my mind, willing my magic to bend to my will. The shadows hardened, condensing in on each piece and crushing it. Muscles I didn't know I had begged me to stop, to give into fatigue, but I kept at it, searching out each piece.

JUST. ONE. MORE.

I pushed again with my will, forcing the magic to stream from my fingertips. A dome of shadows flickered to life, racing down from my fingers to encase the danger. Using the magic was draining my reserves. Tears of exhaustion trickled down my cheeks, but I forced myself to keep channeling the magic, forcing the shadows to coalesce into an unbreakable dome that reached from my palms to the floor.

JUST. ONE. MORE.

I screamed in agony, shadows pouring from my fingers now, but I had to make sure every piece of metal was encased within my magical shield. I had to get every. Single. One.

That poor boy.

JUST. ONE. MORE.

I couldn't even see my hands anymore. All I saw in their place were geysers of shadow flooding over the imminent explosion. Soft darkness blanketed the fiery death. I felt my magic finally touch the cool floor. I threw myself forward, pressing down with my palms on the dome of shadows. Fire didn't scare me. It couldn't hurt me, but it could hurt my beautiful charge, the boy with the scared blue eyes. However, the shards of metal could rip us both to shreds. My magic gave out, the remaining shadows draining into the dome I held. I just hoped I'd done enough, that it would be enough to save him.

*Enough,* echoed my screaming companion. Except she was whispering now.

"Enough," I whispered back. The bomb exploded, shaking my dome of shadows and knocking me flat on my back. My head hit the hard, concrete floor and darkness took me.

# Chapter 41

My eyes fluttered open.

Wow. That was a surprise. I didn't think that would ever happen again after jumping on a bomb. Seeing the light of day again was an unlikely miracle because jumping on a pipe bomb tends to inhibit certain bodily functions. Pain lanced through my body. No doubt about it, I hadn't shuffled off this mortal coil. Not yet anyway. If I had, I wouldn't hurt this much.

I blinked, trying to focus on the bright white ceiling. It hurt. How could blinking hurt? Was there a way to exercise your eyelids to be stronger so the pain would stop? As soon as I thought of pain, my nerve endings flared up like fireworks on the Fourth of July.

The sensation of burning muscles from my quads and calves let me know they were more than slightly displeased with me. It felt like it was the day after leg day at the gym, but instead of Mike, the nice normal instructor, you had the drill sergeant from Hell who wouldn't let you quit until you did just. One. More.

*Why did that sound so familiar?*

I grunted as the muscles in my stomach, back, shoulders, chest, and biceps joined in the fun by letting me know they had a bone to pick with me as well. If my leg muscles were burning, everything else was a four-alarm fire. Except my arms below the elbow. Why couldn't I feel my hands?

I tried to sit up to look and ended up just mewling in pain as soft cotton dragged against my skin. Cotton? I thought I was wearing leather and loaded with so many knives a porcupine would've been jealous. I glanced down. A soft cotton nightie covered me from the neck downwards, disappearing under a beautifully pieced quilt. A movement in my periphery caught my attention. I convinced my neck muscles to move so my eyes could focus.

*Mama.*

Mama was sitting next to my bed knitting. She didn't even look up as she finished her row. "Good to see you are back with us, Cameron. The wolves thought they had lost you for a moment there. Of course, I knew better. You're a fighter." She winked as she slid the finished row fully onto her needle and set her woolly project to the side.

I groaned as I tried to inhale enough to verbalize my question. My ribs let me know they weren't going to expand without protest. Somehow, I gasped through the aches peppering my body. "What happened? Andrei! Is Andrei okay?"

"He is. Minor cuts and scrapes. Whatever you did saved him and the rest of the Pack. Unfortunately, you took the brunt of the explosion. You've been asleep for a few hours, child. Enough time for your supernatural healing abilities and my concoctions to pull you back from the brink. I've kept you sedated. To be honest, you should probably rest more. You need to give your body the chance to recover. Sleep is its own kind of magic when it comes to healing," Mama informed me.

If it hurt this much now, I was glad she had kept under as long as she had. I held up my hands. The movement was excruciating. Mama had bandaged my hands and arms to the elbow in white gauze, but I could see blood and pus leaking through in places.

"Mama, tell me this is better than it looks," I said.

Her eyes were stormy and sad at the same time. My heart plummeted.

"I don't know, child," she sighed, regret coloring every syllable.

That scared me. Mama always knew.

"The lacerations on your palms are deep—in some places, down to the bone. The wolves got you to me as quick as they could. We worked quickly to stitch you up and get the poultices in place, but only time will tell." Her shrug spoke volumes. This was not good.

"How bad?" I wish my voice hadn't quavered.

Her eyes filled with sorrow. "It depends on what kind of supernatural blood flows in your veins. In the best case, you'll only have a little stiffness and slight loss of dexterity." She tried for levity, "And perhaps some mild talent in weather prediction." Her attempt at humor fell flat, but I wasn't about to tell her that.

"What's the worst case, Mama?" My voice cracked at the end.

She looked away from me but didn't mince her words. "Worst case is that you'll lose most of the motion in your fingers. Your hands won't be able to grip anything again fully."

My mouth opened and closed in horror.

She leaned in and kissed my forehead. "We should have a good idea of your prognosis in a few days. For now, get what rest you can, child."

I turned my head away from her, trying to hide the hot tears scalding my cheeks. Mama touched my shoulder gently. I couldn't face her right now. She squeezed my shoulder lightly. A moment later, I heard the door open and close as she left.

Once I was alone, I let out a shaky breath. I knew injuries like this would take a Norm weeks or months to recover from, if they ever did. At least it would merely take days for a Supe to heal sufficiently for a long-term prognosis. Right now, a few days of uncertainty, of not knowing if my hands would ever heal, was an eternity away. I gave into the feeling of hopelessness sweeping over me and wept, pain wracking my body with every gasping, silent sob.

I dozed fitfully, trying to escape my painful reality by diving into the dark bliss of sleep. However, whenever the darkness took me, it wasn't bliss or silence I found. Every time, the same scene replayed behind my closed eyes. An explosion of fire and shrapnel in agonizingly slow motion.

*What was I? What kind of magic had the disintegration of my mother's charm released?*

Questions circled my head, maddeningly. What sort of supernatural blood did I have pumping through my veins that allowed me to survive jumping on top of a bomb? What about my hands? What would I do if I couldn't use my hands again?

Every time my mind turned down that path, I tried to hold back the grief. Every time I failed. The agony I felt when body-wracking sobs ripped through me was nothing compared to the torture of not knowing what the future held.

# Chapter 42

The sound of shuffling feet woke me. I looked around groggily, trying to locate the sound. Andrei stood in the middle of the room with a big white box in his hands, looking at me with a mixture of concern and teenage awkwardness. Damon shut the bedroom door as I finally blinked enough sleep away to focus clearly on the two werewolves.

Andrei approached the bed, holding out the box. "This is for you. For, you know, saving my life." He thrust it forward. Aww, the kid has gone from grabbing me in a bar to bringing me presents. Cute.

Damon came up behind him and placed a hand on his son's shoulder. "I am in your debt, Cameron Blaze. For the honor you've shown, the bravery you've lived, and the future you've saved, I thank you from the bottom of my heart."

Andrei spoke in a rush, "I don't know how you did it, but whatever it was you did, thank you." He glanced at his father and then back at me.

"I owe you a blood debt, Cameron Blaze. I am yours until I repay it, or my life is forfeit." The words sounded more than heartfelt thanks. They sounded almost ritualistic. Damon watched his son with a sense of resigned pride.

A thump echoed in my chest cavity, eerily like what had occurred when reaching my agreement with Kingsley. Like the metaphysical wind had been knocked out of me. Andrei's words distracted me from the sensation as they finally registered.

*Wow.*

A blood debt from an Alpha's son? I didn't know much about were-wolves beyond what I had experienced this week, but I guessed that non-wolves weren't often granted such a thing.

Wait. Did that mean that Andrei would be Alpha someday? Shit. What did Damon think about this? What did the Pack think? Various implications rushed through my mind. This was some heavy stuff to process.

I pushed it to the back of my mind for the moment and coughed, trying to buy myself time to formulate a response. Formal oath speaking wasn't my forte. Give me an agreement over shots in a bar or a firm handshake any day.

"Uh," *Great start, Cam.* I thought to myself. *Auspicious.*

"Thanks? I guess? Andrei, buy me a beer or something and we'll call it square. Wait, can you even buy beer legally? I don't want you going to jail over something so stupid. Tea? Can you do tea?" I was pretty sure I was rambling now. I blamed the blood loss.

Andrei looked passionate. Damon looked amused.

The older werewolf interrupted my verbal diarrhea. "Cameron, we would be honored to supply you with a beverage of your choice, at your convenience. However, you and my son are tied together until he fulfils his oath." Well, that answered that I supposed. Behind Andrei's back, Damon's eyes glittered with a warning that I could clearly read.

*Make sure that you are worth any danger you drag my son into.*

My mouth was suddenly as dry as the desert at high noon. An angry Alpha will do that to you.

Damon stepped forward, settling himself in the chair where Mama had been knitting. Steepling his fingers in an eerie imitation of the Fae Ambassador, he calmly said, "Perhaps we could save the exchange of drinks for a later date? After all, a mutual enemy sent a pipe bomb to a peaceful meeting with the presumed intention of killing one or both of us. Personally, I would like to repay the favor." Damon actually licked his canines.

I shivered. *Friendly PSA: don't piss off werewolves.*

Although he presented a refined face to the world, Damon was the Alpha of a Pack of werewolves. He looked ready to rip Aldrich's throat out. Without shifting into his wolf form. From the way he bared his teeth, I knew he would smile the entire time as his teeth sank into the Fae's flesh if he got the chance.

I tried to focus. "Okay," I said. "Let's start at the beginning. Walk me through what you saw, heard, smelled, whatever, at the warehouse. My memory gets a little fuzzy past a certain point." I held up my hands to emphasize my words.

Andrei set the box he held on to the bedside table and leaned against the wall, seemingly happy to let his father do the talking. Damon cleared his throat and laid it all out for me.

"After the Fae's glamour was dislodged, you and my wolves reacted quickly. Will and Julius shifted and found limited shelter before the blast. Your quick thinking put me out of harm's way entirely," Damon put a hand to his heart and bowed his head slightly in my direction, "For which, you have my gratitude and thanks."

I nodded, relieved that he had been unscathed by the bomb. If the bomb had hurt the Alpha of the Pack, it would have likely ignited an all-out war between Fae and the werewolves, with New Orleans as the hapless battleground. There was also the likelihood that I would've been pulled into the conflict if I survived. Or been blamed for the explosion, especially if I was blown to smithereens. Dead Camerons make great scapegoats.

Damon continued, "None of us got a close look at what happened next. The best that we can piece together is that you jumped on the bomb. Shadows engulfed you and Andrei. None of us could see through it from where we were in the warehouse. Not even Andrei, even though he was the closest." The teen wolf nodded his head, confirming his father's words.

"Seconds later, the bomb exploded. Somehow, the explosion was contained. When the shadows cleared, you were curled around Andrei, with your back to the bomb. Neither of you suffered any burns from the blast. The same can't be said for your clothing, unfortunately." His blue eyes flickered to the remains of my leather coat draped on a chair across the room.

"Damn. It took me ages to find a leather coat I liked," I muttered angrily.

"Indeed. One can empathize," the Alpha intoned drily. Andrei's mouth twitched as he tried to hold back a smile.

"After the explosion, we thought you were both dead, blown to pieces. However, we discovered both you and Andrei unconscious, presumably from the blast. The only visible injury to either of you was the extensive damage to your hands, Ms. Blaze. Once we saw you were alive, we rushed you both here." Damon summed up the story succinctly.

I raised an eyebrow. "Why here and not the hospital? Or the local coven?" The local witches took care of most of the healing needs of the Supernatural community of New Orleans. I knew they were excellent healers from experience. I was good at my work, but my jobs had an alarming tendency of not always going to plan.

"Mama has a reputation," Damon said with a gentle smile.

That she did. Her reputation as a healer spread far outside New Orleans. It didn't surprise me that the werewolves knew of her.

"Perhaps you can inform us how you and my son walked away from the epicenter of a bomb with, all things considered, relatively minor injuries?" The Alpha was probing carefully, trying to figure out what kind of creature had saved his son. What kind of creature his son was now tied to by a blood debt.

I looked at the bandages on my hands. He was right. The damage to my hands was bad enough to have Mama worried, but I should have been dead. Blown to itty bitty Cameron chunks.

I rolled my shoulders, trying to feel for the pain or tightness of skin that would indicate recent burns from the explosion. Nothing. No excruciating pain greeted my movement. My back was completely unharmed. In fact, there was no more pain anywhere. Damn. I didn't know if it was Mama's healing or my magic or a combination thereof, but I knew luck didn't even begin to cover it.

I met Damon's eyes. "I honestly don't know how either of us survived or how my hands got ripped to shreds."

His eyes hardened fractionally. He must have assumed that I was hiding my powers from him. I rushed to explain, "I don't know how much Mama told you about me..."

"Nothing," he interrupted.

Good. I shouldn't have worried. Mama's dedication to privacy was far superior to anyone else I'd ever known.

"Right. Well, I have a lot of questions of my own concerning my history and my powers. I have the general supernatural gifts, but the rest is a mystery." I purposely kept my answers vague. Damon could prove to be a powerful ally in the future, but until I got to know him better, I was playing my cards close to my chest.

Damon rubbed his hands together and let out a sigh. "Well, I guess you can add being fire resistant to your list of mysterious powers," he said.

My phone rang before I could formulate an answer. Andrei grabbed it off the nightstand and held the screen up for me to see the caller ID. Logan Wilder. Interesting.

"Umm, would you mind?" I asked, raising my hands. I wasn't confident I could operate the touch screen right now. Andrei slid the accept button over and moved to tuck it between my ear and shoulder.

"Hi you, what's up?" I said, trying to sound breezy. I didn't know how well werewolves could hear, but I didn't want to give anything away beyond what was absolutely necessary.

Logan picked up on my abnormal greeting. "Are you alone?" he asked at once.

"Not precisely." I knew he would couch his words now to ensure that sensitive information remained that way.

"Okay, look Cameron, I know something went sideways with the last job. I am fielding panicked calls from the Embassy. Lady Letitia is upset and wants to talk to you. Now. When can you get yourself over there?" Logan sounded annoyed that he had to deal with complications I had caused. Little did he know.

So, Letitia wanted to talk to me at the Fae Embassy? wondered what she knew. Perhaps this was Kingsley's convoluted way of finishing me off? I quickly ran through my options. I could sit here in bed and learn nothing new about why Kingsley had tried to kill me. Or I could go confront the Fae bastard.

I grinned into the phone as I spoke. "Tell her I'm on my way. And I'm bringing some friends."

I raised my head, dropping the phone into my lap as Logan clicked off. I examined the werewolves. "How do you guys feel about playing bodyguards as I go to confront our little bomb-maker?"

Andrei growled, and Damon licked his lips hungrily.

# Chapter 43

Will drove right up to the gates of the Fae Embassy and leaned on the SUV's horn, long and hard. When the video intercom sprang to life with the face of an angry Fae security guard, Will flipped him the bird. The security guard started shouting about disrespect. Will just leaned on the horn again, drowning out the Fae guard's protests until he threw his hands up angrily and stopped talking.

When Will released his pressure on the horn, I heard Letitia's voice shrilling over the intercom to let us in *immediately.* If it wouldn't have hurt so damn much, I would have rubbed my bandaged hands together in glee. I enjoyed ruffling the prissy Fae's feathers. Life is short. You've got to enjoy the small things where you can.

The gates swung wide and Will drove us right up to the door of the Embassy. He let out another obnoxious, unnecessary blast on the horn. Letitia was standing at the door in a lovely pastel pink pantsuit, waiting for our arrival and flanked by a pair of Fae guards. She literally jumped at the sound of the horn and almost tripped on her matching stilettos. I smiled. It was petty, but it soothed my bitchy itch after a shitty day. I decided I could really get on board with doing things the werewolf way.

Andrei jumped out of the back and opened my door for me. Damon, Julius, and Will stepped out, oozing vicious charm. The four werewolves flanked me as I stared up at Letitia.

She cleared her throat nervously. "Welcome to the Fae Em..."

"What do you want?" I interrupted her, pitching my voice loudly enough to carry to anyone close by.

"I, umm, I would like..." she stumbled over her words in an uncharacteristic display of uncertainty.

"Well, I would like to know why your *ambassador* tried to blow us all up. Are the Fae into assassinations now?" I rudely interrupted her again. Julius emphasized my point by emitting a rumbling growl loud enough to shake the foundations of Hell. Letitia flinched.

*Never play domination games with a werewolf, little Faeling.* My internal voice let out a dark cackle, and I had to fight to keep a cruel smile from twisting my lips.

"Where is your am-bomb-sador, anyway?" I craned my neck, trying to catch a peek inside. "Kingsley!" I shouted, "Stop hiding behind your little niece's skirts. I've got some big bad wolves here and they are ready to blow your house down if you don't show your cowardly face. NOW!"

Letitia looked ready to pee her pantsuit. "He's not here, Cameron. That's what I wanted to discuss with you," she murmured, attempting to deescalate the situation.

I glared up at her. "What makes you think I am stupid enough to come inside? A Fae has already tried to kill us once today." This time, all four wolves behind me growled. The unison rumble made the pebbles at my feet dance and the Fae guards reach for weapons. Oh, werewolf bodyguards were the *best*.

Letitia took a purposeful step forward at the sound, putting herself between her people and the wolves. "I, Lady Letitia, acting ambassador of the Fae kingdoms, do invite Cameron Blaze and company into our Embassy as honored guests with no expectation of obligation or return. They are entitled to all the protections the Fae courts command. Any who harms a guest under our guestright shall be executed. Immediately." She raised an eyebrow at me, obviously recovering some of her spine as she recited the formal invitation.

I nodded thoughtfully as I sifted through her words. If Letitia was acting Ambassador, that must mean Kingsley was missing. Interesting. The offer of guestright was also an interesting tactic for Letitia to take, namely because it was a fairly archaic practice. Essentially, we couldn't be harmed without deadly consequences. However, if I accepted guestright on behalf of our party, we also couldn't harm any Fae until we concluded the meeting. I shot a side-long look at Damon. He nodded tightly at me without taking his eyes off Letitia. So, this was my party then. The Alpha was ceding decision-making rights for me.

"We accept your kind offer, Lady Letitia. However, if your people attack us in any manner, we will respond with deadly force," I stated, wanting our position clearly articulated.

"Naturally." She stepped back and gestured toward the house with an inviting wave of her arm. "Please be welcome."

Letitia turned her back on us, preceding us into the grand mansion. My werewolf bodyguards formed up behind me as we followed her into the Embassy, into the home of the man who had recently tried to kill us all. A Fae security team brought up the rear of the procession but maintained a respectful distance from the seething wolves.

Letitia led us through the Embassy to the manicured garden behind the mansion. The staccato tap of her stilettos echoed through the massive manor, making it sound as eerie and empty as it looked. Walking through the Embassy with the security detail ghosting along behind us made my neck itch. I didn't like being followed by armed guards, even with the assurance of guestright.

Lady Letitia led us outside and through a beautifully curated flower garden. A table set with a china tea service and delicately decorated cakes sat in the middle of the garden. We had come ready to rip out throats. Letitia wanted to have a frickin' tea party.

Letitia turned to the Fae security team following us. "That will be all, gentlemen," she said, raising a hand in dismissal. They hesitated, not liking the fact that they were leaving Letitia alone with four wolves and a pissed-off me.

Her voice crackled with ice. "They are here under guestright. They know the consequences that an unprovoked attack will bring down on them. Besides, a representative of the Fae has done them a grievous injustice. The least we can do is to demonstrate a show of good faith." Ah, there was the icy bitch-queen I knew. Letitia had the potential to be an effective leader given some time and experience.

The guards retreated, looking suitably chastised. Letitia waved her manicured fingertips towards the chairs encircling the beautiful garden tea party. When none of us moved, she sighed dramatically and sank into one at random, raising an eyebrow at me. I waited a beat to let her know that she wasn't the boss of me and then plopped in the one across from her.

Damon elegantly took the chair on my right and Andrei settled in on my left. Will pointedly shifted his chair closer to his Alpha and further from Letitia with an audible sniff, like a putrid scent had just offended his olfactory system. Julius did the opposite, and nearly broke the chair as he crowded into Letitia's space. I allowed the bitchy grin I had been hiding to curl over my lips at her obvious discomfort.

"What do you..." I started, belligerently.

Letitia held up one finger and shot me a beseeching look. "Indulge me for a moment more. Please, Cameron."

My mouth snapped shut at her plea. Silently, Letitia reached across the table to serve us all steaming cups of tea. When she was done pouring, she indicated we should help ourselves to the gorgeous treats by filling her plate to an absurd degree. We followed her lead in silence, but none of us ate anything.

"There," I heard her murmur to herself, "That should be enough."

Letitia's fingers flew through the air, hidden from the mansion behind the elegant tea service, but easily apparent to the werewolves and me. A pressure built on my ears, like I was deep underwater and needed to equalize. I yawned, popping them.

Letitia turned to me. "I have woven a glamour to keep our conversation private. My people have a nasty habit of eavesdropping. I would prefer to keep this between us, if you don't mind."

Andrei rocked back in his chair, poking at the air around the table. "Kind of like a cone of silence?"

"Yes. Stop that!" Letitia hissed at him. The young wolf settled his chair back on to all four legs, not looking the least bit apologetic.

I nodded, somewhat surprised that she had the power to create and maintain a glamour strong enough to encompass all of us and keep out any eavesdropping Fae. She was more powerful than she had let on. It made me wonder if the party-girl persona was really Letitia or if it was some sort of false face.

Letitia distracted me when she leaned forward urgently and said, "Cameron, what have you done with my uncle?"

# Chapter 44

My eyebrows shot skyward, taking up residence in my hairline. "Good Lord! What is wrong with you, Letitia? He's the one who tried to kill us!" I was shaking in barely restrained fury as I tried to keep my voice low. I didn't want to test the bounds of her glamour by shouting.

Letitia shook her head. "Cameron, you must know what the situation is here. You had a meeting with my uncle, the ambassador to Fae. He is one of the most powerful Fae in this realm. Perhaps *the* most powerful Fae in this realm. Several members of the Fae delegation witnessed you leaving the property in a rush. There has been no trace of my uncle since your meeting with him."

My blood ran cold. Suddenly I was extremely grateful that Letitia had offered us guestright. "What are they saying, Letitia?" I asked, trying to keep my face impassive.

"Most people here think that you kidnapped him somehow. That's the best-case scenario. No one knows precisely how you might have accomplished such a feat within our wards, but then again, no one knows precisely what you are or what you are capable of." Letitia's words came out in a rush, but she kept her voice and eyes lowered to prevent provoking the wolves.

"He tried to kill us! With a pipe bomb! Today! He did *this* to me!" I waved my bandaged hands at her as I whisper-shouted, not sure of how well her spell contained sound.

Damon laid a calming hand on my bicep, interrupting my diatribe smoothly. "Lady Letitia, I believe that Ms. Blaze is trying to say that if she had kidnapped Mr. Kingsley, why would she return to the scene of her supposed crime? Especially after he sent a glamoured bomb to a meeting with my Pack without her knowledge? If he were in her power, she would have no need to return. In fact, it would be the height of foolishness to do so." His eyes gleamed with sophisticated savagery.

Letitia nodded, a contemplative look on her face as she digested Damon's logical points. I took a calming breath, suddenly thankful for the Alpha's calm presence and rational experience at this meeting.

Damon continued, "Regardless, neither Ms. Blaze nor my Pack would've come here if we had done Mr. Kingsley in. What would be the point?"

I could see the werewolf's cool words penetrate Letitia's fear for her uncle. She drew in a deep breath, apparently having come to a resolution.

"Cameron," her beautiful blue eyes swung to me. "I know you have no reason to trust me. However, as acting ambassador to Fae, I would consider it a kindness if you would tell me of your dealings with my uncle. I could likely uncover them myself, but I fear that time is not on our side. In return for your trust, I will repay you with a small favor of your choosing."

I contemplated briefly. There was nothing in my dealings with Kingsley that needed to be kept private. There was no point in withholding information. Especially if I was getting an undisclosed favor out of the agreement.

"Deal," I said. A thump resonated in my chest. It was becoming familiar sensation whenever I struck a bargain with someone. Like someone had directed a concussive blast directly at my soul. I wondered if it was something that happened to all Supernaturals or if it was unique to me. I needed to ask around about it discreetly. Something to consider later.

I recounted the pertinent details of the past few days for Letitia and the werewolves. When I finished my recitation, Letitia let out a long sigh and shook her head. "I knew this was serious, but I didn't realize just how dangerous the situation had become," she muttered.

I leaned forward. "What are you talking about, Letitia?"

"Come. I have something that you all have to see. Immediately," she said, rising to her feet so suddenly that she upset her untouched cup of tea, sending it crashing to the ground.

Letitia led us through the Embassy to what looked like a private office. It was decorated in the same dark wood and rich furnishings as the sitting room where I had met Kingsley. The Fae guards that attempted to follow us into the office were surprised when Lady Letitia shut the door firmly in their faces. It surprised me when she turned the key in the lock, then wedged a heavy chair under the door handle, ensuring our privacy.

Letitia marched across the room and rummaged in the drawers of the desk. It drew my attention towards Kingsley's workspace. Assuming no cleaners had been in, he was a tidy man. Fastidiously so. Every item on his desk was neatly in its place. He even had a miniature of the portrait that I had seen leaning against the wall of the foyer on my first visit: A tiny Kingsley and a gorgeous lady Fae smiled adoringly down at a beautiful blonde Fae child. I picked up the miniature, studying it.

"Letitia, who is this?" I asked, holding it up for her.

She glanced at the picture before returning to her search of the desk drawer. "That is Uncle Aldrich, his wife, the Lady Carina, and their daughter, Blythe." She then held up a ring of large wooden keys in triumph.

I traced a finger over the tiny faces. They all looked so happy. A perfect, beautiful family moment preserved in the brush strokes. A pang of jealousy buried its way through the core of my soul. I didn't have any memories of my family, beautiful or otherwise.

An inconsistency niggled at me, causing me to ask, "Why was Lady Carina removed from the painting in the other room, but not from this one?"

Letitia shrugged as she moved across the room towards the bookcases. "Uncle Aldrich said it was too painful to have a daily reminder of his wife. He asked that the portrait in the sitting room be re-done with just Blythe and himself. The original was to be shipped back to his estate in Fae. I didn't know he kept a copy of the original here."

"Seems strange that he would remove her from one, but not the other," I mused.

Damon spoke over me, "What happened to the Lady Carina, if I may ask?"

Letitia turned to face us, tears suddenly glittering in her eyes. "My aunt was killed by a drunk driver almost a year ago. There were those in the Spring Court that feared her death broke something in my uncle. He hasn't been himself since. He has only been back to Fae a handful of times to visit Blythe in the past year. It was finally decided that someone needed to make sure that he wasn't a danger to himself or others."

"You volunteered? Weren't you missing out on all your Fae parties?" I asked, incredulity coloring my tone.

Letitia's icy blue eyes bore into me. "Uncle Aldrich sent all the others home. I'm sure that he only tolerated my presence because I'm family," she stated coldly. I nodded slowly, unsure of what to say and unwilling to add to her pain. Losing a family member was a unique form of daily torture. I knew that firsthand.

Letitia turned back to the wall and lifted a painting off its hook, revealing a hidden lock in the wall. She selected a wooden key from the ring and inserted it into the lock. When she turned it, a panel of the wall swung inward.

"There is value in distraction, sleight of hand," she waved her hands holding the keys and they seemed to disappear, "or wearing a false face."

Letitia's countenance changed from serious and composed to lively and bubbly in an instant. She jumped up and down a little, clapping her hands in front of her. Her voice was higher and a little ditzy-sounding as she said, "I just *love* a secret passageway!" She dropped the sorority girl cheerleader act so quickly that it jarred me. If she'd been playing the part well enough to fool Kingsley for the duration of her stay at the Embassy, she was more capable than I'd given her credit for.

Letitia's face then took on a carefully composed blank expression that gave nothing away. There was no hint of either the bubbly party girl or the serious woman. Spooky. I'd underestimated her. It wouldn't happen again.

"One makes use of the tools one is given when gathering information. It is helpful when no one thinks you are watching. Or particularly capable." Letitia allowed a small smile to break through her impassive mask. I nodded, impressed.

Letitia turned towards the opening in the wall. "My uncle took great pains to keep this place a secret. I think that what is down here will greatly interest you."

# Chapter 45

Letitia walked into the dark passageway hidden in her uncle's study. I looked at Damon, who shrugged. We had come this far. Might as well see why Letitia had summoned us to the Fae Embassy. The dim light reflecting off the stone walls from the study provided enough of a glow for me to see easily enough in the darkness. Andrei grabbed his phone and flicked on the flashlight app, providing extra illumination as we followed Letitia into the dark tunnel.

We walked further than I thought was possible, given the dimensions of the house. I wasn't sure if Mama's herbs were messing with my head or if we had entered some funky Fae pocket dimension or something. However, when Letitia finally stopped in front of a heavy oak door, I had a faint sheen of sweat on my forehead from the walk.

Letitia paused in front of the door, turning to us. "I don't know what my uncle was up to, but whatever it was scares me." She didn't elaborate further, just opened the door and led us into the room.

The dark, dank cellar stank of mold and decay. The smell of it hit us like a physical blow a moment after she opened the door. Letitia flipped a switch near the door and a couple of flickering bulbs did what they could to beat back the darkness. As soon as the lights blinked on, I wished they hadn't.

There were cages stacked against every inch of wall of the entire cellar. Every single one was filled with dead, rotting animals.

I turned my face away in horror, trying to breathe through my mouth to lessen the stench of decaying flesh. As I did, I saw the wolves weren't faring much better than me. The reek of rot was overwhelming, especially if you had a sensitive nose. I took a deep breath and forced myself to look back into the room of death.

Kingsley had set up an elaborate ritual space. There were strange symbols painted all over the floor in various shades of orange and red. I was pretty sure from the shade of red that it wasn't blood. Old blood turned a nasty brownish-reddish-black. However, I wasn't willing to test that hypothesis. I moved carefully so as not to disturb any items or step on the dried paint. You never knew what kind of residual magic might linger in a ritual space this elaborate. The werewolves followed me into the room. Letitia watched us all from the door. I didn't blame her. I wouldn't want to walk through this carnage more than once, either.

I forced myself to focus on the dead animals in my first circuit of the room. Kingsley had stacked the cages on top of each other up to head height. Every cage had two animals of the same species in it. The cages just to the right of the door held squirrels, rabbits, rats, and chickens. Beyond these were larger cages holding goats and sheep.

Then things got a bit more exotic. There were a variety of breeds of dogs and cats, peacocks, even a pair of monkeys. It was hard to tell because of the decomposition of some the animals, but it looked like one of every pair had a gaping chest wound. The other looked like it had its throat neatly cut. I shivered. Kingsley must have been at this for months to have such a wide range of dead animals in varying states of decay.

When I reached the doorway, I started a second circuit of the room. I put my back to the murder cages and focused on the interior of the room. There were two concentric circles on the floor divided by four lines into eight equal sections. Painted in each section of the two circles were a variety of symbols. I was no tweed-wearing professor of iconography or symbology, but I was certain that the pictures came from different cultures. I didn't know what any of the symbols meant, though. In the middle of the circles, at the bullseye formed by the bisecting lines, was a large, raised dais stained in blood. Kingsley had painted unique symbols on each corner of the stained makeshift altar. I squinted, trying to make out the crude drawings without stepping on the ritualistic painting. It gave me the heebie-jeebies.

"What are those things?" I pointed vaguely at the drawings. "I think I see a sphinx at the bottom here. Maybe some kind of dog too, but it has a human body. A werewolf maybe?"

"That's a bird in the upper corner there," Damon said, pointing from across the room.

"I think that's a circle across from the bird," Andrei chipped in.

Will corrected him. "No, it's a snake eating itself. Like that symbol in *The NeverEnding Story*? Except instead of two snakes, there is only one."

Letitia spoke from the doorway. "At the top is a triskele. The Celtic triple spiral. Fae use it to symbolize infinity."

I took a deep breath, trying to center myself. It was a mistake. The smell of the rotting corpses hit the back of my throat, making me gag.

"Letitia, is there anywhere we could talk that isn't, you know, *here*?" I asked, trying to fight down the bile my roiling stomach was threatening to heave up my esophagus.

She nodded. "Let's go back to my uncle's study. We can talk there."

The wolves murmured agreement and hurried from the room.

I fumbled my phone in my back pocket and took a couple of photos of the ritual set-up. It was hard to manage with the bandages, but I wiggled them down far enough that I could manipulate the phone's camera. I moved around the room, snapping several pictures of the symbols painted on the floor and altar from different angles. I wanted to show Ben. The necromancer might have some insights into the symbols painted in this room of death.

Finally, I turned away, leaving the disturbing scene behind. As Letitia shut off the lights and relocked the door, I murmured a prayer for the departed under my breath to any gods who would listen. No creature should end its existence locked in a cage, having its life stolen to fuel a spell and then left to rot.

# Chapter 46

The plush furnishings of Kingsley's office seemed overly opulent after the hidden den of decomposition and death. The werewolves pulled the chairs into a rough circle while Letitia poured us all a whisky from her uncle's liquor cabinet. Although it wasn't my drink of choice and I had to hold it awkwardly between my bandaged hands, I was happy to have the liquid fortitude. By the way the wolves chugged back the generous pours, I was confident I wasn't alone in that sentiment.

We sat in silence for a minute or two, trying to process what we'd seen in the murder dungeon.

Finally, I sighed, looking around the circle. "I don't know about you all, but I'm confused as hell. I have more questions than answers. What was *that?*" I jerked a bandaged mitt towards the hidden door and the unsettling ritual space. "How long has he been doing this? And more to the point, why? What is the endgame here?"

Damon cleared his throat and raised a finger. I nodded in his direction. "Perhaps we should pool what we know. We each might hold a piece to this puzzle. Perhaps it is a piece that we are unaware we even possess, but by sharing our knowledge, a picture may become clear?"

His proposal was sound. I nodded slowly. "Okay, sounds good," I said. "Lady Letitia, do you have any additional information that could help us understand your uncle's creepy lair of death?"

She grimaced, shaking her head slowly. "I moved to the Embassy about three months ago. Ever since I moved in, he has been different.

The man I remember from my childhood was full of laughter and joy. Recently, Uncle Aldrich seemed to alternate between sadness and intensity. He was laser focused on his work. I thought it was his method for dealing with his grief at my aunt's passing. It seemed like he'd lock himself away in here for hours. I thought he was studying or making deals or whatever it is ambassadors do. When I discovered the hidden passageway, I realized he was spending his time…differently." She paused, licking her lips nervously. "Beyond that, I know little else."

I nodded, trying to digest the information. It wasn't much. I wish she'd spent more time on her assignment of watching her uncle rather than shimmying the night away in barely-there dresses. I sighed. Wishing wouldn't change the past.

Damon spoke next. "I'm not sure how this connects with what we just witnessed, but a Shadow Shard was stolen from my Pack's protection recently. Do you know what a Shadow Shard is, Lady Letitia?"

At her nod, he continued. "The theft brought my Pack to New Orleans. We tracked the Shard here. We lost the trail soon after arriving in Louisiana and I ordered the Pack to track down any lead, no matter how tenuous, which led us to Ms. Blaze here. She kept popping up in all the wrong places. It seemed too coincidental to ignore, so I ordered my men to keep an eye on her."

I spoke up then. "Kingsley hired me to find the relic, this Shadow Shard. He didn't tell me why he needed it, just that it acted like a super-charged magical battery or something. He gave me a deadline, which expires at midnight tonight." I glanced at the clock on the wall. "Which is in just a few hours."

Letitia asked, "Is that it?"

I realized no one had likely told her of the relic-slash-bomb that Aldrich had passed to me. I quickly recapped the events leading up to the explosion. Damon corroborated my story, filling in a few details I left out that he thought pertinent.

When he finished, silence crowded into the room. I could almost hear the gears turning in everyone's heads as they struggled to find connections to link everything together.

I suddenly raised my head as a memory struck me. "We forgot about the ghosts! My necromancer friend, Ben, told me that ghosts were disappearing."

Andrei rolled his eyes at me. "Isn't that kind of their schtick?" he asked. "I feel like that's in the job description, right next to hanging out in graveyards and shouting 'Boo!' at people walking by."

"Yeah, I said the same thing, but according to Ben, they are completely disappearing. Like, nobody can find them. Not other ghosts, not necromancers. Nothing. Gone without a trace. And then you showed me those pictures," I said to Damon.

Damon shook his head, eyes squinting thoughtfully. "Interesting. Kingsley is harvesting ghosts, presumably to power his ritual."

I spoke up again. "Stick with me here for a second. We know Kingsley killed animals in his murder-lair. From the rate of decay of the remains, it looks like he started with small animals and progressed. He obviously didn't get the result he wanted from the little ones and worked his way up. If he had gotten what he wanted, he would have stopped. No more corpses. Right?"

Grudging nods greeted me. I continued, working my way towards an answer that made sense. "We know he is on a deadline. Whatever he wants to do, he needs to get it done by midnight tonight. So, maybe he starts looking for something to amp up the power of his ritual. He hears that there is a Shadow Shard in play on the black market or maybe he hires the thief to steal it from the Pack. Maybe he starts collecting ghosts to use as a power source once he finds the Shard to fuel his spell, but it's lost. Until I hand it over to him."

*Like an idiot.* I didn't say that last bit, but my subconscious was playing it on repeat. The bitch.

"When I let it slip that I was meeting the wolves to give the Shard back, Kingsley saw a way to take some of the heat off. An explosion that killed any of the Pack or me would have distracted everyone until after he completed his—well, whatever he's doing." I shrugged at the lame finish. It sounded far-fetched even to me.

Damon didn't look convinced. Neither did Letitia. Will and Julius kept their emotions masked and a careful eye on their Alpha. Only Andrei nodded along, following my conjectures.

The Alpha cleared his throat, not swayed by my theory. "That doesn't tell us where Kingsley is now or what he is planning. I think you are correct on one point. Whatever he is doing, it is happening at midnight tonight. Which means we need to find him immediately."

Nods greeted Damon's statement. I bobbed my head along with the rest of them, swayed by the Alpha's ability to command a tense situation.

"Here is what I propose," Damon continued. "My Pack will break off into teams of two to be safe. We try to trace Ambassador Kingsley and his magical residue. Fae tend to have a very..." he paused delicately, "distinctive scent." Will and Julius nodded emphatically.

He turned to Letitia. "If the Lady Letitia would allow it, my wolves could pick up the Ambassador's scent here and track him down. If he's attempting this ritual tonight, he'd need to find a secluded place that would allow him the time and space to reconstruct what we witnessed below."

Letitia agreed. "That seems sensible. I will send along some men to support your endeavors. The more people we have looking, the more territory we can cover."

Damon didn't look pleased at the thought of working with Fae. "It may be best if you remain here, my Lady, in case your uncle returns to carry out his ritual in the space he has already prepared. If he returns, detain him until we arrive. You'll need your men here to support you. From what I've witnessed, Kingsley isn't to be trifled with."

Letitia nodded graciously, seeing the wisdom in his directions. She also looked mildly relieved. Convincing the Fae guards to cooperate with the werewolves would have been an arduous task.

I was impressed. Damon was like a general, maneuvering troops on a battlefield quickly and efficiently.

I spoke up, "What about me? Kingsley pulled me into this. I want to see it out."

Damon eyed my hands pointedly, silently reminding everyone that I was worse than useless in a fight. Currently, I wasn't an asset or able to pull my weight. I was a liability. I blushed, having forgotten my injuries.

"I think it would be best if you returned to Mama Atli's house." Damon raised a hand as I started to protest. "You said that the necromancer might have more knowledge of the symbols or the ritual set-up. Any information would be helpful. If he can deduce the goal of this ritual, that may give us a probable location. Even if he can share a likely ingredient or important situational element, it might narrow down the search area." I grimaced. I could see the Alpha's logic, but I didn't like being benched.

Twenty minutes later, I was standing outside Mama's house, staring unhappily at the taillights of the Pack's SUV. I kicked at a loose stone on the curb. I hated feeling inconsequential, shoved to the side, or worse, unable to help. But Damon's plan was as solid as we could make it. He'd dispatched everyone, given their unique strengths and abilities. I was no good in a fight with my hands torn up the way they were. According to Mama, I wouldn't be in fighting shape before this whole thing played out. As much as I hated to admit it, the best I could offer was being a glorified researcher. Perhaps I could uncover some useful information. I sighed and headed inside, hoping that I could discover something that would help us find a needle in a haystack. Or a Fae in New Orleans. Whatever.

# Chapter 47

Mama greeted me at the door, pulling me inside. Her eyes, normally so full of good humor, were deadly serious.

"Cameron, we need to talk. Now." Mama grabbed my arm above the bandages and hurried me through to the kitchen. Ben waited for us, drumming his fingers on the heavy kitchen table. He leapt to his feet as we entered, pulling out a chair for me.

Mama settled herself across from me. "Child, we need to talk about the company you've been keeping."

I groaned, "I know, I know. Kingsley's not a good guy. I never should've taken the job. I get it. But that's why I'm here. I need help." I fumbled my phone out of my pocket to show them the pictures as I filled them in on what we had discovered in the Fae Ambassador's bloody hidey-hole.

"I don't recognize these painted symbols or what they do. Anything you can tell me would be helpful. Especially if it helps us narrow down the options for a new ritual site. Even better if you can pinpoint him for me." I shrugged, feeling helpless. I hated it.

Ben started flicking through the pictures on the phone. He looked up at me with sudden enthusiasm. "I've never seen this complexity or combinations of symbols before. This is excitin'!"

I looked at him in horror. "Didn't you hear a word I just said, Ben?"

"No, no, no. I didn't mean excitin' like it's good. It's just been a long time since I seen somethin' this complex. This interestin'. I mean, who would've thought to..." Ben was rambling now, and I couldn't help but stare at him. He wasn't making much sense to me. I snuck a look at Mama. She looked confused too.

Ben suddenly jumped to his feet. "I'll be right back! I need to check on a couple of symbols in my library. If I get these wrong, I'll be about as useful as a screen door on a submarine." With that, his lanky legs propelled him from the room, his wild white head bent over the eerie images displayed on my phone.

Mama and I watched in surprise as Ben flew out of the kitchen and pounded up the stairs. Mama recovered her wits first and turned to me with a grim expression creasing her normally cheerful face.

"Child, you've been keeping mighty poor company," Mama said sternly.

"I know," I groaned, dropping my head to my hands, "Kingsley..."

Mama's tone was deadly serious when she interrupted me, "Not the Fae, although he also proves my point. No, child, I'm talking about the demon."

I raised my head to stare at her incredulously, "What the what now?"

"The *demon*." Mama enunciated the words like she thought I was suffering hearing loss from the bomb. "You remember? The one you asked me to look into?"

I shook my head slowly as my mind raced back over the events of the last few days. I couldn't make her words fit into my memories. The only person I'd asked her to investigate was...

"Meridiana?" I squeaked. "That sexy redhead is an actual, honest-to-goodness demon ?"

"Well, demoness if you want to be persnickety," Mama corrected. "From the demons I've met, they appreciate when you acknowledge the nuances."

I took a deep breath, closing my eyes and trying to find some calm as her words rocked my world. "Mama, let me get this straight. You're telling me that demons are real?"

Mama looked at me like I was touched in the head. "Of course, child. You accept that werewolves, Fae, and vampires exist without question. Witches have healed you. You are aware Ben is a necromancer and

Goliath is his reanimated familiar. Your best friend is a leprechaun. The existence of demons throws you?"

"Well, sure," I grumbled, "When you put it like that..."

Mama shook her head slowly. She leaned her arms on the table and spoke urgently, "Cameron, please pay attention. I'll only say this once. All the gods, all the myths, all the stories. They're all real. The trappings of the stories may have been embellished or forgotten over time, but everything, at its essence, is real. Gods, goddesses, angels, demons, supernatural creatures of all kinds. They. Are. All. Real."

My world shattered and rebuilt itself as Mama spoke. I'd assumed that Supernaturals were at the top of the food chain. Even though I didn't know who or what I was, I joined the rest of the supernatural world in looking down our collective noses at the poor, unenlightened Norms. Being told that there were entities a step or five above me who viewed me in the same way I looked at Norms rocked my world. Mama had just served up a big ol' slice of humble pie topped with an ego-reduction sauce made special just for me. Gulp.

"Tell me what you know. Please, Mama. I need to know everything. I don't want any more surprises tonight." The earnestness in my voice surprised me. Never in a million years did I think I'd be begging for more information about demons. Mostly because I viewed demons as the Bible's boogeymen to scare non-believers onto the straight and narrow path. Appreciating the irony, I acknowledged I was now a believer. In demons, at least. But I wasn't on the straight and narrow. More like the rocky and occasionally drunken.

Mama cleared her throat before starting. "The name confused me when you first asked me to do some research into your new, shall we say, *friend*? I thought you said Mary-Diana. As in two words, a hyphenated name. When that name returned nothing, I started getting creative with the spelling. Eventually, I used Siri."

"No way!" Incredulity bubbled out, causing me to interrupt Mama's story.

"Way," she said.

I briefly wondered if she knew she had quoted the classic line from *Wayne's World.* Demons. Right. More important things.

Mama continued, not noticing that I'd taken a slight mental detour. "When I spoke the name along with some other keywords, it took me to a webpage all about Meridiana, the demoness who corrupted a Pope. From there, I could conduct my own, more esoteric research into your demoness."

I bit my tongue to keep from interrupting her again. But really? My newest drinking buddy was a demon? Sorry, *demoness?* It made me question why that tequila had been so delicious. The devil's drink indeed.

"Meridiana appears to be a type of succubus," Mama explained. "A succubus is a type of demon, usually female, who uses her charms to divert her victims from life's noble purposes. Most succubi live in the shadows, shrouded in anonymity even as their victims stumble and fall from positions of power or wealth. Meridiana broke with tradition. She seduced a young up-and-coming cardinal in the late tenth century. He fell in love with her and kept her by his side as he progressed through the ranks of the Catholic Church. Eventually, he became Pope Sylvester II. Meridiana stayed by his side as his unofficial consort and confidant for the duration of his papacy. When he fell ill, Pope Sylvester denounced her on his deathbed."

My eyes had grown wide, engrossed in the morbid tale. "But how did they know she was a demon?"

Mama shrugged. "Supposition? I assume they thought her a witch. Witches can be burned, but demons can't. It would be ridiculous if a little thing like fire could destroy them. It wouldn't do to have all your employees working in an office that could kill them, so to speak. Poor management, on Hell's part, if that was the case."

*Oh. Right. Hell. Eternal damnation. Fiery pits of unending torment. Where Meridiana, the demon, worked. It wouldn't do to burn the help to a crisp in the middle of a torture session. Got it.*

"So, why'd she turn up now, here in New Orleans, of all places? I mean, wouldn't Vegas be a better place for a demon? Sin City and all that?" I was truly perplexed by Meridiana's presence in my town, let alone in my life.

Mama raised one finger towards the ceiling. "That's one question, child, but not the most important one."

I swallowed hard, understanding what Mama was getting at. "What does she want with me?" I managed to squeak out past the lump in my throat.

Mama tipped her finger down to point at me, "Bingo."

# Chapter 48

Heavy footsteps pounded down the stairs and interrupted any further conversation about demonic appearances in my life. Ben burst back into the kitchen. His long arms were full of thick books and wrinkled papers. He unceremoniously dumped the lot in a pile on the kitchen table. Goliath followed him in, dragging a small scrap of paper behind his wildly excited master. Ben scooped the little mouse up and tucked Goliath into his spot under the necromancer's left ear.

"Where is it?" Ben muttered, leaning over the pile of papers and shuffling through them. Goliath flapped the piece of paper he held, which was a card of some sort.

"Ah, thank you, Goliath." Ben snagged the card and patted the tiny mouse gently on the head. He thrust the card at me. "Look at this!" he said excitedly.

I took the card, studying it carefully. It looked like a tarot card. It was a black and white drawing of a wheel with eight spokes radiating from a central point. The image reminded me of an old sailing ship wheel. I compared the card to the images on my phone. It wasn't an exact copy, but it was close. Too close to be coincidence.

Ben's excitement was obvious as he said, "This image pops up in several religions and cultures worldwide. It's an important part of the tarot deck, as you can see. In ancient Egypt, it's called the Wheel of Fortune. Several other religions refer to it as the Dharma Wheel or the Wheel of Law. Each culture uses this wheel symbol to represent life."

I was a little lost. "Ben, I got to tell you. Those pictures I showed you, well, I'm pretty sure they had nothing to do with living. From all the dead animals around, it seemed like Kingsley was focused more on death and dying."

Ben shook his head, trying to erase some misconceptions. "Not living," he said. "*Life*. As in the cycle of life. Birth, living, death. Occasionally rebirth as well, depending on the religion. This wheel is a symbol of the never-ending cycle of birth and rebirth. Life." He gestured wildly with his arms, waving them in ever-widening circles.

I nodded slowly, understanding sinking in. "Okay, so what about the rest of the pictures?" I asked, pointing to the images painted on the corners of the dais and in the different sections of the circles. "This one looks like a dog or something? But it has a human body. Does it have something to do with the werewolves?"

Ben waggled his flat hand back and forth in a 'maybe' gesture. "Because of the Wheel, I would guess that it's a crude depiction of Anubis."

I raised my eyebrow. "Ben, it's probably best if you assume that I'm dumber than a doornail with this stuff. Spell it out for me. Like I'm a four-year-old."

Ben nodded, apparently grateful to delve into his area of expertise. "Anubis is an Egyptian god of death and the afterlife. His job is to weigh the hearts of the deceased to determine their place in the afterlife." Ben grimaced, "Some of the stuff those old Egyptians came up with was pretty grim. I wouldn't want to be spending eternity in any of their versions of never-ending punishment."

I could tell that Ben was in danger of going off on a tangent about death. Necromancers. I pointed at the crude drawing of the sphinx on my phone to keep his attention focused. "Is that why the Sphinx is here? In Egyptian legends, does the Sphinx work for Anubis or something?"

Ben's eyes refocused on the glowing picture on my phone. "Yes, and no. They used the Sphinx in a guardian role. Which is why you often see them depicted in front of temples or tombs. Their job is to protect those inside and deter outside disturbances. However, they also fulfill the role of an adjudicator in some legends. When you see a Sphinx with a sword, the creature is sitting in judgment."

I swiped at the phone to zoom in on the picture of the Sphinx. "Maybe it's holding a sword? It's hard to tell. Kingsley needs to work on his painting skills," I complained.

Ben continued as if I hadn't spoken. "The other symbols seem linked. The triple spiral triskele is a Celtic symbol of infinity or the cycle of life, afterlife, and rebirth. The snake eating its own tail, also known as Ouroboros, is an ancient symbol in many cultures that represents the same thing. Life, death, and eventual rebirth." Ben's finger poked at the crude drawing of a bird. "This is most likely a phoenix, if the Fae kept to the same general theme."

"The bird that dies, bursts into flames, and is reborn from the ashes," I said. Even I knew that one. Team Dumbledore all the way.

"Exactly!" Ben nodded excitedly. He pinched his fingers on the phone, zooming out for a wider look at the ritual site. "The rest of these symbols are a collection of iconographies from different cultures, referring to life, death, and rebirth. There doesn't seem to be a particular rhyme or reason to their placement in the circle. More like the one who drew them didn't want to leave anything out."

"Okay," I drew out the word. "So, Kingsley wants to do something with the cycle of life and death. I'm guessing that he isn't focused on the death part. He wouldn't need an elaborate ritual set-up for that. Just a gun or a sword. Ba-da-bing, ba-da-boom, ba-da-stabby. Death."

Mama leaned forward in her seat, speaking for the first time since Ben had crashed back into the kitchen. "I think you're overlooking the main point of the ritual space, child. Yes, there are elements of life and death, but many of the symbols include an element of rebirth. Too many to be a coincidence or a secondary element of this ritual."

My mind raced back to the cellar where we had discovered the ritual set-up and all the dead and decomposing animals in cages. Kingsley's office. The tiny miniature painting. Everything suddenly clicked into place.

Each pair of animals had been murdered in the same way. One had its throat cut. The other had a gaping hole in its chest. The first had been the test subject. The one that Kingsley was trying to bring back from the doors of death. The second was the fuel for the ritual.

My eyes snapped up to meet Mama's. "He's trying to bring his wife back from the dead."

She nodded seriously. "From what you said about those animals, I'd guess he's been practicing, but hasn't been successful. Yet. Perhaps he is not powerful enough on his own. Which means he would need..."

"The Shadow Shard," I whispered.

"And the missing ghosts," Ben added.

"Remember the time frame," Mama continued, ignoring our interruptions.

"Conducting the ritual on Halloween is smart. The veil thins on All Hallows' Eve, bringing our world closer to the afterlife than normal. Conceivably, he could rip a hole in the veil large enough to pull her soul through to our world. Which is terrifying enough. But if he isn't careful, he could rip a hole larger than he expected. Or he might not have the power to close it back up. Either way, what other nasties are waiting on the other side of the veil, just itching to be set loose in the mortal realm?"

I shivered. Halloween was spooky enough, but with a crazed Fae armed with a supercharged magical relic? Well, it seemed like a good time to take my trick-or-treating far away from New Orleans.

My phone buzzed. I jumped and nearly fell out of my chair. I was wound tight to be startled by the vibrations from the little device. Peeking at the screen, I saw Sloane had texted me a picture, but I couldn't puzzle it out from the tiny notification icon.

Ben spoke, distracting me from the message. "From what you've shown us and the events of the past couple of days, I'd wager you're on the right track, Cam. You need to track this crazy-ass Fae down. He ain't got the sense God gave a goose if he's been messin' about with this nonsense." I noticed his Southern twang thickened up again after he set aside his academic persona.

Mama nodded in agreement. "The faster you find him, child, the better. For all of us."

I scrubbed a hand over my face, forgetting that it was covered in rough bandages. I held it up for both of them to see. "What am I supposed to do? I can't hold a pencil, let alone a knife or a gun. I can barely even operate my phone." Annoyed, I shoved the thing for emphasis. It buzzed back at me. Another message from Sloane.

Mama and Ben exchanged glances. Nodding at the phone, Ben said, "Right. You get on that there horn then and you holler at them wolf-y fellas runnin' around in the dark. Let 'em know what you know."

I threw my hands up in the air, letting my emotions take the reins. "And tell them what, exactly? That Kingsley is trying to resurrect his dead wife with some kidnapped ghosts? How does that help us narrow down where to look? We're on a clock. If we don't find him by midnight, then all hell could break loose!" I snorted at the unintentional turn of phrase. "Literally!"

Ben rubbed his hands together as he thought out loud. "So, this Fae feller is gonna need somewhere that has some space to paint his little doo-dads on the floor. Somewhere indoors. You don't want the wind blowing a stick and breaking your circles. That'd lead to a whole lotta stuff and nonsense he don't need right now. Demons escaping, spirits runnin' wild, that sort of thing."

Mama chimed in, "If he's smart, he'll be looking for a transition point. A place where the living pass through the veil to the other side. Somewhere like a morgue or a cemetery. The veil is especially thin in places like those. It'd be easier for him to tear a hole in a thin part of the veil and then pull his wife's soul across to this side."

"He's also gonna want somewhere isolated. It takes time to set these types of shenanigans up. If he gets caught in the set-up or has to find another new ritual site, that's gonna eat into the time he's got left," Ben added.

I nodded, absorbing what they said. "So, we're on a clock, but so is he. Which means that he's only got one shot at this. He has to get it right the first time. It also means that he couldn't have traveled too far to find his new creepy ritual site, which works in our favor."

Mama and Ben nodded along with my assessment. For the first time since walking into Kingsley's murderous hidey-hole, I felt flickers of hope spring to life in my gut. My phone buzzed again. I peeked. Sloane. Again. She must really need something.

Grabbing my phone, I pushed to my feet. "Mama, I know you've got connections. Could you reach out to see if you can uncover anything else?"

Mama nodded seriously. She headed up the stairs to her office immediately. I looked over at Ben. "Would you mind driving me home? I know it's not far, but speed counts right now. I think I might have a way to track Kingsley down, but I need to visit my armory. Knives might be out of the question for me to use effectively, but guns aren't."

If the tracker could locate the relic once, it could do it again and, by extension, Kingsley. I was hoping against hope that I could find him before he ripped a hole in the veil between our world and the afterlife big enough to drive a bus through.

# Chapter 49

I pulled up Damon's number as I waited for Ben to grab his keys to the old death-trap he called a truck, walking slowly out the front door. The Alpha answered on the first ring. As quickly as I could, I filled him in on the information we had discovered. I told him to focus on things like morgues, cemeteries, mausoleums, and other transition points for the dead. My phone buzzed with yet another message from Sloane while I was talking to Damon. We wrapped up quickly, and I flipped over to my chat with Sloane. And swore.

"That bastard. I'm going to kill him," I hissed at the phone.

I was staring at a photo of Sloane. She was tied to a chair and staring defiantly into the camera. Bruises covered her face and arms. She must've put up a fight. Two messages had popped up after the picture.

*Willing to trade your friend for you. 30 minutes. A.K.*

The second message simply read:

*Tick tock, Ms. Blaze.*

Cursing under my breath, I tapped out a message as quickly as I could.

*Let her go, asshole. When I find you, I'm going to tear you apart with my bare hands.*

The response came a moment later. *Not with those hands.*

I looked around, taken aback. How had he known about my hands? I hadn't seen him after the pipe bomb explosion. Had I? I tapped out a message, carefully.

*How do you know about my hands?*

*Magic.*

I rolled my eyes and then gave his message some serious consideration. I didn't know what kind of magic Kingsley had, but he must be powerful if he was both the Ambassador to Fae and a member of the Collective. Maybe he'd slipped me some sort of spelled talisman that I hadn't noticed? Was it possible that he laid the spell directly on me? Ignorance was not giving me bliss right now.

Another message popped up. *Say anything to anyone and I will know. Her death won't be the only one on your head. Get yourself to the Old Absinthe House on Bourbon Street. You have 22 minutes left.*

I stared at the screen, trying to puzzle out a meaning. What was Kingsley's game here? The door banged open, startling me. Ben hurried down the steps as fast as his long legs could carry him.

As Ben triumphantly held up his keys, I saw a red dot appear on his sternum and trace its way up to his heart. I froze.

*The fae bastard. He was dead. As soon as I could get my hands on him.*

I schooled my face into a blank expression. If Ben thought there was a threat, he might do something stupid and get us both killed. The red dot suddenly blinked off. Fighting down the anger inside of me, I followed the murderous Fae's commands.

"Ready to go?" Ben asked, hurrying over towards the truck.

"All set," I managed through a dry throat. I swung myself up into the cab, using the motion to get a bead on the unseen gunman. Nothing. Damn it.

Ben handed me my bag. "Mama said you left this upstairs earlier, and you'd want it."

"Thanks, Ben," I muttered, settling the bag over my shoulder.

Ben's truck roared to life as we sputtered our way down the darkened streets of New Orleans. I had four minutes, five max, to formulate a plan that wouldn't get Ben or Sloane killed by the end of the night.

As we drove, I punched out another message to the Fae who had just been promoted to the place of honor on my shit list.

*Can't make it in 20. If I tell my driver to change locations, he'll get suspicious. I need at least 45 minutes to get to you alone.*

I waited anxiously, tapping my phone on my knee. Ben looked over at me. "What's up?" he asked.

"Just waiting to hear back from Sloane," I lied. My mind was racing frantically. How could I swing things in my favor?

Ben nodded, keeping his eyes on the road. "Haven't heard from her in a while. Let us know if she needs something."

"Sure," I said as my phone vibrated. "That must be her now."

*You have 30 minutes. Come alone. Leave your phone in the truck. Remember, we're listening.*

Ben snuck a look at me. "Everything okay?"

I nodded. "She's tied up with some things. Looks like she will be freed up soon to come and help." I didn't know if they had a listening device in the car or if Kingsley was just playing with my mind and trying keep me isolated. I wrote a terse message on the screen, but didn't send it, waiting for a response from Kingsley. If he had cloned my phone somehow, I was in trouble. I tapped the phone against my knee as I waited impatiently.

Nothing.

I gave it another thirty seconds to see if Kingsley was monitoring my phone. When no outraged messages popped up, I let out a quick breath. So, he was listening, not watching. It was a calculated gamble. If the Fae was monitoring my phone, there wasn't much I could do to pass along a message. If I couldn't send out some sort of distress signal, Sloane might not live to see 12:01 tonight.

As Ben turned onto my street, an idea popped into my head. It wasn't a great one, but my choices were limited. I smiled grimly as I tapped frantically at the screen, changing a couple of settings as quickly as I could with my bandaged hands. I didn't want to put him and Mama in any more danger than I already had done by dragging them into this mess, but I knew I needed help.

I pressed send on my pre-typed message as I leaned over kissed Ben on his weathered cheek. "Thanks for the ride! I'll be in touch."

With his head turned away, Ben couldn't see as I held up the phone for Goliath. The little mouse's red eyes watched me carefully as I tucked it into the seat of the truck. I jumped out of the cab, leaving a glowing picture of Sloane tied to a chair on the home screen of my unlocked phone. I sent up a brief prayer to the gods of technology and stupid ideas that my gambit would pay off.

# Chapter 50

I rushed up the stairs to my place. Fumbling the keys out of my bag, I eventually got the door to my apartment open. Closing it behind me, I let my head bang against the door. What was I going to do?

*Think, Cam!*

Kingsley had effectively isolated me by making me leave my phone in Ben's truck. I had no way of communicating with anyone in time to get help. Who had a landline these days? Not this girl, that's for sure. Well, I had one way of reaching out to my friends. A long shot, but what the hell? What did I have to lose by trying?

I ran to the kitchen and pulled up my laptop. I tapped out a brief email with the pertinent details. My hands were screaming at me in pain for making them do so many fine motor movements by the time I pressed send. My message in a binary-coded bottle zipped off to Mama, Ben, and Logan. Hopefully, they'd get it in time to help. I wasn't holding my breath, though. I knew I needed to be the first one on the scene to help Sloane.

*Focus, Cam.*

What could I do right here, right now? Dumping out my bag on the kitchen table, I pawed through it. I pushed everything that wasn't a weapon onto the floor. An unfamiliar tinkling sound rang up from the floor. I scoured the ground until my gaze fell on the silver and quartz ring that had been hidden with the relic. It glinted at me from the tile of the kitchen.

I scooped it up and toyed with the strange ring as I examined the assortment of knives and guns on the table. I let out a heavy sigh and dropped into a chair. A fat lot of good my weapons did me. I couldn't hold any of them, let alone use one with any accuracy. I held up my hands, looking at them in disgust.

Good Lord, I really wanted to put something pointy right through the asshole Fae's eye. Or maybe not pointy. Something dull would hurt more, wouldn't it? I wasn't fussy as long as I could wiggle said object around in his skull. What I wouldn't give for two working hands! Ain't that the way of it? Always wanting what you can't have? Coveting your neighbor's...

A Hail Mary of an idea popped into my head. I grinned darkly. More like a Hail Meridiana.

"Meridiana!" I shouted into the empty apartment. "I could use some damned help. Get your damned ass in here!"

Between one breath and the next, the demoness appeared, sitting in the same chair she had before. Even though I'd been half expecting it, her sudden appearance startled me enough that I took an involuntary step backwards.

"So, you've figured me out then?" Meridiana said, as she inspected her perfectly manicured nails.

"Whoa!" I shouted, trying to get my racing heart to slow down. "You need a bell or some sparkly smoke or something. You appearing out of the shadows? Not cool. You're going to take years off my life."

She tossed her long red hair and twisted her scarlet lips into what I identified as her signature sexy smirk, warm brown eyes lighting with good humor. "Shadows are more of your thing than mine, my dear. I'm into fire."

Her eyes gleamed wickedly before sliding to the space over my right shoulder, her gaze shifting from curious to excited. "The charm is disintegrating faster than expected! How are you feeling?"

I held up my bandaged hands. "I've been better."

Her eyes lost all warmth, turning dark and menacing in a heartbeat. "Tell me everything," she commanded.

I summed up the events of the past few days as quickly as I could, ending with the threat to Sloane's life. Despite my best friend being in grave danger, Meridiana seemed unduly focused on my experience with the werewolves in the warehouse.

"What did you feel when you were in the place between? What did you see? Colors? Shapes? Items? Anything you can remember would be helpful," she asked intently, leaning forward.

"Honestly, it was really hazy. Smoky or shadowy, I don't know Hard to see. Except for me. My shadows came more easily than ever before though and I was able to use them to contain the blast of a pipe bomb. I have no idea how, but..." I leaned forward. "What does it mean, Meridiana? I know you know. Tell me."

Meridiana let out a low whistle. "It sounds to me like you created a null shield."

I shook my head, never having heard the term before. "What's that?"

"Incredibly advanced shadow magic. Essentially, a null shield acts as a barrier between the caster and whatever she is trying to protect against. However, unlike most shields, a null shield will eat any energy it comes into contact with."

"Eat it?"

She shrugged. "It's the best way I know how to describe it. Magic that comes into contact with a null shield, vanishes. Ceases to be. Leaves this realm. Gets eaten. It all amounts to the same thing in my book. One second the magic or spell or whatever is there, the next, it isn't. The thing becomes void. Null. Hence the name. Null shields are a nasty, but effective bit of magic."

I held up my bandaged hands. "If null shields destroy any magic that comes in contact with them, how do you explain this?"

Meridiana tipped her head like a curious cat and then lifted a slim shoulder. "You suck at null shields?"

"Gee, thanks," I said dryly.

"Give yourself time. It was only your first attempt after all. I'm sure you'll get better."

I rolled my eyes, but then an idea occurred to me. "If you know enough about shadow magic to have detailed info on null shields, help me out. What else can I do that I could learn in, oh say, less than thirty minutes?"

Meridiana glanced out the window, furtively reminding me we had unseen listeners observing our conversation. Damn eavesdroppers. As soon as I dealt with this mess, I was upping my security. Both the mundane and the supernatural.

She sighed and leaned back in her chair. "I really can't say anything more on the matter."

I mirrored her posture. "Well, it was worth a shot."

"What do you want from me, Cameron?"

My grin looked feral, and I knew it. "I want to make a deal with the Devil, but since he's not here, you'll do."

Meridiana clapped her hands in excitement. "Oh, I knew I liked you! Tell me what you're thinking."

I laid out the plan that I'd cobbled together with wishes and hopes. I tied it together with a wisp of smoke and a prayer that a demoness would do me a solid.

The demon nodded slowly. "That might work, but you'll need a lot of luck. Perhaps that little talisman will bring the luck you need." Meridiana tipped her head towards the ring I still held.

I raised it, letting the kitchen light glimmer within the rose crystal. "This? It's just a ring I found. Nothing lucky."

Meridiana held out a hand, and I passed the ring over. She examined it thoughtfully. "Still, it's pretty. Excellent craftmanship."

"Not that it matters. It's not going on these mitts anytime soon. Not that it fits anyway." I waggled my heavily bandaged hands at her to emphasize my point.

"Indeed. Well, we can fix that." Meridiana snapped her fingers. The necklace that I'd forgotten I was wearing unlatched itself from around my neck and floated over to her. She looped the ring onto the chain, letting it fall to join the carved gold charm she'd given me earlier. The demoness leaned forward to drape the necklace around my neck once more, latching it firmly in place. The ring hung low, hitting just between my breasts.

Meridiana eyed me and nodded in approval. "There. That's better. Where were we now? Oh yes, your plan. It might work, but there'll be a price to pay."

"Whatever it is, Sloane is worth it," I interrupted her.

She nodded thoughtfully. "You must love her dearly."

"She is my family. I love her as dearly as any sister." The words poured out of me, but I knew the truth of them as they fell from my lips. I'd do anything, pay any price to keep Sloane safe.

"Yes, this should work then," she said, tapping a red-tipped finger against her chin. "Like Cinderella, I can give you until midnight. After that," she shrugged, "you're on your own."

I nodded sharply at once. "Good enough. I'll make it work." I tipped my head to the side contemplatively as the rest of her words sank in. "Does that make you my fairy godmother?"

Meridiana put her hand to her chest in feigned outrage. "Please, my dear! Never lump me in with the Fae again! Although, the godmother in question is from my side of the fence so, perhaps? Do you want me to be your godmother, Cameron?"

Wow. That was a loaded question if ever I heard one. "Let's start with drinking buddies and see where the night goes," I demurred.

The demoness across from me shrugged easily. "Can't blame a demoness for trying."

I didn't know what she meant. I made a snap decision that not knowing what she meant was probably a good thing for me. Demons, am I right?

"However, like Cinderella's fairy godmother, I can only provide assistance until midnight." She glanced at the clock on my microwave. "Is an hour and forty minutes going to be enough time?"

I grimaced. "It's gonna have to be. It's not like I have any other choice."

Meridiana spat in her hand and extended it to me. "Then I offer you a favor for a favor, Cameron Blaze."

"Deal," I said, spitting into my bandaged hand and reaching across the table to shake hers. I winced when she lightly gripped my hand and shook it just once.

This time, the thump wasn't just in my chest. It reverberated through my entire being and down my arm to where I clasped Meridiana's hand. Her eyes flew up to mine, surprised by the sensation.

I had half-expected the reaction to the deal. It had seemed to occur with frightening regularity, but it was interesting that it surprised the demoness. I masked my reaction because, well, badass points matter.

"And that's why you shouldn't make deals with the Devil, whether you know her or not," I said.

"Quite," Meridiana answered, looking for all the world like I was the Devil in this deal.

# Chapter 51

The green shuttered doors on the Old Absinthe House were thrown wide and costumed merry-makers spilled out of the bar onto Bourbon Street. I leaned a shoulder against the lamppost on the corner of Bourbon and Bienville, trying to avoid the drunks and keep an eye out for Kingsley at the same time. A group of men dressed in identical red jerseys swayed their way down the street, singing something that might have been a song at the top of their lungs as they tried and failed to keep their beers from sloshing all over the pavement. Normally, I would've found it hilarious to watch them try and navigate Bourbon Street clutching huge ass beers, but not tonight.

Tonight, I had other business.

Someone crashed into me, almost knocking me sprawling into the sticky road. Trust me, face down on Bourbon Street is not a good place to be. Especially on Halloween. The guy who knocked into me, held up one hand in apology while he placed the other next to his mouth, trying to keep his drinks on the inside. Sweat dripped down his face, running rivulets in the poorly applied white face paint he wore in lieu of a costume. He heaved into his fist a couple of times before taking a long inhale and shooting me a thumbs up.

A woman tottered out of the bar behind him looking like she'd been attacked by a clown's make-up artist bent on revenge. She was wearing a massive top hat with such a nauseating array of colors in eye-gauging shades that I was surprised the guy hadn't puked when he saw her heading his way. Instead, he let out a long, loud blech and blew beer breath right into my face.

The woman cackled and threw an arm around his waist. The guy caught her in a drunken hug, spinning her around as she flung out her arms and sang out, "We're all mad heeeeere!" They collapsed in a pile of limbs and giggles in the middle of the road as the rest of the street applauded them.

I rolled my eyes, ignoring the drunks once more. I needed to find Kingsley. I didn't want him to think I'd missed the deadline. Who knows what he would do to Sloane if he couldn't find me among all of the costume party-goers? It wasn't like I could call him either. Not after he'd made me leave my phone in Ben's truck.

I scanned my little corner of Bourbon Street again, searching for anyone who could've been Kingsley in disguise. As much as I didn't like the Fae, I had to hand it to him. Setting up a meet here ensured I wouldn't see him make an approach. All he'd have to do to blend in seamlessly with this crowd would be to slap on a mask and stumble over his own feet occasionally. I'd never see him coming. Turns out, I was right.

A hand grabbed my elbow. I wheeled to see Kingsley glaring down at me as he held me in a vice-like grip just above my bandages.

"Who did you bring?" he demanded.

I shook him off. "It's just me, asshole. I'm not messing with her life," I said, shifting my weight to rest it all on one cocked hip.

The Fae took his time looking around to make sure that the area was secure. I used the time to evaluate him. Kingsley looked the worse for wear. He was still wearing the same suit from our earlier meeting, but it was wrinkled and disheveled. His shirt was unbuttoned at the collar and his entire ensemble was speckled and spattered with paint. There were even splotches of paint in his long silver-blond hair.

"Doing a little late-night arts and crafts?" I asked, raising an eyebrow at his scruffy appearance.

"Come with me," he said shortly. He reclaimed my elbow and used his hold to steer me across the street and up Bienville. He stayed silent, watching the drunks stumble towards Bourbon Street as he guided me away. Two blocks later, we turned left onto Burgundy. Although we weren't too far off the party center of New Orleans, the drunken crowd had dissipated completely.

Kingsley pulled me into a packed parking lot on the corner of Burgundy and Iberville, shoving me up against a black Mercedes. "Spread your arms and legs," he growled.

"Usually, I insist that a man buys me dinner first, but as it's you..." I drawled, stretching my arms straight out to allow him to frisk me.

He grunted when he saw my bandaged hands. "I hadn't realized that the damage was so extensive. What happened to you, anyway?"

"Your bomb did, asshole."

He grunted again and gave me a thorough, professional frisking. He untied the knife in my thigh sheath that Meridiana had helped me secure and carefully pulled the two throwing daggers out of my boot by their hilts. Sadly, he'd worn gloves and the iron in the knives didn't immediately burn his skin. Well, it was worth a shot. I hadn't really expected my ploy to work.

Kingsley stepped back and raised an eyebrow at me, holding the knives up in a silent question.

"Habit," I said with a nonchalant shrug.

"Can you even hold these right now?" he asked, eyeing the bandages that ran from my palms to my elbows.

I leaned in, channeling all my crazy into my grin. "Give 'em back and let's find out."

Kingsley curled a lip in a snarl and tossed my knives in the gutter. I looked after them regretfully. Those were some of my favorites. I hoped I'd see them again, but I knew better. Those blades would disappear into the seedy depths of New Orleans before the night was out. I'd never see those beauties again. I silently swore to avenge them.

Sloane first, though.

Kingsley stepped back in, completing his weapons search. When he got to the bandages around my arms he hissed, pulling back. "There's iron in there!"

I shrugged, keeping my voice neutral. I hoped the sweat dripping down my back didn't give me away. "It's a splint or something. I don't know. I was unconscious when they put it on."

He leaned forward, peering more closely at my bandaged hands. "Why do you have a ring around your fingers then?"

Time for some top-notch dancing around the truth. I flipped my hands back and forth like I was examining the rings poking out from under my bandages. "Mama swears it's the best way to make sure her healing poultices stick. Something about the alchemical properties of the gifts nature gives us combined with the magic infused metal for longer absorption rates or something. I'm no healer. I don't know if that's true or just some bullshit she told me to make it seem like I had a chance at regaining the use of my hands. Between you and me, I started to zone her out once she got on her soapbox. Don't tell her though, she'll have my hide."

Kingsley shot my hands one more look before shrugging. "It's not going to matter anyway," he muttered and then gestured towards the car. "Get in. You're driving."

I shook my head. "No way. Free Sloane first. That was the deal."

The Fae flicked his wrist. A glowing green ball of fire sprang to life in the middle of his palm. "Life magic can be so, *unpredictable*. Why, I could convince the grass pushing up through the pavement to trip you and tie you up before you could get out of this parking lot."

I shrugged, nonplussed. "Cities must suck for you if all you can manage is grass."

"Ah, my magic is so much more insidious than that. I encourage *life*, Ms. Blaze. You see, with a simple scan of my magic, I can find a benign growth such as a tumor or blood clot or lipoma. Something small. Something that wouldn't kill you. Unless I pour life magic into it that is. I can make that small, inconsequential whatever inside of you grow and grow until it presses up against something vital. Plugging an artery perhaps? Stopping your heart? Pressing against important parts of the brain and causing a stroke?" He turned his hand over, letting the green magic trickle across his knuckles. "I suppose I wouldn't have to make it life threatening. I could just hurt you. Something like making your bones grow until they burst out of your skin. Gory, I'll admit, but it does so make the point," the former Fae Ambassador said with a smirk. Good Lord, even his smile was slimy. His smirk made me want to punch the Fae in his all too perfect face even as his threats turned my stomach

He let the magic pool in his palm again. "Get in the car, Ms. Blaze."

I crossed my arms over my chest, refusing to give in to his demand, despite the queasy roiling in the pit of my stomach. I glanced at his flickering ball of green magic and the roiling increased to full-on churning. "Sloane first," I said, stubbornly.

Kingsley shook his head slowly. "I think not. I'm changing the terms of our agreement. Get in the car and you can see the leprechaun one last time or I can shoot you here."

"That wasn't the deal," I said, stubbornly.

He raised his hand holding the ominous green ball of magic. It snapped as it licked out towards me like living flame. "Choose."

I got in the car.

Kingsley slid into the back seat, keeping his magic pooled in the palm of his hand and ready to use in an instant. "Drive," he said.

I sighed and put my bandaged hands on the wheel, wincing for effect as I tried to grip it. No harm in highlighting that I was suffering from my injuries. Anything to get an edge.

"Where to, asshole?" I asked, keeping my voice low and my eyes straight ahead. I needed him to believe that I was weak and beaten. That I was submitting to his superior cunning and firepower. For now.

Kingsley gave me an address of a funeral parlor on the outskirts of town. My subconscious started cheering. Mama had been right! A transition point between life and death. A place where the veil would be thin on All Hallows' Eve. Unfortunately, a funeral parlor wasn't at the top of the priority list that I'd given the werewolves. The mental cheering stopped abruptly, and I tried to suppress a shudder as I drove. I wasn't confident that anyone was going to find out where Kingsley had set up his ritual space. At least not in time. If I couldn't swing this situation in my favor somehow, either Sloane or I were going to end up fueling this gruesome ritual of his with our life's blood.

I rolled down my window, needing some air. I leaned my left arm on the open window of the Mercedes, enjoying the warm evening breeze dance over my skin.

"What are you doing?" Kingsley's voice broke the tense silence in the car.

"Needed some air," I muttered. Speaking louder, I said, "You know that there's a special place in Hell for people who break deals, right?"

He grunted behind me. "It can't be any worse than the hell I've been living in for the past year."

I fidgeted with the bandages on my left hand, toying with the plain metal ring on my finger as I tried to keep him talking. "So, what are you doing? You're obviously not planning on letting me walk out of here alive, and we've got time to kill. One last wish? Satisfy my curiosity?" I shrugged, trying to keep the morbid line of questioning as light as possible.

The Fae was silent behind me. I drove in that tense silence for almost two minutes, feeling sweat slide down my back, my mind playing out all sorts of horrible variations of how this night could end. The fingers on my left hand kept worrying at the bandages in a nervous tic. I was almost thankful when Kingsley cleared his throat and began to speak.

"My wife was killed last year by a drunk driver." He paused, and I could hear him swallow back his emotions. I tried not to roll my eyes. There was no way that I was going to fall for some phony sob-story from this Fae who had kidnapped my best friend, used a threat to her life to kidnap me, and was likely planning to kill one or both of us. Cry someone else a river, asshole, because I wasn't getting dragged in by some crocodile tears.

"Have you ever been to Fae, Ms. Blaze?" he asked, jerking me back from my musings.

I shook my head once. "Haven't had the pleasure."

His voice took on a wistful note, like a traveler reminiscing about this one magically beautiful spot from the 'Best. Vacation. Ever.'

"It's a place unlike any other. Fae is an amalgam of contradictions. It's a beautifully violent place. The inhabitants are straightforward in their attempts at trickery. Magic, mayhem, and murder go hand in hand with normalcy, order, and life. The politics of the Courts are fascinating and deadly. Those who live outside the elegant brutality of the Fae Courts are both honorable and deceptive. Everyone wears multiple masks to hide their true intentions and identity." He sighed in pleasure, lost in his memories. "It's a fascinating, wonderful place."

"Sounds twisted," I said. "Who would want to always hide their intentions or whatever? Doesn't that get exhausting?"

In the rearview mirror, I saw Kingsley's attention snap back to me. He tipped his head to the side, like he was searching for the right words.

"It does, and it doesn't. Do you find walking exhausting? Or breathing?" he asked. Without waiting for my response, he continued, "It's like that for the Fae. Deception. Trickery. Playing a beautiful, convoluted game is ingrained so deeply within us that it's burned into our bones. It's in our DNA, as the Norms here would say. We can't live without it, nor do we want to."

I nodded slowly. That fit with what I knew of the Fae. It'd also bumped Fae way down my list of top vacation spots. Murder with a side of mayhem? No, thanks. I'll take a beach and a Mai Tai any day.

Aldrich continued, "My Carina, my lovely wife, she loved the game of it all. She was brilliant. Beautiful, deadly, graceful, cunning, caring. When I met her, I was entranced. She was my everything, and then she fell pregnant."

I couldn't help myself. "You fell in love or lust or whatever it is Fae do and had a kid. So what? How does that justify any of this?" I waved a hand vaguely in the air.

"You don't understand," he insisted, his voice dropping. I couldn't tell if it was from grief or anger, but knew I needed to proceed with caution. When emotions ran high, people did stupid things.

"Those Supernaturals who are gifted with long life are also cursed in different ways. For one, we cannot procreate as swiftly or as easily as our human counterparts. If we could, long-lived Supernaturals would soon overpopulate all the realms. Some Supernaturals cannot procreate at all. Others find it merely difficult. The vampiric virus, for example, kills more than it converts. Werewolves have their elaborate rituals surrounding infection, or dire consequences ensue."

His shrug caught my eye in the rearview mirror. "Different species of Fae procreate at different speeds. The Fae nobility in the Courts are some of the slowest to conceive. Even then, a fetus surviving to term is rare. To have found my Carina, to have bonded with her, and then to have Blythe? My life was complete. It filled me with joy unlike I had ever known. I lived in a blissful paradise with my wife and our beautiful baby girl. Until my Carina was taken from me."

His voice caught, and he took a moment to regain his composure before continuing.

"My Carina was killed here. A Fae of noble blood dying in the mortal realm hasn't happened in a millennium. When we die in Fae, things are different. The rules surrounding death are different there. The deceased can come back to comfort loved ones; they can reach out across the veil during certain times of the year. Carina can't. We don't know why, but she can't return to Fae to visit us. To visit Blythe. To visit me."

"Death. You are describing death." I tried to soften the tone of my voice, but found it difficult. He sounded like a petulant child who was told he couldn't have his cake and eat it, too. "It sucks, but it happens to everyone. We all deal with it, eventually." In an attempt to avoid antagonizing the man with the deadly magic, I left the next part unsaid, but it rang loudly in my mind.

*What makes your loss so special?*

"My Carina's death was a blow to us all. Eventually, we discovered we couldn't reach out to her, that we couldn't find her across the veil. My daughter," his voice caught on a sob this time. "My darling daughter went mad. In one blow, she found out her mother was dead and there was no way to reunite with her, even for a moment. The trauma of the loss caused her mind to break, and she retreated into silent madness."

He paused again, collecting himself. I snuck a peek in the rearview mirror at the Fae behind me. The streetlights painted intermittent bars across his face as I drove. He looked overwhelmed by his grief. A heavy silence settled over the car as I drove as slowly as I dared through the darkened streets of New Orleans.

Kingsley took a deep breath and continued, "As much as I loved my Carina, my love for Blythe was more. More pure, more selfless... just *more.* She brought out the best in me. I would do anything, *anything*, to have a chance at reuniting my child with her mother. It's my last hope to bring my darling daughter back from the brink of her madness."

I thought I caught a glint of tears rolling down his cheeks as a streetlight illuminated the interior of the car for a moment. I didn't want to feel anything for this asshole. He had kidnapped my best friend and me. Threatened both our lives, for all the gods' sakes! But…

If it were me, wouldn't I have done anything to see my mother again? To hold on to her for as long as possible? To find comfort, joy, peace, and love in her arms? I drew in a shaky breath.

I didn't want to empathize with Aldrich. He was insane! Without knowing what the potential consequences were, he was casually discussing magically resurrecting his dead wife in the hopes of saving her or his child's sanity, or both. I didn't want to, couldn't want to empathize with him.

But I did.

I understood the bone-deep ache that kind of loss could create. It was the pain of heartache that woke you in the dark hours of the morning, carving away at your core like someone had repeatedly stabbed you in the soul. That kind of loss, that invisible hole in your heart, *hurt.* I knew how the pain must be eating away at Aldrich, eroding his sanity, because I'd experienced it firsthand. It didn't surprise me Aldrich jumped at the opportunity when he found a way that might bring one or both back. I would've been tempted if I'd been in his shoes.

Aldrich interrupted my thoughts. "I pieced together an ancient ritual that can bring my Carina back to me. If I can pull her soul across the veil and take it back to Fae, I may be able to help my darling daughter heal as well. I've tried for months to perfect it, but time is running out and I'm not powerful enough. If I cannot drag my Carina back from the Abyss soon, she will be lost to me forever. If she is lost, then so is Blythe. My heart and my soul gone in one fell swoop."

Aldrich's eyes met mine in the rearview mirror. Their green depths were burning with an inner fire that bordered on psychotic passion. I could see tears coursing down his cheeks as he leaned forward in his fervor. Kingsley's deadly magic crackled as his emotions flared. "And you, Ms. Blaze, are going to help me bring her back. To bring them both back."

# Chapter 52

Kingsley directed me to pull around to the back of the funeral parlor. His big black Mercedes wouldn't seem out of place parked outside it, even at this late hour. I slid out from behind the wheel, careful not to move too quickly. The last thing I needed was to alert the Fae's suspicion. He was twitchy and still held his magic at the ready. I leaned a foot up against the side of the car and made a show of fumbling with my shoe. I grunted and dropped to a knee on the pavement.

"Hey!" Kingsley hissed, rushing around the hood. "What are you doing?"

I raised my head slowly as I rose from my crouch, pressing my hands against the ground. It was a long shot, but I was trying to lay a scent trail, just in case the werewolves managed to track us here. I kept my voice calm, "Just adjusting my shoe, man. It was rubbing. That's what I get for wearing boots in this heat. Sweat makes nasty blisters, am I right?"

Aldrich looked around warily. I raised my hands and stood leaning a hip against the car door. I knew that the likelihood of the werewolves tracking the car here through the urban sprawl of New Orleans was next to zero, but I had to try. Even if it was the slimmest of hope. I stood there, rubbing my scent against the car and waiting for Kingsley to regain his composure. He finally turned back to me, waving towards the funeral parlor.

"Let's go," was all he said.

I preceded Kingsley into the building. He gave terse directions as we crept through its dimly illuminated interior. He kept a careful distance, and held his magic ready at all times. I wasn't sure that I could've taken him in a physical fight, but he didn't give me the opportunity to try.

At Kingsley's direction, I opened the door and stepped into the chapel. The pit of my stomach dropped. He'd converted it into a hellish scene designed precisely for my personal, eternal torment. If I lived past tonight, I knew I was going to have nightmares on an epic scale.

Kingsley had painted designs in scarlet all over the floor and walls. The paint was so fresh that it glinted eerily, like spilled blood in the dim light. The designs were identical to what we had discovered in the hidden cellar of the Fae Embassy. A shudder I couldn't suppress ripped through my body as the memory of all the decaying animal corpses came into focus in my mind's eye. I pressed my hands to my stomach to fight back my gag reflex as Kingsley pushed me deeper into the desecrated chapel.

Then I saw her. Sloane. She was unconscious and laid out on top of a closed coffin in the center of the ritual circles painted on the floor. The coffin was raised off the floor on what looked like a table with wheels. Sloane's hands and feet were tied to the handles of the coffin, securing her unconscious body firmly in place for whatever horrible plans Kingsley had in mind. He'd placed another coffin beside Sloane's. I had little doubt who Kingsley intended it for.

He waved towards the second coffin. "Please take your place, Ms. Blaze." The bastard was almost courteous.

I realized in that moment that I could empathize with the man's emotions and still hate him. Holding both emotions felt strange, until Kingsley gave me a shove. He pushed my empathy for him right out the darkened window into the Halloween night with that one motion. Hatred welled within me, but I put it firmly to the side. I didn't have the luxury to deal with emotions. I had to figure out how to escape.

I hoisted myself up on the coffin, wincing at the pressure it put on my hands. The metal inside the bandages dug into my flesh painfully as I scrabbled up to sit on top of the coffin. I grimaced. This could very well be *my* coffin. I glanced over at Sloane. She had taken a beating. I was glad that she was unconscious and unable to feel any pain.

I hadn't meant to drag her into a dangerous situation when I asked for her help. I thought this job was an easy track-and-recovery gig. If I'd known it would put Sloane in danger, I would have thrown it back in Logan's face. No amount of money or information was worth losing Sloane.

"You've got me here. Let her go now. You don't need both of us." I tried to keep the desperation out of my voice. I didn't succeed.

Aldrich tossed me some zip-ties. "Tie your feet together," he said. I fumbled the zip-ties around my ankles, trying desperately to think of a way to convince him to let us go. Or at least let Sloane go.

"I saw your cellar, Kingsley. You don't need both of us to fuel your ritual when you've already got the ghosts you kidnapped. You only need one of us, so use me." My fumbling with the ties was embellished, but only marginally. It was tricky with the bandages wrapped around my hands, especially now that the left one was flapping loose from all the fidgeting I had done in the car. I finally got the zip-tie secured around my ankles and glanced up.

The Fae shook his head as he moved closer to zip-tie my hands to the rails on the coffin. "You don't understand, Ms. Blaze. You see, I was never able to actually bring back any of my test subjects. Oh, I got close a few times, but the energy from a single ghost or even up to five ghosts wasn't enough to bind body and soul together. Five was the most I could manage with my resources. However, since you've brought me the Shadow Shard, I have more power that I could imagine at my disposal." He tried to fit the zip-ties over my bandaged arms. The bandages were too thick. Kingsley sighed, annoyed. He secured me to the coffin by looping a second zip-tie through the one at my ankles and fixed it to the railings of the coffin.

"What do you mean?" I asked, tugging at the restraints. They held firm. Kingsley nodded, confident that I couldn't go anywhere and started searching for something to restrain my arms. I watched him move around the room as I continued to try to work my way free.

"The Shadow Shard has the potential to hold many more ghosts than anything I used in my previous experiments. It also has the added bonus of being able to harvest magic from Supes. According to my calculations, draining your magic and combining it with the energy derived from the ghosts will provide ample power to combine my Carina's soul with a body. Your body."

My mouth opened and closed in horror. I froze for a moment as my mind churned. My body was going to house his dead wife's soul? That's what he intended? What did that mean for me? Would two of us be sharing this body, having a constant struggle for domination? Or would I be kicked out? My body turned into an empty receptacle for this Fae lady's soul? Panic started welling up in me. I hadn't anticipated any of this. I had to get both of us out of here, fast.

I struggled to loosen the tie around my ankles, but tried to keep my voice level and logical. Maybe I could talk my way out of this situation yet. Or at least convince him to let Sloane go. "You still don't need both of us. Let Sloane go."

Kingsley shook his head as he started unwinding a thick cord holding back ornate curtains. "There are two essential parts this ritual. Opening the veil to allow Carina's soul to cross back over from the Abyss and cementing her soul with her new body. You will house Carina's displaced soul. Your friend will assist me in opening the veil."

I shuddered as his meaning became clear. The resolve in his eyes terrified me more than anything else. Somewhere in the last twenty seconds, he had taken the final, irrevocable step. Sloane and I were now just magical fodder to him. Fuel for his deranged ritual. I knew he would feel no more remorse for killing us than a farmer does for slaughtering a pair of chickens. Kingsley had already decided. Now, he just had to do the deed.

"You say that like she has a choice! Like she's helping you out of her own free will. She is not sacrificing herself, you maniac! You are murdering her!" I was screaming at him by the end. He ignored my tirade.

I looked over at my best friend, reaching out a hand desperately to try to release the ties binding her to the coffin-altar the deranged Fae had created. Maybe, if I could free her, the movement would wake her. Then she might be able to get away on her own.

A hand grabbed my shoulder and slammed me down onto my back, knocking the breath from me. I hit my head against the lacquered wooden coffin hard enough that I saw stars dancing across my vision. By the time I blinked most of them away, Kingsley had secured my right arm above my head to the railing running around the base of my coffin with a thick tasseled rope he'd torn from the curtains covering the window. I tried to fight him off with one arm, but he was strong. With a dispassionate look on his face, Kingsley walked between the two coffins to secure my other arm to the railing as well.

"You bastard! Let us go!" I screamed, thumping my body futilely against my restraints. It wouldn't sway him, but perhaps someone would hear me? I knew that to be false hope. There was no one here. My murderer-to-be had made sure of that.

I tried to watch him as the Fae moved around the room, setting up the final touches for his soul-snatching ritual. I pulled at my restraints, trying to loosen them. Was there a little bit of give in the rope? Maybe, but not much. I looked over at Sloane. She was still out.

"Sloane!" I hissed. "Wake up! I need you. You need to wake up! We need to get out of here. Sloane!" Her head rolled towards me, but her eyes stayed closed. I snuck another look at Kingsley. His back was to me. I guessed he was busy preparing something for his damned ritual.

I spoke louder, rocking my body to try and touch her hand. "Hey! If you wake up and get us out of here, I will buy you a bottle of that tequila that you like! The really expensive one from our vacation to Mexico last year!" I raised my head to take another look at the Fae. He held something in his hands that was giving off a faint light, easily discernible in the dim interior of the chapel.

"Two bottles! Just! Wake! Up!" I hissed urgently.

Sloane's head rolled back, her eyelids fluttering slightly, giving me hope. A breath escaped her slack lips and her eyes stayed closed. Not good. I pulled at my restraints again, trying to loosen them even more. Maybe I could slip a hand free? If I could, I might be able to get us untied before he noticed.

Kingsley wheeled to face us. In his hands was the Shadow Shard and it was glowing.

The Fae moved with serene grace towards us. I pulled desperately at my restraints. The more slack I had, the more likely I could do something to protect Sloane. Kingsley approached Sloane's side of the makeshift altar, the Shard in his hand. He laid it carefully next to my best friend and pulled out a long, wickedly sharp knife. I caught a glimpse of faint engravings on the blade in the dim light, as Kingsley calmly moved over to Sloane and raised his knife.

"Wait!" I shouted, grasping at straws. "What are you doing to her?"

He paused, looking like I had shaken him from whatever murderous reverie he had sunk into. "I am preparing her for the ritual," he said, slicing open her shirt. He peeled the two halves of the mangled fabric back, revealing her taut belly and lacy black bra. He ran a finger from her naval up to her clavicle, finding the hollow at the base of her throat. I watched his finger move slowly up my friend's helpless body. That motion captivated my attention with its horrific slow precision. He used the point of the knife to make a small nick just above her clavicle. Dark blood beaded on her pale skin instantly.

I yanked at my restraints again, striving to find any slack. I needed to work my hands loose before time ran out. Sloane's life hung in the balance. I had to protect her. I gained a few more millimeters. Not enough. I worked my fingers back and forth, trying to get an angle on the ropes before it was too late. My breath hitched as I panted in desperation. My restraints were too strong. I wouldn't be able to help Sloane.

Kingsley grasped the Shard. He ran a finger gently over its length. It responded to his touch by flaring to life, the brighter glow sending shadows dancing around the room.

"What was that?" I gasped in surprise.

"The ghosts. I promised them a peaceful transition to the other side of the veil. Some came joyfully, glad to accept such an offer. Others," he paused, stroking the crystal again, "weren't so willing to depart this world." The light from the Shard flared angrily at his words.

Shadows danced against the edges of the walls. My eyes tracked them frantically, hoping that one of my allies, one of my friends, had somehow followed me here. That they were waiting in the shadows to free me, to save Sloane.

But I knew that wasn't possible. Everyone was out hunting for Kingsley in all the wrong places. No one even knew that Sloane had been taken, or that I was here. I sent up a silent prayer that Mama and Ben had found my phone. Maybe they could piece things together in time. Maybe they could find us.

Giving up on trying to free myself, I scrambled to find a way stall Kingsley. Any minute I could keep him talking was a minute more that Sloane and I stayed alive. A minute more for Mama and Ben to find my message and send the werewolves to track me. I didn't know how well they could track in a city, but I was hoping it was well enough. They had a certain reputation in the supernatural world, after all. I had to buy them the time they needed to get their furry little asses here.

"Well, aren't they enough? You didn't have the Shard for your little trial-and-error experiments in the Embassy cellar. Why do you need both of us? Use me to open the veil and the ghosts to power the spell. See, you don't even need Sloane." I was feeling frantic as I tracked the timeline in my head. Even if they had found the clues I left, I wasn't sure that the werewolves would make it here in time to save us.

Kingsley traced his index finger along Sloane's collarbone and made a little 'x' in the blood pooling at the base of her throat.

"Perhaps, perhaps not," he whispered. His eyes met mine. The dark intent in them was petrifying. "I only have one more chance. I won't risk using too little power. No, I must not fail. Better to have an excess of power than too little."

He touched his bloody fingertip to the tip of the crystal. The relic flared brighter as it drank down the drop of Sloane's blood. I watched in horrified fascination as the lights held captive in the crystal swirled around the dark red smear, pulling it deeper inside until it disappeared completely. The crystal flashed ominously.

My mind raced back to my conversation with Mama and Ben, searching for anything to stall Kingsley. "How are you going to close up the tear in the veil? I'm sure that there are some big bad nasties just itching to get across and into the mortal realm. Especially on a night like tonight when the veil is thin. You wouldn't want them slipping through and messing with your plans to save Carina, would you? It'd be a shame if you pulled her soul across and then her new body was killed by a demon or something, wouldn't it?"

The Fae shook his head. "I should easily have enough to hold back any that wish to slip through until my Carina is settled in her new home."

"My body. I'm not moving out without a fight. I'll fight her with everything I've got."

Kingsley shot me a look filled with pity for my stupidity. "You won't have any magic left to you. I'd be very surprised if you were able to resist her dominance. Admittedly, no one is precisely sure if you would be pushed to the side like a repressed identity or completely displaced, but it is doubtful that you would be able to best my Carina in a battle of wills."

I blinked as a crazy, desperate idea occurred to me. Kingsley was unsure that Carina's soul could beat mine in the battle for my body. Which meant there was hope. It was a slim hope, but still a hope. At the moment, I'd take even the merest sliver of hope that Sloane might be able to survive this encounter. All I had to do was convince a madman to kill me.

# Chapter 53

I kept my tone cool, acting almost dismissive. "You're an idiot. You've overlooked something so basic that is going to cost you everything." Kingsley glared at me. I met his gaze and gave a derisive snort. "Moron."

"What do you mean?" his tone was cold when he spoke, but something in my ridiculous declaration had at least halted the descent of the Shard.

"I mean that tearing a hole in the veil sounds like it would take a lot more energy than binding a body and soul. I mean, necromancer's do that all the time. I've never even heard a whisper of someone tearing a hole in the veil. If you don't have even power to do that, then all of this," I nodded my head around the ritual space, "has been an epic waste of time. Sloane is a low-leveled Supe. I'm not."

"I checked your powers at the Embassy. They were unique, but not terribly high-powered."

"Check again, asshole."

Kingsley rolled his eyes, but he must have switched over to his second sight or whatever because he stumbled back a pace a moment later.

"Your powers! They were warded when I checked at the Embassy!" he hissed.

"They're here now. In full," I said flippantly, baiting him. Switching places with Sloane wasn't ideal, but at least it gave her a chance to survive tonight. All she had to do was fight off the displaced soul of a High Fae on a murder-spree. However, if my shadow magic was the carrot that enticed Kingsley away from Sloane, then I was happy to dangle it in front of him.

Kingsley glanced at his watch and moved swiftly to my side of the coffin table. It looked like my gamble had paid off. I glanced over at Sloane as he nestled the Shard against my right side. His knife ripped through my shirt. The cool air from the darkened chapel kissed my bare skin as he traced his finger up towards the hollow of my throat, sending shivers dancing along my skin.

"I'm sorry, Sloane," I whispered to my best friend. Her eyes were still closed. I doubted she even heard me. "I tried. Please know that I tried. Fight hard. Don't let that bitch push you out of your body."

A quick, sharp pain at the base of my throat tore into my awareness. Kingsley had marked his target for the sacrificial killing blow. I refused to look at him. If I had to die tonight, I wanted my last view of this world to be Sloane. My gaze roved across her slack face, branding the memories we shared into my soul. Sloane, laughing at me over drinks. Enjoying the New Orleans nightlife together. Watching stupid TV at even stupider o'clock. Coaching each other through hangovers the next morning. A hot tear slid down my cheek. What I wouldn't give for more time with Sloane. I was going to miss those little moments with her the most. The insignificant ones, the ones that made life, well, *life*. Tea. Walks. Eating out. Hugs. Laughter. Love. All of that was about to disappear forever into the void of whatever came after this life. My mind stuttered, focusing on a single thought.

*Void. Null. A null shield. Stop feeling sorry for yourself and get your act together!*

I whipped my head back to Kingsley. He had put his knife down and was holding the crystal relic flat in his outstretched palms, like he was offering it up to some murderous deity. The light inside was growing brighter. I saw his lips moving silently. The crazy asshole was praying over it. Right before he intended to use it as a murder weapon. As *my* murder weapon.

I struggled again, but this time to recall what I had done when I'd made the null shield. What had triggered me to tap into that power in the warehouse? If I could figure that out, maybe I had a chance to save

Sloane. Faint shadows gathered at the corners of my vision. Not enough, not nearly fast enough. Kingsley finished his whispered incantation and raised the Shard over his head with both hands.

I pulled on the shadows in the corners of the room all my might while reaching down into the depths of my soul. I tried frantically to tap into whatever power had spilled out of me when I jumped on the bomb to save Andrei. My body thrashed as the primal side of my brain took control and magic roaring to life as shadows flooded into me, erupting from my fingertips. My gaze locked onto Sloane's face just as the Fae slammed the radiant Shard down towards me. The world flashed black.

I turned my head back towards Kingsley, surprised I could still move. Shadows poured out all around me, obscuring Sloane completely. The High Fae was fighting to press the relic through the haze, but its burning light was muted by the shadows. By *my* shadows. He looked furious as he bore down with all his might, pushing the Shard closer to my exposed throat, one millimeter at a time. The shadows flickered and the relic slipped closer. I couldn't focus my magic. The null shield wouldn't hold. I smiled grimly. I still had one last card to play.

There were mere seconds left on Meridiana's Cinderella time frame. We had struck a bargain back in my apartment. Meridiana agreed to give me the full use of my hands back until midnight in return for a future favor of her choosing. The kicker was that if I did any further damage to my hands while I was under her demoness hoodoo, it would likely be permanent. My hands for Sloane's life? It was a simple choice for me.

I kept the shadows pouring out of my right hand. They slowly formed a dome between me and the relic, but I knew it was going too slowly. Kingsley would force the crystal through my defenses before I could solidify the magic.

The fingers on my left hand curved around the plain metal ring I had looped on my index finger. The safety ring of my karambit, keeping it tucked securely inside the bandages. Meridiana had helped me re-wrap the knife into my decoy bandages in my apartment after she had worked her demoness magic on me. The same bandages Kingsley had failed to check completely when he frisked me. The ones that I had been loosening ever since the treacherous Fae had double-crossed me. At first, I had been trying to rip pieces of the bandage off and drop them outside the car, hoping the werewolves could use the scraps of cloth to track me. The closer we had gotten to our destination, the more important it became for me to have easy access to the knife. I just hadn't gotten it free in time before Kingsley tied me to the coffin.

I worked my fingers and wrist desperately, wincing as the double-edged blade caught the delicate skin just below my palm, but the blade's edge also cut into the bandages. The more I worked the karambit back and forth, the faster the cloth bandages parted. My gaze swung back up. The relic was within a foot from ending my desperate ploy. I was sweating, trying to maintain my hold on the shadow dome while also focusing on freeing my knife. I just needed to hold on so I could get one more slice in.

Just. One. More.

The knife finally broke free of the bandages and I sliced through the cord restraining my wrist. I reacted on instinct, falling back on my training. Instead of pressing the half-formed null shield forward and hoping I had enough power to maintain it, I just let it go.

The shadows dissolved, revealing Kingsley. His eyes gleamed in first surprise and then triumph as his thrust seemed to speed up. I desperately threw my entire weight onto my left shoulder, forcing my right shoulder up to meet the descending Shard. Effectively, I impaled my shoulder on the relic. I screamed directly into Kingsley's surprised face as he held the relic embedded in my shoulder. At least it wasn't my throat.

With another scream of agony, I ripped the relic out of his hands. Wrenching my shoulder to the side was excruciating, with the crystal firmly embedded in my flesh. Despite the agony of torn muscles and tendons, I continued the roll to my right, swinging my now free left hand up towards Kingsley. The one clutching the karambit. With as much force as I could manage, I stabbed at his throat. I felt the blade tear through skin and flesh as it sank home. I twisted it, using the curved blade to rip as much as I could into his jugular. Blood sprayed across my face. Then I stabbed him again and again.

Kingsley stumbled back, his hand flying to cover the gushing wounds in his throat. Ignoring the pain from the crystal pulsing with light from within my shoulder, I leaned awkwardly on my elbow as he fell to the ground. Grimly, I watched as the Fae tried to staunch the blood dripping from between his fingers.

His eyes met mine, and he tried to shove to his feet. He scrabbled his way towards me, determination lighting his eyes. I screamed as I rotated enough to free my other hand from the rope tying it to the coffin. I pushed myself forward with my good arm so I could also free my feet.

I wasn't even close to fighting shape, but there wasn't a chance in hell that I was about to let Kingsley regain his feet. I was the last line of defense for Sloane. Kingsley lurched again, trying to convince his legs to keep him upright. He never made it. I watched remorselessly as the Fae crumpled to his knees for the last time. I held my knife ready in case he managed a final burst of strength.

His eyes flew to meet mine. They were no longer filled with madness; only terror lurked in those emerald depths. Blood frothed on his lips as he tried to form words, but he wasn't able to push sound out of his ruined throat.

My pitiless gaze pierced the darkness as I stared down at him. The crimson pulsing light from the relic embedded in my shoulder was the only light illuminating the gruesome scene. I slowly shook my head, never breaking eye contact. "Say hello to your wife."

Aldrich Kingsley's eyes flared wide for a moment, the blood bubbles on his lips bursting as he tried to respond. Then his strength gave out. He collapsed in a puddle of his own blood. The dark crimson pool oozed across the chapel floor. I watched it mingle with the fresh paint the Fae had so carefully painted. I silently witnessed his last breath. It sent ripples dancing along the pool of blood seeping out from under his body. Then, there was nothing.

I fell back on the coffin top. My shoulder blazed in agony as my slight fall jarred the relic still embedded in my body. I reached up to grab the crystal, either to stabilize it or rip it out. I hadn't decided yet. When I tried to grasp the faceted face of the relic, my hand cramped up in painful misery, knocking the relic out of my shoulder and to the floor with a crash, rolling to stop right next to the Fae's dead body.

I screamed and suddenly felt all the slices and tears that Meridiana had blocked as part of our bargain. I felt every. Single. One. Another scream of pain echoed through the chapel, as the runes painted on the floor flashed a dark crimson. As red as Kingsley's blood. Time had just run out, in more ways than one.

# Chapter 54

My eyes tore around the chapel. It was illuminated by a faint flickering red light that bled from the Shard into the runes painted on the floor. The light seemed to pulse like it was throbbing along with a heartbeat. As quickly as I could, I freed myself from my restraints. However, I overestimated my pain tolerance. Agony ripped through my shoulder, and I collapsed on the floor, eye level with the glowing, bloody paint.

*Shit. Shit. SHIT.*

Between Kingsley stabbing me, and me spilling his life's blood on the painted floor, we must have triggered the ritual. My eyes darted frantically around the room, searching for anything that could help me stop the magic throbbing up from the runes. I couldn't see anything that could help me. No notes or books. Nothing. The crazy Fae must have been working from memory. He'd had enough practice in his murder den.

Trying not to scream, I crawled over to the Fae to feel for a pulse. The ritualistic painting must have sucked it all out of him. I shivered violently. It could've just as easily been my blood lighting up the room instead of the Fae's if I hadn't been able to call up my magic.

The runes on the floor flared and a long dark crack in reality sprang to life, hovering just above Kingsley's body. I watched in horror as the crack expanded, growing wider by the second. Momentarily paralyzed in fright at seeing the unimaginable, I couldn't react fast enough as a blue spiral of light erupted from the now gaping tear between this world and the next. The light plowed straight into my chest, knocking me onto my side.

I gasped for breath, half laying on the dead Fae with the wind partially knocked out of me. Gritting against the pain, I forced myself to sit up. As soon as I saw what was waiting for me inside the tear, I wished I hadn't.

The glimpse I caught of the other side of the veil was enough to make me want to embrace religion. Any religion. Anything at all that would guarantee that I wouldn't end up *there*. A swirling vortex made up of millions of different malevolent lights of every color rushed towards me. There was a great shriek and a scrabbling of souls as they exploded towards the tear in the veil. While I knew it would be bad if those unhoused souls were released upon the city of New Orleans, they were nothing compared to what was clawing up through the middle of the vortex.

Grotesque faces, distorted by rage, growled up at me. I saw fangs, horns, hooves, and wings in that mass. Demonic creatures clawed over each other to be the first to reach the tear. They were nothing like Meridiana. The demons fighting their way towards me were terrifying. The obscene, deformed, and monstrous *things* battling towards the tear in the veil scared me shitless. They were slashing, scratching, and scrabbling to be the first to break through into New Orleans.

Guess who would be the first one to greet them? No way was I going to be the welcoming committee to Hell.

The glowing light emanating from the crystal relic flared brilliantly. I grabbed the relic instinctively, holding it up between me and the tear in the veil like it could hold back the oncoming horde. White fragments of light swirled under my hands. I gasped as I realized the ghosts were still contained in the crystal. Kingsley death hadn't released them.

"Who you gonna call?" I muttered to myself. The white lights flared menacingly. "Chill out!" I said to the relic, "I'm a friend of Ben's. He sent me to find you." The entire host of white lights contained within the crystal seemed to perform a swirling little bow to me, acknowledging my words before continuing their frantic swimming back and forth within their faceted prison.

"Okay, I'm guessing that means we are on the same side." I slurred. The pain from my injuries was making me woozy.

A spear of orange light lanced straight out of the dark tear between worlds, rocketing off into the night. I couldn't afford to get distracted now. This was a horrific turn of events. Souls were escaping, set loose upon New Orleans, but it could get so much worse. I needed to close off the tear quickly. We could deal with any escapees later, on a one-to-one basis. Right now, I just had to limit the prison break. But how?

I saw claws reach through the edges of the tear. The horned demon hoisted itself through, growing in size by the millisecond as it set foot in the mortal realm. It grinned at me, showing wicked-looking fangs and a forked tongue. I expected it to eat me right then and there, but apparently the demon had more pressing matters to attend to in the mortal world.

"I'll be seeing you soon. Mark my words," it hisspered before darting off into the night.

My energy was draining with every heartbeat. I looked around for help, but there was no one in the hellish chapel. I had to figure out a way to close the veil by myself, to be my own savior. My vision dimmed, and I shook my head drunkenly.

*Focus, Cam.*

Red fingers suddenly gripped the edges of the tear in the veil. I stared in horror at Aldrich Kingsley's face. Beyond the tear, his insubstantial body drifted like it was made of nothing but smoke. However, the hand gripping the edge of the veil was as real as I was. He looked up at me with wild eyes.

"I did it!" he cried in triumph. "I found her! Did you see her? Isn't she beautiful, my Carina?"

"Go back to where you belong!" I screamed at him. Terror burned away the fuzziness in my brain. Using the last scrap of willpower I possessed, I hurled the crystal relic at the tear in the veil, hoping to knock Kingsley back into the Abyss. However, I'd vastly underestimated the damage my body had endured in the past few days. The relic dribbled out of my hands rather than flying forcefully at Kingsley. The crystal landed on the point on the hard floor under the rip in the veil and shattered.

I was knocked backwards as white lights spiraled up from the broken fragments of the relic. The ghosts swirled in front of the tear. A single spark of inspiration spiraled through the fog clouding my thoughts. If Kingsley could use the ghosts to power a spell, then maybe I could too. The only spell I knew that might have a prayer of destroying the tear. A null shield.

"Guys," I said weakly, not knowing exactly how to address the swirling spirits. Nothing happened. I cleared my throat and tried again, "Ghosts, I need your help. Please."

The lights stopped swirling, appearing to turn to face me. I'm not sure what gave me that impression as they had no faces or bodies, but I knew that somehow, they had heard me.

"If that tear stays open, I don't know what else is going to be able to get across the veil. We have to close it. Kingsley was going to use your energy against your will to power his ritual. Will you power my spell instead? By choice?"

The white light paused, almost like it was considering my words. I held my breath, waiting. I was still new at using null shields and was going to throw the best one I could at the tear, hoping it would eat the magical energy of the rip in the veil like it had consumed the bomb's energy. However, if they agreed to help, the ghosts might be able to give me a little extra magical boost, and I needed all the help I could get. Finally, the white lights dipped in what I imagined to be a slight nod. I let my head fall to the floor in relief. With not a moment more to waste, I used the dregs of my energy to pull on the shadows, sucking them into my body. I crammed as many shadows inside me as I could hold and then cupped my hands to hold even more. It only took a moment, but it felt like I'd just drunk a river full of whisky. The magic *burned* within me.

Unable to hold anymore, I directed my magic at the tear in reality and screamed as the shadows flooded towards the opening. The white lights swirled around the shadows as they streamed towards the rip, somehow igniting my shadow magic. Brilliant flashes lit my darkness from within. I gasped at the flood of magic that flowed through me, around me, out of me. It was both freezing and burning me all at once. A massive dome of shadows sparking with white light roared to life in front of the tear, decimating it. The dome expanded, growing to touch the ceiling and floor before collapsing in on itself with a concussive blast.

The last thing I saw before the darkness took me was the alter at the front of the chapel. The tear had vanished. I surrendered to the encroaching blackness with a peaceful smile gracing my lips.

# Chapter 55

The snickety-snack of knitting needles intruded upon my dreams. My eyes fluttered open to see afternoon sunlight dripping across my bedspread in lazy beams. Mama sat next to me in her chair, working on her latest project.

"Welcome back, child," she said, eyes fixed on her knitting as she finished the row she was working on.

"We've got to stop meeting like this, Mama," I groaned, reaching for the glass of water on the bedside table to ease the sandpaper stuck inside my throat. My hands sported new, thick white bandages, causing me to hold the glass awkwardly.

"Stop making reckless, impulsive decisions, and we might." Mama spoke drily, but a relieved smile deepened the wrinkles at the corners of her eyes.

The cool water trickled down my throat, filling in the crevices that had cracked open since I had last had any liquid. I sighed in relief, taking another sip. Mama and I sat there in silence, simply enjoying each other's company. Mama put her knitting to the side as Ben pushed the door open with his elbow. He moved carefully, balancing a tray of tea and chocolate chip cookies.

He broke the companionable quiet, sending pieces of the silence scattering to hide in the shadows. "Well, don't you look prettier than a glob of butter meltin' on a stack of wheat cakes!" he called out merrily to Mama as he bustled into the room and kissed her on the cheek.

Addressing me, he said, "You look like a wolf chewed you up and shit you over a cliff," as he set the tray down on the bedside table.

"Whatever chewed me up was in dire need of a breath mint," I groaned. Switching gears, I asked "Are those for me?" I pointed at the cookies hopefully. They looked like they had just come out of the oven. I was already salivating as the delicious aroma wafted up.

Ben nodded as he poured tea for all three of us. "I've been as busy as popcorn on a skillet while Mama kept an eye on you. Cookin', cleanin', shooin' that teenage werewolf boy of yours away."

"Andrei?" I asked.

"Yeah. He was here so much I was worried his butt was gonna be permanently imprinted in that there chair. It's been a couple of days, you know," Ben said.

I looked up sharply as he handed me my mug. "How many?"

"This is the afternoon of November the second," Mama said calmly, settling back in her chair with the mug that Ben offered her.

The old man snagged a couple of cookies and perched on the foot of my bed. He broke off part of a cookie and passed it up to Goliath. The mouse was nestled in his customary place on Ben's shoulder, half-hidden in the old man's wild white hair. The little familiar popped out long enough to snag the cookie before darting back to nibble at his prize.

I'd been asleep for almost two days. At least I'd woken up.

"Seems like I missed a lot. Fill me in?" I grabbed a cookie myself. There was no way I was letting Mama's efforts in the kitchen go to waste.

Ben and Mama took turns sharing what had happened while I'd been unconscious. Apparently, they had pieced together the scanty clues I'd left for them soon after Ben returned to the house. They reached out to the werewolves and redirected their search efforts to find me.

After finding Sloane in the parking lot of the funeral parlor, the Pack split up. Some stayed to protect Sloane and called Mama to come with her healing kit. Damon led the rest into the building. They had to enter cautiously, just in case there were any booby-traps rigged to surprise them. By the time the wolves made it to the chapel, they found me passed out on the floor with Aldrich Kingsley's corpse lying next to me.

The werewolves extracted me from the chapel of death and handed me off to Mama when they saw the deep lacerations on my palms. They'd also delivered Kingsley's body to Letitia at the Fae Embassy. Damon personally notified the Collective of the events that had transpired.

I choked on the bite of cookie I'd been eating. "The Collective knows what happened? I thought Kingsley was doing this on the side, without their backing."

Ben winked at me. "The Collective knows what that there Pack reported happened. Namely, Kingsley attempted some sort of ritual and failed. He ended up deader than a doornail and the werewolves recovered the relic."

Mama shrugged. "These kinds of things happen all the time when you mess with magic above your weight class. Everyone assumes that Aldrich went mad with grief and overstepped his abilities. With no one to provide evidence to the contrary, that has become the official story. Any other versions would invite too many questions. Too much scrutiny from powerful beings." Her eyes flashed a warning at me. I understood. If I wanted to continue to fly under the radar, I needed to keep my mouth shut.

Ben smiled at me, "But if you'd happen upon an interestin' story and want to share with some very curious friends, that'd be okay with us."

I grinned up at the lanky old man. He was incorrigible.

"Maybe another time, Ben. I think I need some time to process. Try to make sense of it myself, you know?" I demurred.

"Sure, sure, when you're ready, of course," he mumbled into his teacup.

I held up my hands. "What's the prognosis on these, Mama?"

I wasn't hopeful. I knew that I'd likely caused more damage to them in my fight with Kingsley and then by mending the veil. Meridiana hadn't been able to heal them after all. She had just given me enough demonic pain blockers to let me survive the night.

That reminded me; I owed her a favor. I shivered involuntarily wondering what kind of favor the demoness would demand.

Mama interrupted my dark thoughts, "Well, let's see, child." She set her tea aside and slowly moved to get her supplies.

She removed the bandage from my shoulder first. I'd almost forgotten that Kingsley stabbed there. Although it was a bad angle, I could tell that Mama had done her best to stitch me back together. I would have a scar to remember my close call, though. I was practically bouncing in the bed as Mama unwrapped my hands.

Ben grinned at my impatience. "You rush a miracle man, you get rotten miracles, girlie."

My gaze shot up to him, wondering if he knew he quoted one of my favorite movies of all time. Although he looked more like Miracle Max than Mama did.

When the final wrappings fell away, all three of us stared. Scars covered my hands, but they looked months old, not days. I curled my fingers slowly into fists and then extended them fully. It hurt and they were stiff, but at least I could move them. I flipped my hands back and forth, clenching them as I marveled at the flexibility in my fingers. Physical therapy would likely help the stiffness and the pain would fade in time, but the damage could have been so much worse. It *should* have been worse.

My confused gaze met Mama's serious one, asking the question without giving it voice.

She shook her head slowly, "I think your magic is more potent that we imagined."

I nodded silently, unable to verbalize my thoughts past the lump in my throat. Grateful didn't begin to cover what I was feeling. I couldn't imagine life without full use my hands and, although I'd resigned myself to the probability, it hadn't come to fruition. Tears welled in my eyes and spilled down my cheeks. Mama and Ben surrounded me in a massive bear hug as I sobbed out my relief and joy. Directly into my hands.

Mama released me from her care the next day with a healing poultice to help with the stiffness, orders for daily exercises, and a stern word to come back to visit soon. Ben dropped me off at home. He insisted on carrying all my things up to my apartment. Even with the necromancer at my side, I followed my extensive security protocols just in case Kingsley had arranged retribution from beyond the veil. I wouldn't put it past him.

I thanked Ben and gently shooed him out of my apartment. I needed some me time, and I was desperate to see what I had missed in the last few days. When I tried to turn on my phone, the black screen refused to spring to life with the comforting blue glow. I sighed at being forced to wait and plugged it in.

While the phone was charging, I engaged in a lackluster, superficial tidy-up of the apartment. It was a mess from my hurried exit. Weapons and gear were strewn everywhere. Everything needed to be checked, cleaned, and returned to their proper places. Eventually. The comforting idea of a steaming mug of tea distracted me from my well-intentioned cleaning, so I boiled the kettle while I checked my phone. Still dead. I fidgeted with the quartz ring on its chain around my neck as I searched for something more interesting than tidying to keep me occupied while I waited.

My eyes landed on the large white box that Ben had set on the kitchen counter. The one Andrei had given to me. In all the hubbub, I'd forgotten about the werewolf's gift. Curiously, I carefully slid a fingernail under the tape and lifted off the top. I folded back the wrapping slowly.

A small moan of pleasure slipped out from between my lips. Nestled in crisp white tissue paper was a beautiful new leather jacket. I think the best term for it was 'sexy'. My hands ran over the cool black leather, delighting in the suppleness of the butter-soft material under my fingertips. A little tingle of anticipation danced along my spine as I slid into the jacket. It molded itself to my curves perfectly. Some tension I'd been carrying for the last week finally eased out of my shoulders. I ran into my bedroom to examine my reflection.

I admired the sexy badass who peered back at me from the mirror. I spun around, running my hands over the buckles of the new jacket. "It has pockets!" I squealed at the discovery. Pockets in a variety of sizes sewn into the lining. Oh, this werewolf was *good.* He could stay.

My phone dinged to tell me it was finally charged enough to use. I hurried to the kitchen and flicked it open, unsurprised that I had messages waiting. Sloane's text popped up first, asking me to call her when I was feeling better. I knew she would want the entire story. I wasn't up to recounting it all just yet. Perhaps I would head over to the Forge for a drink later. I also had messages from Mama, Ben, and several of the werewolves, checking in to see how I was doing. I replied to all of them saying that I was recovering and would be in touch soon.

A message popped up from Magnus as well. He wanted to talk, to smooth things over between us. I ignored it. I didn't know how I felt about the handsome man. Somewhere along the way, I'd caught the start of feelings for him and then he'd betrayed me. Lied to me. Led me on. I wasn't ready to forgive and forget.

I kept scrolling, surprised when I saw Logan had even sent a text to see how I was recovering. He casually mentioned that Lady Letitia wanted to meet with me at my earliest convenience. Which really meant as soon as possible. She could wait. He also hinted at a potential job waiting for me. I sighed. I wasn't up to working right now. A couple of days of recuperation and relaxation sounded good to me.

Speaking of relaxation, I headed towards my kettle to refill my tea. I toyed with my necklace again as I waited. The rose-colored crystal in the silver ring caught the light pouring through my windows. Twinkles of blue flashed in the sunlight. I hadn't noticed the dimension of color before. It was pretty. I let it fall to my chest and the ring tinkled pleasantly against the carved charm my mother's note claimed was from my father. In all the recent excitement, I hadn't been able to try and uncover any further information on that particular front. I decided that pursuing any lead I could uncover on my father's identity would be my first priority. A rumbling boil burbled from the kettle. Well, my first priority after I made myself a cup of tea.

I reached over to pour the hot water into my mug. My eyes snagged on two large white envelopes that were laid carefully on the counter. I hadn't noticed them before now. Curious, I tore open the thinner one. It was from Meridiana.

*I'm calling in my favor. Girls' night out. Drinks are on you. —M*

I grinned. Leave it to a demoness to spend a favor so frivolously. Secretly, I was already looking forward to it. I was excited to see what shenanigans we could get up to.

I turned my attention to the second envelope, only now recognizing it as the one Kingsley had given me as payment. A jolt went through my body as the enchanted wax seal broke easily under my thumbs. I held my breath as I ripped it open, tearing it further in my haste, and pulled out the pile of cash. Enough money to buy me some peace and quiet for the next few months.

"Ouch!" I glanced down. Blood welled in a surprisingly deep papercut on my index finger. I stuck it in my mouth, sucking the droplet of blood away. It hurt more than such a small cut should've. I pulled my finger out of my mouth and looked at it again. Blood sprang up along with a tiny spike of pain. I danced around my kitchen, waving my hand back and forth in a futile effort to get the pain to subside. The only thing I managed to do was to flick a few droplets of blood towards my torso.

"Damn," I said, pulling my chin in to look down. I wanted to wipe the drop of red away before I ended up with yet another blood stain on my clothing. I'd have to start setting aside a larger budget for clothes if I kept ruining clothes at this rate.

I jerked back in shock. The carved golden talisman on the necklace was glowing.

I jumped when a deep, male voice rang out from the oblong charm, "It's about time you opened up this thing, Sophia!"

I yanked on the necklace, breaking the thin chain and hurling it across the kitchen with a clatter.

"Sophia! Sophia? Where are you? What's going on?" The male voice shifted from annoyed to concerned.

I grabbed a kitchen mug and carefully crept towards the talking necklace.

"I can hear you moving around. Just answer me already, damn it." The tone of command in the voice raised the hairs on the back of my arms.

Without saying a word, I plopped the mug over the necklace, muting the noise. Confident I'd contained the thing for now, I hurried to my bedroom. I whipped open the closet door and fell to my knees, using a dull practice blade to wiggle some of the floor boards loose. Soon, a small iron safe glinted at me dully front the floor. I'd had it installed to mute the effects of magical items I procured for Logan. Magic and iron didn't mix. I spun the dials and it clicked open.

Snagging a playing card from a deck on my coffee table, I crept back up to the mug. I heard annoyed buzzing from the voice on the other end of the necklace, but it was muted through the thick ceramic. Careful not to touch the enchanted item for fear of what it would do to me, I wiggled the card until I flipped the necklace into the cup, much like one would to capture a spider. Except spiders didn't talk.

The volume rose from the oblong charm, but I ignored it. Moving swiftly, I carried the mug to my bedroom with my arm fully extended to keep the talking necklace as far from me as possible.

"Who are you? Where is Sophia? Tell me!" The voice roared. I ignored it.

Carefully, I set the mug down in the iron safe and slammed the door shut. The voice cut off abruptly. I spun the dials and sat back on my heels, considering the safe with a furrowed brow.

Who was on the other end of that necklace? And why did he call out my mother's name?

THE END

# Thank you!

Thank you for picking my book. If you enjoyed it, please consider adding a review. I would be grateful if you could spare a couple of minutes to leave a review. It need only be a line or two and it makes a massive difference. It's easy to skip this step – I often did myself until I realized how much authors count on these reviews. I'd be so grateful if you would take a moment to post a rating and a few words. More reviews help other readers discover this series and, as I now realize, it helps your humble author enormously.

Best wishes,

L.L. Gray

Turn the page to read a sample of **FELONS AND FANGS** - Smoke and Shadows Series Book 2

# Don't forget, your FREE book is waiting!

**A killer pair of shoes, a party of a lifetime, and a demon.
What could possibly go wrong?**

Cameron Blaze owes a demon a favor and what better way to pay off a debt than to have a girl's night out? The plan was simple. Find a killer pair of heels, go to a great bar, and party into the early hours of the morning. Cameron thinks that she has everything planned. The shoes on are, the drinks are poured, and the party is in full swing. She just forgot to account for one small thing. Magic going haywire.

# Sign up here to get your free book!

https://www.subscribepage.com/llgray

# Felons and Fangs - Chapter 1

I threw myself into a forward roll, narrowly avoiding the sledgehammer-like haymaker aimed at my head. The half-ogre grunted, stumbling past me in a barely controlled fall. I grinned. He hadn't expected the speed. I sprang to my feet, spinning on a heel to face my lumbering opponent. The big man pawed the sweat from his eyes before setting himself to attack again.

I raised my short sword, bouncing lightly on the balls of my feet. Deep-set eyes burned with intelligence. The half-ogre wiggled his fingers before clenching his fists, stretching the skin tight across his broad, hairy knuckles. The grayish-greenish tinge that betrayed his supernatural ancestry caught the evening light. I could see why people assumed that ogres were the villains. Ogres were big, ugly, and brutish, but also clever. Imagine someone with the brawn of Hercules and the face of a billy goat meeting the business end of a frying pan, who was also a grandmaster at chess, and you'll get an idea why ogres are considered among the most dangerous Supes.

A growl brought my attention back to the business at hand. The half-ogre wasn't as big as his full-blooded cousins, but that didn't matter when he lowered his head and charged, relying on his bulk to pummel me into submission. The drawback was that he had to haul all that muscle around. Nothing about my five-four, lean athletic build would've inspired fear in the big guy, but I was quick. As long as I could stay out of arm's reach, I had a chance to tire him out.

As the ogre rushed towards me, I dodged again. This time, he was ready for it. He spun with me and feinted a jab at my head, testing my defenses. I danced backward slightly, using the movement to search for an opening. He left his right arm hanging out between us for a breath too long. I could've struck, but I knew from experience that this ogre was wily. I couldn't afford to get lured into his long reach. Not without a plan at least.

The ogre shuffled forward again, his large, hairy feet squelching on the mat. I didn't look down. Not just because he was in desperate need of a pedicure. No, the attack would come from his shoulders and chest, not his feet. He preferred the noble art of boxing to MMA-style fighting. Me, I didn't care, as long as I won.

With a roar, the ogre sprang at me, arms outstretched to capture me in a sweaty bear hug. I dodged to the left and yanked on my shadow magic. I blurred out of sight. The ogre's eyes went wide as I apparently vanished right before his eyes. I used the momentary advantage to swipe up with the flat of my blade and rap him painfully on the wrist. The ogre hissed, yanking his arm back to his side as he whirled around. I let my shadows fall away as I pressed my advantage, hitting with two lightning-fast taps to his torso before dancing out of his reach once more.

The ogre let out a bellow of pain, batting the tip of my wooden sword aside with one meaty arm. He closed the distance between us. His fist flashed out as jabbed me with a quick combination. Despite his speed, I dodged easily, noting that he left that right arm hanging in midair too long once again. I whipped my blade up, hoping to catch the nerves running along his forearm. The ogre surprised me. He opened his fist and caught the blade, jerking it and me forward.

*Damn ogres and their damn feints! Why couldn't they all be stupid like the stories said?*

I stumbled forward, caught off balance by the unexpected move. The half-ogre wrapped one massive arm around my biceps and chest, effectively pinning my arms to my torso. He lifted me up so my feet flailed helplessly in mid-air. With his free hand, he palmed my head like a basketball and *squeezed*.

"Call it, Cam!" the ogre grunted.

"Never!" I shouted, trying to wriggle out of his iron grip.

"Admit it, I won!"

"Inconceivable!" I shouted. I whipped the wooden training sword up to kiss the ogre's forehead between his eyes, almost hitting myself in the face. "If I die, I'll take you with me!"

The ogre batted the wooden blade aside, sending it spinning into the corner of the gym. "Fine, if you won't concede, then suffer the consequences!" he roared in my ear. I had a moment to wonder what he meant before massive ogre knuckles ground into my scalp. "Noogies!"

"Hey!" I batted ineffectually at the big guy's hand. "Hank! Hey! Stop it! You're messing up my hair!"

"Not like anyone would know. Concede!"

"All right, all right. You win!" I laughed. He released me immediately. I slid to the floor gasping with laughter.

Hank chuckled with me. "That'll teach you! Never mess with the mighty Hank!" He flexed his impressive biceps, striking a victorious pose.

Hank was a half-ogre who worked security for the Fae Embassy. He was also a great guy to train with because of his size and his fighting expertise. Whenever I went toe to toe with Hank, I always felt like I could really push myself to my limits without fear of injuring him or me. While he was a nice guy and a great sparring partner, Hank wasn't always around. He was often sent off on mysterious assignments and could be gone for weeks at a time. However, since Halloween, he'd been sticking closer to home. Which was great for my training and bad for my scalp.

I made a show of sniffing at my shoulders and back where I was drenched with his sweat from the unexpected bear hug. I wrinkled my nose. "The *smell* will teach me," I said.

"Be faster," Hank shrugged.

I rolled my eyes. "Remind me what the score is, big guy? Four to one in my favor, isn't it?"

"The only bout that matters is the last one. Which I won." Hank struck another pose, sweat making his muscles glint in the fading sunlight.

"Well, let's have another round to see who's the champion," I suggested.

Hank glanced at the clock on the wall of the gym, the grin dropping from his face. "I can't. I need to get cleaned up and back to the Embassy. The Interim Ambassador has an engagement tonight and I don't think she'd approve if her bodyguard turned up like this." He waved a meaty hand at his sweat-drenched clothes.

I nodded. Lady Letitia was a stickler for propriety when it came to appearances. Especially since she had been made the Interim Fae Ambassador following her uncle's death on Halloween. Aldrich Kingsley had tried to open a portal to Hell to bring his dead wife's soul back, by using my best friend and me to fuel his magical ritual. Needless to say, I objected strongly and let him know. Repeatedly. With my knife to his jugular. Letitia had been doing everything in her power to demonstrate to the greater New Orleans area that Kingsley's crazy hadn't tainted all the fae.

"Fine," I said, moving with him towards a bench on the far side of the padded mats. "But before you go, can you help me with these?" I held up my hands that were wrapped tightly with extra padding.

"Sure." Hank started loosening the wraps. As he worked, a pair of werewolves in human form took our place on the sparring mats and started their workout. I glanced around at the gym. It was a swanky place full of high-end equipment and lots of padding for the Supernatural clientèle. Most Norms didn't set foot in the place more than once. They were scared off by the amount of muscle on display, the exorbitant prices, or a well-developed sixth sense for survival.

Hank dexterously worked the knots loose. "Hey, you're getting better with your magic. Your disappearing act really threw me off my game and *I* know you can do it."

I grinned. "Yeah, I've been practicing. It's getting easier to use, but I still feel like I've got a way to go."

Hank nodded. "I've heard that learning magic takes a while. Be patient. You'll get there." The last of the wraps fell away. Hank let out a low whistle when he saw the barely-healed lacerations crisscrossing my hands. "Are you sure it's a good idea to be sparring this much? I mean, this is the fourth time in as many days. Shouldn't you be resting those hands?"

I jerked my chin at the training blade lying on the floor. "That's why I get the sword instead of punching you, you big lug."

"I suppose," Hank said, unconvinced. He handed me the wraps. "But Mama would have your hide if you mess up all of her hard work."

"Well, we wouldn't want that now, would we? Speaking of Mama, she sent along some of her chocolate chip cookies."

His eyes lit up. "The ones with the bits of toffee that take her two days to make?"

"The very same."

He stuck out a massive hand, "Give 'em here!"

A wicked twinkle lit my eyes. "Can't. I ate them."

"No you didn't!" His eyes widened in disbelief. "She only makes those a couple times a year and they're my favorite."

I chuckled. "You're right, I didn't." I dug into my bag under the bench and pulled out a plastic box filled with the cookies. "Here you go," I said, offering it to him. Hank's eyes locked on the box, and he grabbed for the treats eagerly. I pulled it back, holding up a finger. He cocked his head questioningly. "These are all yours. If you don't tell Mama about all this." I spun my finger to indicate the gym and the sparring mats.

"Deal!" The ogre said, grabbing the box. I let him have it this time. "Although, she's gonna figure it out eventually, Cam. How are they feeling anyway?" he asked, popping the lid and jamming an entire cookie into his mouth.

I flipped my hands back and forth, flexing the fingers. "Stiff. Mama told me to keep working on the flexibility. If I don't, they'll stiffen up permanently."

He shook his head somberly. "That's shitty. Do you know if the damage is reversible?"

"A couple more days and she should be able to tell exactly how much dexterity I've lost. Thank the gods for Supernatural healing, am I right?" I grinned, trying to keep my words light and unconcerned. The reality was that I was nervous I'd never regain full flexibility in my hands. A knife-fighter with stiff hands wouldn't survive long in my world.

Mama was the best Supernatural healer in New Orleans but hadn't been willing to give me a full prognosis. Not yet anyway. However, she had cleared me for light activity, encouraging me to stretch and move my hands now that the worst of the superficial damage had healed. I was sure that she didn't mean sparring with an ogre, but what she didn't know wouldn't hurt her. Besides, I was going crazy just sitting around.

Hank interrupted my thoughts, "Right. I gotta go or I'm gonna be late, and the boss lady doesn't like that. Thanks for the cookies!" The half-ogre grabbed his water bottle from the bench, carefully tucked the box of sweets under a huge arm and headed for the showers.

"Same time tomorrow?" I called after him.

"Can't. I gotta work. Call me next week, Cam," Hank said over his shoulder before disappearing into the locker room.

Two dwarves with massive beards that could have concealed entire menageries gave me a side eye as they walked by. I sighed, collapsing on the bench and sipping on my water while I watched the werewolves spar. My life was a whole lot of crazy right now. I'd become a celebrity in the Supernatural circles of New Orleans overnight, and not necessarily the good kind. Something about being at the epicenter of the murder of a powerful and respected member of the Supe community while he was attempting a black magic ritual will do that to a girl's reputation. Even if it was self-defense.

Besides, there was the whole mysterious issue of the enchanted talking necklace that I had locked in my safe at home. Eventually, I finally conceded that I was avoiding my apartment and the idea of dealing with the magical necklace. Still, questions chased each other around my mind.

*Why did my mom arrange for me to receive the enchanted necklace after she passed away?*

*What was I supposed to do with a talking necklace?*

And most importantly, *who was doing the talking?*

I grabbed a towel from the pile near the bench and mopped my face free of sweat as I watched the werewolves put on a show. A Pack had just officially moved to New Orleans. Technically, they had been welcomed by the Collective, the ruling body for Supes in the Louisiana region, but that was the only welcome they'd received. Everyone else was trying to figure out where the Pack fit in with the Supe hierarchy, which led to tensions running high and more fights than normal breaking out. I wondered if the sparring match on display was an effort to integrate with the local Supes or to show off the prowess of the werewolves. Knowing what little I did about the Alpha, it was probably both.

A stranger sat down on the end of my bench. I glanced at him out of the corner of my eye, appreciatively noting the handsome physique through his fitted T-shirt. The stranger sucked in a breath as one of the werewolves tackled the other to the floor with a vicious snarl.

"I wouldn't want to get on *his* bad side," the man said to no one in particular.

"Which one?" I asked, using the opportunity to turn and examine the stranger more completely. He had golden-blond hair that was cropped stylishly short. It accented his ruggedly masculine
features to their full advantage. A wide, intelligent brow cut down to sky-blue eyes. Attractive stubble covered his defined jawline. The man's full lips curved into an amiable smile as he continued to watch the wolves.

"Either one, really. Pissing off werewolves never seemed like a particularly wise choice if you ask me."

I nodded, sipping on my water. I wondered what kind of Supe he was if he mentioned werewolves so casually. "I don't believe I've seen you around. Do you come here often?" I asked.

"No, I'm a first timer. I'm here on a job and Logan Wilder pointed out some local spots that would be of interest," the stranger said, turning his attention fully to me.

"Ah, you know Logan then?" I asked, convinced the name drop hadn't been accidental. The stranger was showing his bona fides. Logan was my job broker. My middleman, who communicated with clients and kept me out of the public eye. As much as possible, anyway. It was an expensive service, but worth it.

"Tangentially. I've employed his services before, but never in New Orleans. It's a lovely city. One I look forward to exploring more fully." His eyes sparkled with deeper meaning as he met mine boldly.

I kept my face bland as I replied. "Yeah, I love living here. There's always something to do and something new to see. If you're looking for a spot where the locals hang out, you should give the Forge a try. Best cocktails in town, Mr...?" I left the last part hanging, offering him the opportunity to introduce himself.

"Otto," the man said, extending his hand.

"Cameron," I returned, shaking his hand firmly once before turning back to the sparring match. The last time I'd encouraged the attentions of a handsome stranger, he'd turned out to be a werewolf who tricked me to further his own ends. Fool me once, shame on me. Fool me twice? Over your dead body.

"Not Cameron Blaze?"

I looked back at him in surprise. "Yes," I said slowly. "That's me."

"Logan Wilder speaks highly of you," Otto said, smiling disarmingly.

I relaxed slightly. Logan was my job broker. I wasn't surprised my name came up if Otto had spoken to Logan recently.

"He's a good guy," I said noncommittally.

"Indeed. He mentioned that you were one of his best agents, but were taking some time off for personal reasons. I'm curious. What would it take to procure your assistance on a time-sensitive job?"

Tension crawled up my back. I worked with Logan precisely to avoid cold approaches like this. Besides, Logan knew I was taking some time off following the fae fiasco. So, why would he send this stranger to hunt me down?

"Not interested," I said coolly, jamming my water bottle into the bag at my feet.

"It pays well," Otto said. "Very well."

"Then you shouldn't have trouble finding someone to help you out. I'm on vacation."

"Well then, perhaps I could take you out for a drink?" He held up his hands as I shot him a dark look. "Just a getting-to-know-the-neighborhood drink. No ulterior motives."

My mind flashed back to Magnus. The treacherous werewolf had said something similar, but his motives were solely ulterior. He'd used me to find an ancient missing relic for the Pack and then tried to steal it from me. I didn't handle betrayal well. "No. Thanks," I said shortly. Then, so as not to appear rude, I smiled and added, "Enjoy your visit."

I grabbed my bag and retreated to the ladies' showers. I took my time, washing the sweat away and lathering up my long, honey-streaked hair. One great thing about the gym was that the water always stayed hot. By the time I dried off and put my street clothes on, Otto had vanished.

# Felons and Fangs - Chapter 2

I shrugged into my leather jacket and shouldered my gym bag as I pushed through the doors of the gym into the early November evening. The jacket had been a gift from the same werewolves who were causing territory disputes in New Orleans. I had saved the son of the Alpha, but lost my favorite jacket. To be honest, this one was an upgrade. The leather was as soft as butter and there were a ton of pockets hidden all over the garment. It was the type of jacket every woman wanted. Sexy as hell and super practical. Winner, winner, chicken dinner.

I hit the street and looked around, trying to decide what to do. The sun was setting, but I didn't want to head home just yet. Heading home meant addressing the issue of the mysterious necklace and I didn't feel up to it right now. I knew I had to figure it out sometime, but that didn't mean it had to be today. I tucked my bag into the small storage space behind the seat on my Rebel, pulled on my helmet and threw a leg over the motorcycle as I tried to figure out what to do with myself. My Rebel roared to life and I drifted into traffic, letting my mind wander. Finally, I decided some company, a drink, and dinner sounded like an excellent way to avoid my apartment a little while longer. I turned the Rebel towards my best friend's bar in search of all three.

Sloane O'Shea owned a bar that catered primarily to the Supernatural population of New Orleans. The Forge was aptly, if not creatively, named. Sloane had turned an old blacksmith shop into a lively night spot that served imaginative cocktails. She'd even kept the giant anvil in the middle of the largest room as a repurposed table for her patrons. The heavy iron anvil also acted as a fae deterrent. I'm pretty sure that was the main reason Sloane had kept the monstrosity. The leprechaun barkeep had a less than cordial relationship with the fae.

Sloane and I were best friends, although you wouldn't know it to look at us. We were as different as high heels and combat boots. Sloane was a petite leprechaun, with Black Irish coloring. She had pale skin, dark hair chopped fashionably short over slightly pointed ears, and luminous blue eyes. On the other hand, I towered over her at my distinctly average height. Honey-streaked brown waves fell past my shoulders, complementing the caramel of my skin. Startling golden eyes framed by long dark lashes were my most notable feature, which Sloane kept telling me to play up whenever we went out on the town.

I parked the Rebel in the small lot behind the Forge and went around to the front, dodging around the massive anvil and weaving my way through the crowd to the bar. Sloane waved at me from behind the heavy wooden bar and waved me towards the far end.

"Hey! How are you doing?" Sloane asked loudly over the pounding of a classic rock song.

"Same old, same old," I said, offering my hand. Our fingers flew through the complex series of movements in our secret handshake. The ritual belonged in middle school, but part of me enjoyed the fact we could buck convention by doing it in a bar.

Sloane shot me a knowing look. "Still avoiding your problems?"

"Giving myself space. They say it's healthy."

"Avoidance is never healthy," Sloane pointed out.

I glared at her. "The only unhealthy thing I want right now is some of those cheesy fries with loads of candied bacon, a beer, and maybe a shot of tequila."

"Oh, it's *that* kind of a night then?"

"Don't judge me. I'm on vacation. No vacay-shaming from you," I said with mock severity as I shook my finger at her.

Sloane laughed and held up her hands in self-defense. "Never! Just gotta watch out for my girl!"

"Well, come and share some fries with me then."

Sloane looked around at the bar. It was still early, but the place was already filling up. Rudolph, a wood elf bartender and Sloane's second-in-command, must've caught the tail end of our conversation because he came over and patted her shoulder. "You go visit with your friend. I've got this."

Sloane shot him a worried look. "Are you sure?'

Rudolph nodded. "Yeah. Don't worry. If things start to turn hairy, maybe Cameron can give the new bouncer a hand?"

I raised a hand. "Wait! Where's O'Malley?" The shifter was a loner who kept to himself, but he also helped to keep Sloane's bar a peaceful place to drink without drawing much attention to himself.

Sloane drummed her fingers on the bar. "He had some family business to deal with. He recommended another shifter to fill in for him while he's away." She pointed at a man in dark jeans and a fitted black shirt sitting near the door.

I glanced over at the new bouncer. I didn't recognize him, but that wasn't saying much. The were-community typically didn't welcome in outsiders too easily. "I've never known there to be a problem here that you two or O'Malley couldn't handle. Are things really that bad?" I asked.

Sloane nodded. "Things have been tense ever since the werewolves were officially welcomed to New Orleans. We've had multiple fights almost every night this week."

Rudolph snagged a couple of his home brews from under the bar and flicked the tops off with practiced ease. "All the more reason to take advantage of the quiet now. I'll put your order in and send those fries right over." He pushed the beers into Sloane's hands and made a little shooing motion.

"Are you sure?" The leprechaun still looked concerned.

Rudolph smiled warmly. "You'll be right over there. If anything goes sideways, I'll give you a shout."

Sloane came around the bar and I linked my arm through hers, pulling her towards my favorite table in the back corner of the bar. Rudolph shot me a thumbs up behind Sloane's back. I winked in return.

Settling in at the table, we clinked bottles, drank deeply. I felt tension start to drain out of my shoulders.

"Rudolph sure knows his stuff," I said.

"Tell me about it. I'm lucky to have him here."

One of Sloane's servers, a witch named Mia, hurried over with a bottle of tequila, a plate of limes, and two glasses. She set them down between us with a cheery smile. "Rudolph said it was urgent. Let me grab those fries for you and I'll be right back!" She tucked her tray under one arm and wove through the crowd easily.

I eyed the bottle curiously as Sloane poured two generous shots. "Cheers!" Sloane said as we clinked glasses.

I sipped, enjoying the sinuous burn the liquor left from the tip of my tongue to my empty stomach. My eyes widened. "What kind of magic is this?"

"A sprite in Texas owed me a favor. In repayment, she flew across the border to grab a couple of bottles of this liquid gold. Apparently, some demigod down in Mexico makes it. It's supposed to be amazing."

"It is! Damn, that's a smooth burn," I said, eyeing the unmarked bottle curiously.

"Right?"

We sipped. I sighed in contentment. Tequila really was this girl's best friend. Next to my leprechaun bartender, of course.

I lifted my glass to Sloane. "You go first. Tell me who is causing the problems. Whose ass do I need to kick?"

Sloane ran a hand through her short, choppy hair. "That's a tricky question. By my best guess, there's somewhere between twelve and twenty werewolves in Lykaios' Pack. That many Supes appearing here at one time? Well, it just seems like they're everywhere. Sniffing around at everyone. The locals don't like it. I mean, we get the odd Supe moving to town all the time. Sometimes a couple, and on the rare chance, a family or something. But a Pack of shifters? Nothing like that for a while now. And it's ruffling more than a few feathers."

"How so?"

Sloane held a hand parallel to the floor and waggled it back and forth. "The Pack is bringing business in, and keeping it to mostly Supe-owned places, which is nice. But they're also bringing in trouble, whether they want to or not." Sloane shrugged, sipping her tequila. "I think people are just settling into the new normal, you know?"

"Yeah, because Supes are *so* good at adapting to change," I said dryly.

Sloane pointed an index finger at me in agreement. "You've got it in one."

"You'd think the werewolves would know better than to stir up trouble when they're new to town," I observed.

"To be fair, they aren't the ones starting the trouble, but they sure as hell are finishing it."

I rolled my eyes. "Domination games. I should have known."

Sloane nodded. "It's all one big pissing match at the moment. I just wish they wouldn't do it at my bar."

"Sounds gross," I observed.

She rolled her eyes at me. "You know what I mean. I know that some folks need to hammer out their place in Supe society, but you think they could do it somewhere else. Hell, *anywhere* else!"

"Amen to that," I said, raising my glass. We clinked again, hit the table with the bottoms of the shot glasses simultaneously and then downed the tequila.

"Another?" Sloane asked, reading my mind.

"Make mine a double, bar wench!" I said with an imperious flourish of my hand.

She laughed and poured. "Thanks for listening to me vent."

I shrugged. "There's not much I can do besides listen. It's not like I'd make the best bouncer right now." I held up my healing hands for emphasis.

"How's that going anyway?" Sloane asked, jerking her chin towards my hands.

"As well as can be expected. Mama says there'll be minimal scarring if I keep healing at this speed, but loss of flexibility is still on the table. She says she could give a better prognosis if she knew what kind of Supe I am, but…" I trailed off with a shrug, taking a long drink from my beer.

"No news on that front? What about the necklace?"

I made wet circles on the tabletop with the bottom of my beer bottle. "Yeah. No. I still don't know what to make of that nonsense."

"Break it down for me. What's going on? Why are you so afraid of confronting this?" Sloane said, sipping her drink and licking droplets of the delicious liquor from her lips.

"What? Are you my shrink now?" I asked.

"Bartender. Shrink. It's all the same in the Supernatural community," Sloane said easily, leaning her forearms on the table.

"Do you play shrink to everyone who walks through the door?" I quipped.

"I'm everyone's *bartender*. I only do double duty for those I really like. There's no way in hell I'd want to be a vampire's therapist. Or a werewolf's. Could you imagine pushing one of them for a breakthrough?" An involuntary shudder rippled along Sloane's tiny frame.

"Could you imagine being Meridiana's shrink?" I asked with a laugh. "She'd send any therapist running for the hills."

"Or her bed," added Sloane with a lecherous grin.

I pointed a finger at her in agreement. "Speaking of, have you seen her recently?"

Sloane shook her head. "Not since we took her on that girls' night out. She kind of dropped off the radar after that."

Meridiana was a sexy redhead who had done me an invaluable favor. As thanks, Sloane and I had taken her out. A few too many drinks led to a pixie picking a fight with us. That had resulted in all three of us temporarily switching powers, and I may have accidentally kicked off an entire bar fight in a place filled with powerful Supernaturals. Oh, and gods. Did I mention the gods? Throw in a couple of sexy Vikings and you get the idea. Meridiana had dubbed it one of her best nights out. Ever. Which is saying something, coming from a demoness.

After our return to New Orleans, Sloane and I had poured ourselves into bed to recover. Meridiana had vanished. I'm all for leaving each to their own, but dropping off the face of the Earth because of a horrible hangover was a touch dramatic. Apparently, not so for the demoness. I didn't even have a number to contact her.

Come to think of it, I wasn't sure what the policy was regarding having a demoness on speed dial. It seemed like a good method to get a one-way ticket to the Bad Place.

Sloane snapped her fingers, bringing me back to the present. "Tell me, Cam. What gives? This isn't like you."

I sighed and toyed with the shot glass in front of me. "Cards on the table?" Sloane nodded so I continued. "I'm scared. I've gone through life with my shadow magic apparently on mute and now, all of a sudden, it's like the magic is blaring out at full volume. On top of that, I'd come to grips with never knowing who my father was and what I am and now..."

"Now there's a chance to find out," Sloane interjected kindly.

"Yeah," I said. My voice dropped, "But what if I'm something bad, Sloane? Like, *really* bad? Like, people want to hunt me down and mount my head on their wall for a trophy kind of bad."

"*What* you are doesn't change *who* you are," Sloane pointed out, smiling warmly at me.

"Maybe for you, but what about everyone else?" I gestured around at the noisy bar. "Look at the hubbub the werewolves have caused just by living their lives."

"There's a big difference between a Pack of shifters and you. What are you going to do, anyway? Just sit around in limbo? Avoid your apartment for the rest of your life?"

"The thought had crossed my mind," I muttered.

Sloane leaned across the table. "Look, Cam. I love you, but you need to put on your big-girl pants and go talk to that necklace," she said earnestly.

A crash interrupted us from the other side of the bar. I looked over to see the new bouncer headed towards a group of belligerent-looking men with a grim expression on his face. Sloane noticed it too. She let her head fall to the table with a thump. She lifted it, shot back the tequila, and bit into a lime wedge before groaning, "Whereas I need to put on my big-girl pants and deal with the werewolves and whoever decided to tangle with them tonight." She pushed back from the table.

"Trade you!" I called after her.

"Not a chance!" she shouted back. "Save some of that tequila for me, or else."

"No promises!"

Sloane flipped me off before disappearing into the crowd.

# Felons and Fangs - Chapter 3

Mia bobbed over and delivered my fries with a tight smile. She turned back to help with the minor ruckus at the bar without a word. I stretched in my seat, craning my neck to see what was going on. A couple of angry shouts arose, followed by the crash of glass breaking on the floor. I pushed to my feet, considering wading into the fray, when loud laughter rang out followed by cheering.

Sloane's voice cut through the crowd, "And that's how it's done, folks! Sorry for interrupting your evening. Shots are on me at the bar!" A cheer met her words as the crowd surged towards the heavy wooden bar.

I settled back into my seat, reaching for a fork to happily dive into the mountain of fried carbs dripping in cheese sitting in front of me. A familiar voice interrupted me before I could take my first bite.

"Well, you weren't wrong. This place is certainly full of ambiance."

I glanced up to see the man from the gym. What was his name? Oh, that's right. Otto. He looked sexy as hell in a crisp white button-down shirt with loosely cuffed sleeves pushed to his elbows and dark tailored jeans. Impeccably polished shoes peeked out from under the jeans. Otto raised an eyebrow, noting how my lips curved into an appreciative smile.

"What are you doing here? Stalking me?" I glowered at him, trying to hide the flare of interest under bad manners.

He held up his hands in protest, waving a familiar chunky brown bottle at me. "No, no. Just lucky happenstance. I had a tip that this was a good place to grab a drink with like-minded individuals."

"You can say Supes. Norms don't usually come in here and those that do think that we just really love comparing tomato to chicken noodle."

Otto smiled broadly, "Oh, chicken noodle *has* to win every time."

I shook my head. "You've obviously never had a Louisiana gumbo and cornbread. Hands down the best thing as far as comfort food goes."

"And here I thought you were going to support the grilled cheese and tomato-basil combo."

I tipped my head. "Nothing wrong with that, but you haven't *lived* until you've tried the gumbo at Cafe Sbisa. What they can do with vegetables and seafood is magical." I emphasized my point by blowing a chef's kiss into the air.

"Your recommendations haven't steered me wrong thus far. Where can I find this famous palace of gumbo then?"

"On Decatur, on the fringes of the French Quarter. Ask any local, they'll send you in the right direction," I said, pointedly turning my attention back to my fries.

"Ah, I see. Well, I do have one more question, if you can bear with me for a moment longer."

I set down my fork and looked up with the smile of a beleaguered cotillion hostess. "Yes, darlin', how can I be of assistance this evening?" I drawled in my heaviest Southern twang.

"I have just become aware of a place that serves excellent gumbo and I was wondering if you would care to accompany me to sample this delightful local delicacy?" Otto quirked a roguish eyebrow my way.

I snorted back a chuckle at his blatant, charming flirtation. I pointed my fork at my cheesy fries. "I do love their gumbo, but I'm all set tonight, thanks." I speared a wedge of potato and shoved the fried piece of heaven coated with gooey cheese and crispy bacon into my mouth. My eyes rolled back in my head.

"I'd hate to interrupt your, ahem, *meal*, with an impromptu dinner invitation. Truly, how rude of me. Perhaps I could join you instead?"

Otto asked. I couldn't tell how sincere he was, but that cheeky smile was attractive. And he knew it.

Not ready to fall on my face for another handsome stranger, I glared at him, putting a protective arm around my next good-bad choice. He held up his hands. "I assure you; I have no intentions to touch your...food."

I swallowed the lump of half-chewed potato. "Well, on those conditions, you may stay," I said, waving at the empty chair across from me with my fork. On the other side of the bar, the piano jangled to life. The pianist ran a promising arpeggio up the keyboard before breaking into a lively classic. Soon, the entire bar was humming along with the recognizable tune.

I speared another cheesy fry. "So tell me. What are you doing in New Orleans? Really?" I asked, popping the fry into my mouth.

Otto sipped from his bottle and nodded his approval. "Drinking beer and planning shenanigans."

I snorted, speaking around the fry. "Aren't we all? But you could do that anywhere. Why New Orleans?"

Otto gestured at the crowded bar as the pianist shifted into an upbeat jazz number. "The ambiance. The music. The company." He winked in my direction. "Take your pick."

"Thanks, but no. I'd rather know the real reason why you're here. What's your business?" I asked.

Otto ignored me, nodding towards the bottle of tequila and the empty shot glasses on the table. "I've always found that tequila and truth go hand in hand. Care to test the hypothesis?"

I rolled my eyes. "That's true more in the drunken-confession way than in the universally-profound-insight way," I said, finally putting down my fork and facing the gorgeous man full on. He had the over-confidence of an attractive man oozing off him. He was dripping flirtation pheromones all over any eligible female in the room, including me.

"When one is searching for truth or drinking, I find it is terrible form to do so alone," he said, reaching across to grab the bottle and pour two shots. He raised his glass.

*What the hell? Might as well put the tequila on his tab.*

I shrugged and grabbed my own glass. "So, what are we drinking to then?"

Otto clinked his glass against mine. "To new friends," he said.

"To truth," I countered.

"I wouldn't wish for that too much. Too much truth is dangerous," my new drinking companion said seriously.

"Only in the hands of liars," I returned, not knowing exactly where the quip had come from. It sounded vaguely familiar, but that could've been the tequila talking.

"Granted. Are you a liar, then?" he asked, a small smile tugging at the corner of his sensual mouth.

"I have lied," I prevaricated, trying to stop my lips from twitching upwards in response to the verbal repartee.

"Ah, but is that the truth or another lie?" The smile bloomed fully, curving the harsh planes of his face into something softer.

"I'll never tell," I said, returning his smile against my better judgment.

"I see. You are a philosopher then," he said.

"Only when I've been drinking," I replied, shooting my tequila for emphasis. I grabbed a lime wedge from the plate on the table and sucked the tart juice. It was an excellent complement to the liquor.

He tipped his head back, downing his tequila as well. The movement gave me an excellent view of his chest and arms on display under his crisply ironed shirt. Long, lean, and tan. A swimmer's body, built for efficiency. Among other things. I felt a warmth build low in my stomach and move downwards.

"Surprisingly delicious. Tequila is not my first choice of beverage," he said as he examined the unmarked liquor bottle on the bar curiously.

"Would you believe me if I told you a little fairy dropped it off?" I asked with a roguish wink.

"I would indeed. Fairies always know where to find hidden treasures. In my experience at least," Otto said, placing his shot glass carefully on the bar.

I chuckled. "What would you know about treasures?" I asked, starting to feel the effects of drinking a little too quickly after my sparring match with Hank, despite the fries.

Otto winked at me, pouring another shot. "About as much as you, Cameron. From what I've heard, we are in the same line of work."

I raised an eyebrow. "Oh, and what line of work is that?"

"Larceny. Pure unadulterated thievery for the sheer joy of outsmarting the mark." Otto cocked his head to the side, considering for a moment. "Although the beautiful things I'm hired to steal do hold their own sort of allure."

I leaned forward across the table, cupping a hand to my mouth and stage whispering loudly, "I hate to break it to you, but I'm on vacation. And I never, *ever,* work while I'm on vacation." I swayed in my seat a bit, finally feeling the alcohol take a hold of my better senses.

Otto leaned across the table, brazenly brushing a strand of hair back from my face and stroking my cheek lightly with my thumb. He whispered back, "And what would it take for you to break that rule, just once?" Otto leaned forward across the table until I could feel his breath on my lips.

My heart stuttered and my breath hitched. Warmth pulsed in my cheeks as I leaned into the caress.

*Wait. What was I doing?*

I was in the process of jerking back from the sexy stranger when a strong hand gripped my arm tightly and wheeled me away.

Suddenly a very angry werewolf stood between me and my cheesy fries. I mean, Otto. A werewolf. Otto. Between. Something like that.

I glanced up at the man standing in front of me as recognition broke through the tipsy.

Oh, this was not good.

# Enjoy the book?

**Y**ou can make a big difference.

Reviews are the most powerful tools in my arsenal when it comes to getting attention for my books. Much as I'd like to, I don't have the financial muscle of a New York publisher. I can't take out full page ads in the newspaper or put posters on the subway.

(Not yet, anyway).

But I do have something much more powerful and effective than that, and it's something that those publishers would kill to get their hands on.

**A committed and loyal bunch of readers.**

Honest reviews of my books help bring them to the attention of other readers.

It's easy to skip this step – I often did myself until I realized how much authors count on these reviews. If you've enjoyed this book, I would be very grateful if you could spend just five minutes leaving a review (it can be as short as you like) on the book's review page.

More reviews help other readers discover this series and, as I now realize, it helps your humble author enormously.

Thank you!

*L.L. Gray*

Don't forget! VIP's get early access to all sorts of book goodies, including signed copies, private giveaways, advance notice of future projects, and a FREE NOVELLA.

Join here: www.llgray.com

# Also By

**Smoke and Shadows Series**

Shadows and Relics - Book 1

Pixie Pranks (exclusive novella)

Felons and Fangs – Book 2

Bones and Blades – Book 3

# About the Author

L.L. Gray was born in Wisconsin and split her time being a musical theatre nerd, a book worm, and a burgeoning coffee addict. She began writing her debut novel after obsessing over fantasy books for most of her life. When she's not writing, she can be found playing soccer (or football for you non-American folks), singing loudly to any and all showtunes, or traveling the world in hopes of trying out new coffee shops. L.L. Gray currently lives in Abu Dhabi with her husband and two daughters.

**Psst, it's me. L.L. Gray. Nice to meet you! Connecting with fellow lovers of the written word and crazy adventure stories is important to me. If that sounds like your cup of tea (or coffee, or other beverage) please hop over to my website (www.llgray.com) and join my newsletter where you can grab a FREE, exclusive goodies or hang out with us on my Facebook readers group.

However, if email is more your speed, then please feel free to drop me a line at info@llgray.com should the mood strike.

I hope you stay in touch!

# Acknowledgments

First, I need to thank my fabulous team. They have become like a second family to me. I couldn't do it without die-hard supporters like them.

I'd also like to thank you, the reader. I hope you enjoyed reading Cam's wild adventures as much as I've enjoyed writing them. If you'd like to stay in touch or be kept up to date with upcoming releases, please head over to my website. If you'd like to hang out with some like-minded readers on Facebook , come and join our wonderful community.

And last, but definitely not least, I'd like to thank my wonderful husband. Without your support, none of this would have been possible.